LOTUS AND THORN

Also by Sara Wilson Etienne

HARBINGER

LOTUS AND THORN

SARA WILSON ETIENNE

G. P. PUTNAM'S SONS

GABRIEL
Pleiades
The Dome
Festival Grounds
Reclamation Fields
Tierra Muerta
Shuttle
Suji's Ravine
IAN SCHOENHERR © 2016

G. P. PUTNAM'S SONS
an imprint of Penguin Random House LLC
375 Hudson Street, New York, NY 10014

Copyright © 2016 by Sara Wilson Etienne.
Map illustration copyright © 2016 by Ian Schoenherr.

G. P. Putnam's Sons is a registered trademark of Penguin Random House LLC.

Library of Congress Cataloging-in-Publication Data is available upon request.

Printed in the United States of America.
ISBN 978-0-399-25669-1
1 3 5 7 9 10 8 6 4 2

Design by Ryan Thomann.
Text set in Bembo.

To my own beautiful sister, Megan—
who always believes in a world of more.

Sail those waves and make them yours.

ONCE UPON A TIME . . . *there was a sorcerer who disguised himself as a beggar. He went from house to house stealing beautiful girls. He spirited them away and no one knew where, for none of them were ever heard from again.*

One day, he came to the door of a house belonging to three beautiful sisters. The beggar carried a tall basket made of reeds and his back sagged under the weight of it. His hands shook with age. Still, when he rapped his knuckles against the door, his knock was strong and loud and could not be ignored.

The oldest sister answered the door—she was lovely and kind and offered the beggar a piece of bread. But at the touch of his hand, the sister was spirited into his basket. He carried her away, striding across broad rivers and green fields, until he reached his great house in the heart of the dark woods.

But the sorcerer was a greedy man, and one sister was not enough. He went back to the house, and this time the youngest sister came to the door, dressed in black. She refused to give him any bread, but still, the beggar took her hand and she, too, vanished into his basket.

Time passed and the sorcerer found he was no longer content. He returned to the house once more. The last sister—the middle one—was known for her cunning. But she was also determined to find her stolen sisters. So when she answered the door, she looked straight into the beggar's eyes. Then she reached out and took his hand.

FROM *FAIRY TALES OF THE BROTHERS GRIMM*
BY JACOB AND WILHELM GRIMM,
EARTH TEXT, 27TH EDITION, 2084.

"FITCHER'S BIRD,"

PART ONE

PROLOGUE

All objects recovered from beneath the desert sandline, excepting those vital to the health and survival of the Citizens, shall be traded and surrendered to the Curadores. Any infraction shall render the Citizen forfeit. May God find us worthy and in His wisdom allow us to return to Earth once more.

THE FIRST LAW OF PLEIADES,
ORAL TRADITION, 2085–PRESENT DAY [2590].

SARIKA WAS STILL BOTTLING the last of the mezcal as I slipped past her into the bedroom. I blinked hard—my eyes stinging from the fumes—as the alcohol gushed from the copper still into mismatched glass bottles. Sarika could've used plastic, but no. She said it killed the mezcal.

The Abuelos suggested she make the switch . . . once. She'd given them her look—impassive and absolute—and said, *Surely God made certain there was enough glass left on Gabriel to hold a drink worthy of Him.*

It would've been blasphemy coming from anyone else, but

there was nothing Sarika took more seriously than God and mez-cal. And, on these points, the Citizens of Pleiades agreed with her. So the Abuelos gave Sarika her glass bottles.

I hesitated in the doorway, making sure everyone was too busy to notice me—half hoping someone would. But they were consumed with preparations for the Festival. Sarika topping off each bottle in turn, never spilling a drop. Lotus dutifully capping and loading them into crates. Taschen oblivious to all, cross-legged in a cramped chair, putting the finishing touches on her dress.

The bedroom was stifling, but I slid the door shut behind me anyway. Wishing, not for the first time, that our doors had locks.

Kneeling by the mattress Lotus and Tasch and I shared, I felt for the hidden seam. Tiny, invisible stitches only Taschen could make. Finding it, I pulled my knife from my belt and paused, listening again to be sure: clinks and chatter from the kitchen. Then I sliced through the stitches and reached inside.

I dug through the stuffing—years worth of old, worn-out clothes—until I found it. The book. Even after all these years, the faded painting on the front made me catch my breath. I crawled across the mattress, brushing lint off the battered cover, and held the book up to the light of the window. There was the blond girl standing in her shady grove, tossing a golden ball. In the distance, a castle was perched at the top of a hill. Gleaming silver in the cheery sun. Earth's sun.

But it wasn't the girl, with her simpering smile, that I cared about. Or the magnificent castle. It was the trees. The girl was surrounded by a thousand shades of green. And I swore I could feel them . . . cool and alive and whispering. So far from anything I knew on this godforsaken planet.

From six stories up, I could see all there was to see of the deserts of Gabriel. Below my window, a steady stream of eager Citizens passed through the gates and out onto the Festival Grounds. Stalls and people and bright flags already crowded the dusty plain, but no one ventured beyond its walls to the Reclamation Fields. Not today.

Good. I ran a finger along the frayed binding—*this was going to work.* Get out to the Festival Grounds. Get through the gates to the Reclamation Fields. Get rid of the book. Don't get caught.

I wouldn't have to go far. The ugly expanse of pits and digsites started just outside the walls of the Festival Grounds and stretched on for kilometers. Studying them now, the Fields looked wrong without their usual haze of excavation. No scouts crawling in and out of tunnels. No Finds being exhumed from the recesses of the planet's former Colony. And beyond the Fields, nothing but blue-grey dunes stretching out to bleak mountains. A long valley of nothing.

"So whaddya think, Leica?" Taschen burst through the door. "Ta-daaaaaaa!"

I shoved the book behind my back as my older sister swirled into the room wearing her finished dress. She'd been obsessed for months—scrounging for fabric, her hands perennially stained with dye as she assembled her masterpiece.

"Oh, were you making a dress?" I tried hard to keep my voice light and teasing, even as my heart panicked loudly in my ears. "I hadn't noticed."

She glared at me and I blinked innocently, tacking on a too-sweet smile for good measure.

"I'll make my grand entrance again, and *this time* I expect to find my loving sister in here." Tasch stalked out in a fake huff and I scrambled across the mattress, jamming the book under me, managing to cover up the hole just as Tasch strutted back into the room.

"Spin! Spin! Spin!" I chanted this time, and she grinned, indulging me.

Patches of purple and blue spiraled into each other as the skirt flew out. Tasch was radiant—long black hair fanning around her. And the sadness of the last year cleared from her face.

Lotus looked in from the doorway—already dressed for the fighting ring in meticulously mended pants and a loose shirt, black hair tied back tight. My younger sister added her voice to mine. "Spin! Spin!"

But as she watched Tasch laugh and show off her skirt, Lotus's face folded into a scowl. Anyone else might've thought Lotus was jealous of Tasch—but I understood the truth of it. Because the same anger clenched my heart.

After the outbreak, we let ourselves get used to the faded, shadowed, grieving Taschen. Got so used to it that we'd forgotten this bright, dancing Tasch even existed. And among all my tiny daggers of grief, this was the sharpest.

But I wouldn't dampen Tasch's joy; I made my face relax into a smile. "The boys will trip over themselves to get to you."

"As long as I get to dance, I don't care who with. I'll take Lotus if I have to!"

"Not on your life!" But Lotus let Tasch whirl her into a polka anyway.

The closed-off look fell away from Lotus's face and it was like watching someone dancing with their own reflection—black eyes shining, skin glazed golden-brown by sunlight. They were practically twins, despite the two years separating them.

Sarika chided us from the kitchen. "No one'll be dancing if we don't get these bottles down to the Festival."

"Coming!" Tasch waltzed the two of them out of the bedroom and into the other room.

"Be there in a sec!" I called.

Heart pounding, I pulled the book out from under me and slipped it in my pack. Then I thrust my arm back into the mattress and pulled out the other two treasures. The old camera—the name we shared elegantly embossed on its tarnished chrome. And the silver necklace, with its strange black metal pendant. I nestled them into my bag next to the book and smoothed the blanket over the gap in the mattress. I'd fix the hole tonight. After I told my sisters what I'd done. After I'd somehow convinced them to forgive me.

We hauled crates of mezcal and pulque down the five flights of stairs and across the courtyard. For the first time in eight months, the gates leading to the Festival Grounds were open and unguarded. The tall walls that usually isolated the buildings of Pleiades from each other were not barriers today. Citizens flooded from Pleiades' nine glass apartment towers, out onto the Grounds, and into each other's company.

As I stepped through the gates, the wind picked up, flapping the strings of colorful flags against each other. Despite the heaviness of my pack, despite what I had to do today, it was impossible not to feel that tingle of excitement—like I was a kid again. As the streamers played against the warm breeze, I could see it on everyone else's face too. All the people waiting for marriages to be sanctified by the Abuelos. All the babies that'd been born but hadn't met their grandparents. All the wooing couples who'd been separated by walls for months and months, until the flare-up of Red Death was finally under control.

"I can already hear them tuning their guitars!" Tasch said as we wove our way through the labyrinth of stalls to Sarika's large, stately booth. There were many brewers in Pleiades, each with their own tables and crates of pulque and mezcal—but there was no question that Sarika was the best.

"Well, *I* can smell the tamales." Lotus grinned at us as she put her bottles down next to mine.

"Mmmmmm . . . sweet corn." Tasch swooned into me, draping herself over my arm.

"Kabocha pumpkin." Lotus grabbed my other arm, as if she was too weak to stand.

"Cinnamon and nutmeg and honey!" I clamped my hands to my heart and sank to my knees—taking them with me, so we landed in a ravenous, gasping pile.

Sarika glared down at us, her silver-streaked hair framing a frown, her curved nose making her look like a hawk surveying her prey. Then a smile twitched on her face.

"Useless." She prodded our bodies with her toe. "Fine . . . off with you! You'd better hurry while you can. I'll see you after the Remembering."

The first bite was heaven. Warm, ground corn and cinnamon-laced pumpkin. I hadn't had anything sweet for eight months. Not since the New Year's Festival. Not since the sudden, devastating wave of disease had swept through Pleiades. Not since we'd lost Mom and Dad. And suddenly the mouthful felt grainy and too rich.

I squeezed my eyes shut, remembering my mother's beautiful eyes turning pink. Blood leaking from her mouth. Her ears. Her eyes. Dad wouldn't let us go near her, wouldn't even let us say good-bye. *I'm not losing all of you,* he'd said. But when Mom had cried out for him, he couldn't stop himself, cradling her in his vast arms.

And he held on tight. Even as he surrendered them both to quar-antine, he refused to be separated from her. Red Death was always a threat in Pleiades, but it usually just took a few dozen a year—those who were already old or sick. But that day, my parents were just two among hundreds who were infected. And I remembered the silent Curadores, faceless in their isolation suits—hauling their bodies away to be burned in the Dome. The endless bodies.

Now, chewing in silence, my sisters and I were each trapped in our own nightmare of memories. And when the guitars started up and the trumpets called to the dancers, Tasch used the excuse to escape. I wished Lotus had too, but she seemed to think it was her duty to stay with me. So we wandered aimlessly through the maze of booths, my eyes darting in the direction of the gates on the far side of the Festival Grounds. Toward the Reclamation Fields.

Usually Citizens were allowed to gather every two months—a relief from the isolation which was supposed to keep the plague in check—and the Chuseok Harvest Festival had always been my favorite. But not this year. Despite the sunshine and the scent of grilling bulgogi and corn cakes, there was an uneasiness about the day. And I couldn't wait anymore. I steered us away from the market and toward the fighting rings, knowing Lotus wouldn't be able to resist.

Fighters were already gathering—boasting and clacking their sticks together in good-natured taunts. Watching their easy camaraderie, I longed to shed my pack and join them, to step into the ring and show what I could do. My body quick and ruthless. My eyes taking in every movement, every twitch and feint. The wooden sticks in my hands lending me their solidness.

But, of course, I didn't do any of those things. Instead, as Lotus glanced at the fighters, then back to me, I said the words she needed to hear.

"Go sign up. You know you're ready." I played the older sister for all it was worth.

She was fourteen this year—finally old enough for the ring. We'd been training hard, even after, especially after, Dad died. She still hesitated and I put my hand on her arm. "You're a natural, like Dad . . . the best I've ever seen. You're going to make him proud."

Lotus shook her head, her dark eyebrows pulling down. "Not as good as you." She squeezed my hands and I realized that it wasn't Dad's memory that was making her hesitate.

No. Not as good as me. I squeezed back with my six-fingered hands—my Corruption—trying to keep bitterness from twisting my face. It didn't matter how good I was. I would dishonor the ring with my aberration. "Then you'll fight for both of us. Your victory will be my victory."

Lotus nodded and darted in to kiss my cheek. Then she ran off to join the rowdy crowd.

"New blood!" one of the fighters shouted. And a heckling, hooting call went up from the ranks—folks clapping Lotus on the back as she was assigned a match for the evening. It stung more than I'd imagined to watch her step into that world that was closed to me. But I also realized I was excited to watch her tonight. What

I told her was true . . . she was gonna win. And Dad would be proud. *I* would be proud.

But first, I had my own task. I was afraid if I put it off any longer, I might discover I didn't have the nerve. So I told myself I was just going for a walk.

I kept my mind busy as I zigzagged through reunited families. Women showing off pregnant bellies. Little kids trying to keep up with older cousins. All the while, heading for the entrance to the Reclamation Fields.

But when I reached the gate, there were guards posted. There were *never* guards posted at the Festivals. Yet there they were—five or six of them huddled, talking solemnly near the entrance. I panicked, feeling like they could *see* my treachery. *See* the sinful items in my pack.

I took a deep breath and I reminded myself that this was exactly *why* I needed to do this. For my sisters. For myself. With the Abuelos' recent raids on Citizen apartments, our naming gifts weren't safe anymore. *We* weren't safe. I would have to find a way through.

But as I started to evaluate my options, the enormous bonfire was lit—calling everyone to the Remembering. Suddenly, Citizens were moving toward the stage, closing in around me, anxious to show off their faith. Four thousand people all suddenly moving in one direction. Or was it more like three thousand now? And as Sarika's voice boomed over the Festival Grounds, I was swept along with the press of people.

"For millennia, Earth was our home. It was beautiful and lush and people were happy."

This was not good. I'd hoped to be out and back by now. I

caught a glimpse of the gate as the crowd funneled by it—it was open and unguarded now.

I swung back around—determined not to miss my chance—and smacked straight into a stranger. I grabbed on to him to keep from falling. "Sorry!"

The man, about my dad's age, reached out to steady me with an indulgent smile—assuming I'd drunk too much. Then he saw my hand—my fingers—on his arm. I watched his face contort in disgust and he pushed me away, spitting the insult at me. "Indigno!"

I shoved my hands in my pockets, trying not to draw any more attention to myself. Still, people stared. So I buried myself deeper in the mass of Citizens gathering for the Remembering. Feeling the word branded on me.

People always found my hands unsettling—my Corruption had isolated and defined me my whole life. But it was so much worse since the outbreak. Everyone wanted someone to blame for all their recent suffering. And everyone wanted to prove they were loyal.

"But there was a snake in Earth's Garden! A restless serpent who poisoned our ancestors with lies. Whispering to them, 'You are Gods!'" Between the heads of the people in front of me, I could see Sarika now, her arms spread wide in the middle of the stage. The Abuelos—dressed in dark, formal hanbok robes—sat in a circle around her, their wrinkled, somber faces ready for prayer.

Suddenly, I realized I could still make this work. Because in a few minutes, Sarika herself would provide me with just the moment I needed. I started inching my way back through the throng—working my way to the side.

"The snake told man, 'God is not the only one who can make life! Why ssssettle for Earth when you can make your own world?'"

The slyness of the snake was alive on Sarika's face, and her slithery words were echoed by the crowd. "Why sssssssettle?" As if a thousand snakes writhed at our feet.

By now, the crowd was pressed up against the edge of the market. A few kids had climbed the wooden stalls so they could have a better view, and I remembered being fascinated once too—fervent even. That was before I'd understood the Remembering wasn't *for* me. Now I didn't know what to believe. But the rest of audience was captivated, a hush falling over them as they listened to the words they already knew by heart.

"So the Colonists journeyed through the constellations themselves, until they found their way to Gabriel. They took this dusty planet as their own and built Ad Astra Colony. They terraformed this valley. They built tall cities. One sun and one moon—they made Gabriel in Earth's image."

Every eye was on Sarika when I ducked between the rows of booths and slipped away—the crowd caught in the spell of her story. "And God punished the Colonists for their arrogance. He sent Red Death to show our ancestors that, for all their cleverness, they were *not gods*! He returned his children to blood and bone. He crushed their cities with his almighty fist."

I raced down the paths of the empty market, my pack slamming against my shoulder blades—keeping low as I wound my way toward the gate. My mind silently recited the remaining lines along with Sarika, urging my feet to hurry. Marking time with the rhythm of her words.

"But God is merciful. He saved some. Made them immune. Made others strong enough to survive the plague. Scattered that strength through the generations."

Shouts of praise rose up from the crowd, and I put on a burst of speed.

"But God is merciful! He saved Pleiades for them!" In my mind's eye, I could see Sarika pointing to the nine blue glass towers behind the stage. And my eyes were pulled, as always, to the Curadores' Dome perched in the foothills above us. "We have spent the last five hundred years doing God's work. Undoing the sins of the Colonists."

I reached the edge of the stalls with enough time to catch my breath. From here I had a clear view of the gates. There were no guards, but there *was* an empty stretch of nothing between me and the opening—nowhere to hide. I'd be seen by anyone who was looking. So I crouched behind a kimchi booth—the spicy, sour smell making my mouth water—and I waited for the moment I knew was coming. Ready to run.

"On the occasion of Chuseok, let us bow our heads and thank God. We are humble in His eyes. We cleanse the land in His name. Let us pray that someday He will find us worthy and return us to our home. Return us to our good, green Earth once again."

The world fell quiet and I took off for the gate. My boots silent on the packed sand. My path unseen by the righteous. And as I made it past the wall, it felt liberating for once not to be praying for a future I would never see.

For the good, green Earth was not for me. As long as I could remember, there had been someone there to remind me that I would not be going to that promised land. *I* was Corrupted. *I* was a sign that God had not yet forgiven us. *I* was sin incarnate.

Indigno.

I hurried through the Reclamation Fields, careful to avoid the huge, deep pits riddling the desert. The sun was easing behind the mountains—casting blue shadows across the already blue sands of Gabriel. I suddenly felt a lightness, and soon I would be lighter. I skirted around rusted beams and stacks of old tires ready to be traded with the Curadores, taking cover behind the heaped Finds.

Then, finally kneeling at the side of a pit, I pulled out the book. As I held it over the bowels of what had once been a Colony building, a song of praise drifted over the wall. I only had a few minutes. I needed to be done by the time the crowd broke up and the guards returned to their posts—slipping back inside during the chaos.

"For the hundredth time, I don't *care* if you haven't gotten a corn cake! The Abuelos *told us* to be on the lookout for dissidents and that's what we're going to do." An Abuelos guard—wide face, wide neck, wide shoulders—suddenly came into view, wandering out from behind a mound of tires.

Fear flooded through me as I tried to freeze, to hide the book, to hide myself. But I was out in the open and the massive guard was coming toward me and it was too late. It'd been too late the second I'd stepped through that gate.

Another guard—smaller, but meaner looking—followed him. "All I'm saying is, if *you* were gonna plan some kinda . . . *rebellion* . . . wouldn't you choose to do it around a mezcal bottle rather than a pile of old—"

Then the smaller guard saw me, a smile creeping onto his face. "Well, if we haven't trapped ourselves a little rat *after all*."

I almost ran, but where would I go? Beyond these fields was nothing. Only the wasteland of Tierra Muerta and the mountains marking the end of the habitable world.

The guards weren't gentle when they grabbed me. Despite the

XXVI • Sara Wilson Etienne

fact that I didn't fight back, I got an elbow in the gut for my trouble. Their fingers dug into my shoulders as they started half carrying me toward the gate, and pain overtook fear.

"I can walk on my own," I growled, trying to pry their hands off. But they ignored me—as if I was a thing, and not a person they were dragging through the pits.

"Will you look at those hands?" There was a gleeful malice in the massive guard's voice. "Abominations . . . God might as well've spit on her."

"Never should've been allowed to live in the first place," the smaller one said as they bullied me through the gate.

As we entered the Festival Grounds, Sarika was offering her closing prayer. Her moment of glory. "God, we are all sinners in your eyes. Only with your guiding . . ."

But the audience was no longer paying attention to her. Whispers hissed through the mass of people and every eye turned to me as the pair of guards split the crowd down the middle. It was a nightmare—one guard on either side of me, crushing my arms as they "restrained" me. They made a show of jostling me and hustling me, making me lose my footing so they could drag me every few steps.

"Leica!" I heard Tasch's shout and Lotus's more muffled exclamation. My eyes found my sisters in the crowd—still cut off from me by thirty or forty people—Taschen worried, Lotus angry. And for a second I watched with wonder as they pushed their way through the mob. A force of nature moving mountains.

Then the smaller guard knocked me off my feet again and my knee smashed into the ground. Pain lit up my world and the real danger of the situation hit me—Lotus and Tasch couldn't get mixed up in this. No matter what else happened, I must keep them safe.

I was fifty meters from the stage when Sarika finally saw it was me—the scene playing out across her face. Shock. Then concern, as she took in the guards. And finally, a startled, wounded look that didn't fit on her usually stoic face.

That was the worst part—the instant Sarika understood I'd done more than steal her thunder. I'd betrayed her, betrayed the laws she revered and preached. It was her daughter, Marisol, all over again—running off with a Curador. Only, I'd humiliated her in front of everyone. After Sarika had taken us in. After she'd made us her family.

As the guards hauled me up onstage, I ached to explain myself to Sarika. More than anything, I wanted to say *I'm sorry*. But I was too afraid to face her.

The pair of Abuelos from Building Nine stepped out from the circle of elders. Their long robes added to the gravity of their movements. I attempted to bow—out of habit—forgetting the guards were holding me.

The first guard—the hulking one—went over and spoke to the pair of Abuelos. After a whispered exchange, the guard bowed and left the stage.

"Release her," the Abuela told the remaining guard. Her white hair was pinned high on her head—giving a sense of tallness despite her stooped frame. The Abuela reached out her hand. "Give me your pack, girl."

This woman had known me since I was born, but now she denied me even the respect of my name.

I hesitated, knowing if I obeyed, I'd be lost. Knowing I was already lost. The guard wrenched the bag off my back, nearly dislocating my shoulder in the process. I struggled to stay upright, to stand tall, as the Abuelo now stepped in to take the pack.

"You were caught out in the Reclamation Fields." The Abuelo's voice was croaky, his creased face pulled down in reproach. "For what purpose?"

When I didn't answer, he yanked open my pack and dumped its contents on the ground. A jug of water. A knife. And, of course, the book, the camera, the necklace.

My eyes flicked to the crowd. And there were Lotus and Tasch—not five meters from the front of the stage—their eyes unbelieving as they stared at the objects. As if our mother herself was sprawled there. Rage won out on Lotus's face, while Tasch's was raw with grief. And seeing the pain returned there, I wished I could undo every moment of this horrible day. I could only hope my sisters' shock would keep them silent. And safe.

The fact that my mother had been fascinated with the vestiges of the ancient Colony had been a badly kept secret. But only my sisters knew that our mother's fixation had gone far beyond giving us blasphemous names. Even Sarika, her best friend, had no idea that our mother had risked exile, smuggling these Finds back into Pleiades with her. One for each of her daughters—naming gifts, she'd called them.

"I charge you with the theft and hoarding of objects found beneath the sandline," the Abuelo said. "These Finds are the sins of our ancestors. Now you have made them *your* sins. And our sins as well."

The rest of the Abuelos nodded their heads solemnly, their

wide robes swaying with the movement. Whispers snatched up the accusation and carried it through the audience.

He asked the next question in a rasping bark. "What do you say to this charge?"

Slowly, I picked up the book from where it'd fallen. There was no winning this fight. There was no other verdict—I knew the consequences if I got caught. And yet, I heard the word come out of my mouth before I even thought it.

"How?"

"What did you say?" The old man loomed over me; he used to be a fighter and I could see the sinews of muscle tensed through his ceremonial sleeves. I wondered if he'd hit me. I wondered if I'd hit him back before the guards got to me.

"How is this a sin? It's a storybook. It holds nothing but tales of princes and dragons." I heard my mother's words coming out of me. Years of whispered conversations. Of hushed arguments with my father. "And this thing"—I pointed at the camera—"used to take pictures. And that"—I gestured to the necklace—"was a trinket someone wore. *How* are they sins?"

"You know Technology is not a sin in itself." The Abuelo's voice took on a sanctimonious tone, somewhere between reverence and indignation. "But when the Colonists used their technology to turn their back on Earth . . . to place themselves among the gods . . . *that sin* summoned the wrath of the Almighty. In every way, we are the children of that sin. And our planet is the vessel which holds it."

The Abuelo was relishing his moment. He spread his arms wide—a poor imitation of Sarika—embracing the rapt attention of his Citizens. "You do not see the danger in these *trinkets*, as you call them, because you are young and you only see the dreams of what *could* be. That is why the survivors made the law absolute."

The Abuela placed a tempering hand on his arm, eager for a turn of her own. "It is not entirely the girl's fault." Her face was all sympathy and sorrow, but as she stepped toward me, her eyes were full of a spiteful joy. "Your mother had this sickness in her heart too. How else do you explain being born . . . Corrupted."

The Abuela's eyes lingered dramatically on my six-fingered hands, but my eyes were already looking to my sisters. The two of them were trying to fight their way up onto the stage, their faces masks of fury. I saw now that the Abuelos were toying with us. The elders had long suspected my mother's sins went beyond outspoken words. As soon as they'd seen what was in my bag, they'd guessed rightly that *she* was the one who had stolen these things—but they had no proof.

Now they were baiting my sisters and me, hoping that in our passion to defend our mother, we'd admit her crime. And then her sin would be inherited by *all* her children. Why punish one sister when you can punish all three?

The bigger guard grabbed Tasch and Lotus. I don't know if he was planning to help or hinder their path to the stage. Either way, it was over. The Abuelos would question my sisters and they would slip. In my attempt to protect them, I had condemned us all.

Then, suddenly, Sarika was down there among them. A word from her and the guard was gone. Another word and Taschen and Lotus went silent.

I met my sister's eyes without fear. Without anger. But I couldn't keep out the sadness. And I shook my head just the tiniest bit. Forbidding them to come to my defense. To our mother's defense. The Abuelos had hated our family—our strange names, my Corruption, our mother's obsession with what was forbidden—for as long as I could remember. We would not let that hate destroy us.

Finally, seeing that we were not going to give her the family confession she craved, the Abuela grabbed me by the hair. With one great yank, she pulled me down to my knees. Then she picked up my knife. She couldn't implicate my mother or my sisters, but she still had me.

"You have sullied your hands and your heart for the love of these . . . these trinkets. For your worship of the corrupt. You have sullied all of us." Her eyes shone with satisfaction—the only hard thing in her round, sagging face. Then she raised the knife and brought it down on the coil of hair she was still holding. Hacking it off with brutal slashes. "You will be exiled to Tierra Muerta for the remainder of your life."

Then, with all of Pleiades watching, she performed the ritual, shaving my entire head. The blade scraped at my scalp, leaving it raw and red. I kept my eyes fixed on the ground—lengths of straight black hair falling around me, drifting like crow's feathers.

When my humiliation was complete, the guards dragged me to my feet. I held my sisters' eyes, realizing this was the last time I would see them. We'd never been separated—not for a night. And I didn't even know how to begin processing the idea, because in truth I didn't fully understand where I ended and they began. We slept, legs overlapping, elbows digging into ribs. We ate in a constant flurry of unnoticed, automatic trades. Removing unwanted carrots from each other's plates, exchanging bread crusts

XXXII • Sara Wilson Etienne

for centers. We drank from each other's cups and ran outside in whoever's shoes were handy and made a shield with our bodies when one of us cried.

How can you be exiled from yourself?

I don't know if I was crying, but I watched tears stream down Tasch's face. Red blotches appeared on Lotus's cheeks as the Abuelo made a show of placing the forbidden gifts back inside my pack. Walking to the edge of the stage, he opened the jug of water. He took a drink, then poured half of it out on the thirsty sand—the sin of wasted water underscoring the sin of my crimes. Finally, he put the half-empty jug and my knife back inside the pack.

"Take your sins and your Corruption." The Abuela took the pack from him and handed it to me. I forced myself to look away from Tasch and Lotus as I slung the bag over my shoulder. Knowing that time was already eroding their faces from my memories. "Go through that gate and never return. You are considered Indigno for the rest of your days. *May they be thirsty ones. May they be few.*"

CHAPTER 1

657 Days Later

I CROUCHED BEHIND a crumbling wall and pulled out my scope. Through two scratched camera lenses and a bit of plastic pipe, I scanned the blue haze hovering over the ridge of dunes. Something was moving on the other side. And nothing that moved was good.

Right now, I was weak, and I was trapped. Our crewboss, Suji, had chosen this ravine—a little pocket between the mountains and the dunes—after the first symptoms of Red Death had shown themselves. The crescent of cliffs at our backs meant we only needed one lookout to keep an eye on the desert to the east. And there were enough decaying buildings to hide our movements. Suji said if we were lucky, no one would notice us.

But we were not lucky.

Yesterday, the vultures started screeching and circling, signaling to everyone in Tierra Muerta that there'd been death. That we were vulnerable. And by tonight, the stink would lure the wild dogs down from the mountains.

But the dogs hardly mattered, because the men would get

here first. I'd spotted them a few hours ago, a flash high up on the dunes—the noon sun bouncing off something metal. Now, as the sun dropped behind the mountains, the men had given up on even the pretense of stealth. I watched them through my scope . . . exiles with mangy beards sharpening knives. Swigging mezcal. Always keeping one eye on what they could see of our camp.

They were waiting till dark. Then they'd come down here and pick us clean—food, scrap, and any recruits who might be willing. Or unwilling for that matter. And they could afford to wait to attack because we had nowhere else to go. It wouldn't be long now. The only good news was that it looked like there were two different crews—they'd have to fight each other as well as me.

Keeping low, I scurried back through the maze of ruins to camp. Though after two days without food and one without water, it was more like a limping stagger. "There's two groups waiting to ambush. Thirty, maybe forty men in all," I said.

"Time for you to go." Suji groaned as I ducked into the tent; she started coughing, blood splattering out of her mouth. Seizures racking through her.

I'd thought she was too far gone to speak, but evidently she was still in the fighting ring with Red Death.

My teeth clenched, crunching grit between them. "How many times do I have to tell you, I'm *not* going to abandon you."

I was fighting too. For the past three days, I'd been battling to save Suji's life—to save *all* their lives.

Suji managed to open her eyes. They were two gaping red holes in a sea of bruises. She looked like a monster from a fairy tale. She looked like Death.

"Water." The word gurgled up from her, as she forced air through the blood filling her lungs. And the surge of energy was gone. Seeping out with her blood. Her body curling her into a tight ball—as if death was unmaking her, returning her to the womb.

"It's okay." I dropped to my knees and laid my hand lightly on her chest, breathing with her. Aching to breathe *for* her. "I'm here."

Suji reached for the water jug strapped to her nearby pack, but she was too weak to manage it.

"I got it." It was empty—had been since yesterday—but I doubted she'd notice at this point. Pulling the knife from her belt, I sliced through the rope holding the jug in place. Carefully, I managed to coerce a tiny droplet down the side. She closed her eyes as it reached her swollen tongue.

"Are they *all* gone?" Her hand searched the empty sand next to her for her wife—forgetting we'd lost Maria yesterday.

I was glad there was no water left in me for tears. I owed it to Suji to answer her with clear eyes. "Yes. They're all waiting for you."

Three days ago, after we found the ancient remains of the shuttle, Suji had been the first to show signs of Red Death. It'd happened so fast. If Red Death found you, it usually made itself known in a matter of days. But her symptoms had appeared in minutes.

The sudden fever. The speckled rash. And the undeniable bloodshot eyes. One by one, the women of the crew had followed, as they had always followed her—their organs liquefying inside of them. But Suji had outlasted them all, making sure they'd been taken care of before she would let go.

And she'd never flinched. Not when she'd held the body of her dying lover, not when the pain was so fierce she'd passed out. Suji had clawed and spat and fought the plague every second. There was a reason she was our crewboss even though she was young.

Only twenty-two to my seventeen. Then again, no one lasted long in exile.

Now the fight was almost over. Red Death had stolen even her bitter smile and mutated Suji's brown skin into an unrecognizable purple bruise. Her lips were cracked and red pus oozed from them. Her body had broken down until it could no longer hold its own blood—it leaked from her eyes and nose and ears. Streaking her skin.

"Then . . ." Suji's bloodshot eyes struggled to focus on mine again. "You're the only one. You have to go back for it . . . Just don't let me rot out here."

I knew what she was asking of me, but I had no words to give her. If I tried to speak now, I would fall apart. There's only so much ripping a soul can take before it shreds to pieces. Before it disintegrates. My body ached with hunger and thirst and exhaustion, but it was this soul death I truly feared. Because in my deepest of secret places, I knew that all I wanted was to lie down there next to Suji. To fold in on myself. To let this desert take me.

But she deserved better than that from me. Because if Suji had the choice, she would live. She would fight.

And I would too.

So I used the first trick Suji'd taught me when I got to Tierra Muerta. *The world wants you to believe it's all noise and bigness,* she'd say. *That's how it thinks to beat you. But survival is in the details . . . If you look close enough, there's* always *a way.*

I sat in that treacherous valley—watching, listening for it.

The wind gusted, slap-slapping against the tent. Trying to pull it from its anchors.

Night shadows crawled their way across the ravine. Snaking between the dunes standing guard at its mouth.

Bright red blood trickled from Suji's eye. One drop among thousands that'd already been lost in this place.

And I saw it. Saw how I would make it out of there alive. Or at least, how I would try to.

But first, there was Suji. I wiped the blood from her face with the sleeve of my tattered shirt—one more stain wouldn't hurt. I'd been coughed on, bled on, puked on, and a lot of other things I didn't want to remember, and I hadn't so much as spiked a fever. Red Death always passed over a few. What would the Abuelos say if they knew someone so Corrupted as myself had survived out here? Their God certainly had a twisted sense of humor.

"Promise you won't leave me here." Suji forced me to face her, laying a burning hand on mine—her five fingers against my six. She'd never been one to shrink away from my Corruption. Not like the others . . . even here in Tierra Muerta.

I opened my mouth, but the words stuck in my scorched throat.

"I'm your crewboss." Her eyes flashed with the last of the light inside her. "Now promise me!"

I still had her knife in my hand. I gripped the handle hard, letting the metal edge bite into my skin—the pain driving out my grief. Fortifying me. I touched Suji's chest, her heart beating weakly, the heat of her fever searing through her soaked shirt.

"I promise."

The knife glinted in the hot afternoon sun. And—with a single slash—I slit her throat.

CHAPTER 2

IT WAS OVER in seconds. Suji didn't have much blood left to spill. The blade glistened red and I thrust it into the sand to clean it. Then I slid the dagger back into her belt.

Only when I looked at her face—at the shell of what had been Suji—did I cave. My stomach cramped, doubling me over in the sand. But there was nothing in there to lose. As my forehead pressed into the hot grit, I let the smell of dust and sagebrush and sweat blot out everything else.

You don't know what you're capable of until you're doing it. I didn't make the mistake of looking at Suji's face again as I wrapped the blanket around her and dragged her into the pile with the rest. There were sixteen bodies on the pyre now. I forced myself to think of them like that. Not my crew. Not my friends. Just bodies.

I wouldn't let the horror of it swallow me whole. But I knew it would be there . . . waiting for me. If I'd learned anything in Tierra Muerta, it was that you couldn't escape retribution. I'd seen it a hundred times in the desert. Greediness and cruelty always met themselves in the end. And grief was the same. Even now, I could feel it pooling inside of me—a kind of liquid ache seeping into my hollow, fractured places. I knew I would have to pay the price of the last three days. But that would have to come later. Because right now, there was no one coming to save me.

When I'd first been exiled and walked out into Tierra Muerta, I was dehydrated and starving and too stupid to know not to travel at night or in the worst of the sun. And it'd been Suji who had found me and given me her share of water and made me part of her crew. And now she was dead, and the only single fucking thing I could do about *that* was to save myself.

A kind of holy anger seized me as I hauled everything in our camp to the pyre. Tents, blankets, scrap, I threw it all on. I wasn't about to leave anything for those bastards on the dunes to scavenge. Finally, I added the tires—our makeshift chairs—so they formed a ring around the edge of the unlit bonfire. Everything was brittle-dry in this barren desert on this barren planet . . . It might take a few minutes, but they'd burn. Everything burned.

Finally, I uncorked the last bottle of mezcal and took a swig— letting it roar down my throat. We might have broken the law, we might be Indignos, but we still deserved respect. So I intoned the cremation prayer freeing their souls from their bones.

"May the fire cleanse you. May you take wing from the ashes and be remade. May God find you worthy." But the words felt feeble in the face of such loss, their meaning robbed by what I'd seen of God's "mercy" over the past few years. I wasn't sure I could believe in a God who was this cruel. I threw the rest of the alcohol over the mound, dousing the bodies. Then, taking a glowing stick from the morning's bonfire, I lit the pyre.

Fire ate around the edges—first tracing the path of the alcohol. Then the blankets caught, the flame sinking its teeth into the pile of debris and corpses. Smoke stung my eyes. I wanted to think it could burn away the hell of the last three days, but all that happened was the stench of burning flesh and plastic filled my nose. I pulled on my sandmask but it barely dulled the smell.

Turning my back on the pyre, I darted through the rubble and half buildings to the low wall where I'd left my belongings. I loaded up my pack—my empty water jug, my blanket, my book. Then I tied the whole thing onto the long plastic sledge we used for hauling Finds across the sand. A door from the shuttle we'd found was already strapped to the slideboard—the only piece small enough for us to salvage—and I cinched my pack on top of it. Then I grabbed one of the harnesses, but they were all tangled up together. As I worked on the knot, my extra fingers caught on the straps, pulling the mess tighter. I tried again, but I couldn't loosen the snarl.

"*Mierda!*" I threw the harnesses on the ground and buried my face in my hands.

Then I heard my dad's voice in my ear, his massive hand on my shoulder, saying, "Loosen your grip. Loosen your breath. Loosen the knot."

He wasn't there, of course, but I heard his words anyway. They were sewn into my center.

I took a deep breath, picked up the harnesses, easing the thick straps apart from each other—taking my time, even as I knew I was running out of it. When I finally untangled them, I sliced away the extra sets of harnesses. When fully loaded with salvage, the slideboard would be hauled by four or five people—but right now, the extra straps would only get in the way.

The air was growing hazy by the time I finally slipped on the remaining harness. I triple-checked the fastenings on the shuttle door and my pack, then eyed my route out of there. A small dip between the two sand dunes. Dusk already draped the path—but the mountains were still rimmed with reds and purples—there was enough light to see where I was going. And any second, the men would spot the smoke from the pyre and realize I wasn't going to let them take what was mine. I made myself focus.

I needed to get out of there. I needed to get past the men without being seen. I needed to make it to the Exchange to trade for water and food. I needed to survive, not just for myself, but because I was the only one alive who'd heard the voice over the shuttle's radio. The *only one* who knew how to contact Earth. After all the sermons and laws and Rememberings, this could be the Citizens' chance.

A shout went up from the dunes and all at once, the men came pouring down the hill. Sunset gave their faces a gruesome cast and their mouths gaped, howling in anger and battle—knowing I was burning the very things they needed to survive. I stayed crouched behind that wall, inhaling acrid smoke through my sandmask as they charged toward me. Pulling out my knife, I got ready.

My heart was racing with the same call to battle. Suji liked to call it *the euphoria.* It drowned out fear and reason, and by the time the first of them reached the ruins, everything inside was screaming at me to fight. The men were already wheezing in the smoke, their shirts torn and their rank beards matted with sand. *You can take them,* a voice shouted in my head. But this time it was *not* my father—it was the madness of the fight.

One of the men sprinted right past me—so close I could smell the putrid sweat of him. His eyes were crazed as he started pulling things from the mass of bodies and flames—salvaging what supplies he could. The wind pushed the smoke farther out into the ravine, not enough yet to truly hide me but enough to tighten my lungs. I tried not to cough, counting the men as they passed, knowing that any second one of them might notice me.

Six. Eleven. Seventeen.

Almost.

Then, when I couldn't risk waiting any longer, there was a loud popping and the tires finally caught fire, spewing thick, dark smoke into the camp.

Now.

I plunged out from hiding place—dragging the slideboard with me—and into the oncoming flood of exiles. Making for the cleft between the two dunes, I let the adrenaline take me, running faster than I had in my entire life.

They saw me, but not well. The noxious smoke was already filling the ravine and none of them had masks on. They hadn't had time. Some made a grab for me—I dodged, giddy with the game. But most were on their knees, choking. Even with my own filter, I was gagging as I sprinted.

I could barely see either—but I focused on moving in a straight line, keeping the trailing slideboard balanced. Ahead, I could just make out the space between the dunes. Shapes emerged out of the smoke and disappeared again. Soon dusk would enfold us and I'd be safe. I'd almost made it. A sharp call of triumph barked out of me.

Then a face solidified out of the smog. It was different from the rest of the frenzied mob. This one had a sandmask on and he was just standing in my path. Like he'd been waiting for me. He reached out and I swerved, dodging past him.

But I went barreling headlong into a second man. My brain isolated every detail, searching for weaknesses, like in the final blows of a fight. The man's beard was threaded through with grey, but it was trimmed neatly—square along his jawline. A sandmask hid most of this one's face as well, but what I saw in his eyes was disconcerting. Not anger or greed or lust. But a patient cunning. Like he knew whatever he wanted would simply come to him.

And I had. Despite my careful plan, I'd run straight to him. I managed to dance away, but barely—my slideboard made me clumsy. And not two meters on, there was a third man . . . They were everywhere. I switched directions again, but the sand slid out from under my feet. I skidded sideways and the man with the grey beard grabbed my arm.

"Over here!" He shouted to the exiles around him. But I'd come too far to be taken as some man's Find. His words turned into a howl as I jabbed my knife into his ribs.

I shook him off, but there was another one. And another. I ran, lashing out with my blade as I went. Screams telling me when I'd connected with flesh.

The slideboard was heavy with the shuttle piece strapped to it and the thing almost took me down a couple times—swinging wide whenever I changed directions. But I couldn't cut it loose. No point making it to the Exchange with nothing to trade. It'd simply mean I'd die there, rather than here.

The wind shifted and the black smoke thickened, pressing down on us. The last of the light tried to filter through, but I could barely see anything.

Not even a meter away from me, a man shouted, "Where'd she go?" and an arm jetted out of the swirling clouds.

I froze, then backed away from his grasping hand.

Another man tore out of the haze and snatched at me. This time, I darted to the left, jerking sharply as I did, so that my slideboard whipped around behind me, knocking him down. Running him over.

The surge of smoke pushed its way between the dunes—and I pushed with it. Dusk and haze were swallowing the desert, and I disappeared into it. Running low and fast. Staying in its shelter.

Soon there were no more grabbing hands. And eventually even the screams and shouts faded. I don't know how long I snaked through the shadows of the dunes. Until the smoke cleared and the stars were the only light left in the sky.

The frenzy of the fight cleared too and left me vulnerable. In my head, my blade sliced through the thin skin at Suji's throat over and over. One by one, I hauled the bodies of my crew onto the pile, heavy arms dragging—leaving gouges behind them in the sand like the tracks of some nightmare animal. I jabbed my knife into the bearded man again, feeling it slide between his ribs.

I tried to focus on something, anything, but there were no details out here. Only vagueness of the night desert. I plodded through the punishing sands, my feet sinking deep into the grit. Stumbling over half-buried ruins. The dunes and winds waging their constant war across Tierra Muerta—covering and uncovering its bones.

Crossing the moonlit wasteland, it was hard to imagine that there was once a working colony here. The Rememberings described blue glass towers reaching for the sky. Millions of people filling the streets, living their lives, dreaming dreams I couldn't even imagine. It was impossible to believe that we were all that was left of that world.

Soon my thirst drove even those thoughts from my mind, the craving singing through every inch of my body. I was headed northeast toward the Exchanges. But every step was a battle, the harness digging into my skin. There was something else keeping me moving, though—something stronger than my desperation. A tiny thought that had been born in my mind when I first laid eyes on the shuttle. When I'd heard the voice over the shuttle's radio, breaking through the static. Flying across the stars. Calling to us.

What if I was the one who found the way back to Earth? Me—the Corrupted one. What if I was the one who saved my people from their eternal penance? Would I be Indigno then?

And with that thought goading me on, I sunk one foot in front of the other. Finally, when my urge to collapse had almost overcome my thirst, I came around a dune and saw the narrow strip of metal cutting across the desert. Catching the bright moon. All the Exchanges sat along the magfly tracks. Most of them weren't much more than a bit of roof, a clump of cactus, and a couple of lights. But walk far enough along the tracks in either direction and you'd find one. And with them, the Curadores.

I was in luck. A silvery magfly was loading up at an Exchange just to the south, a breath of light and noise in the dark. Relief broke over me as I walked along the track toward it. I would not fail Suji. I would not fail my sisters or myself. A pulse thrummed through my feet as if lending me its energy. The deep vibration always ran through the tracks, keeping them free of sand and the trains suspended in the air, though no one knew how.

In fact, very little was known about the Curadores. The Abuelos preached that the Curadores were on Gabriel by the grace of God—to help us reach atonement. After all, hadn't God spared their Dome, just as he'd spared Pleiades? Sarika had felt differently, though.

She'd always been devout. But after Marisol ran away to be a Curador's Kisaeng and the outbreak had swept through Pleiades, her beliefs became more extreme. *The Curadores are a temptation . . . demons put here by God,* she'd said. *We eat their food. Trade with them, in their magflys and suits. We allow their sin to dwell alongside us and yet we cry out, "Why hasn't God forgiven us? Why hasn't He delivered us to Earth?"*

It wasn't only Sarika's attitude that changed after the resurgence of Red Death. Before that, the Curadores had simply been a necessary evil. Every animal on Gabriel was contaminated—a carrier of Red Death—and very little grew outside the carefully tended gardens of Pleiades. So the Citizens needed the food the Curadores provided. More than that, they hauled away our scrap and cremated our dead so infections wouldn't spread.

But in the days after the outbreak, I heard more than one person wonder why the Curadores should stay fat and safe in their Dome and isolation suits, while we died out in a wasteland. Some had even whispered that God had abandoned us . . . though only after a few shots of mezcal.

My mother's obsession with the Colony had extended to the Curadores. Once when I was twelve, Mom and I were weeding the gardens together. She'd stopped midrow and I watched her just kneeling there, staring up at the Dome. Then she asked in a hushed voice, "What if God *wasn't* punishing us with Red Death? What if we didn't have to live like this?"

I'd sucked in my breath, stunned by the extent of her blasphemy. Then I'd looked around, afraid someone else had heard. But Mom just squeezed my hand and looked at me in this wide-eyed way she had and said, "Oh, Leica, do you think it's very beautiful inside?"

Now, as I made out the gleam of the Curadores' white isolation suits under the lights of the Exchange, I wondered the same thing. But then the door of the magfly slid shut, the metal disappearing seamlessly into its streamlined shell. And it started moving toward me.

"No!" I shouted, the wind whipping my words away.

The train picked up speed, flying inches above the track. It was a long silver blade slicing through the sand and I had no way to stop it or slow it down.

I needed to find my way back to that half-buried shuttle. And for that I needed water. And food. I would not fail now. I would not let them leave me.

So I simply stood there, in the middle of the tracks, watching the headlights grow bigger and bigger. The buzzing of the metal rails crept up through my boots, echoing in my hip bones and chest, all the way to my jaw. It eclipsed my parched throat, my cramped belly, even the grief sitting on my chest, until I was only this one single thrumming sensation.

And still the massive beast rushed closer. A blast of the horn blanked out the world and shuddered my eardrums. They had seen me.

But it still kept coming. Whipping the wind around me, knocking me off my feet so my kneecaps cracked against the rails. I kept my eyes wide—facing the glaring lights head-on—daring them to try. Rudders jammed into the sand and I was swallowed by a dust cloud. I shut my eyes against the stinging grit, bracing for impact.

It never came. When the air cleared, the pointed nose of the magfly was so close I could touch it—when I pulled off my sand-mask, my breath fogged its surface. I pressed my forehead grate-fully against the cool metal. Death had been after me all day, but he hadn't caught me yet.

Then a Curador in a white isolation suit was towering over me. The lights of the Exchange reflected off the clear plastic face, mak-ing the Curador into a featureless giant. His nasally voice blared from the speakers of the suit. "What the hell do you think you're doing?"

I forced myself to my feet—taking a step back to put distance between me and the Curador. My legs barely held.

I swallowed but I had nothing left to moisten my throat. I pushed the words out anyway. "I'm here to trade."

"Get off the tracks!" His hands clenched and unclenched, as if he wanted to physically remove me. But he didn't dare touch me, even with his suit on.

I squinted up at him, the beam of the magfly blinding me, my whole body numb with exhaustion and adrenaline. I'd never spo-ken to a Curador before. In Pleiades, the Abuelos council dealt with them. Out here, it'd been Suji. I remembered the way she'd talked to them, though—respectful, but uncompromising. Si-lently, I asked Suji to help me to stay calm. I *had* to make them listen to me, one way or another.

No one was leaving until I got my supplies.

"We found uncorroded metal." The *we* scraped in my throat and I swayed a little on my feet.

"Get her out of here." Another Curador joined the first. He switched on a headlamp and scanned the desert around us—the light only making a small dent in the dark. His voice was tentative. Nervous. "We should've been back by now."

"I need you to listen—" But the first one was trying to move me off the tracks, without really touching me. He sort of shoved me with his foot.

Instinctively, I grabbed it and twisted. These were men used to being obeyed, and the faceless Curador went down with a surprised yell. But I had no strength left and I went down with him—a tangle of slick white suit and harness straps.

The Curador on the ground fought to get away, striking out at with me with his huge fists, panicked blows thumping my gut, my shoulder, my face. The other one kicked me in the ribs, yelling for me to get off. But I was still strapped to the slideboard, and the most I could do was protect my head.

Then there was a commanding shout and the blows stopped. A third Curador joined the others.

I blinked up at the new headlamp starbursting above me and struggled to hold on to consciousness. But the voice was gentle. "Are you okay?"

No. I wasn't okay. The world was closing in on me.

"I have to go back . . . I have to find it . . ." Before it went dark, I managed to push the last word out of my raw throat. "Earth."

CHAPTER 3

"WHAT WERE YOU THINKING, PLANCK?"

It was the third voice. The gentle one. Except it wasn't gentle anymore. It was angry and authoritative. "Couldn't you see she was half dead on her feet?"

I opened my eyes, but the men were just out of view. My body was tangled in the harness, my slideboard and its haul twisted alongside me. Being trapped made me nervous, but at least I still had my pack and something to trade.

"I'm sorry." The one I guessed was Planck answered in a nasal whine. "I was just trying to follow Jenner's orders about getting in before nightfall."

"Let me worry about Jenner," the third one said.

"Edison . . . I think . . ." The second Curador—the nervous one—came around the slideboard. I half closed my eyes as he crouched just a couple meters away. His suit was lit from the inside now and he frowned from behind its plastic window. A few brown curls stood out against his cheeks, a shade darker than his skin. He switched the headlamp of his suit brighter and wiped the dust from my Find. "I think you'd better come see this."

The third Curador, Edison, came into view. He was impressive. At least a head taller than the other two. Something about him—his walk, the way he stood—made it clear that he was in charge. But despite his importance, he dropped to his knees, brushing away more of the dust. "What did she say before she passed out?"

"Something about Earth."

I shifted, propping myself up a little to see better, and the movement caught the eye of the nervous one—his eyes darted toward me. His bushy eyebrows raised and his bright green eyes went wide.

"She's awake!"

Planck joined the other two. His blotchy pink skin matched his nasally voice—bright yellow hair standing out against it.

Even in my exhaustion, I marveled at how different they looked. From each other. From me.

Since the Citizens had all descended from such a small group of surviving Colonists, we were like slight variations of the same song—straight black hair, dark eyes, light brown skin.

But the Curadores were different. Their variations were endless. Blond hair, brown hair, black, curly, straight. Skin from pale moon to the darkest dusk. The only thing they all had in common was their size. The smallest of them were still larger than the biggest of the Citizens.

Edison helped me to sit up, his suit warm where it touched me—heated in the chilly desert. I groaned involuntarily as I moved, my body throbbing from the blows of the other Curadores. From escaping the exiles. From the grief of the last days. He took my hand—pausing for the slightest of seconds as he stared at my fingers—before molding them around a heavy plastic jug.

"Here. Drink." His voice was quiet, but insistent.

And suddenly the mad thirst reared up through the pain. Not able to stop myself, I grabbed the jug, gulping the water in giant, greedy swallows.

"Slow down." Edison eased the plastic jug away from my lips. Precious drops spilled across the sand but he didn't even notice. "You'll make yourself sick."

I nodded and tried again. Forcing myself to take small sips, catching my breath in between.

"I'm Edison. This is Planck"—he jerked his head first toward the pink-faced Curador, then at the nervous one—"and Sagan. Let me apologize for what happened. My men shouldn't have treated you like that."

There was true concern in his eyes as he knelt in front of me. Unlike Planck and Sagan, Edison wasn't afraid to get close to me, and it was impossible not to stare.

He was perfect. Like someone had taken the best parts of every face and arranged them in complete balance. High cheekbones that gave his face a sleek, angled look. Matched with a straight, broad nose. And skin that gleamed deepest brown with a hint of purple. The color of the mountains at dusk. It made your eyes drift to the brightness of his mouth. Making his smile or frown matter that much more. But his eyes were the finishing touch. Yellow-orange eyes. Like the blaze of firelight through a glass of mezcal.

"I'm Leica." I tilted my head in greeting and gave him my name as a way of accepting his apology. This was the Curador to trade with. It wasn't just that he was in charge, which he obviously was. Something about him made me sure he'd give me a fair deal. He was the kind of Curador who would fit inside the lovely Dome my mother had imagined.

"What happened to you?" Edison squinted into the dark behind me. "Where's your crew?"

No Citizen was fool enough to wander Tierra Muerta on their own. Especially no woman.

I couldn't begin to describe the past few days, so I simply said "Gone." The single syllable sounded harsh and cold, so I added "Red Death . . . May God protect them." The last words spilled out of my mouth—half habit, half prayer.

"Looks like it's too late for that." His words were sharp and I was reminded that there was a much bigger difference than what we looked like. The Curadores lived with the luxury of isolation suits and the safety of the Dome, whereas Citizens spent our lives exposed, at the mercy or wrath of God.

"Though he seems to have had a soft spot for you." And there was an eagerness in his eyes now, something he was trying to rein in. "Is this all you found? Or is there more?"

His hint of eagerness infected me. I managed to pull free of the harness and get to my feet. I tried to plant myself in a confident fighter's stance, but I imagined what I must look like to him in the glare of the magfly. A short girl with lukewarm brown skin smeared with blood. Wild black hair that I'd kept short, barely long enough to cover my ears. My freakish hands covered in bluegrey dust.

Together, we looked down at the oval door with a small window in it. Uncorroded metal—worth a fortune in Gratitude. The headlights shone yellow against the tarnished letters that'd been stamped into it over five hundred years ago: *Lockheed Martin*.

"There's more," I said. My neck ached as I looked up at Edison. He was one and a half times my height, his wide shoulders stretching out the white plastic of the isolation suit. "The whole shuttle is intact and—"

But Edison interrupted. "Is that how your crew got sick?"

I nodded and touched my aching head, trying to block out the memory of what we'd found inside the shuttle. "We were forced to abandon it, but I have to go back. There was someone . . . on the radio. Someone from Earth."

And in a voice used to giving orders, Edison said, "I'm going with you."

"No." A Curador was not going to be the savior of my people.

A flicker of anger crossed his face. It was a risk to refuse a Curador. I tried to backtrack. "I mean, the whole thing is infected with Red Death . . ."

"So you said. But I'm wearing an isolation suit and you appear to be immune. So we're just the people to go after it."

"No. Just trade me for supplies and I'll be on my way." This was a *Citizen* matter. When Sarika preached of God returning us to Earth, I'd always imagined the Citizens being miraculously transported to a divine realm. But maybe *this* was what forgiveness looked like—a long-forgotten shuttle and a staticky voice. I looked down at my hands—maybe I had been marked, not for suffering, but for salvation.

"And what will you do when you find it? Will you haul it back by yourself? On your slideboard?"

There was a smugness in Edison's voice that made me want to hit him, but he was right. What had I expected to happen when I got there? Did I think that God would reach down from heaven and take the shuttle to Pleiades himself? No, the truth was, I hadn't thought past making it back to the shuttle.

"There will be no trade—no food, no water—unless you take me with you." Edison smiled as he said it. There was no threat in his voice. No malice. It was just a simple fact from a man, a boy really, who was used to getting his own way. And he was about to get it this time too.

CHAPTER 4

"IN THE NAME OF the Curadores, I claim this object, found beneath the sandline. It will be used for the good of all who live on Gabriel and all those who will live." Edison intoned the words of the trade ritual. Behind him, Planck and Sagan were distracted, scanning the darkness that pressed in around the Exchange.

We didn't haggle about the Gratitude—enough food to make the journey there and back. The shuttle would be the real prize. And as long as I made it back to the radio, I didn't care what happened to the rest.

As I made the proper response to Edison, the other two hauled the shuttle door into the magfly and loaded my slideboard with bowls of chiken, beeph jerky, five jugs of water, a packet of salt, and two bottles of mezcal. "I accept your Gratitude. In the name of the Citizens, I surrender these sins of Gabriel into your hands. My hands are clean."

Then while Planck went from pink to red trying to convince Edison to come back to the Dome with them, I filled my belly with a tepid slurry of chiken and water and unrolled my blanket. I lay down, exhausted, on the hard grit, but the voices of strange men were the least of what kept me awake. Knots of grief sat tucked behind my shoulder blades. Tied themselves around bruised ribs. Banded themselves down aching, tense arms.

It hurt to breathe. It hurt to close my eyes—as everything I'd lost came rushing back. It even hurt to look at the stars. There were just too many of them.

And yet, sleep must have taken me. Because at some point I opened my eyes and the magfly was gone and Edison sat alone by a fire. The weight of night had settled itself on the valley. *Had Edison slept at all? Do Curadores sleep?*

The cold had deepened too and I walked over, letting the flames warm my stiff muscles. "We should get going. It's sandstorm season and the desert's already got three days' head start."

But there was another reason I wanted to get moving. As soon as the sun rose, we risked running into another crew. More than likely, they'd leave a Curador alone, but I didn't want to chance it. I had enough strength left to get back to the shuttle. But not enough to fight anyone else off.

Edison pulled a bowl from the edge of the fire and sat it steaming on a nearby rock. "Then taking another few moments for you to eat something won't matter."

It smelled like beeph. Something—aside from the jerky—I'd only ever had at Festivals. My stomach groaned. Then Edison brought out a jar of kimchi and started heaping it onto the meat. My hands moved without my permission. I was lucky I didn't burn my fingers as I snatched the bowl from the rock and pulled my whittled chopsticks from my pack.

The beeph was rich and tender. But after more than a year and a half in exile, it was the kimchi that I craved. The sting of vinegar and peppery heat hit my nose, waking me up. Crunchy and soft at the same time, fire exploded on my tongue, playing against the sourness as I chewed.

"Where did you get this?" I couldn't help the awed tone that crept into my voice.

"From the Abuelos. We trade for it along with the scrap. We have to decontaminate it before it comes into the Dome, of course . . . but it's worth it. I figured you could use some to warm you up."

It was odd, thinking of the Curadores inside their dome eating our kimchi. It was something so rooted in Pleiades. I took another bite and when I closed my eyes, I could *see* home. Cabbages growing in the Commons—rows of bright green heads in the dirt. Chiles just ripening—flashes of red hidden among the leaves. My sisters on their knees weeding and singing—their voices weaving a dizzying harmony, each trying to catch the other.

It wasn't until I was almost finished that it occurred to me I was eating alone.

"Do you want some?" I panicked, wondering if maybe it was the custom of Curadores to share from one dish.

"No thanks." He laughed at the sad remains in my bowl. "My suit takes care of all that, releasing nutrients as needed, filtering and recycling . . ." He trailed off, almost looking embarrassed. "Suffice it to say, nothing in or out while we're away from the Dome. It's safer that way."

I shrugged, happily running my finger around the inside of the bowl, savoring the very last bits. Then I scrubbed the bowl out with grit and stood up. Edison was on his feet a second later, throwing sand on the fire and slotting his arms through the slideboard harness. I started to object, but shut my mouth. Right now, I could barely carry myself, let alone my supplies.

We traveled in silence—keeping our feet and eyes moving. Edison's headlamp lit up a broad swath in front of us, but I watched the edge of the beam. Wild dogs were calling to each other in the distance. Though not as distant as I would've liked. There's a reason you don't usually travel at night in Tierra Muerta. Anything the dogs outnumber they considered food.

Even without the slideboard, my bruised body was painfully slow. I longed to run across the desert—to reassure myself that the shuttle was still there. At first, Edison stuck close, but his impatience won out. His vast, long legs strode out ahead; then he'd have to wait for me to catch up. As the hours wore on, he crept farther and farther ahead—leaving me only a puddle of light. I knew why I wanted to find the shuttle, but what was at stake for him? I always assumed the Curadores were happy in their Dome. But was it possible they also prayed for God's salvation? And it hit me how little I knew about my companion.

I kept my eyes on the stars, my only guide in the darkness. Once I had to call Edison back to make a course correction. I crouched in the sand, drinking water while he retraced his route.

"Sorry," Edison called as he climbed up the dune again to reach me. He sounded almost embarrassed.

I shrugged. "Your legs, not mine." Then I couldn't help myself. "What exactly are you doing out in Tierra Muerta in the middle of the night?"

"I thought we were looking for the shuttle."

"But surely you could've sent your lackeys. Why are *you* here?"

Edison sat in the sand next to me. "We heard your voice on the radio."

"You and Planck and Sagan?" I didn't understand.

"Actually, everyone in the Dome heard you. Your signal was picked up by the Curadores' receivers . . . in fact, it broadcast across all our channels."

It was strange, thinking that my voice had traveled into the Dome without me knowing it. That others had been listening to Suji and me that day. Then again, if the signal could travel back and forth from Earth, why wouldn't it travel across the valley too?

"And you heard the response from Earth too?" The idea was both reassuring and deflating. If the Curadores had heard the message from Earth, it made it so much more *real*. But at the same time, somehow it made it less *mine*.

"No, actually. A few receivers picked up a second set of transmissions, but it was nothing but a garbled squealing. Still, we guessed where that second signal must be coming from. Though, honestly, it was *you* that got my attention. There was . . ." And he paused, as if trying to put something into words. "There was triumph in your voice."

And I remembered standing in the shuttle, grabbing the radio— as if this was a moment I always knew would come—and shouting *"This is Ad Astra! We're alive!"*

"So you came out to find the radio," I said.

"I had to. My whole life, I've been stuck under that Dome. Or in this damn suit. I want to know what it's like to walk under the open sky."

"To be in a place that isn't trying to kill you?"

"Exactly." And Edison gave me his wide grin. His amber eyes flared in the light of his suit. "I'm hoping that place is Earth."

And it was that spark in his eyes that caught *my* attention. The men in Pleiades trudged through life, spending their days erasing the past. Praying for a future they didn't believe would come. And the men in Tierra Muerta were angry, just trying to live for another day. Trying to keep hold of anything they could get their hands on. None of them had anything like that spark.

I looked up at the thousands of tiny lights glowing above us. Earth was out there somewhere. We *would* reach it again. But right now, I saw something else too. The line of mountains, black against the less black sky—dawn wasn't far off.

"We've got a lot of ground to cover. Let's go." I stood, dusting sand off. Not that it helped much.

"Okay." Edison kept pace next to me as we headed in the right direction. "It's your turn now. You've been through hell and yet here you are, dragging yourself across a freezing, dark desert. Why?"

The prophesied return to Earth was such a central tenet of Pleiades, it seemed impossible Edison could even ask that question. Perhaps Citizens were as big a mystery to Curadores as they were to us. "How much do you know about the Rememberings?"

"A bit. But if your God *is* calling the Citizens back home, surely he wouldn't show you the shuttle just to bury it again."

I glanced down at my hands, then gave him a bitter smile. "Let's just say I don't completely trust God."

As dawn came, so did the wind. My book of fairy tales described Earth as having seasons like Summer and Winter, but Gabriel only had Dry, Less Dry, and Windy. It's why Pleiades had regular

Festivals—to mark the passage of the year. If I'd counted right we were still a few months shy of two years since I'd been exiled, and that put us right in the middle of Windy.

But today, the sun never properly took to the sky. The desert picked up sand and threw it in my face. Reluctantly, I admitted to myself that this was more than just wind—a sandstorm was building. I forced myself to walk faster, but the wind pushed at us so we were moving even slower than before. We were running out of time.

My eyes—trained to scan for salvage even in the dust—kept catching on right angles jutting out of curved dunes. Rust red against the blue sand. Ancient buildings finding their way to the surface only to be buried again by the next sandstorm. None of them were the shuttle.

I was so focused on the dunes that I almost ran into Edison and the slideboard when he suddenly stopped.

"What's wrong?" I pulled my knife—turning in a slow circle—searching the desert for signs of another crew or dangerous animals.

"Look at that!" Edison pointed at the sky. A shaft of sun had pierced the murky grey-blue haze. High above, grains of sand caught the light—swirling and dancing—before swallowing the sun again. "I've never seen anything like it!"

There was gleeful awe in Edison's voice, clueless to the danger we were in. I, on the other hand, had seen something like it. This was no passing dust devil. It was a Hwangsa—a wall of unforgiving sand rising straight up into the sky.

"Let's hope you live to remember it."

Edison heard the fear in my voice and his smile disappeared.

His words—amplified by his suit—rose up over the wind. "How much farther?"

"Just a kilometer or two, I think. But we'd better cover them fast." I had an extremely good sense of direction, even in Tierra Muerta, where dunes shifted and disappeared every day. But there was nothing of the mountains or sky left to navigate by. Only clouds of sand churning on the horizon.

I pulled on my sandmask and we fought our way up one dune and then another, and with each aching step, I went over our choices in my head. We had no shelter. No sand anchors. And no tarp to attach them to even if we did.

There it was—there were no choices. There was only sand.

And then . . . a tiny bit of not-sand.

"There!" Edison saw it too. He pointed down at a silver wing sticking out of the ground. The shuttle was already half buried and the Hwangsa was coming to finish the job.

Edison lunged down the dune toward the shuttle. But I grabbed his arm, stopping him.

The first rule in Tierra Muerta was: head to high ground. When making camp, it gave you a defensible position. When scavenging, it gave you the best vantage point. In a sandstorm, assuming you could anchor your shelter, it gave you a fighting chance. It only took one mistake for you to learn that rule. And by then you were dead.

Edison's voice was low and calm, but there was a cord of urgency running through it. "Tell me what to do and I'll do it."

"Do you have any way to communicate with the other Curadores? Can they send help?"

"Yes." Then Edison was quiet for a second. His lips moved, but no sound came out of the speakers. He shook his head. "The storm's messing with the signal. I'm not picking up anything."

And he switched on the speakers so I could hear the hiss of static coming through them. It matched the hiss of the wind in my ears.

"In that case, if we stay up here, the sand will blast away your isolation suit and tear off my skin. If we go down there, we'll be buried."

"Well?" Edison flashed me a manic grin. "Which is it?"

"Well?" The wind lashed and pulled at my hair—raking through the tangles. Its hunger hot on my face. "Well . . . what are you waiting for? Run!"

And I rushed down the dune. Edison gave a sort of battle cry, sprinting after me. Soon, he was in the lead, his giant legs pulling him and the slideboard across the sand. In spite of everything, it was magnificent to see. Almost like the magfly skimming across the ground—impossibly fast. He reached the shuttle long before me and was on his knees, clearing the door hatch and throwing the contents of the slideboard inside.

The storm was on us now, scouring my skin. Sand clogging the filters of my sandmask. Sneaking in the edges. I ripped it off. Gasping for breath and getting a mouthful of grit.

I couldn't see anymore. I let the sloping ground pull me forward, hoping to God I hadn't veered off course. Then I saw it, the outline of the shuttle visible only as an absence of sand.

Edison pulled me in. But the sand easily followed us inside the dark, cramped shuttle. The shuttle was probably fifteen meters long, but we couldn't move any deeper into its shelter because the narrow aisle was crammed with crates and bags. I dumped everything off the slideboard, and with Edison's help, shoved it in front of the door.

"It's not enough!" I said, coughing as the insidious sand still found its way in. Edison grabbed a crate and started building a makeshift wall, and I joined him, stacking anything I could find, until finally, we'd barricaded ourselves in. I let myself sink to the floor and Edison put the jug of water in my hands—threading my fingers through the handle, like he did before. Making sure I could hold it.

"We made it." He smiled again, but this time it was a quiet smile. And he nodded to himself.

But I didn't find any comfort in his words. After all, I understood what we'd just done. *Barricaded ourselves in.* Now all I could hear was the howl of Tierra Muerta as it buried us alive.

CHAPTER 5

"OKAY," EDISON SAID after I'd caught my breath. "Let's see this radio of yours."

He upped the brightness on his headlamp and the shuttle was illuminated around us.

"What the hell?" Edison's breath rasped against his microphone as he took in the terrible scene.

I'd known what to expect, but that didn't make it any less grisly. The dead were everywhere—their mouths pulled tight in fear. Skin still covered their bones, stretched and molded like leather over the shape of their skulls. The desert had taken all the water from them but nothing more.

Their matching clothes were still bright. Green jackets still buttoned up and khaki pants still creased. Like any second they would just get out of their seats and walk through the door.

"May God find you worthy," I murmured.

Edison's light reflected against a necklace on one of the corpses. He gingerly unfastened the clasp, pulling the necklace off so he could see it better.

A black metal tag dangled from a chain of tiny silver beads. And

I didn't need to get any closer to know what was printed on it. It was a twin of the one in my pack. Lotus's naming gift.

"Ad Astra Research Colony." He read the tiny letters engraved on one side, then flipped it over. There was a simple outline of a flower and more engraving. "LOTUS 900167845003."

"They're all wearing them," I said.

"Maybe they're for identification," he said.

"But they all say the same thing. Same words. Same number."

"You can read this?" Edison sounded surprised.

"Not all Citizens believe curiosity to be a sin." Just most of them. Very few Citizens could read. Writing was considered to be one more relic of the Colonists' arrogance. The Abuelos preached that illiteracy was a sign of humility. And to be honest, there was very little opportunity to learn. But my mother had taught us in secret. Thinking of the book, heavy in my pack, I didn't know whether to hate her or love her for it. Either way, the book had brought me here.

Edison and I moved farther into the claustrophobic space. I tip-toed past the bodies, like I was afraid we'd wake them. I brushed against one of them, knocking off its hat. There was a crunch of glass and Edison looked down to see what he'd stepped on.

"Don't touch it." I knew Edison was wearing an isolation suit, but all I could see was the scene playing itself over again. Edison's eyes growing bloodshot. The fever raging though him. Blood leaching out of him until there was nothing left.

"What is it?" He peered down at the shards.

"It was a glass tube . . . from that box." I pointed to the fluorescent orange plastic case lying open on the floor. Thick black foam lined the inside, with a space hollowed out for the now-broken glass tube. There was a second orange case nearby. This one was still closed, but a huge crack ran across the lid. And there was an emblem on the broken case too—three overlapping circles with a fourth in the center. Judging by the passengers in the shuttle, that didn't mean anything good.

"I was up front trying the radio when Suji opened the thing."

"Tell me everything that happened."

I shut my eyes, and as I told him about that day, it replayed in my mind. Like a vivid nightmare before it fades. How I'd spotted the shuttle after a dust storm—silver against the bluish sand. How Suji and I had pried off the door and pushed our way inside while the rest of the crew worked to uncover the body of the shuttle. How we played with the radio, pressing buttons until we found something. At first, it was just a recorded voice playing over and over.

"Lotus Colony, this is Homebase. You are under temporary quarantine. Enter verification and transmit on priority frequency so emergency evacuations can be coordinated."

"Emergency evacuations," Suji snorted. *"Probably been saying that for five centuries."*

"Then why didn't anyone ever answer?"

"Maybe they did. Maybe Earth didn't give a shit."

"Then why keep playing the message?" It didn't make sense. Everyone always assumed that contact with Earth had been cut off when the plague started. That Earth had abandoned us. And yet, here was this message, traveling through the stars to reach us. *"Someone must have heard it."*

"Well, these folks weren't in any shape to do anything about it." She looked over her shoulder at the desiccated corpses.

"But surely someone else on Gabriel had a radio."

Suji shrugged. "Maybe no one had a chance. Imagine it, Leica. There were millions of people in this colony. Not hundreds. Or thousands like Pleiades, but millions. The fact that anyone was spared the first wave of Red Death was a miracle in itself."

"Then, at least we should answer it."

Suji rolled her eyes, but she played along anyway. We took turns pushing glowing buttons and twisting knobs and shouting "Hello? Hello?" into the microphone.

Suji gave up first. "No one's gonna answer. Not after all this time." She turned away and I could hear the bitterness in her voice. "They probably think we're all dead."

But I kept trying. It was impossible not to.

Suji went into the back and I remembered hearing the pop of the brackets on the orange case. And an explosive hiss of air. I was just about to ask Suji what she'd found when the message cut out and a real voice blared across the radio.

"Ad Astra? Is that you?"

I stared at the flashing dashboard light in shock.

The shaken, high-pitched voice spoke again. "Hello? Is someone alive out there?"

There was a sudden crunch of glass and muttered swearing as Suji hurried to the front of the shuttle to join me. "Was that a real person? Was that Earth?"

I grabbed the microphone. "Hello? This is Ad Astra. We're alive!"

Static poured through the speakers. But no voice. I twisted the knob and repeated myself. More static.

"Put it back where it was!" Suji ordered, and as I turned the knob, a man's voice emerged from the noise. "Identify yourself. What is your location and stat—"

That voice cut off as well, and the recorded message started repeating again.

Suji grabbed the microphone. "Hello? Hello?" She started mashing buttons. "Come back!"

That's when I noticed the trickle of blood dripping down her fingers. I grabbed her hand, and when Suji turned to me, her wide eyes were already streaked with pink. And her skin had flushed a coppery red.

I closed my eyes, forcing the tears to stay locked behind them. I would not allow them to come in this place. In this moment. No. Right now, I would be the Leica I needed to be to get through the sandstorm. To survive. To find a way home.

"Then that's what made your crew sick." Edison nudged the broken glass with the toe of his boot. "And these unlucky suckers too." He squatted by the broken case. "I mean, why have something like that on board a shuttle? You think they brought it from Earth? Or maybe they meant to take it back with them?"

"Do you think they even knew what they were carrying?" I shuddered, thinking of the dead people around us. Of Suji. "The thing is . . . the fever came so fast. Minutes, not days. As soon as we figured out what'd happened, we abandoned the shuttle . . . before I started showing symptoms too."

"But you never *did* show symptoms."

"No. That's the funny part." I gave him a grim smile and I recited the words of the Remembering. *"But God is merciful. He saved some. Made them immune. Made others strong enough to survive the plague. Scattered that strength through the generations."*

There was irony in the idea of God wasting immunity on someone he'd already damned. And there was that wheedling thought again: *What if I'd been marked for another purpose?* But that would mean God had just let everyone else die. *Why?*

I was shocked to realize that I didn't care what the answer was. I wasn't sure *what* I believed anymore, but I was certain of one thing: if God did exist, he was a bastard.

"Suji pretty much collapsed before we made it to the ravine, and by the time we made camp, two more of them"—I refused to say their names, refused to see their panicked faces—"had fevers. It came for them one by one . . . but not for me."

Edison reached out for my clenched fist, trying to loosen it, to soothe me. I had the urge to punch him—my anger, my pain, was mine to feel. I had no wish for it to be soothed away. I glared up at him and was surprised to see my own pain reflected in his eyes. And I reminded myself that I had no idea what Edison might've lost in his own life.

I let him ease open my fingers. He ran his gloved thumb over the five half-moon indentations I'd left on my palm.

I pulled away and swiped at my face. Forcing myself back to the here and now. "So the upside is, I should be perfectly fine in here until I run out of oxygen." I breathed in—hot and musty. It was a big shuttle, but the air wouldn't last forever.

"Well, I certainly don't want that happening. I mean, these guys don't look like very good company." Edison put on a cheesy grin and said, "Let's see if we can't use the radio to get ahold of the Curadores . . . see if we can't talk them into paying a visit and hauling us out of this thing."

"Right." I headed back up the aisle to the front of the shuttle. Then froze.

"What's wrong?" Edison asked.

"One of the bodies. It's been moved." When Suji and I had first investigated, there'd been a corpse sitting in the front seat, straight up, like the others. But now the dead woman was sprawled across the aisle.

Edison's headlamp illuminated the cockpit. Instead of panels of lights and dials and glowing screens, there were only loose wires and gaping holes.

It was all gone. I felt like I'd been punched in the throat. That radio had been my way out of exile. Its link to Earth had been my way home.

"Dammit." Edison's jokes disappeared fast. He slammed his fist into the ceiling of the shuttle. The whole thing shook—dust kicking up into the air, plastic windows rattling against their frames.

"Careful," I hissed. "All we need is for this thing to fall in on us."

"Sorry." His face was contorted in what almost looked like pain. This was more than simple curiosity about Earth or yearning for open sky. And I wondered again if the Curadores wanted to find a way off Gabriel too.

Edison closed his eyes, breathing deep. When he opened them again, the frustration had been cleared away.

I was glad. There was something untethered about his anger.

"Someone else beat us to it." I stepped over the woman's body, looking for anything useful that might be left. But whoever'd been here had done a good job of it. They'd gutted all the electronics for salvage and snipped the wires close to the ends. There was nothing left to work with. "Does that mean whoever did this got sick too?"

Edison considered for a moment. "Probably not. The hiss you heard when Suji opened the case was probably some kind of coolant system. The case must've had its own power source . . . and even then, after all this time it's surprising the virus was still alive. If Suji hadn't cut herself on the contaminated glass, I doubt it would've been strong enough to infect any of you. My guess is that any trace of the disease died minutes after the test tube broke. But as it was, the virus went straight into the bloodstream, allowing it to hit hard and fast."

It made it worse somehow—the happenstance of Suji's death.

"Now what?" Edison asked, looking at the scavenged cockpit.

"Now?" Sand had climbed past the tops of the windows, muffling the Hwangsa until it was only a faint moan. I sat down on the floor, leaning against the slideboard and the makeshift wall of bags holding it tight against the hatch. "*Now* we wait."

Automatically, I slid the knife out of my belt. When you were exhausted . . . when you were resting . . . these were the times to be at the ready. Only then did I relax enough to have some water and jerky.

Edison sat against the opposite wall, leaning forward against his bent knees, facing me. He was trying to make himself as small as possible in the cramped shuttle—putting as much distance as he could between himself and the dead. He was like a giant from the pages of my book, only folded up and shoved in a cupboard.

In the quiet, I could feel the weight of the sand bearing down on us—blanking out the world. How long until we were just another piece of salvage buried beneath the sandline? But it was a different question that kept going around and around in my head until it spilled out. "What if that was our one chance and we missed it? What if we can never contact Earth again?"

Edison shook his head. "I don't believe that. I won't. You know how I told you that we couldn't understand the reply from

Earth . . . that the signal was garbled over our radios? It wasn't the first time we've heard unidentifiable transmissions like that. In fact, we usually have to avoid that channel on our coms."

"Do you think the transmission was garbled on purpose?"

"I think it was some kind of code." He nodded, his eyes bright. "And more than that, I think there was something about this radio and this shuttle that let you ungarble it."

His excitement was contagious. I tried to picture all the buttons and flashing lights and switches Suji and I had hit. There'd been much more than just a radio on that dashboard.

"And something that allowed us to respond."

"Exactly!" A grin spread across his face. "A descrambler. *And* when the exiles who took the equipment bring it to an Exchange, we'll have it! Then we can try again."

We. We can try again. *We* is the problem. Because I wanted the radio for Pleiades and Edison wanted it for the Dome. But the Rememberings said nothing about Curadores. Even if I no longer believed God had much to do with all this, the Abuelos certainly did. And if I wanted to see my sisters again . . . if I wanted to prove myself a devout Citizen . . . I would need to play by Pleiades' rules.

"Yes." I tried not to let my doubt show in my face. "As long as *we* manage to get out of here." I leaned my head against the make-shift wall. "Let's get some sleep while we can. If we're lucky, when the storm passes, you can reach your buddies and they can get us out of here."

"And if we're not lucky?"

"Then we'll need all the strength we can get to dig ourselves out." I closed my eyes.

But no sleep came.

After a few minutes, Edison's voice broke the quiet again. "Will you tell me about Pleiades?"

"Why?"

"Because when you're talking, I can't hear the sand burying us alive."

"What should I tell you about?"

"How about your sisters?"

I usually tried not to think about them. In some ways, I'd always been an exile from Pleiades, so leaving my home was not the burden it might've been. But leaving my sisters . . . that was different. "We were born, one after the other . . . three children in three years."

"Sounds nice."

I laughed. "Sometimes it was. Sometimes they drove me crazy." I remembered the sudden isolation of those first days in Tierra Muerta, before Suji found me. I'd never been without my sisters before. "But it meant I always knew my role. I was the damaged one." I glanced down at my hands. "The one who knew how to break the tension with a laugh. I was the lightening rod." And then suddenly, I was nothing.

"And what about them?"

"Taschen's the oldest. She's the peacemaker. She knows what to do to keep everyone happy." But that wasn't right. Not happy, so much as, make everyone okay. I struggled to explain it. "Like just before I was exiled, I was . . . anxious."

That was putting it mildly. The Abuelos had been going after rumors of unrest. They'd been raiding apartments, sometimes to look for salvage smuggled from the Reclamation Fields. Sometimes just to show they were in charge. My extra fingers and our family's reputation made us the perfect target. "And Taschen slipped this bit of lime peel into my pocket. It was a scrap of nothing, but when I found it later in the day, I was deep down in the pits and the smell was like a bit of sunshine. And I felt . . . cared for, you know?"

My chest burned and I was surprised by how much that memory still hurt. Then Edison asked, "And your younger sister?"

"Lotus." I thought about her hesitation that day at the Festival. "It's strange. Even though she was the youngest, she was the protector."

I remembered her as a little girl, frowning the first time one of the older boys spit at my feet and told me I couldn't play some game or other. Lotus studied my extra pinkies as if seeing them for the first time. *But that's stupid,* she said, *that's just the way you were born.* "She plays things close to the chest . . . watching. Thinking. It made her a good fighter, but it also made her hold back."

Until it didn't. A week after the incident, six-year-old Lotus had been working in the garden while the other kids were playing tag. She waited until the older boy ran past, then stuck out her rake and sent him sprawling into a heap of compost. Then she'd disappeared into the rows of blackberries before anyone could figure out what'd happened. But she'd made sure I'd seen it.

Lotus had an innate sense of righteousness. Like the sudden rainstorms that hit the desert—unrelenting as they gouged a path through the dunes—her vindication was swift and absolute.

"Lotus. That's what's printed on the necklace." Edison looked up at the corpses.

I shrugged, feeling protective of my family. The old habits of hiding were hard to break. "You find the word everywhere out in the Reclamation Fields."

It was true; in the lowest levels of the pits the word *was* everywhere. Printed in chipped paint on the walls. On fragments of equipment. And, of course, on the necklace. The gift hadn't been arbitrary, though. The oblong pendants were made out of a curious metal—something I'd never seen anywhere else in Pleiades or the Reclamation Fields. The black alloy wasn't rusted or tarnished and its matte finish was so dark, it seemed to absorb light rather than reflect it. My mother wouldn't have been able to resist such a Find.

Edison said, "I thought everyone in Pleiades was named after the original survivors . . ."

I nodded. "When my mother was pregnant, Lotus came too fast . . . she was actually born down in a digsite Mom was scouting. And my mother had a thing about the Reclamation Fields. In fact, she named us all after Finds she salvaged while she was pregnant." I didn't mention anything about the stealing.

"What about your name then?"

"Leica was a camera. Boxy with curved lenses."

"And Taschen?"

"A book." I glanced involuntarily at my pack. "Our names did nothing to help our popularity."

Edison nodded in the silence—as if he understood something I hadn't said out loud. "My brother and I were like that too. Different from everyone else. Alone."

"What about your parents?"

"It's not the same in the Dome. We don't really do things like that." By the soft light of his suit, I could see the frown pulling down his mouth.

"You don't have parents?" So little was known about the Curadores and their Dome, but I couldn't imagine how that was possible.

"Well, after the plague first came to Gabriel, there weren't enough of us left inside the Dome to repopulate. But we had genetic samples from Earth . . . we used those to prevent inbreeding. So we don't really know our parents."

"How are you born, then?"

"Well, one of the Mothers has to carry us, of course. But we aren't *her* child. When we're born, we become children of the whole Dome. And all the Mothers raise us."

"It doesn't sound like you were alone."

"My brother and I weren't allowed to spend much time with the other kids. We just had each other. And *Jenner*." But the way he said the man's name sounded almost like a curse—I didn't dare ask more about him. "Like I said, Nikola and I were different. We're . . ." And he hesitated before saying, "The *future*."

The word set off a kind of wild combustion in his eyes. Like he'd lost his footing and was falling. His fists tightened into balls and he was almost shaking. I didn't need him punching walls again, so I reached over and put my hand on his leg. I met his eyes—matching the caustic fire with the unflinching blackness of my own. Slowly, the panic eased from his face.

"I wish, growing up, that Nikola and I had known you and your sisters," he said.

"Well, I know you now," I said.

Edison smiled at me and his eyes settled back into a steady flame.

• • •

At some point, I must've drifted off. I was dreaming of wild dogs attacking. Ripping me apart. Then suddenly, my dream self was very alert. Sounds were filtering down to me, through layers of sleep.

Breathing.

Someone . . . nearby. Closer than they had any right to be. Closer to my belongings than was smart.

Careful not to twitch my face or eyelids, I tightened my grip on my knife. Then I launched myself in their direction at the same moment I opened my eyes.

I had my knife at Edison's throat before I even understood who he was or where we were. My pack flew across the shuttle in the attack, but Edison was frozen—wide-eyed, backed against the wall. My book clutched to his chest.

"What do you think you're doing?" I said. Edison made a choked noise and I pulled the knife away.

"I'm sorry. I didn't want to wake you," he said. "I just wanted to see if you had anything in your bag that might help us get out of here."

"Like a working radio?" My voice was a growl, but I stuck the knife back in my belt and checked my pack. Water, scope, jerky. And I felt the outline of Lotus's necklace, sewn into an inside pocket.

Edison looked chastened. But I wasn't sure if he felt bad for rifling through my things or for getting caught. "I don't know what I thought. I was just hoping . . . I'm sorry. I should've realized it would be an unforgivable invasion."

He laid my book gently in front of me. "I'm sorry."

As I picked it up, I was struck by the ridiculousness of the whole situation. Here we were, trapped inside a shuttle. Probably completely buried under the sand by now. Edison wasn't trying to steal anything. I mean, what would he do with it?

Still . . . I ran my hand over the cover. He shouldn't have been going through my things.

"*Fairy Tales of the Brothers Grimm*?" The authority was gone from Edison's voice, leaving it tentative. "Is that the book?"

I stiffened, running my fingers over the gold lettering on the cover. I had to remind myself that the Curadores had nothing to do with Pleiades' laws and its prejudices. In fact, Curadores lived with technology every day . . . they were alive *because* of it. "The book?"

"The book you said your mother named Taschen after."

"Oh. Yes. This is the book." And I showed him where the word *Taschen* was written in gold on the binding.

Lotus had been fascinated by the Grimms' tales when she was little, flipping through the pictures thousands of times. She'd been slower to read than I had, and Taschen had no interest in learning at all. So it had fallen to me to read the fairy tales to both of them.

But once we'd gone through the fairy tales so often we had them memorized, Tasch had taken to making up her own. Ones where, as she put it, the girls just don't wait around in towers and the men aren't quite so stupid. As we got older, somehow the stories had become more real—inspired by the things we'd seen and found out in the Reclamation Fields. We'd whispered them late at night in our bedroom, feeling a giddy rebelliousness as we imagined what the original Colony might've been like. Or the dream of returning to Earth, journeying on great ships through the stars. Living a life that had nothing to do with plagues, hunger, or atonement.

"Can I hear one of the stories?" Edison asked.

I hesitated. The book had been a secret between me and my sisters for so long—it almost felt like a betrayal to read the fairy tales without them. Then again, it would keep back the dark and the nightmares.

And I opened the book to my sisters' favorite. A story I knew by heart.

Once upon a time . . . there was a sorcerer who disguised himself as a beggar. He went from house to house stealing beautiful girls. He spirited them away and no one knew where, for none of them were ever heard from again.

"Let me see that thing." Edison came and sat next to me, flipping through the pages. "Why don't we find one with a valiant prince instead?"

But he got sidetracked, looking at the strange pictures. I understood the fascination—women in beautiful dresses, animals wearing clothes, and rolling hillsides with perfect, rectangular houses. But scattered amongst the playful loveliness were disturbing images as well. Snarling wolves with cruel teeth. Thorns dripping with blood. Lost, weeping children.

"Do you think Earth was really like this? With huge palaces and all those trees?" He pointed to the cover—the girl with the golden ball and the faraway castle. The illustration was from the tale of the Frog Prince. The story read, *When it was hot, the Princess would escape deep into the forest, where even the sun couldn't touch her.*

There were only a few scrubby trees out in Tierra Muerta and small clumps of them climbing up the mountains, nothing like in this book. Lotus and Tasch and I had debated about this a thousand times—in fact, it was our favorite argument. Could there really be so many trees that even the heat of the sun couldn't reach you? So many that you could get lost in them and never found again? But if Earth had been so green and lovely, why would anyone leave? I thought again of the missing radio, wondering if we'd ever get our answer.

"Well, if Earth was like this book, then we finally know why the Colonists left." I made my voice deadly serious as I paged through the pictures to find the right one.

"What?" he asked, tensed.

"Mice in pants."

Edison looked at me sharply, then cracked up, shaking his head. Then he found the story of the three sisters again, continuing where I'd left off. And we took turns like that. Reading to each other from the ancient book.

I don't remember when I fell asleep. I just know that Edison's steady, deep voice was in my ears. And then a thought drifted up from the silt of my mind, like a riddle I'd been trying to solve without even knowing it. Edison had asked me about my sisters . . . before I'd ever told him that I had any.

CHAPTER 6

I WAS SHIVERING and wet. Everything lit up in a flash, and an epic crash of thunder rattled through me. I was on my feet before I was fully awake.

My shoes were soaked and the shuttle groaned. Another flash of lightning showed rain pouring down the windows.

"Get up!" I prodded Edison with my foot and shoved the book in my pack as the whole shuttle lurched forward. A gush of water flooded in through the makeshift barricade in front of the door.

We'd done the one thing you never do in a sandstorm: take shelter in the lowlands between dunes. And *this* was a prime example of why not. Rain rarely fell in Tierra Muerta, so when it did, it came so fast the desert didn't know what to do with it. The paths between dunes turned into raging rivers, drowning everything in their way.

I could hear Edison scrambling in the dark now. The beam of his headlamp strobed around the cabin.

"For God's sake, help me!" I threw on my own pack, then started yanking crates and bags out of the way. Trying to clear the slideboard—even as water rushed in through gaps. The whole tower of bags teetered and I ducked. But the blow didn't come. Edison was beside me now, helping me unblock the hatch.

"We're gonna drown if we don't get to high ground." I went for the opening in the door, just as another flash lit up the world.

And there *was* no ground—only an angry, spitting river. Edison yanked me back just before I fell in. The rain had swept away all the sand and now the shuttle was at the center of a rabid flood surging through the dunes. Carrying us along with it. The shuttle was floating—but not for long.

"Climb up!" I pointed to the roof, screaming over the roar of water.

And Edison nodded, hoisting me out the doorway and toward the roof of the shuttle. Wild panic hit me as I dangled over the waves. I didn't know the first thing about swimming. Even if I did, I'd be pulled under in seconds.

Then from out of nowhere, something swooped down on me— its great wings thrashing against the pelting rain. Luminescent blue eyes enormous in its moon-face. The bird's talons grabbed at my shirt, raking my arm, as if it was trying against all odds to haul me onto the roof.

Before I had a chance to do anything, the shuttle slammed against the side of a dune, spinning the ship madly in the current. My fingernails clawed the roof of the shuttle, trying to hold on. Finally, they caught on a seam in the slick metal. Using it as a handhold, I pushed off Edison's shoulders and scrambled up.

By then, the bird was gone. I reached down for Edison—but he was already leaping up onto the roof next to me. As much a force of nature as the lightning streaking through the sky.

Water streamed down my face, blurring everything. But by

now my panic had morphed into the same rush I felt when I was sparring. I was used to uneven odds.

"We have to jump," I yelled over the storm.

If Edison said anything back, I couldn't hear it. He just shook his head, wiping at the rain pouring down the face of his isolation suit.

I opened my mouth to speak again, but he shook his head and pulled me to him. His arms wrapped around me, pressing the side of my face against his warm chest. And for a moment, we stood there, rocking in the darkness.

"Now, say it again." The voice from his speakers rolled through me like thunder.

"We have to jump." The shuttle was sinking lower and lower as it filled with water. Soon there would be no roof to stand on.

"I can't see anything," Edison said.

"You'll have to trust me."

"Anytime." And there was a smile in his voice, even now.

I pulled away and took Edison's hand. Mine was lost inside his grip and I let the solidness of it ground me. I leaned into him. "One, two . . ."

Water crept over the edge of the shuttle's roof and I waited just long enough for the current to take us a bit closer into the side of the dune.

"Three!" I squeezed his hand and we leapt.

I never would've made it on my own. I know that. But Edison sent us soaring into the air, pulling me along with him. We cleared the river and slammed into the hill of wet sand.

Then we were on our feet again. Clambering up the dune. Trying to find traction in the grit.

"Here!" Edison shouted.

He'd stumbled over the ruins of an old building the flood had uncovered. Clinging to each other and what remained of the structure, we climbed. Pulling ourselves up jagged walls. Half-gone staircases. Steel crossbeams. Anything we could find, as long as it was up. Away from the water.

Rain turned to hail and I scrambled into what was left of an old stairwell. Part of the ceiling was intact and we huddled together, catching our breath.

"Let's wait it out here," Edison said. His headlamp scanned the narrow stairway, but we couldn't see much. Which was fine with me. I had no desire to see how unstable this place was.

I sat there, listening to the rain. Remembering to breathe. Wiping water out of my eyes. My teeth chattering.

Edison pulled me close to him and I let him. Letting the heat from his suit calm me down. Stop my shivering.

"Once upon a time . . ." Edison's voice rumbled through me. "There was a house belonging to three beautiful sisters . . ."

CHAPTER 7

DAWN ROSE SOFT over the desert, the sand drying almost as soon as the sun touched it. I eased away from Edison—untangling myself from his arms—and began to make my way out of the crumbling stairwell and back down to solid ground. Like Pleiades, this building had probably once stretched high into the sky, blue solar glass walls shimmering in the sun. But now it stood exposed, like a person without their skin.

You could see chipped sinks and toilets sticking out of the walls. Decaying furniture and waterlogged computers. Within a day, some crew would run across this place and strip it. Wire from the walls. Metal faucets. Circuit boards. Plastics. All good for trading. And anything wood could be used for bonfires.

I swung down from the lowest beam and dropped into the sand. I pulled off my boots, setting them in the sun to dry. Then I planted my feet and drew my knife. I did a few small kicks first, to work out the stiffness. The sand clung to my damp toes and I kicked high, flinging it off—the energy of the storm still imprinted on my muscles.

But here in the early morning desert, it was impossible not to

0

feel the absence of my lost crew all around me. Right now, they'd be breaking camp. Sparring. Chatting over breakfast. I closed my eyes, imagining them here—testing the bruise. My grief was still so fresh and at its center, I hit a wall of isolation so concrete it knocked me to my knees.

I forced myself to open my eyes and see its truth. That there were not friendly spirits bustling around me. That I knelt alone in the empty sand.

The only one of them left.

I clutched my arms to my chest as if they might keep in the pain—as if they might be able to hold me together. And this time when the tears came, I let them. It seemed right to let them fall on the damp sand.

It would not be the last time I'd cry for my friends, but when the tears were gone, I understood something new. I would have to speak louder now—because their voices had been lost. And I would be able to do so because the might of their voices had been added to my own. I wiped my eyes and got to my feet, steeling myself. Remembering what Suji and those women had taught me about surviving in a place that wanted to kill you.

Planting my feet again, I closed my eyes and tried to clear my mind again. But it was still crowded and clamoring. Bit by bit, I cleared away the terror of last night's flood. And the implications of losing the shuttle. I tried to clear Edison away too—the image of him sleeping slumped against the wall of the stairwell, mud streaking his isolation suit.

But my thoughts about him were too messy. This man—this Curador, I reminded myself—I was drawn to him in a way I didn't understand. He was so confident and full of bravado and yet, when he'd talked about his brother . . . about being different . . . I'd understood him. Or rather, we'd understood each other. I'd never had that before. Not with anyone who wasn't Tasch or Lotus. But I wasn't sure what to do with that yet, so I tucked it away for now.

The memory of the bird was not cleared away easily either. Wings pumping. Talons curled.

Had it survived the storm?

I hadn't gotten a good look at it and I didn't need to. I'd glimpsed that same bird many times before, when Dad and I were training out in the Commons. Or in the firelight of the Festivals. It wasn't easy to spot, just a flash of blue eyes in the night. I didn't even remember anymore the first time I'd seen the creature—but I felt like I'd spent my life peering into the shadows, watching for it.

I told my sisters about it once but I got the feeling they thought it was one of our stories. Taschen had slid her arm through mine and said, *Maybe it's watching over you*—as if it was part of our make-believe world. In truth, the bird seemed so fantastic, I wasn't sure I'd truly believed in him myself.

Now I traced the pink ridges running up my arm—the scratches from its claws were real enough.

"Are you hurt?" Edison crossed the sand, worry in his voice. And for a second, I was back in the storm—balanced on the roof, his arms locked around me.

"It's nothing." And knowing he wouldn't give up so easily, I showed him my arm. "Just scratches."

"Well, I feel like I've been through a meat grinder."

"You're injured?" The possibility hadn't even occurred to me.

"Like you, just a little . . ." Edison trailed off, something catching his eye. "Will you look at them!"

He gazed around the dunes in amazement. The sun was all the way up now, and the thunderstorm had done more than simply gouge a trench through the desert.

Overnight, the Tierra Muerta had come alive. Tiny flowers graced the wasteland—yellow, orange, and red speckling the grey-blue sand. And the gully the flood had left behind was blanketed with blooms—a river of color.

"There was nothing! Nothing here yesterday!" he shouted. "Give them some water and they just spring up out of nowhere."

"And they'll probably be dead by tomorrow."

He picked a flower, twirling it between his fingers. "But not before they shed their pollen. Don't you see? That's the whole point! They've been waiting months, maybe years, for this exact moment. The elegance of adaptation. Of evolution." He held the tiny blossom in his outstretched hand, as if he was reaching for the right words to wrap around the ideas in his head. "That something so fragile could grow in this desert should be impossible. But against all odds, here it is."

Without thinking, I repeated what Sarika said when she was collecting spices for brewing. "God loves all things beautiful and delicious."

"God has nothing to do with it. It's genetics. Years upon years upon centuries of this brutal place pushing life to evolve better, stronger, in order to grapple with this desert. You of all people should understand that."

"Me?"

"You're proof positive." Edison reached out carefully and took my hands—running his gloved thumbs across my extra pinkies.

Then he looked into my eyes as if he was searching for something. Some sense of understanding, of validation. And I found myself, more than anything, wanting to give it to him.

"Leica, can't you see this world was made for you? Or more accurately, *you* were made for it. Immune to Red Death. Fast, strong. Your extra fingers must give you an edge!"

An edge? What had my dad told me over and over again? *Your opponent is the least of your worries, Leica. If you believe you are weaker than him, if you believe his five fingers are better than your six, then you have already handed him your sticks.*

I'd always imagined that I compensated for my Corruption with speed and strength and cunning. But was it like Edison said? Were my hands actually an improvement on the rest of the world? I'd never gotten a chance to try myself against the best of Pleiades; maybe I was stronger.

"Gabriel *made* you better. And for the sake of your people, you should accept that." He laid his great hand against mine. "And Jenner? The Dome? For the sake of my people, they made *me* better. We are the same."

Edison looked at me the way he'd looked at the wildflowers. I thought of the careful way Edison had talked about his brother and him being "the future." I wasn't sure exactly what that meant. But I realized, stunned, that I'd never really had a future before. In a group of people who lived their lives in anticipation of a paradise I was never invited to, I'd only ever had an existence.

The same. I'd be lying if I said I hadn't liked the sound of that.

There was none of the grinning exuberance in Edison's face now. Only a promise as he folded his fingers with mine. "The same."

• • •

With only a half jug of water left, it seemed smart to see if we could find the shuttle. We followed the riverbed, picking through debris as we went. Broken crates. One of the orange boxes. Nothing useful.

"Maybe some of the supplies are still intact inside the shuttle," Edison said.

We didn't have to go far to find out. Around the bend we found the shuttle on its side, dug into the sand. Happily, it had flipped door side up when it sank.

The metal groaned as we used the wing to pull ourselves up onto the side, and drop in through the door. The shuttle was filled with wet sand and I dredged through it to find anything of use. The slideboard was smashed. Jugs were split open.

"Find anything?" Edison was rummaging through the back.

"One unbroken bottle of mezcal, for all the good it'll do us." I pried it out of the sand anyway and slipped it in my pack. I squinted into the dim shuttle. "How 'bout you?"

"Nothing here either." Though I swore he slipped something into his pocket. Still, it wasn't anything to eat or drink, since that would be useless to him while he was wearing his suit. Past that, I didn't care. "At least the frame's still worth salvaging for scrap."

As I followed him back outside, I heard the static of his intercom. "Let's see if they can get a reading on me now."

"Ad Astra, come in. This is Edison. Come in." More static. "Let's try from the top of the dune."

We climbed up and tried again. There was a hiss, and then: "We have a fix on your location, Edison. Jenner will be glad to hear you're alive. He's livid you didn't come back with the magfly and wants a full report."

"At least he can't kill me till I get back." Edison grinned, and though I heard the undercurrent of tension, the man at the other end laughed. "Tell him I've found something interesting. We're heading to the Exchange now. Send a magfly to meet us."

"Us?" the voice asked.

"Just do as I say."

"Us?" I echoed the Curador's question when Edison was done with the transmission.

"Only if you want to." And the tentative expression looked strange on his face. "The radio is still out there, some exile has it right now, and soon enough, they'll bring it to an Exchange. And then we'll have it. And you'll have your Earth."

But for me, finding Earth meant finding a way home to my sisters. Edison guessed at my hesitation. "This may not be how you expected salvation to look. But the truth is, your best chance of finding the radio is with the Curadores." Then he was the one who hesitated. "With me."

Edison was right, this wasn't anything like I thought it would look. And I wondered if he really understood what he was asking of me. If I became Edison's Kisaeng, it would sever any remaining threads that tied me to my people. Even if we found the radio, even if I managed to make contact with Earth again, would the Abuelos accept a savior who'd betrayed her people twice?

"I'm sorry, Leica. If I could make it possible for you to go home, I would. But you know Curadores have no say in Citizen law. All I can do is offer you a way out of Tierra Muerta."

And like a reminder of the ugly realities of this place, a large group of exiles slipped into view—crossing the lowlands at the bottom of the dune. I pulled Edison down into the sand, simultaneously weighing and discarding all of our escape routes. We couldn't hide; we were too far from last night's ruins. And we'd never outrun them.

"Maybe they haven't seen us." But even as I said it, I knew it was unlikely. We'd been standing on the ridge of the dune, Edison's suit glaring white against sand and sky. Still crouching, I put my hand on the knife in my belt. Not wanting to draw it. Not yet.

"They're hauling something big," Edison said.

He was right. The men were headed southeast, moving in two lines across the sand with a deliberate, steady rhythm—neither clumped together nor spread too thin. In the center, protected by the others, a group of five hauled a slideboard piled high with salvage catching the sun.

"The shuttle!" Edison exhaled the words. "They're the ones who gutted the shuttle."

It was possible—the crew would've gotten caught in the sandstorm, just like us. They would've had to hunker down and wait it out in whatever shelter they could find or make.

"How can you tell?" Their Find was definitely metal. But it could be anything.

"I can see the radio components."

I squinted at the slideboard, but it just looked like a mass of scrap to me. Could he possibly see that far? Then I thought of his enormous leap last night in the storm . . . what else was he able to do?

I was willing to believe him. I wanted him to be right. After all, what was my other choice? Follow Edison into the Dome, become his Kisaeng, and what? Wait around and hope the radio showed up? No. My people had turned their backs on me, but that didn't mean I had to turn my backs on them.

It was like Edison said: *Some exile has the radio, and soon enough, they'll bring it to an Exchange. And we'll have it. And you'll have your Earth.*

I stood up.

"What are you doing?" Edison was alarmed, but I didn't answer as I headed down the dune.

He followed me, like I knew he would. "I'm doing exactly what you said. They want to trade it for supplies, right? I'm just skipping the waiting part." We skidded down the slope, sand billowing up behind us. "We'll promise them a huge Gratitude, escort the crew to the Exchange, and reclaim the radio."

"And if they refuse?" Edison said, his voice strained.

"Wait—why would they refuse?" I stopped and looked at him, not understanding his hesitation. Crews fought each other over Finds, but never Curadores. Why else would they salvage the radio if not to bring it to the Exchange?

"Well, some of the exiles have been less . . . friendly toward us lately," Edison said.

The crew had altered its direction to intersect with us and now we could see that this was no straggling mess of exiles. Aside from the double lines protecting their Find, another three men took the lead—walking in a V—and three men kept watch in the back. There was something disturbingly familiar about their neat formations.

"Meaning?" I asked.

"Meaning that there have been incidents." I glared at his vagueness and Edison gave in. "There's been attacks on the Exchanges."

I didn't understand. Exiles looting supplies? But it was too late to do anything with the information anyway—the crew was practically on top of us now.

Edison stepped forward. "Hello, friends!" The words boomed from his speakers. Commanding, but friendly.

"Hello . . . friend." A man with a greying, neatly-trimmed beard and a bandaged side stepped to the front of the group. He gave a deferential tilt of his head but there was no respect there, and his gravelly voice was cut with bitterness.

He was the man who'd grabbed me in the smoke. His face was narrow and reserved. And there were the same eyes, calm and cunning. A chill went through me.

He was clearly the crewboss; all it took was a tiny nod, and his men—twenty-five or so of them—spread out in a circle around us. They were stone-faced and silent in their movements. Everyone out in Tierra Muerta was a criminal, and it didn't take long for the desert to teach you its savageness. But this group had a cohesion I'd never seen among the makeshift bands of exiles. It was daunting.

At least Edison had been right about the salvage. The slideboard was piled with circuit boards, wires, and panels from the shuttle. Edison said, "I see you've got some good Finds."

"Yes, the storms certainty uncovered some treasures. But these aren't for trade," the crewboss said. His words were relaxed, but careful. And he blinked at us slowly, as if everything about him was deliberate.

I didn't understand what was going on. What good would this junk be to exiles, if not to trade for food and water?

Edison didn't let his broad smile falter. "I can give you a hand-some Gratitude for them."

"We don't need your Gratitude. We grow what we want. Or take it." His voice was cold, almost amused. He nodded to his crew.

As if they'd been waiting for the signal, three men stepped forward—the ones who'd taken the lead in their formation. One pulled his knife from his belt while the others took Edison's arms.

Edison glanced at me. I gave the tiniest shake of the head. He could take these three easily, but what about the rest? We weren't going to win this in an outright fight.

The trick was figuring out what these men wanted. I scanned the impassive, focused faces of the crew looking for clues about how this was going to end. Their steady eyes, their fierce discipline—these were not your ordinary exiles. It was more than just the fact that their beards were trimmed. Or their clothes, though threadbare, were patched and cared for. They had a pride. A sense of purpose about them.

These men were not hungry. Not greedy or lecherous. Even their anger was contained. A jolt of fear shook my core. They didn't want anything from us. And that was very bad news indeed.

"Now," the crewboss said, a sneer creeping into his voice, "what are a Curador and his Kisaeng doing wandering about in Tierra Muerta?"

"I'm nobody's Kisaeng!" I injected emotion into my voice, let-ting fear stain the edges of my words. I needed to upset the tightly controlled balance of this situation. And I needed to do it while not seeming like a threat.

The crewboss pulled a long, curved knife from his belt and

came closer, looking me over. I held his gaze defiantly, but added the tiniest lip tremble. The man looked old—his long brown face wind-blasted and scarred—but his black eyes were sharp and bright. In truth, he probably wasn't much past thirty-five. Even back in Pleiades, you were one of the lucky ones if you made it into your forties.

"I believe you." He ran the point of his knife along my cheekbone and up into my scalp, using it to lift up a clump of my butchered hair. "Clearly you're one of us . . . forgotten out here while your own people make deals with the devil."

The thing is, I was sure I'd seen a flash of recognition in his face, just as I recognized him from the other day.

"Well, the boys are always happy to make a new . . . friend." There was cruelty in his voice, but it didn't reach his eyes. With an unsettling realization, I understood he was like me—playing a part. Trying to get a response. And as his knife slowly ran down the length of my neck and came to rest between my breasts, he got one.

"Don't touch her!" Edison *wasn't* pretending. He strained at the men holding him—anger and frustration spilling out of his suit's speakers. "The Curadores will come looking for me . . . *and* her. They know how to find us!"

And I remembered that the Curadores were tracking our signal even now.

A smug grin widened the crewboss's face. Evidently, that was the information he'd been looking for.

"And so they *will* find you . . . a tragic victim of the sandstorm. After all, we can't let you report back that we're collecting equipment." Then the man's face went deadly serious. "Kill him."

Edison went wild, struggling to get free. He was huge and powerful, but he couldn't take on all twenty-five of them. Five closed in on Edison, knives out. Next to me, the crewboss looked on with a grim satisfaction. He thought the fight was over, but I was just getting started.

The heel of my right hand slammed up into his chin—snapping his neck back—while my left hand grabbed his knife. He stumbled away from me and I kicked him in the ribs, right where I'd stabbed him the other day. He moaned and collapsed on the ground.

It only took seconds. And before any of the men could reach me, I had my boot on the crewboss's sternum—knife at his throat. "Let the Curador go."

The men around Edison lowered their knives, but they didn't release him. Even now, the crew stayed calm, if hyperfocused.

"Let him go, or I'll kill your crewboss." A trickle of blood ran down my fingers from where I'd grabbed the crewboss's blade, and I wiped it on my pants.

"Six fingers!" one of the men shouted, pointing at my hands now. "She's got six fingers."

I held the knife steady—but the balance around me was changing, a crack finally appearing in the crew's restraint. A split second before, everyone had been ready to give up. To lay down their knives at the boss's signal. Now there was a growing restlessness.

Would they want to kill me now too? Would their hatred for my Corruption trump their concern for their leader? Suddenly, one of the younger exiles let go of Edison.

"It's her . . . she's alive!" He put his knife away and crossed to me, face breaking into a grin. "Leica! It's you, isn't it?"

CHAPTER 8

HEARING MY NAME from that stranger, that exile, unsettled me. Like I'd suddenly lost my footing. I looked closer at the crew, who'd fragmented into several excited, whispered conversations, studying him. Under all the dirt and scruff, I finally made out a familiar face—a man from Building Nine. Well, not man—boy. Too young even for a proper beard. If I remembered right, he was a year younger than me . . . Lotus's age. And last time I'd seen him, he'd been part of a mob of kids who liked to torment me. His hair was shaggier now, but I recognized his stubborn chin and rebellious eyes.

Alejo. Yes. That was his name.

"I'm Leica. What's it to you?" This set off a new wave of whispers and my neck prickled with alarm. My name meant something to them.

"It's okay." Alejo came toward me with open palms, showing me he was unarmed. "We're not your enemy."

But a few of the exiles were still holding Edison, looking unsure. *Unsure* was dangerous. I adjusted my grip on the knife at their leader's throat. "Then why do you still have my friend? If you're not my enemy, then tell them to let him go."

Alejo looked to his crewboss. "Jaesun?"

I backed off the knife, just enough to let the crewboss—Jaesun—speak.

"Do what she says," he ordered.

"Now." I eased my boot off Jaesun's chest as they released Edison. "Someone better tell me exactly what's going on."

"Alejo thinks you're one of *us*. Not just an exile, but an *Indigno*." Jaesun's eyes glinted as he uttered the Abuelos' insult—full of challenge. "So . . . are you?"

I made my face and my words hard, crouching in the sand, so Jaesun and I were face-to-face. "Am I what?"

There's a moment in every fight when you win or lose . . . and it's rarely a showy punch. It's usually something too small for the spectators to notice. A clever feint. A tiny hesitation. An opening. Whatever this man's challenge was—this was the moment.

Jaesun smiled. "One of us."

"*Michinnom!* I don't even know who you *are*!" I laid the tip of the knife so it tucked, ever so gently, just under his rib cage. "And you don't know me or what I'm capable of."

"I know that you accepted your exile with bravery and honor. That you protected your sisters with your silence," Jaesun said.

Evidently this is what it meant to have your humiliation take place in front of thousands. And my hackles rose up, my instincts from that day at the Festival kicking in again. "My sisters have nothing to—"

"I know that your crew is gone," Jaesun interrupted. "And I know that we have more in common than you think."

"He's right." Alejo took a step closer.

I pulled my own knife from my belt—one in each hand now, trying to keep control of the situation. "Back off."

Alejo put his hands up again. "Jaesun, we'd better take her with us. She needs to *see* to understand."

I laughed, the noise coming out a little strangled. "What part of my blade gave you the impression I would go anywhere with you?"

"'Cause it's better than dying out here alone," Jaesun said. "No supplies. No allies."

Alone? I looked to Edison, confused . . . but he was gone. Then I spotted him, already halfway up the dune—heading in the direction of the Exchange.

The shock must have shown on my face. Because Jaesun got to his feet, brushing sand from his beard. "And here was me . . . hoping you two kids were gonna work it out."

"Should we go after him?" Alejo tried to sound tough, but I could tell he was hoping Jaesun would say no.

I hoped so too. My chest was cold with Edison's desertion, but I didn't want him dead.

"He's not worth it." I hoped that—if these exiles believed I was one of them—my words would hold the necessary weight. "He wasn't lying . . . more Curadores are already on their way."

Jaesun's eyes were glued to Edison's receding figure, like he couldn't stand to let a Curador get away. But eventually, Jaesun turned back to his crew. "Leave him. We need to get back to camp before it gets dark."

I turned my back on Edison too—I had no choice. I tried to reconcile the Edison who'd raced against the sandstorm. Who'd told me stories in the flood. Tried to reconcile *that* Edison with the one who was disappearing over the dune and leaving me with these exiles.

It stung. And worse than that, I felt stupid. Had I misunderstood his offer to come live in the Dome with him? But then I thought of Edison standing in the desert of wildflowers, amazed and grinning. *We are the same.*

No. I hadn't imagined it.

But the crew had already returned to formation and were heading off—I didn't have time to waste trying to parse what Edison had or had not meant. They didn't bother trying to corral me. Jaesun was right. I was exposed out here. I was almost out of water. Plus, they had the radio . . . and making contact with Earth was still my best and only path home. I might not trust this crew, or even understand who they were, but my choice was already made.

I fell into step behind them. I'd keep my knife close, my eyes open, and see how this next round played out.

It was another few hours back to their camp. Most of the crew kept their distance, but Alejo stayed close to me. And I stayed close to the salvaged radio—trying to tell what kind of shape it was in. There were other Finds piled on the slideboard alongside it. Old computer components and bits of metal.

"If you're not going to trade that salvage with the Curadores, why collect it?" I kept my voice even, trying not show it was important to me.

"We're always on the lookout for intact electronics. In fact, that's why we were staking out your camp." And Alejo looked just a little bit ashamed. "We ran across the shuttle a couple days ago and knew someone had gotten there first. Later, when we found your camp, we were hoping to trade for whatever you guys might've salvaged. But then the other crew showed up. And there was all that smoke and you made a run for it and . . ." He paused, as if stuck in that moment. Finally he said, "I swear, we didn't know your whole crew was dead. We thought it might be some kind of ambush or something."

It seemed an innocent enough explanation . . . if it was true. Then again, they'd just tried to kill Edison. "Intact. Does that mean those gadgets work?"

Jaesun sidled up next to us, cutting into our conversation. "*Your* crew found the shuttle . . . why don't you tell us?"

The edge in his voice told me that Jaesun didn't trust me, despite what he'd said about my *honorable* exile. And the feeling was mutual. Still, Suji had been a good teacher—never lie if it might be found out. Plus, information was the currency of more information. "Well, we *did* hear something on the radio . . ."

"Yeah, we heard too, before we gutted the thing," Jaesun said, and I knew I'd made the right choice. "Some kind of recording. Figure it's been broadcasting since the very first outbreak of Red Death."

So the crew hadn't tried to respond—or if they did, no one answered. Good. "What are you going to use it for?"

"Anything we can." Alejo looked to Jaesun and Jaesun nodded his permission. Evidently my honesty had bought me a little credit with the crewboss. It felt like a small victory in a day, a week, of losses. Alejo went on. "We're not like everyone else out here. We're exiles by choice. We call ourselves Indignos."

"Last time I saw you in Pleiades, you were calling *me* that, along with a few other choice names."

Alejo stopped for a second and the man behind him almost ran into him. Then Alejo remembered where he was and scuttled to take his place in formation again. I matched my pace with his while Jaesun discreetly dropped back, rejoining the rear guard of our procession. Alejo's mouth kept twisting into different frowns, as if he was struggling to find the right words.

"I think, *I'm sorry* is what you're looking for," I said.

"I know." His messy hair fell over his eyes and he shook it out of the way impatiently. "And I *am* sorry. My dad and little brother had just died and I was *so angry*. I took it out on the wrong people."

"And now? Who do you think are the right people?"

Alejo looked away and shrugged.

I let it drop. No need to alienate my only supporter. "Exiles by choice. Does that mean you left Pleiades on purpose?"

"Yes, to see if we could create something new . . . without the Curadores."

When I gave Alejo a blank look, he smiled. "You'll see when we get to camp."

After hours of walking east, we crossed the magfly tracks and turned south, the peaks rising up in front of us. The loose sand hardened into cracked mud—scattered with boulders and scrub brush. The crew seemed to relax as we got close to the mountains, their formation looser, their faces less somber. But the nearness of those cliffs made me nervous and I rested a hand on my knife.

As I did, a group of exiles—guards by the look of it—stepped out from behind a patch of boulders. Three men and two women blocked our path, weapons drawn. But when they saw Jaesun, they nodded respectfully and let out a piercing whistle. From about fifty meters up along the ridge, the whistle was returned.

"You have men up on the mountains?" I gaped. No one went into the mountains. It was the domain of wild dogs and diseased animals.

"We do lots of things other folks don't consider smart," Jaesun said by way of answer. "Don't want any other crews *accidentally* wandering into camp."

The guards seemed to think this was funny—their sandmasks muffling their laughter. Jaesun asked them, "Any news while I've been—"

A dog came bounding around the corner. Mouth open, running hard. I drew my knife, but Jaesun crouched down and flung open his arms.

"Hey, girl! Did you miss me?"

Instead of baring her teeth, the dog flopped down—rolling over for Jaesun to rub her tummy. And more unbelievably, he did. Speaking of doing stupid things.

But the dog didn't *look* sickly or particularly aggressive even. In fact, she looked ridiculous—tongue drooping out of her mouth—as she jumped up again and inspected the troops. And the previously menacing group of Indignos pulled their sandmasks off and stood at faux attention while the dog sniffed and investigated them. A few of them even cracked a smile.

Though none of the guards were from Building Nine, I recognized all of them from the Festival ring. Life on Gabriel was hard. The people of Pleiades didn't have much, but our fighters were our soul. The ring was a place where Citizens could *see* we were still strong. That despite unrelenting penitence, our lives had worth. Good fighters were revered by their buildings—a sign that God smiled on its Citizens—and these men and women standing in front of me were some of the best. Over the years, I'd seen each of them fight—and lose to—my dad. They'd been heroes, symbols of pride for Pleiades, and now incredibly, here they were in the wasteland of Tierra Muerta.

When the dog got to me—ridiculous or not—seventeen years of instinct kicked in. I froze as the dog sniffed every inch of me. Animals brought death. Everyone knew they carried disease, they stole food, and they attacked when you were vulnerable. When the dog jumped up to snuffle at my pack, it was all I could do not to give in to the all-encompassing, head-buzzing panic.

I only started breathing again when the dog dropped down on all fours and trotted over to Jaesun, wagging her tail.

"The pup approves." Jaesun was holding back a smile, enjoying my discomfort. But his smugness didn't last long because suddenly pebbles were skittering down the mountainside, gathering at our feet. Dust billowed along the ridgeline above us and, in the wake of a small rockslide, another guard in a sandmask came skidding down the steep slope, charging at me.

Before I could even raise my arms in defense, the guard tackled me. Knocking me to the ground.

"You're safe!" The guard ripped off the sandmask. Blue dirt smudged every inch of skin and the black hair was short and messy, but the grin was the same. Reaching all the way up to her eyes, making them sparkle.

"Lotus!" I hugged her with all my strength, wishing I could cement myself to her. But there was so much less of her than the last time I'd seen her. She'd been stretched thin and I could feel her ribs under my hands.

But still. She was here. And it was like finding myself again.

"When I saw you through the binoculars . . . How did you . . . I can't believe you're here!" She hugged me again, laughing.

And I was laughing too. The belly-deep, whole-body kind of laugh, which shakes your soul loose. Questions and worries and thoughts spun themselves around, but there was no room for them. There was only room for my sister.

I grinned at her. "I never thought I'd see you again. I *wanted* to believe it, but now I see I never did. Not really."

Lotus nodded. "Tasch swore somehow that you'd come back in one piece and she was right, as always!"

"Where is she?" I glanced around, as if Tasch might suddenly appear down the mountain too. It was then I noticed that Jaesun's crew—except for Alejo and the guards—were already heading into the ravine. Lotus was terribly quiet and I pushed her sand-mask farther down so I could see her clearly. Her skin was drawn tight over her cheekbones. Her whole face was pinched, except for under her eyes, where it was puffy and bruised-looking. "What happened?"

Raw pain flashed across Lotus's face and she opened her mouth to speak; then she closed it again and stood up. It was as if she put away the sister I knew—simply took it off, like it was a dress or a shirt—and carefully folded it up and tucked it away inside herself. "A lot's happened since you left."

"That much is clear. And I didn't leave. I was exiled." I stood up, putting myself in front of her, even though I had to crane my neck to look at her. Not giving her an out. "Where's Tasch?"

Tasch and Lotus would never intentionally be separated. Surely she was here somewhere. Surely if something had happened I would've known. Would've woken up in the middle of the night. Surely my heart would've stopped, at least for a moment. I scanned the faces of the guards, even though I knew that was the last place Taschen would be. All I found was pity in the eyes of the toughest people in Pleiades.

No. I survived. I'd made it here. I'd done the impossible—I'd found Lotus. *This isn't how it happens.*

I turned away as a fissure formed inside of me. Fracturing me. Schisming me. My soul shredding and evaporating in the sun.

Not wanting to hear the answer, I asked the question anyway. "How did she die?"

CHAPTER 9

MY VOICE CRACKED as I asked Lotus the question again. "How? When?"

Even the guards moved off now, giving us space. Only Alejo hung back, looking uncertain.

Lotus faced me finally, straight on—locking her hands onto mine, so we were a circle of two. Her fierce, dark eyes fixed on me, so I could see her pain and rage, still fresh. "A few months ago. A new wave of Red Death swept through our building. I've never seen anything like it. The quarantine shed was full. The Curadores had to come into bedrooms and apartments to collect the bodies. And Tasch . . . she went so quick. The fever burned through her before she even started bleeding."

"It wasn't right." Alejo's voice broke into our tiny circle and Lotus glared at him. "It didn't make any—"

"Now is not the time," Lotus snapped.

Alejo closed his mouth, his jaw clenched. It was clear they'd had this conversation a hundred times. Alejo looked at Lotus with a fierceness that matched her own—but it wasn't anger that blazed there. It was a protectiveness, like he wanted to shield her from her own pain. But to take Lotus's grief would be to take Tasch from her. On some level, Alejo seemed to realize this and relented, following the other Indignos into the ravine and leaving us to ourselves.

"I wasn't there for her. For either of you," I said. There was a numbness to the words, as if the cavern breaking open inside of me had made it impossible to process anything.

"It's not your fault. You were trying to protect us. Taking the Finds back to the Reclamation Fields. You couldn't have known." And the same detachment filled Lotus's answer. As if we were two actors playing out a scene. Saying the things we knew we should.

"I should've listened to you," I insisted.

The night before Sarika had come to live with us, after our parents had died, the three of us had sat—perched on our wide, lumpy bed—trying to decide what to do with our naming gifts.

"We can't get rid of them." Lotus leaned toward us, her hair falling in front of her face as she spoke in an intense whisper. As if she could compel us to agree by sheer force of will. *"They're the only bit of Mom and Dad we have left."*

I wanted to give in, but instead I steeled my heart against her. "No. We can't keep them anymore . . . not with Sarika moving in and the Abuelos searching for dissidents."

I looked to Tasch for support. But Taschen surprised us both, clutching the book of fairy tales to her chest. "It's my birthright."

The stubborn streak—so obvious in Lotus and me—rarely surfaced in Tasch. But when it did, there was no hope of changing her mind.

She stuck her chin out, face unrepentant. "Why should we be condemned for stories?"

I'd known then that we had a problem. Tasch's words were

treasonous. For all of Lotus's brashness, she knew when the words she spoke were dangerous, and she knew when to keep quiet. But Tasch's idealism could get her into trouble now that the world was a lot less ideal. It could get us all into trouble.

Sarika being in our house made things extra tricky. She'd changed after Marisol left. Sarika became fervent in her belief that the new outbreaks were punishment for questioning God and our way of life. And there was nothing Marisol could've done to hurt her more than falling for a Curador. I suspect Marisol *knew* that. She and her mother had never gotten along and Sarika had seen Marisol's decision to become a Curador's lover—a Kisaeng—not just as a personal attack, but as a message from God. One more sign of how the Citizens were going astray.

So even as we had cut open the mattress and hid the naming gifts, even as Tasch had closed the hole with her invisible stitches, I'd known the Finds would have to go. Before we all got exiled. I just hadn't known it would take eight months before I'd get the chance to do something about it. And in the end, hadn't I made it worse?

It hurt to looked at Lotus, standing there on the outskirts of the Indigno camp—her whole face taut with the effort of holding herself together. Of being strong.

And like earlier that morning in the quiet of the desert, I opened my eyes and let myself see the truth, as it was.

"I am so sorry I left you alone. I'm sorry I wasn't there. I missed you . . . I missed you both so much . . ." But words were such useless things. So I pulled Lotus to me. And she broke, sobbing in my arms.

I knew that that was the first time she had cried for Tasch. And that she'd saved her tears in order to share them with me.

I returned her gift.

And something happened. As we cried there in the desert, Lotus's tears filled in the rifts. They pieced together the shreds. Putting me back together. Because in all the world, only Lotus knew my grief over losing Tasch. Only Lotus knew what it meant, not only to lose Tasch now, but to have lost her two years ago. To have lost them both. And what it was like to be together again, but still incomplete, fractured even in our reunion.

Our tears didn't lessen the pain of losing Taschen. In fact, the pain was bigger between us, but it was shared now. And that made it bearable. That made it right. That made it possible to carry.

When we came down into the Indigno camp, we were sisters again. And it was like a broken miracle. I never thought I'd get to see Lotus again. Never thought I'd get to have a family again. And I tried to imagine what it must have been like for Lotus. No sisters, no parents. It was no wonder she'd left Pleiades . . . she'd already lost her home.

Lotus led me down into the valley and introduced me to her new home with obvious delight. Actually the place was less like a valley and more like a wide, multilayered reclamation pit. Stretched out in front of us was a maze of exposed ruins, just below ground level. Half of the ruins were covered with tarps and makeshift roofs. The other half were open to the air.

There were lower levels as well—stair-stepping down toward a wall of mountains. The bottom one was planted with corn and beans and swaths of other vegetables. Just like the name Indignos, they had taken the curse of Tierra Muerta and claimed it for their own. Filling the empty spaces and bringing the crumbling buildings to life.

And everywhere there were people, men and women doing a hundred busy things. Patrolling the boundaries. Making dinner. Chopping wood.

"How many of you are there?" I asked.

"Probably about eighty or so, by now. The first Indignos left Pleiades about seven months ago, when Red Death got really bad. But the number grows every week."

When we finally reached the bonfire in the center of camp, Alejo was waiting for us. He handed us plates of food, piled with vegetables and thick stew. Unseen by Lotus—who dug into her food like she hadn't eaten in weeks—Alejo studied her for a moment, his eyes lingering on the grimy tear tracks snaking down her face. His worry was replaced by relief and Alejo gave me a slight bow of gratitude as he handed me my own plate.

I nodded back, equally grateful that Lotus had someone, as I took a seat on one of the old tires arranged in a huge circle around the flames. I didn't realize how hungry I was until I smelled the meaty stew—likely contraband from one of the Indignos raids. The dog was evidently hungry too. Eyeing my plate, she came right up to me. Light brown patches rimmed her eager eyes, making them stand out against her otherwise black fur.

Her closeness made me nervous and I kept one eye on her as I picked up a bit of squash. Her ears perked up. She licked her lips, exposing a mouthful of white teeth. And when the dog nosed at my knee, I instinctively flung the food as far away as possible. Anything to get her away from me. She ran over to it—all lanky legs and giant feet—and gulped it down without chewing. Then she came back for more.

One of the Indignos laughed. "The pup always knows who's a chump!"

I glared at the dog. "Well, *pup*. You'll have to fight me if you expect to get any more."

I forced myself to ignore her, giving myself over to the meal. Pausing just long enough to guzzle some of the drink I'd been given. You could barely call it mezcal, it was so bland and weak. I dug my own bottle of mezcal out of my pack. After they'd reunited me with Lotus, I was glad I had some way of saying thank you to the Indignos.

Alejo cracked a smile. "I *knew* we should take you with us! She comes bearing gifts!"

He raised the bottle up high and a cheer went up from the crowd around the fire. Then Alejo offered the bottle to Jaesun, who unscrewed the cap and took a swig. A look of total pleasure came over his face. "Now *that* is mezcal." His voice was almost reverent.

A profound hush fell over the fireside as the bottle was passed around—sip by sip—and by the time it got to me, I was bewildered by the spell this mezcal had cast. I took a drink and memories of Pleiades flooded over me.

This was Sarika's brew. I knew every subtle taste. Every secret ingredient. Hell, I'd probably stood side by side with her and my sisters, helping to craft this batch. In fact, I was sure I had. There was a strong scent of strawberries to it and I remembered the huge floods that spring—a little over two years ago—that'd caused the red berries to pop up everywhere.

A little sunshine for the winter, Sarika had said, her hands stained red with the juice. Grinning, Tasch had dumped them into the pots by the handful, infusing the whole batch with berries before we bottled it. And when we'd first tasted it, it'd had the same effect on us. A sort of joyous, burning euphoria warming our throats.

What were the odds that Edison would give me *this* bottle—Sarika's bottle—of mezcal? It was hard to believe it was a coincidence. And he'd known about Lotus and Tasch too—asking about them before I ever mentioned I *had* sisters. The puzzle of it turned uneasily in my mind.

The bottle was finished off, and as dusk descended on us, strings of lights flickered on around the camp—giving it a bright, festive feel.

"How did you manage that?" I asked, instantly wondering how much power still ran to this place. How much of the wiring was still functional. What that could mean to a group of exiles trying to build a new community.

Jaesun flicked his head toward Lotus. "It was your sister's doing."

"Yeah?" I turned to her, taking a sip of the Indignos' poor excuse for mezcal. Lotus looked proud and there was an open confidence there. Despite everything that'd happened, this place and these people had clearly been good for her. I found myself wanting to understand more of what was happening here.

"When we were digging out the fields for crops, we found power lines and water pipes that were still intact. I figured out how to splice into the circuits and ta-da!" Lotus put her hands up, gesturing at the lights.

"We'd like to get lighting inside the camp too," she said, pointing at the tarp-covered ruins behind us. "But the wiring in the walls is kind of a mess. And I only know what you taught me."

Lotus raised an eyebrow at me, her question implied.

I took after my mother—because we were both small, we'd been scouts out in the Reclamation Fields. This whole valley was basically one vast graveyard. According to the Rememberings, the Colony had been smashed by the fist of God.

But under the sandline, a whole world remained. Basements and underground apartments. Winding concrete tunnels. Rows and rows of rusty vehicles. This is where Pleiades' salvage came from.

In the Fields, whenever they were ready to open a new pit, small test holes were dug until someone hit something promising. The holes were barely big enough to crawl down into, but there was less risk of a cave-in that way. Scouts like me were the first ones in, checking if the ruin was worth excavating or not. It also fell to us to make sure none of the wiring was still live when the blasters and diggers moved in.

It was dangerous work. And it wasn't pleasant. Sometimes the ruins were caved in, unrecognizable. But other times, it was like walking into a frozen moment. Tables set for dinner. Little skeletons tucked into bed.

And every scout had their thing—the thing that kept you from going crazy while you were down there in the crushing dark, with the dead. Mom's was books. Mine was electronics. Switching gadgets on, seeing if they still worked. Peeking inside. Most times the power was already dead when I got there. The sockets and switches useless. But if I was lucky, electricity was still flowing. Scouts were taught enough about wiring so they could cut the power safely. But before I cut . . . I learned.

"Already trying to get me to do your work, huh?" But Lotus knew me too well. She knew I was itching to get a look at this place. "Fine. I'll check out the wiring tomorrow." And I'd find out what shape the radio was in too. Though now that I'd found Lotus, it seemed almost like an afterthought.

I helped myself to more stew and asked, "How do people find out about this place? I mean, my crew didn't have any idea you guys were even out here."

Jaesun took a slow sip of the Indignos' mezcal, then answered. "First thing you need to know is, a lot's changed while you've been out here. Red Death's getting worse and the Curadores' Gratitudes are getting smaller. More salvage for less food. Most folks inside Pleiades aren't ready to give up on it yet, but tensions are running high. People are hungry and desperate and searching for hope wherever they can find it."

I looked around the fire. Despite the generous meal, the Indignos were still too thin and too tired, but there was a sense of purpose about them. They held themselves tall and seemed to trust the others around them. I found myself wanting to trust them too.

"And what do the Abuelos have to say about this place?" I asked, taking another bite.

"Nothing," Jaesun said. "They pretend we don't even exist. They want to go on acting like everything's fine in Pleiades. Like nothing's happening. Same with the Curadores mostly."

"Why?"

Jaesun tossed back his mezcal and locked eyes with me across the fire. "Because a place like this calls into question everything our society is built on. Cleansing the land. Redemption. If those things weren't the core of our life . . . if Citizens stopped digging the reclamation pits . . . how else would the Curadores get their supplies? How else would the Abuelos stay in power?" Jaesun challenged. Then he asked casually, "How do you like your dinner, by the way?"

The beeph was flavorful and tender, and much richer than usual. "Best meal I've had in almost two years." I thought of the tamale I'd eaten at the Festival and took another big bite.

"It's rabbit, trapped out here in Tierra Muerta."

I spit out the half-chewed food and the pup snatched it off the ground—gulping it down. The Indignos around the fire laughed.

"Don't worry." Jaesun speared a bite from my plate. "We've been eating them for months. Not a single soul here has gotten sick."

"It's not true, then? The animals aren't infected?"

"Not that we've seen," Jaesun said.

"That means . . ."

"Here it comes." Alejo grinned. "She's got it."

"That means that we don't need the Curadores' chiken," I said.

"Take it further," Lotus said, nodding.

"You said you found working water pipes?"

"Yep," said Alejo. "And you saw the crops."

"Then . . . maybe . . ."

"Maybe we don't need the Curadores for anything." Lotus grinned.

The idea felt almost blasphemous. Trading with the Dome had been our way of life for so long. Without the Curadores, the Citizens wouldn't survive long enough to find redemption.

But what if we didn't *need* redemption?

CHAPTER 10

THAT NIGHT, I slept next to Lotus in one of the tarp-covered structures. Lotus, Tasch, and I had always shared a room. So lying there in the dark, listening to the rhythm of Lotus's breath, to her getting settled in her sleeping bag, was a little like being home again.

But something kept needling at my thoughts. "What did Alejo mean about Tasch? About her death not being right?" I hated to bring it up. Hated to hurt Lotus more, but I needed to know. Lotus stayed silent, but I knew she wasn't asleep—her thoughts were loud in the little room. "Tell me."

"When Tasch got sick . . ." Lotus was so quiet I could barely hear her. "Her symptoms were strange."

"Strange?"

"Not at first. She came back from the Reclamation Fields with her eyes bloodshot and then the fever came on, like it always does. But it was too fast." The awfulness of that day was heavy in her words. "Like she was being burned from the inside out. One moment, she was begging us to help her and the next"—Lotus's voice went cold—"she was just gone. There wasn't even any blood."

"Did anyone else get sick?" I thought of Suji's symptoms

coming on fast like that. But it'd been different in my crew. There had been blood. More than I wanted to remember.

"Fifty people in our building alone . . . in barely more than a day. They all died. All went the same way. And then the sickness disappeared again as quick as it came. It wasn't like any epidemic I'd ever seen. It was . . ." She hesitated, then repeated Alejo's word: "Wrong."

"You think Red Death is changing?" I thought about what Edison had said about evolution. About things adapting.

"Maybe. Or maybe someone's changing it."

I wasn't exactly sure what Lotus was getting at, but I'd seen the look she and Alejo had shared when he'd brought it up—the conversation they'd had without ever speaking. There was more to this than she was saying. But I'd learned not to press Lotus, not if I wanted answers.

Instead, I let her ask her own questions. "What was it like out there?"

I knew what she meant. Technically, this camp was in Tierra Muerta, but it was nothing like the rest of the wasteland.

"It was dangerous." I thought of Suji's blood dripping from my knife. My silenced crew, dead and burnt to ash. "It was terrible."

"I missed you." Lotus rolled over and laid her head on my shoulder.

"Me too." And the feeling of my sister next to me made me feel more whole and more broken at the same time. Searching for comfort, I said, "Once upon a time . . . there were three beautiful sisters—"

"No." Lotus's voice was tight. "Not without Tasch."

I tucked my arm around her. "You're right. Not without Tasch."

Lotus's head grew heavy on my shoulder. I closed my eyes too, but sleep left me stranded. Everything from today—the Indignos, Edison, Tasch's death, the radio—ran around in my brain, arranging and rearranging themselves. Trying to find a shape that made sense. I'd been tossing for an hour when I heard scratching noises near my sleeping bag.

My eyes flew open to see the dog staring back at me. I held still, not daring to move in case she turned on me. But the pup just sniffed my blankets and flopped down on Lotus's and my legs. As her warm body heated my feet, sleep called to me and I finally answered.

The pup was gone when I woke up. I climbed out of my sleeping bag, feeling restless and exhausted at the same time. It was still early and only a few other people were up. I found an empty patch of sand by the fire and started running through fighting maneuvers by myself.

I wasn't alone for long. I did a spin kick and found it parried by Jaesun. He threw a punch and I blocked it. Then he pulled two pairs of fighting sticks out of his belt and tossed me a set. "Let's see if you're your father's daughter. Your dad was always bragging about your extra fingers. Your secret weapon, the way he told it."

With the Pleiades' fighting elite as the camp's guards, it didn't surprise me that Jaesun had known my father as well. There was a challenge in Jaesun's words, but it seemed more curious than malicious. I made a show of getting a feel for the sticks—weighing them in my hands—all the while sizing him up. Tall for Pleiades. Big arms.

But I was short—so *everyone* I fought was bigger than me.

As we circled each other, I came awake. A quiet alertness flowed

LOTUS and THORN · 91

through my muscles as I studied the way Jaesun moved. And the way he watched. He was older, slower, still stiff from the injury I'd given him a few days earlier. Grey tufts marked his eyebrows, and beneath them were cautious eyes. This was someone who'd experienced pain and assumed life had plenty more of it to give him.

I was used to using my compact body and my speed as my primary weapons, and that would work well here too. That, and the fact that everyone underestimated me.

Jaesun swung out, his impassive face giving nothing away. I dodged his stick, then came in with a blow to his stomach with my own. I skittered out of his reach—the satisfaction of a good hit still ringing through my muscles. His beard camouflaged his twitch of a smile, but I still caught it as we circled each other again.

My goal was to make as little contact as possible. Only strategic strikes. If Jaesun got a grip on me, the fight would be over. So it became a game of cat and mouse. A dance almost. The kind I loved.

Jaesun feinted to the right, then moved in left, kicking up. I dodged again, but this time his kick landed, knocking the wind out of me. "Careful, little mouse."

But even as Jaesun goaded me, I was riding the kick's momentum—using it to spin out so I ended up behind Jaesun. Then, with my stick, I thwacked the back of his supporting leg, buckling it.

"Don't *have* to be careful when I have such a lazy—"

I don't know how, but Jaesun managed to catch himself. Just barely. And he rammed his elbow back into my ribs.

Just before I went down gasping, I thrust my stick into his back—knocking him off-kilter again. Then he was belly down and I was on top, holding his face to the sand.

Muffled laughter came from him and I rolled off, catching my breath—letting my own smile out.

"Well," he said, "that was fast. I can't say if it's your extra fingers or not. But you certainly got *something* going for you. We're lucky you and your sister are on our side."

Our side. Was I?

Still shaking the sand out of our pant legs and hair, we joined the group over at the bonfire. The smell of cooking food woke up my stomach too.

"I see you've been making friends." Lotus wiped a smudge of blue dust off my face before handing me a steaming cup of something. I took a sip from the mug and spit it out. "What *is* that?"

A smile quivered at the edge of Lotus's mouth. "Nettle tea. It's not so bad once you get used to it."

I took another sip. "Mmmm . . . Dear sister, you're right. A little like chewing grass." I tried to sound grumpy, but I broke. That made Lotus crack too and her laugh sounded like the most right thing in the world.

I'd barely shoved a corn cake in my mouth when Lotus said, "Time to get going."

"But . . ." And I looked longingly at the fire and the hot griddle lined with baking golden cakes.

"Cakes or wires, your choice." But she knew my curiosity would win out.

"Fine." I compromised, grabbing a still-doughy cake off the griddle, almost burning my fingers. Then I followed her through the layered ruins—making our way down winding, broken cement steps.

So far, the Indignos were only using the top level of the ruins for their camp and the bottom for fields. But in between was a sort of tiered city. Each level had a long row of houses facing the nearby mountains. The houses all shared walls with each other, so they were a little like our apartments in Pleiades.

"Why haven't you opened these up? The Indignos could be living here." I peered into the dim spaces; plenty of room for a family.

"That's the hope. But we've barely had time to get a sense of what's down here. Or whether it's stable enough. Right now, the top camp has electricity and water and latrines. But if we can get this up and running, the place would start to feel like a real home." She didn't ask the question, but I heard it anyway.

I gazed around at the crumbling buildings. What treasures were hidden inside them? What possibilities? What if we actually *used* the things we've been purging all these years?

"You were born to do this, Leica! You were always the practical one—logistics and plans. Even out in the Reclamation Fields, you were clever about this stuff."

And I knew she was sweet-talking me. But the thing was, she was right. I could do it. Not alone, of course. But I could do this. "Okay. We're gonna need a light and some paper to map this place out with. A pickax, pliers—"

"You'll find everything you need in the workshop. And if not, you'll find something else that can do the job." She led me down more stairs, past a cornfield and another field that was only dirt—either just planted or about to be—and finally to a wide shed.

Inside, lights blinked and flashed everywhere. Wires and cables coiled across the dirt floor like snakes. The whine of live circuits sang deep in my bones. The sensation was heady and disorienting at the same time.

"What *is* all this?"

"It's not nearly as impressive as it looks." Alejo ducked out from behind a jumble of machinery. He flashed Lotus a smile and I could see why she liked him. A couple of years had turned his injured stubbornness into a kind of roguish strength. "Mostly it's just bits and pieces we've salvaged and cobbled together."

"What for?" I left the sunlight behind, walking deeper into the flickering, whirring rhapsody. I'd messed with some of this stuff—computer monitors and beeping toys—while I was scouting. But there were new things here too. Things I'd never seen before.

"Well, some of it runs the lighting for the camp." Lotus pointed to nest of power cords running from a large, humming control box. There must have been fifty circuit breakers inside—handmade labels haphazardly stuck next to switches. "We're experimenting with other stuff . . . trying to figure out what it does. And then there's a whole bunch of salvage we're just breaking down for parts."

I had a horrible thought—my eyes scanning the piles of scrap electronics for the radio. "And the stuff from the shuttle?"

"Over there. We haven't even had a chance to see what we've got. Wanna do the honors?"

I nodded, kneeling by the slideboard, which hadn't even been unloaded, and started sorting through the parts. It was slow going. I picked out pieces I remembered from the shuttle's dashboard—knobs and buttons, the radio's microphone—but they were mixed in with all the other salvage.

"What's so special about this thing?" Lotus grabbed the transmitter, turning the black box in her hand, as she and Alejo crouched next to me on the dirt floor.

All the fairy tales Lotus and Tasch and I had made up about Earth came flooding back to me. What would Lotus think about a real one? I took a deep breath, and told her about the voice on the radio.

Lotus looked skeptical at first, then stunned. But Alejo was shaking his head.

"Earth." The word came out hushed, but he didn't seem happy about it.

I spotted another knob and fished it out. "I thought if we could get the radio working—"

"No." Alejo sounded angry.

Lotus wasn't exactly overflowing with enthusiasm either. "But we can't exactly ignore it, can we? If Earth *is* out there, we can't just pretend we never found this."

"Why not?" Alejo said.

Their reactions confused me. "But this is what all the Rememberings talk about."

"Exactly. It's *exactly* like one of Sarika's stories. And people like us"—Alejo spread his hands out, including the whole camp in his assessment—"never fare too well in those, do we?" He got to his feet. "If you'll excuse me, ladies, I have some burned-out bulbs to change." He gave us a faux bow, making light, but his face was deep in thought as he left.

"And you?" I half expected Lotus to follow him.

But Lotus just frowned as she started sorting through the pile— laying out more components on the dirt. "I'll help. But mostly 'cause I can't get Mom's voice out of my head." Then she gave a sad smile. "She'd love this, you know?"

It was true, and it made me smile too. Lotus and I weren't the enthusiastic team I'd anticipated, but it didn't matter.

"Okay, then. We'll have to figure out what was attached to

what and splice them all back together. Find out how rough the trip was on them. And we'll obviously need a power source."

The equipment was mostly intact, but the storm had done some damage. The day slipped away as we cleaned off exposed wires and corroded electrical contacts, clearing sand out of everything as we went. And it was so easy between us, chatting one minute, falling silent when one of us was concentrating, passing tools back and forth without asking. It was a way of being I'd forgotten even existed.

Once everything looked right, we wired and rewired the different components together, trying to get the right combination. I had no idea if the descrambler Edison had talked about was something inside the radio itself or a different piece altogether. Or what it even looked like. So we had to try everything.

It was so good being with Lotus again. After our parents died and Marisol left, my sisters and I had gone to work for Sarika— cooking up endless and varied batches of mezcal and pulque. Lotus had a keen mind for experimentation and I was good at tracking what we'd already tried and with what results. But Tasch was the one who always saw the big picture—and the space where she should've been grew more pronounced the further we got.

Finally, we got the radio's power lights to come on, but nothing came out of the speakers. Then, after a little tweaking, we managed to get weak static. But no matter what I did, I couldn't get a better signal.

"Any ideas?" I leaned back on my elbows. The dirt under me was cool in the stuffy workshop.

"Well, I know what Tasch would say." Lotus looked at me and together we recited, "Fresh air is food for the brain!"

Then I remembered Edison's intercom—him climbing up to

the top of the dune to get a signal. "Of course! That's *exactly* what we need."

The sun was straight overhead by the time we got everything set up again at the top of the camp. But once we did, the static was much louder. But it was still static.

"Hello? Hello?" I tried out the microphone as I punched various buttons. "Crap."

"Maybe it's time to take a break. There's no shade up here and we need lunch."

I nodded, peering inside the radio with my flashlight. "You go on, I'm just going to see if any connectors came loose. If I can get it working, I could find that signal again. Can you imagine it? Us? Finding a way home?"

"Leica, I'm *already* home." Her voice was careful. "Don't you see? All those years spent making up stories about another world. *This* is that world. *This* is our chance to make Gabriel beautiful and green."

She reached out and turned off my flashlight, waiting till I met her eyes. "You could find a hundred Earths and the Abuelos would still call you Corrupted." Lotus squeezed my hand. "But not here. This can be your home too . . . if you want it."

I blinked hard. I shouldn't have been surprised Lotus saw through me. And I wanted to believe her—to believe in the Indignos' dream. I wanted to say something like *our side* and mean it.

I wasn't ready to give up on Earth. But Lotus was right. And for now, I reached out and switched off the radio.

CHAPTER 11

AS WE PUT the radio away in the shed, I noticed the empty field was now filled with people working. I recognized the green glossy leaves on the tiny saplings they were planting. "Lime trees? Where did you get those?"

"I brought them with me," said a voice as familiar to me as my mother's.

I turned and there was Sarika. It seemed impossible that she was standing in front of me. And in the Indigno camp, of all places. I'd dreamed of and dreaded this moment, this moment I never thought I'd get—my chance to explain myself to Sarika. I'd failed her, even more than I'd failed Tasch and Lotus. I would never forget her face when the Abuelos pulled the naming gifts out of my pack in front of all of Pleiades—like I'd physically hit her. One more daughter who'd betrayed her.

Now that the moment was here, my mouth was dry—empty of words. Sarika stared at me hard, her hair falling around her like a silvery-black curtain. Her nose cut a sharp line across her strong, weathered face. Then she opened her arms to me and I let myself collapse into them. As they wrapped tight around me, I disintegrated.

"I was just trying to protect them." My voice was muffled against her shoulder. "I was just trying to keep Tasch and Lotus safe."

"I know you were." Sarika soothed my back with her hand. "You did well. You were brave and you survived."

I gripped her tighter, the horrors of my exile pushing out of me in a primal sob. "I thought I'd die . . . without . . . without getting to say it." I forced myself to meet her eyes as I said the words that'd been heavy in my chest for so long. "I'm sorry."

"I know you are." And I was amazed to see understanding in Sarika's stern eyes. "I blame myself for not being vigilant. For not seeing what was right there in front of me." And for the barest fraction of a second, Sarika's eyes flicked down to my hands.

It was so quick, it was easy to believe I'd imagined it. And the next second she was wiping away the tears that were still streaming down my cheeks. Then Sarika held me at arm's length. "It's okay. I forgive you. You're safe with us now."

I nodded, feeling as if a slideboard harness had suddenly been cut from my shoulders. With Lotus, I'd shared my grief, but Sarika had lifted it from me, even if it was just for this moment. But I discovered something else was left behind—along with relief, there was a tiny grain of anger that I didn't understand. I took a shaky breath, pulling myself together.

Only then did the incongruity of Sarika's presence here hit me. "You're the last person I expected to see with the Indignos."

"Well, I guess that makes you the second-to-last, then." Sarika actually laughed, the lines clearing from her face. I suddenly had a flash of what she and my mom must have looked like, running around together as girls. "I didn't dare believe Jaesun when I got here this afternoon. You, safe and sound and here with us? It felt like a *miracle*." And she said the word with the gravity of scripture, the illusion of youth disappearing.

And there was that incongruity again. "I'd think all of this was against everything you believe in."

"Maybe if I show you what we're making here, you'll understand." Sarika put her arm around me and together we walked through the fields. There weren't just lime trees being planted, but olives and pecans as well. This grove wouldn't bear fruit for at least five years. These people were planning on staying.

Sarika led me to a cornfield. Only when we were well out of earshot did she give me a real answer to my question. "God's work is not always how you imagine it. The Abuelos have gone astray— become too dependent on the Curadores—and so my path has strayed as well. Sometimes the righteous must walk among their enemies. Remember that, Leica."

I squinted down the narrow corridor of corn—who were Sarika's enemies? The Abuelos? The Indignos? The Curadores? But I knew better than to ask.

Once when I was little, I made the mistake of asking Sarika if the Remembering stories were true. She sat me in her lap and said, "Truth is like the agave . . . someone else can plant a cutting, but if you want it to take root, you have to make room for it inside yourself. Even so, it can stay there, small and forgotten for years. Then one day something will happen, and it will shoot up, seven meters into the sky, and give you flowers."

So now I asked a simple question instead. One I might get an answer to. "You said you brought the saplings with you. From where? Is there a part of the camp I haven't seen?"

"You misunderstand. I still live in Pleiades. There's certain advantages to being head brewer. I can journey into the desert to find herbs or harvest agave. It makes me the perfect inside man. Or woman, rather. Still, I usually send supplies and news with defecting Citizens . . . three days across Tierra Muerta is no easy task for someone at my age. But it's the height of planting season now, and the saplings are too valuable to trust with anyone else."

"So *you* are how people find this place."

"Yes. At the moment, the Indignos and I want the same thing—to be independent from the Curadores' technology. That's enough for now."

We walked in silence. Here and there some of the stalks had turned a nasty shade of brown. "What happened to them?"

"Some kind of blight. It's happened in the other fields as well. Whole sections just withering and dying. We're adjusting the water levels and compost, but so far it hasn't made a difference. We'll find an answer, though." Sarika touched the crinkly leaves. "It's just a matter of time."

Time. That was the difference between the Indignos and the rest of Pleiades. Time was not a series of days spent digging for atonement in a hot desert. Time was a building block that created a new future. And it was a tantalizing idea.

I wandered through the uninhabited middle layers of camp as the sun set that night. My headlamp lit up small rooms—sinks, beds, desks all in their own spots. I flipped light switches that didn't work. Investigated computer panels installed in some of the walls. Happily, I hadn't run into any dead occupants so far.

As a scout I'd often explored ruins, but I'd always been dismantling them. No one had ever asked me to put things back together again. And the biggest question was what to do first.

Down below, Indignos were unscrewing the caps from metal cylinders sticking out of the ground. Lotus had told me about the hydrants when she explained why all the fields were planted on the lowest layer of the camp.

I hadn't understood what she was talking about, but now I saw for myself. As the cap came off, water gushed out, flooding across the fields. Aside from storms, it was more water than I'd seen in my entire life—put together. The ground in the grove had been ingeniously slanted so it collected in the middle, pooling around the water-hungry pecans. I stood there in the last of the light, looking down on the water flowing through the trees. Turning the sandy dirt a dark blue. And eventually, the land green.

In that moment, I caught a glimmer. Not of the scrawny twigs or the sandy field. But of tall trees giving shade and food. Children climbing in the thick branches. A world we'd made ourselves.

Awwrawk!

The noise caught my attention and I spotted turquoise eyes glowing in the shadows of a decaying house.

"How in the world did you find me? *I* barely know where I am myself," I whispered. I took a step closer, more fascinated than afraid as I looked into the bird's strange eyes illuminating its round face. It ruffled its feathers, almost like a nervous twitch.

I reached out a hand. "I won't hurt you."

But the bird twitched again, cocking its head like it was listening. Then, with another soft *awwrawk*, it took off. Becoming a silhouette against the evening sky. A second later, angry voices reached my ears as well. Lotus and Alejo—mid-argument.

They were coming up the stairs from the workshop and Alejo's voice rose loud enough that I could hear what he was saying. "You know as well as I do she shouldn't be here."

Then Lotus. "But we *need* her. There's no getting around that." Her voice was light but careful—an offhand tone I'd heard Tasch use a thousand times when she was trying to defuse an argument between Lotus and me.

But it didn't help. Alejo's words were full of venom when he said, "It's a deal with the devil. We're gonna regret we ever brought her here."

I switched off my light and stepped into the doorway of a room as they came up the stairs past me. But they were too engrossed in their fight to notice me anyway.

There was a warning in Lotus's reply. "Sarika is not the devil. She's a true believer. Our goals are the same—to break away from the Curadores. To do that, we need to find a way to feed ourselves, figure out what's wrong with the crops, keep recruiting people from the inside. We can sort out differences later."

"I'm just afraid later might be too late." Alejo's voice faded as they made their way up to the fire.

And I was left alone with my thoughts. Maybe making a new world wasn't as easy as splicing wires and planting seeds. Even if the Citizens managed to feed themselves in this barren desert—managed to grow themselves a forest of lime trees—the real question would still be unanswered.

Who was going to rule this new world?

CHAPTER 12

THE NEXT MORNING, Jaesun was back for more. This time as we sparred, we fell into an easy rhythm. Punch and parry. Kick and dodge. The pup jumped around us, yipping, like a referee. It felt good to have a capable training partner—almost like having my dad back. And after yesterday, there was no pressure to prove myself.

"I have to patrol this morning. Would you like to join me? A few of the other guards are curious about you."

I immediately went on the defensive and it must have shown on my face.

"Let's just say a couple of folks witnessed our fight yesterday and saw . . ."

"Me kick your ass?" I couldn't help grinning.

"Saw your demonstration of skill," Jaesun finished, answering my smile. "It made you a popular girl yesterday."

"In that case . . ." I paused to scratch the pup's ears. Her tail thumped on the packed mud, sending up a cloud of dust. "I'd like that."

• • •

At breakfast, I tried to choke down the nettle tea Lotus gave me, but I was grateful when Jaesun interrupted us.

"You ready?"

"Let me grab my pack."

"You taking her on patrol? Is that safe?" Lotus sounded alarmed.

"No more so than any other day," Jaesun said. "Don't worry, I promise to take good care of your sister."

But Lotus looked uneasy. And I understood. We were still practicing at being sisters again. We might have to let each other out of our sight, but we didn't have to like it.

Jaesun and I climbed out of the Indigno camp in silence—the pup charged ahead, leading the way. Jaesun whistled up toward the mountains before following.

"Always smart to let them know we're coming." Jaesun's shrill whistle was returned and we headed up a gritty trail. It helped knowing there were guards up there, but going into the mountains went against every survival instinct I had. "Lotus told me about your radio. And the message from Earth."

Of course she had. I suppose there were no secrets in a place like the Indigno camp. After Lotus's reaction, not to mention Alejo's, I knew this was my chance to make my case about why the radio was so important. "Not just a message, *voices. People.* We managed to get the power working, and if I can get the signal back, then just think about it! We can contact Earth! They can help us." I glanced at Jaesun, but his eyes were on the steep path that zigzagged back and forth, slowly easing us up the mountain.

Finally, he looked at me. "Well, you're welcome to try keep

trying. But don't be disappointed if no one around here is very excited by the idea of a miraculous rescue."

I kept my eyes on him; he seemed to be leading up to something.

"I was a loyal Citizen once—a digger in the Reclamation Fields. I believed the Rememberings and taught them to my children. Then three years ago, Red Death came to claim them. My wife had already died in childbirth and I was left completely alone in the world. And *still* I believed.

"But the grief wouldn't lift, and so I went to talk to the Abuelos. They told me that God had punished us for our arrogance. That our people must try harder. That we must dig deeper. Cleanse the Fields.

"What kind of God punishes children for the world they were born into? That was the day I stopped believing."

I didn't say anything. I knew the pain of loss. Of doubt. The ache in my chest was from more than the steep climb.

"Everyone here's got a story like mine. They all have different reasons for coming, but this camp works because we all see the same vision . . . a place where we make our own way. The people of this planet are standing on our own feet for the first time in five hundred years. We rescued *ourselves*. The last thing the Indignos want is someone else showing up and telling them what to do. No. Earth turned its back on us a long time ago."

We reached the top of the trail and Jaesun stopped, leaning against a rock. Taking a drink from his water jug.

You could see the whole camp from here, spread out below us. People busy shoring up the stretch of tarp-covered buildings. Moving in and out of the rows of corn. Planting new fields. I suppose Jaesun hoped this view would inspire me—but after all this time in Tierra Muerta, all I felt was exposed, standing on the steep mountainside. Even with the guards, even if wild animals weren't carriers for Red Death, I was still uncomfortable being so out in the open.

"Do you have your scope with you?" Jaesun asked.

"Yes." I dug it out of my bag.

"Do you see that clump of boulders and mesquite west of camp?"

I raised the scope. There were no guards today. Instead I caught a glimpse of white. And as it came into focus, I recognized an isolation suit and the towering Curador inside it. Edison.

The surprise of seeing him there set off a chain of tiny explosions inside my head. Edison . . . who'd saved me. Who'd deserted me. Who'd invited me to be part of his world.

Edison. Who'd known things about me that he shouldn't have known. Who was part of the very system Lotus and the Indignos were rebelling against. Who was risking his life, even now, just by being here.

Edison . . . who was the same as me.

As I looked through my scope, all I said was, "I see a Curador down there."

Jaesun nodded. "Your Curador, I think. We've been watching him since last night."

If I found Edison's sudden appearance near the camp confusing, the Indignos' reaction was even more so. "Why don't your guards grab him?"

"Because he's worth more to us this way."

I lowered my scope. "I don't understand."

"We should keep moving or he'll know we've seen him." Jaesun continued his path along the ridge. "At the time of the epidemic three years ago, when you and Lotus lost your parents, some of the Citizens had already begun questioning the doctrines of cleansing and redemption. You know the Abuelos blamed rebellious Citizens for the new outbreak. But I for one do not believe it was God doing the smiting. I believe it was the Curadores."

It crossed my mind that the Indignos were being led by a madman. "For what possible reason?"

"What do you think they're doing with all that junk we give them? Do you think they're cleansing our sins for us? No. We're sure they *need* those raw materials to keep their Dome functioning."

Our trail was no longer going up, but paralleling the side of the mountain. We walked side by side now as Jaesun explained the Indignos' theory.

"If we find another source of food and water, then the Citizens can live perfectly well without the Curadores. But what about the other way around? The Curadores are stuck inside that Dome, inside those suits. Without us, they will have no way to get enough salvage. We always imagined that the Curadores were doing *us* a favor, but I think it's the other way around."

We met up with a couple of guards—their grey clothes blending in with the mountain. Jaesun stopped to talk to them for a moment, introducing me briefly, and then we moved on, the trail guiding us back down the mountain.

"So you think the Curadores are infecting us with a terrifying disease, just so we'll keep excavating the Reclamation Fields?" I shook my head. The idea didn't match up with what I knew of Edison. Then again, Planck and Sagan had been far from kind to me.

"Yes. That and to keep our numbers down. The more of us

there are, the stronger we are and the more supplies they have to give us."

"And the more salvage we can give *them*." I was relieved to find a flaw in Jaesun's argument.

"That's the thing. The Curadores have managed to get what they want by demanding more salvage for less food. The outbreaks haven't hurt them a bit."

"So instead of helping us, you think the Curadores have been killing us." The idea was impossible and ridiculous, but my mind kept coming back to the bitterness and fear in Edison's voice when he'd mentioned Jenner. When he'd talked about himself and his brother being the future. What had he meant?

And I had to admit I'd learned very little about the Curadores from Edison. All I knew was that his people had mistreated him, the way mine had mistreated me. That didn't speak well for the Curadores.

And there were things about Edison himself. Things that didn't make sense. How he'd known about my sisters even though I'd never mentioned them. How he'd given me that particular bottle of mezcal. And now he was here. Why? To get the radio? To attack the Indignos? And an unsettling little voice inside me whispered, *He came back for me.*

Jaesun came to a dead stop on the trail, turning to face me as he answered my question. "Yes. I think the Curadores have been killing us. Repeatedly and systematically for the last three years . . . ever since Red Death resurfaced. And I know Lotus told you about Tasch. The nature of the disease has changed. It's swifter. More deadly, if that's possible."

His face was intense, but there was no trace of madness in his eyes. Whether it was true or not, Jaesun believed in what he was saying. I made myself ask the next question. "What are you going to do about it?"

"With your help, we're going to infiltrate the Dome."

"Edison." I understood now why Jaesun had brought me up here on the mountain with him. Not just so I could see Edison, but so Edison could see me.

"Yes, he seems to be scoping out the camp. Watching our patrols. Looking for a way in. We think he's going to come for you, maybe tonight. Maybe tomorrow."

"And what if he's not here for me?" Even as I said it, I realized I *wanted* Edison to come for me. And on the heels of *that* realization— another, conflicting one: I also wanted to make a home for myself here, with my sister. And thinking of Lotus, the danger Edison posed felt very real. "What if he brings more Curadores?"

"We're ready for that. But for now, he seems to be alone. I want you to know, no one here will make you go with him. The whole point of this camp is for people to make their own decisions."

"What will you do to him if I don't go?"

"We won't let him hurt anyone or take anything. But if you refuse and he leaves quietly, we'll let him go. But, Leica, if he comes for you, you need to be ready. You need to know your mind. You need to be sure what you want to do. This isn't just your life anymore. It's all of ours."

Lotus was waiting for me when we got back from our patrol, fidgeting by the campfire. As soon as she saw me, she came over and gave me a hug. She must've known why Jaesun had taken me with him—that was the real reason she'd looked concerned earlier.

There was no one else around, so I asked Lotus straight out, "Do you believe Jaesun? Do you think the Curadores are really killing our people?" I asked, hoping that she would say, *No, of course not. Jaesun is crazy.*

But Lotus pulled herself tall and looked me straight in the eyes. "I do."

And looking at Lotus, at this camp of damaged, but determined Citizens, I could no longer deny that something was very wrong in our world. I had gotten one sister back . . . but the other? The other had been taken from me. And I could not let that stand.

I said the words that had been taking shape in my mind as Jaesun and I had hiked down the ridge in silence. "I believe him too."

Still. I was so tired of fighting. So tired of being an exile. I looked around the Indigno camp and, in my mind, I could *see* myself making a home there. I was sitting by the fire scribbling plans for the new houses. Down in the ruins, supervising work. Picking limes for our first Chuseok Festival. Fighting Jaesun in the ring.

I could see myself doing a hundred little everyday things. And I wanted the chance to do them. And yet . . .

Some part of me wanted to see inside that Dome. Had wanted to ever since my mother had dared to ask her question: *Do you think it's very beautiful inside?* It was time for Citizens to do more than gaze up at the Curadores' shimmering glass bubble, wondering.

Carefully, almost casually, Lotus asked, "What are you going to do . . . when the Curador comes back?"

"Do I even have a choice?" I threw the words at her, suddenly angry. Mad that it had to be me. Mad that I had leave my sister. That I had to go into exile again. Like Jaesun said, it was my decision to make—but in reality, there was *no choice.*

And when I was completely honest with myself, more than anything I was furious that some treacherous part of me *wanted* to go with Edison.

"I didn't know he'd come here, I swear. I never dreamed we'd get this chance." Lotus's voice struggled to stay level, but there was excitement underlying her words. "I would go in your place if I could."

When her eyes flicked up to meet mine, there was sadness, but there was no apology in them. The girl I'd once had to push toward the fighting ring was gone. This Lotus was stronger, but there was a hardness there too.

"You know what you're asking me, right? Not only to leave you. Not only to become a kind of spy. But if I go with this Curador . . . I'll as good as belong to him." It hurt to think Lotus would just let me go. Would let me to walk into danger. "Look me in the eye and tell me you understand what you want me to do."

And suddenly the hardness in her eyes caught on fire and Lotus snapped. "When have you *ever* cared about what *I* want you to do? You do whatever the hell you want anyway. Don't you get it?"

She was shouting now. "You left me! You left us! If you'd just told Tasch and me what you were going to do, if you'd asked, we would've helped you. We could've distracted the guards, kept a lookout, maybe gotten away with it. Or maybe we wouldn't have! It doesn't matter, because either way, the three of us would've been together.

"But you didn't do that, did you? You chose to do it yourself. And your *choice*, Leica? Your choice left me alone. Can you imagine what that was like? Mom and Dad dead. Tasch dead. Sister exiled. Ostracized by everyone. Sarika barely speaking to me because of the secrets we kept from her."

Lotus was shaking as she paced back and forth. I wanted to go to her, wanted to comfort her, but I couldn't because I was the one who had cause this pain. And I wished more than anything I could undo it.

She went on. "And I still don't get a choice because *you're* the one the Curador is interested in. Do you know what I would give to infiltrate the Dome? To give Tasch justice? But it's not my choice."

Lotus stopped pacing and turned to face me. Her anger back under control now, her voice calm and confident as she looked me in the eye.

"So yes. I'll tell you *exactly* what I want you to do. Despite the fact that all I've wanted since you left is to have you back . . . despite the fact I'm going to miss you like hell . . . what I want is for you to leave again. When that Curador comes for you, I want you to smile and flirt and do whatever it takes to get inside that Dome so that you can find out what happened to Taschen. And what the hell is happening to our people."

Lotus fell silent, her torrent of words hanging in the air between us. I wasn't sure if she was finished, and she didn't look sure either. So I let the silence rest for another beat while I figured out what to say.

She was right. All of it was right . . . and there, by the campfire, I told her so. It hurt to admit it and I said that too. But the thing that she was most right about is where I started. "I'll miss you like hell too."

CHAPTER 13

HALF ASLEEP, I thought it was the pup.

The almost silent footfalls. The rustling of the sleeping bag. Then I remembered that they'd shut the pup away somewhere so she wouldn't bark—in case he came.

I opened my eyes and there, looming over me, was the white isolation suit. Edison.

He looked happy to see me, if a little nervous. And I was surprised when the same bright agitation echoed through me. But now was not the time for that. I put that feeling aside, tucking it away for later. Edison put a finger to his lips—signaling for me to be quiet—then motioned for me to follow him.

For a second, I froze, understanding that I was about to walk away from everything and everyone I knew. Again.

They took Tasch from me.

And with that thought came movement. Blood rushing in my ears. I slipped out of my sleeping bag, shoved my feet into my boots, and glanced back at Lotus. She kept completely still, but she was watching me. Her eyes were wide, her short hair messy from sleep, giving her a startled look. As if she was truly understanding for the first time what she'd asked me to do. Then Edison took my hand—his heated glove sending a ripple of warmth up my arm—and led me away. Through the Indigno camp.

It was like a dream. We skirted around sleeping bodies and crept along the edge of the still-lit bonfire. Stumbling down the steps in the dark. The whole camp was holding its breath around us. It seemed impossible to me that Edison couldn't hear it. I thought I heard a faint whine and I got an unexpected pang, thinking I wouldn't even get to give the pup's ears a last scratch.

"Where are we going?" I whispered.

Edison pulled me into the shadow of the ruins. His voice was barely a whisper through his microphone. "I've been studying this camp. I found a path along the base of the mountains that's hidden by an overhang. The guards won't spot us."

Maybe not the guards, I thought. But Lotus was tailing us through the camp. Staying ten meters back. For a second, I imagined turning on Edison. Confronting him here and now about the outbreaks and Tasch's death and his questions about my sisters. Then I could stay here with Lotus.

But that was nothing more than a fantasy. Even if Edison answered me, I'd have no idea if he was telling me the truth. And then it would be over. I'd lose my only way in. I'd lose the Indignos' only way in. If I wanted to know, if I wanted to stop what was happening to the Citizens, I would have to infiltrate the Dome.

So instead I asked, "What are you doing here?"

The light inside his suit flicked on. "I'm here for the same

116 • Sara Wilson Etienne

reason I was out in Tierra Muerta when we first met. We picked your voice up over our intercoms yesterday."

"You came for the radio." I was half relieved, half disappointed. "For Earth."

"No. That first time, I came to find the radio signal," Edison said. "*This time* I came to find you."

"But why?"

There was a combination of hurt and confusion in his eyes. "I thought we . . ."

I'd thought so too. "Then why leave me to the Indignos?"

"Well, you seemed to be doing perfectly well on your own. And I thought I'd be more help to you alive than dead." His bright teeth flashed against his dark skin. Then his amber eyes caught the light and beneath his bravado, there was real warmth. I still didn't completely trust Edison, but I wanted to. I looked at his perfect face illuminated by the light. Edison might be one of the Curadores, but maybe he didn't have to be my enemy.

And I realized that going into the Dome was different than being exiled. This time I was choosing. This time I had a purpose. I'd tried to protect my sisters once, and I'd tried to do it alone. Now I looked at the spot where I knew Lotus was hiding in the shadows and nodded. This time I would do it with allies.

"Okay, then . . . now what?" I said.

"Now we get the radio and get out." He pulled me back out of the ruins and down toward the workshop.

I helped him load the radio components on the slideboard. Lotus was still following us, and through the doorway, I spotted her. She stepped out of the shadows, the moonlight lighting up her damp face.

Edison finished strapping on the harness, then took my hand. He looked down at me, his face uncertain and vulnerable. "You know if you come with me, you can never come back."

I met his eyes and the lie was harder than I expected. "I'd never want to."

WHEN SHE CLIMBED OUT *of the sorcerer's basket, the middle sister was amazed to find herself in a great house in the heart of the forest.*

The sorcerer kissed her cheek and said, "My dear, you will be happy here. I will give you everything your heart yearns for."

But after a few days had gone by, he said, "I am afraid I must leave you for a while. I will entrust you with the keys to my house and you may wander everywhere and look at everything . . . save for the one room this key unlocks." And the sorcerer held up the smallest of the keys. "Do not disobey me, or you shall surely perish."

He gave her an egg as well, saying, "You must carry this egg with you wherever you go and keep it safe . . . for you will suffer a great misfortune should it be lost."

She promised to do as he said. But as soon as the sorcerer was gone, the cunning sister tucked the egg away safely in a drawer. Then she began to search the great house for clues to the fate of her sisters.

Every room sparkled with gold and silver. Jewels and delicate glass graced every corner. The sister had never seen such splendor. And at last, she found the forbidden door. She took the smallest of the keys, fitted it into the lock, and turned. With a click, the door swung open.

"FITCHER'S BIRD,"
FROM *FAIRY TALES OF THE BROTHERS GRIMM*
BY JACOB AND WILHELM GRIMM,
EARTH TEXT, 27TH EDITION, 2084.

PART TWO

CHAPTER 14

THERE WERE NOISES coming from somewhere in the camp. The distant clinks and clatters of someone making breakfast. Maybe Lotus had gotten up early and was bringing me something to eat—hopefully not nettle tea. But I really didn't care what she brought . . . I was ravenous. Like I hadn't eaten in weeks.

An idea drifted into my mind . . . or maybe it was more like a memory. Or a voice.

When you wake up, I won't be there. But don't be scared.

I opened my eyes. But I wasn't in my sleeping bag staring at a tarp-covered ceiling. Instead, I was in a wide bed, snuggled up under a gloriously thick purple blanket. There were wide windows at both ends of the room and the light coming through them was the soft yellow of late afternoon.

Another memory-idea floated to the surface.

A white room. Cocooned . . . suspended in a strange sling. The acrid scent of chemicals. I was lost. No.

I'd lost something.

And there was that voice again. Edison's voice.

Don't be scared. I'll see you soon.

But in the memory, I *had* been scared . . . and angry, but I didn't feel any of that now. Like all those emotions had been left behind in that white room.

Instead, my brain felt like the gauzy curtains draped around the bed. I made myself sit up, perching on the edge of the mattress. Cautiously, I touched the black gown I was wearing—not wanting to snag the fine fabric on my rough skin. But my calluses were gone. I marveled at my hands, all twelve fingers practically as soft as the gown itself. And the cloth felt fantastically cool and delicious against my skin. In fact, I realized that right now *everything* felt good against my skin.

I got up and started touching things. The textured coolness of the wooden bed frame. The shiny metal handles on the ornate dresser. The etched stone fireplace. The perfect crystal-clear smoothness of the glass doors leading out to balconies on either end of the room.

Then a different door swung open, a bedroom door that led out to a staircase, and in came Sarika's daughter. She was smiling—like it was perfectly normal for her to be there. She carried a mug of something hot, the steam curling the loose hair around her face.

"Marisol?" Though I'd grown up with her, I hadn't seen Marisol for years. A Curador had noticed her from the window of a magfly one day and she was gone the next—without a word about it to anyone but Tasch.

"The one and only," she said, doing a little twirl to show herself off—without spilling a drop from her mug. There were mirrors decorating every wall of the room and a hundred Marisols twirled with her.

Giddy laughter spilled out of my mouth without my permission.

I'd never made that high-pitched giggling noise in my whole life. I was sure of it.

"Ah," she said fondly. "You've got a good case of Dome-haze. Enjoy it while you can . . . it'll wear off by tonight."

"Dome-haze?"

"It's just what the girls call the aftereffects of the sedation. Makes you a little loopy. But in a good way."

Marisol grinned and handed me the mug, making the wispy curtains sway as she sat next to me on the bed. It was surreal seeing her here. She'd barely changed. Sure, her button-faced proportions that'd made her *just too cute* had settled into a more grown-up beauty now. And her orangey-red hair was longer. But that was about it.

Marisol's hair was a much kinder version of my anomaly. Like my extra fingers, red hair cropped up in Pleiades once every few generations—a legacy of our ancestors. It was still considered a Corruption, a reminder that we had not yet been absolved of the Colonist's sins. But at least Marisol's red curls were a beautiful aberration. And, in Pleiades, she'd always been careful to tamp them down, braiding them firmly behind her back so they wouldn't stand out.

Not anymore. Now Marisol's hair spread out into a kind of fan around her head, jutting high into the air, showing off the unusual color. It was a strange look, but it suited her, accentuating her perfectly turned-up nose and her huge hazel eyes.

She'd been sixteen when she'd left Pleiades over four years ago—a year younger than I was now. Lotus's age.

That's what I'd lost. Lotus. And Taschen. Home.

But there was no pain when I thought of my sisters. No emotion at all. Like someone had stolen the most essential parts of me.

I couldn't even mourn the loss. I could barely even focus on the reason I'd come here. *Tasch's death was wrong. The Curadores were wrong.* I hoped what Marisol said was true, that this vague euphoria would wear off fast.

I wrapped my hands around the warm mug for comfort, blowing on the creamy-looking liquid. A toasty, nutty scent hit my nose.

"You're gonna *love it*," Marisol said. "It's coffee. I can get the food synthesizer to put in more milk if it's too strong." Then she sighed dramatically. "I envy you, ya know? You're about to experience all these delicious, lovely things for the first time. It's wonderful being new."

I could tell that Marisol meant what she said, but there was a glitter in her eye too. I recognized it. Marisol had a few years on my sisters and me—but between our mutual outcast status and our mothers' friendship, we'd all been stuck with each other. More family than friends. The look she had now was the same one she'd had when she talked me into stealing a precious raspberry out of the garden and then tattled on me. Or when she told me a secret she knew would be torturous to keep.

I took a sip of the coffee and let the rich flavors roll over me. Roasted sesame seeds. Caramely agave. And the bitter bite of dandelion greens. But it was none of these things either. Marisol was right. I did love it.

Best of all, the coffee seemed to be clearing away some of the giddiness. And the question I should've asked first thing made its way to the surface. "How did I get here?"

"They took out your last IV this morning and moved you from the isolation room . . . to make your transition more comfortable."

I looked down at my wrist and there was a bandage tied around it. I pulled off the cloth and saw a purplish bruise around my veins.

Sharp pain. Needles pushing through my skin. Plastic tubes, so many of them. Like spider legs stretching out to bags of ruby-red blood. And Edison leaning over me while people in isolation suits scurried around the room, pressing buttons.

"We have to keep you here so we can filter your blood and run some tests . . . eradicate any germs you might bring into the Dome with you."

"How long?"

"Just a few months."

"Months!"

"Yes. But you'll be sleeping the whole time. You won't even know the days are passing. When you wake up, I won't be there. But don't be scared. I'll see you soon."

Edison had been wrong. When I forced my fuzzy brain to focus, I did remember a vague sense of time passing. *Men in white suits coming in and out of the room. Bright overhead lights. A tiny silver knife. And my own voice, crying out.*

"Months." I said the word out loud without meaning to. What had been happening out in Tierra Muerta while I'd been sleeping? And memories surfaced through layers of dust and sand—as if they were being uncovered by a desert storm. My crew dying. Being trapped in the shuttle with Edison. Finding Lotus. Only to lose her again. But they were just *facts*. I still couldn't feel anything attached to those memories.

"Three months. Standard quarantine procedure. All Kisaengs go through it when we arrive from Pleiades," Marisol said. "I know the sedation thing is disorienting, but don't worry about it. Time feels different here. Not so . . ." And she searched for the right word. "Relevant."

Then she changed the subject. "Are you hungry yet?" She pointed to a bowl of red fruit on the dresser. They were like the tiny strawberries that Sarika nursed and coddled in her garden, only these were enormous. My mouth watered.

"Evidently. You look like a feral animal. You can eat them while we get started." Marisol grabbed the bowl with one hand and me with the other and pulled me into a pristine bathroom. She'd been one of the only people in Pleiades—besides my sisters—who hadn't shied away from my extra fingers.

"Tonight there's a dinner in your honor and *everyone* is going to be there." Then she gave me a scathing once-over and said, "Looks like we have a *lot* of work ahead of us."

I'd known Marisol for too long to let her barbs get under my skin. In fact, I was always more comfortable with a prickly Marisol. It was when she was sweet—when she wanted something from you—that you had to watch out.

Marisol twisted the gilded metal taps on the tub and steaming water poured out. I just stared at it. There was no hot water in Pleiades, there *never* had been, as far back as anyone could remember. Though on winter mornings I'd often stared at the *H* on the water taps and willed them to work.

"One of the many perks of living here. Now come on." She grabbed at my gown and started yanking it up over my head.

I jerked away. "I can get it."

I turned my back to her and pulled the gown off, feeling exposed.

"Turn around," she ordered.

I didn't have many other options, so I did. Like in the bedroom, there were mirrors everywhere, reflecting every inch of my body back to me at every angle. I shivered in the chilly bathroom.

"You didn't turn out half bad." She nodded approvingly, staring at my curvy hips, then moving up to my breasts. "Yes . . . those will come in quite handy. I always knew you were gifted."

Feeling awkward, I crossed my arms over my chest. Marisol slapped them down, hard—leaving a red mark on my wrist. "Don't ever do that again. Your body is power. It is the food you eat. It is the roof over your head. Don't do anything that will lessen its value."

My Corrupted body. I looked down at my hands.

Marisol misread my self-consciousness for coyness. "Don't pretend to be naive; it doesn't suit you. You *chose* to come here. What did you think you'd be doing?"

The truth was, I *didn't* think. The idea that the Curadores had killed Tasch . . . that I had to leave Lotus again . . . that I would finally find out what was beneath the glittering Dome—those things had left little room for the reality of becoming a Kisaeng. That night in the Indigno camp, I'd forgotten Suji's most important rule. Survival is in the details.

So now I looked closely. As I saw it, I had two problems. One: I was here to find answers about Taschen's death, but didn't know where to start. Two: I needed to play a convincing Kisaeng—Edison's Kisaeng—but I had no idea what the rules were.

I could only hope that if I kept my eyes open, the first problem would fix itself. But the solution to the second problem was standing right in front of me. Marisol.

"Now. You're going to get in the bath and I'm going to do what

I can for you. Then you're going to wear what I tell you to and do what I tell you to. And you're going to be grateful for my help."

There was an undercurrent of bitterness in Marisol's words that made me alert. But I nodded and climbed into the hot water.

"Now! Tell me everything about Pleiades." And Marisol was back to her chatty self. "Tell me everything I've missed."

She knew nothing about my exile or the Indignos or the recent outbreaks of Red Death. And nothing would be served by telling her any of it. Despite the fact that Marisol was playing nice (or because of it), I didn't trust her. But I had to give her *something*.

"Sarika is well." I hesitated—thinking of the hurt that'd shadowed Sarika ever since Marisol left—then added, "She misses you."

Marisol snorted. "I bet she does."

But I saw the bruise behind the flippancy. Marisol and Sarika had always been opposites; they'd spent more time bickering than anything else. Marisol was difficult on a good day. But, I realized, so was Sarika.

I'd always been too caught up in being annoyed with Marisol, or envious of her, to see the reality of it. It couldn't have been easy growing up as Sarika's daughter, and a Corrupted one at that. And Marisol had never known her father. He and Sarika had chosen to enter into a Reproductive Pact—fulfilling a requirement, nothing more. It must have been a lonely, cheerless upbringing. It suddenly seemed obvious why Marisol had left as soon as the opportunity had presented itself.

Marisol was still silent, scrubbing my head a bit harder than necessary. Finally, pouring a pitcher of water over my hair to rinse it, she said, "Now then. What about the gossip?"

So—while Marisol washed my hair and scrubbed my skin raw

and complained about my cracked nails—I dredged up bits of things I remembered from before I was exiled. I told her about which boys had become worth looking at and who had gotten married or had kids. But the truth was, I'd never really been part of Pleiades. Tasch and Lotus had been my community. So when I ran out of real gossip, I started making stuff up—elaborate stories about who'd jilted who. Family rifts. Illicit love affairs. Anything I thought Marisol would care about.

I was just starting to enjoy myself when she interrupted me. "And . . . Tasch? Did she marry that handsome boy from Building Four?"

I forced myself to look at Marisol when I broke the news. "Taschen is gone."

Marisol's face went slack. But she nodded, accepting what she must've already guessed from my avoidance. "Red Death?"

"Yes."

And finally, I could feel it again—the weight of grief just under the surface. My sisters. Taschen, who made up beautiful stories and beautiful dresses, never doubting that somehow she'd escape this dreary desert. And Lotus, who was still alive, but who might as well be on another planet. The loss of both crushed my lungs so I could barely breathe.

But I was grateful for the pain.

"I wondered what you were running away from. Now it makes sense." Marisol sniffed and splashed some of the tepid bathwater on her face.

"Enough. This bath is turning us into old ladies." And she held up her water-wrinkled hands for me to see. "Let's get you dressed."

I dried off and, while Marisol got a towel for my hair, I grabbed a strawberry, greedy to stuff it into my mouth. But Marisol put her hand on mine, stopping me.

"Not like that."

She stepped in close, so I could feel the heat of her body—her silk dress shivering across my bare skin. She smiled, teasing as she tugged the fruit out of my fingers.

Watch. Learn, I commanded myself. The more convincing a Kisaeng I was, the better spy I would make.

Marisol closed her lips around the berry in one juicy bite, then shut her eyes as if overcome by the flavor. A smile played at the edge of her lips. It was tantalizing—a hunger rose up inside of me that had nothing to do with food—watching pleasure slowly fill her face. It was so very private, and yet, I was suddenly aware that I was watching a performance. A perfect, seductive dance. But a dance nonetheless.

She bit her bottom lip, sucking the last of the red juice from it, in an artful finale. Then her eyes popped wide and she laughed—that bubbling-up laugh that I remembered from childhood. A laugh that made you long to be part of whatever Marisol was doing.

"Now you." She tossed me a strawberry and scrutinized me. I realized she wanted me to mimic her, so I took the fruit in my mouth, feeling ridiculous, my lips feeling clumsy and huge. But the moment I bit into the berry, juice exploded on my tongue. I *had* to shut my eyes, to hold it all—the tart and the sweet, and underneath, the memory of sunshine and damp dirt and rain. This was nothing like the scrawny desert berries in the Pleiades gardens.

When I opened my eyes again, Marisol had an odd look on her face. "I always thought Taschen was the pretty one. But I was wrong."

Then she pushed away whatever was bothering her and grinned

again. "Forget the lip thing at the beginning, you looked like an Abuela without any teeth. But keep the rest. Whatever you did just then, do that tonight. You'll drive all the Curadores mad!"

"Well, I'm not sure I want them *all*!" I grinned as I tried to mimic her flirty tone. *You can do this,* I told myself. But there was an undeniable twist in my gut. Because pretending would only take me so far tonight, and I was not about to admit to Marisol of all people how inexperienced I was.

It's not like I'd never been with a boy before. Once, I borrowed one of Tasch's dresses and worn it to the Seollal New Year's Festival. The long sleeves trailed way past my fingertips—so I could play at being normal. I was curious. I wanted to see if everything Taschen said about boys was true.

As we all lined up to perform our *sebae* bows to the Abuelos and receive wisdom, I watched—singling out a quiet boy from one of the other buildings. Not too handsome. Or too needy. Or too anything.

Despite the cool night, I led him to the outskirts of the bonfire—letting flickering shadows hide my hands. Not that that's where he was looking. He'd been sweet and it'd been fine. Almost nice, even. But it'd also been awkward and messy and not a *little* painful.

"Oh, you do want them," Marisol said. And there was that laugh again. "Belieeeeeeve me. You do!"

And I couldn't help thinking about Edison's low voice reading me to sleep in the stairwell. Him and me, standing in a desert of red and orange flowers, our hands folding together. And the way he'd looked at me when he'd "rescued" me from the Indignos. Maybe . . . maybe things could be different from that clumsy night at the Festival.

"Now come on." Marisol threw open a door opposite the bed.

It led to a huge closet filled with fabrics of every color. The variation was breathtaking—sheer, heavy, silky, bright, and luxurious. Scattered among the meters of cloth were dresses—short, long, of every style imaginable. And many I'd never imagined at all.

And in the middle of the lavish collection hung the most complicated dress I'd ever seen. "*This* will do nicely."

She pulled it out and held it up in front of herself—it was mesmerizing. The dress itself was short in front, stopping well above Marisol's knees. But the back of the skirt flared out in countless layers, draping all the way down to the floor in every color of green. The greens were echoed in the top, a patchwork bodice, pieced together in a nod to Pleiades' dresses. But this was no simple Festival gown. And there was even something that looked like it might be a hood, but I wasn't sure.

"I can't wear that . . . I wouldn't even know how to put it on."

"You can and you will." Marisol searched my face, as if trying to find some answer. "Leica, as of today, you are a Kisaeng. It doesn't matter who you were before, or what you are now, or what you feel comfortable wearing. All that matters is the fantasy. From this point forward, you are only what a Curador wants you to be."

She was right, I *was* here to create a fantasy, one strong enough to hide what I was really after. I closed my eyes and cleared my mind, picturing the girl I was to become. A girl who came to the Dome not to search for secrets, but to be a Kisaeng. And I realized that all those hours my sisters and I had spent reading fairy tales of princesses, knights, and dragons—making up our own tales about Earth—had prepared me for this. I was *good* at stories. I could be whatever I needed to be.

For the next hour, Marisol arranged the dress artfully on my body, so the bodice hugged my hips and curved out with my breasts. The green skirt spread across the floor behind me like a delicate shadow made of sage and vines. The hood turned out to belong to a sheer cape that lay lightly across my shoulders but added no modesty to my obvious cleavage.

Marisol ruffled her hands through my shaggy hair, which had grown wild in my three months of isolation. "Not much I can do with this."

But she fiddled with it anyway, doing something miraculous with the hood—clipping it to my hair so it rested right at the back of my head. It looked exquisitely careless, like it might slip off any moment.

Looking at myself in the sea of mirrors, I had to admit that the effect was gorgeous—but I couldn't help feeling exposed. I started to wrap my arms around me, but remembered Marisol slapping me and dropped them to my side.

"The trick is imagining you're someone else," Marisol said, and I sensed she was talking about more than just wearing this dress.

I stared at the strange girl in front of me. The green tones of the dress warmed her brown skin to a rich bronze. The narrow waist balanced out her height—making her look small, rather than short. And with her cropped hair half hidden by the hood, her dark eyes stole all the attention.

"Being a Kisaeng is like playing a game. A daring, delicious game. Never take it too seriously, Leica. Or you'll get hurt."

"I'm done being hurt." I made myself smile at Marisol in the mirror as I remembered a character from my fairy tale book—a servant who bolted iron bands around his heart to keep it from cracking open.

But Marisol just gave me that look again, like I was a puzzle she couldn't figure out. Finally, she released my gaze and focused in on my hands. "Last, but not least."

Marisol rummaged through her bag and brought out some kind of lotion. Sitting next to me on the bed, she cupped my hand in hers. She spread the lotion onto my backs of my hands, turning my skin a shimmery gold.

"What are you doing?" I tried to pull away, appalled. "Everyone will see them."

"*That* is the point." She gripped my hand tight. "The Curadores revere variation. Each of them spends their life hoping they have *something*—a trait different enough or special enough—that's worthy of passing onto future generations. A tiny scrap of themselves, living on for posterity." She rolled her eyes. "We Kisaengs, of course, are simply fashion accessories. But it never hurts to be a bit of a . . . singularity. This isn't Pleiades, Leica. Above all, you must always remember that."

So I let her spread the lotion over my too-many fingers, working it into my hands. By the time she was finished, the effect was stunning. Every time I moved my fingers, the eye was subtly drawn to them. I'd never hated my hands—my family had never let me—but I'd never thought of them as beautiful either.

As I stared at myself in the mirror, I silently repeated what Marisol had said. *This isn't Pleiades*. I would be someone new here. Someone who discovered new worlds. Someone who fluttered her golden hands and made love to strawberries. Someone who kept secrets and found answers. I would be a Kisaeng.

CHAPTER 15

DINNER WAS LIKE nothing I'd ever experienced. Hundreds of people were crowded into a vast tent. Strings of twinkling lights draped from the ceiling like stars, and swarms of glittering black insects navigated through them.

Marisol and I had taken a silver magfly through the dark streets of the Dome. And though I'd been glued to the window during the short ride to the Promenade, trying to figure the layout, all I saw was a blur of lights rushing past.

"You'll see it all tomorrow," Marisol promised as we padded across the broad lawn to a bright pavilion beside a lake.

The place smelled of savory dishes and crushed grass. There were tables but no one was sitting down. And there was food everywhere but no one seemed very interested in it.

The place had the same feel as the Festivals in Pleiades. Bright clothes, loud music, plenty to drink, and a hundred things going on at once.

It was strange to see the Curadores without their isolation suits. All the men were large and well-built, even the smallest of them would've dwarfed my father. They laughed and chatted as we entered the tent, an endless variety of handsome smiles and strong jaws. I tried not to stare at the unusual skin tones and hair colors from the almost-transparent white of shed snakeskin to the deepest brown of mesquite bark. But it was their eyes that claimed my attention, gleaming in bright hues. The intense blue of the desert sky. Fresh-picked basil. The rich reddish-brown of dried chiles. It was like walking among beautiful giants.

The Curadores wore simple clothes—loose shirts and pants—not so unlike the clothes of Pleiades. Except that none of the cloth was patched or faded. The shirts were all a clean, bright white with gleaming, decorative buttons. And the pants, though muted, came in all different shades.

But this was nothing compared to the women—each one a work of art. Some, like me, were draped in complicated layers of fabric; others wore gauzy dresses masterfully tailored to play a kind of hide-and-seek as they moved. All the women were young and beautiful. All of them had once been Citizens, and yet, they seemed completely foreign to me. Incandescent, decorated creatures.

Kisaengs.

I froze, feeling out of place and intimidated. Beside me Marisol whispered, "Relax, it's just a party." But she was smirking as she said it, knowing full well it was the *last* thing that would make me feel better.

Faced with this mob of strangers, I longed to shove my hands in pockets, but I didn't have any. Marisol tried to get me to keep walking, but my feet wouldn't move and the words slipped out of my mouth. "What the hell am I doing?"

Marisol looked at me sharply, and in a low tone only I could hear, she said, "I've been asking myself that same question, but I was hoping at least *you* knew. The Dome is not an easy place, Leica . . . who a Kisaeng chooses to consort with is her identity. It affects where she lives, what kind of luxuries she has, the power she wields. So you'd better figure out what you want and who's going to get that for you. And you'd better do it fast." Then she smiled sweetly, threaded her arm through mine, and pulled me into the throng.

Marisol's warning churned in my head as we walked through the mass of people, and strangely, her words solidified into courage. I reminded myself that *did* know what I was doing. And I knew very well what I wanted—answers. About the outbreaks in Pleiades. About Tasch's strange death. No one else should have to lose their sister. Or parents. I let that purpose guide me through the crowd.

Though I didn't catch anyone actually staring, I felt their eyes on me. I didn't hide—I couldn't have in *that* dress—but it made me uncomfortable. Whereas Marisol basked under the collective gaze.

She'd chosen a dress that was much quieter than mine. A rusty color that was one shade duller than her hair, and several shades darker than her skin, making her almost luminescent against the fabric. And though her dress was simple, it was exquisite—velvety with lines of brighter red outlining Marisol's narrow curves. Like dunes forming and reforming across the desert.

She didn't need sparkles and jewelry. *She* was the beauty, not the dress. All at once, I felt ridiculous, bedecked in that hooded, corseted thing. Marisol had the same effect on all the women she passed. Hands touched elaborate hairpins and chunky necklaces, suddenly unsure.

We strolled by a girl about my age who was singing. I untwined my arm from Marisol's so I could stop and listen. The song was slow and seductive, nothing like the striding hymns sung at Pleiades' Rememberings. The singer seemed lost inside the melancholy chords, swaying slightly—her eyes closed as she strummed her guitar. She was tall and slender, and her high, haunting voice perfectly matched the sheer, silvery dress she wore.

The people gathered around listening were almost as fascinating. One woman lounged on the lap of a young Curador, arm thrown easily around him, captivated by the music. Another couple danced impossibly close, mouths pressed together, hands roaming across the landscape of their bodies—as if they were in their own private room. But no one except me gave them a second glance.

In another corner, a serious-looking woman in her late twenties argued with a whole group of Curadores. Most of the men around her were older—silver sprinkling their hair—but their eyes were alight with the passion of debate.

One of the younger Curadores attempted to hold his own against her. "Surely in a time of plague or crisis, rules are bent and—"

"Bent. But not broken." The Kisaeng cut him off, pounding her fist on the table. She was compact and tough-looking, despite her long black dress. Her hair sliced across her face at a sharp angle to tuck behind her ear—a complement to the line of her strong jaw. "You cannot just say 'the end justifies the means,' and be absolved. Through chance or skill, the Dome has resources that Pleiades does not—therefore you will always have a responsibility to them. Survival is no longer the goal. *Life* is the goal."

The woman glanced up, hesitating for second as she saw us—a ripple in the flow of words. She raised a narrow eyebrow and a hint of a wry smile hovered on her otherwise stern face.

"Oksun." Marisol nodded at the Kisaeng. "I see you're boring our men again. Gentlemen, when you're tired of her endless prattle, come and join us. One of our ladies can show you what *else* mouths can do."

Under the gaze of Marisol's disapproval, many of the men made excuses and wandered away. Marisol clearly held some sway in the Dome. When I was little, I'd often been at the receiving end of her cutting tongue and I knew the humiliation of it. I gave the Kisaeng—Oksun—a sympathetic look, and I was startled to see her loathing was directed straight at me.

I hurried after Marisol, but she'd disappeared into the crowd, and I was alone in the crush of laughing, drinking strangers. Above me, throngs of insects buzzed here and there in orderly formations. Their endless circling made me dizzy, but like the amorous couple, no one else was paying any attention to them.

A man with sandy hair and watery green eyes bumped into me and steadied himself on my arm.

"Oh! Who have we here?" He was drunk, a messy slur blending his words together.

I tried to slip past him without answering, but he grabbed me, holding my arm tight as he surveyed my body. "May I just say you have the loveliest pair of peaches I have ever seen. But no!" He elbowed the man next to him. "Not peaches are they? Oranges? Grapefruit? We're going to have to dream up a whole new fruit for this one."

Then he wrenched me closer, his wet mouth groping for mine.

His hand reaching for my breast. Instinct kicked in and I grabbed his wrist with my free hand. Wrenching it wrong-ways and up, I dropped him to the ground.

"Dream away. It's a fruit *you'll* never taste." Then I spun back to the crowd, tensed and ready to take on anyone else.

But they were just staring at me—Kisaengs and Curadores, openmouthed and blinking. And my face burned as I remembered where I was and who I was supposed to be. So much for the fantasy. So much for blending in.

Then a couple of Curadores burst into applause and laughter. One of them boomed, "Finally! Someone to put Salk in his place!"

Another man said, "I can only hope someday she bothers to put *me* in my place!"

All around me Kisaengs tittered and the sudden noise made me realize that they'd been holding their breath too. Waiting to see what the Curadores' reactions would be. The singer had stopped her song as well, but there was no smile on her face as she stared at me across the tent. I lost sight of her as one of the laughing Kisaengs jostled me, shoving a glass of mezcal into my hand. I tipped it back, letting it ease my jitters.

And then the crowd shifted and there he was—only a few meters away from me. Edison.

It was the first time I'd seen him without the isolation suit and I wasn't prepared. He was so much *more* now. His head was shaved and the clean severity of it emphasized his sense of power. He dwarfed all the Curadores around him and it was more than just his height. It was like Edison was awake and everyone else was asleep. Like he had a light shining on him that picked up every subtle expression, every gesture, every agile movement he made.

And as he crossed the grass to meet me, he pulled me into his light too. Whether they knew it or not, everyone around us shifted their bodies, their focus, so that Edison—and now I—remained always at the center. The effect was dazzling and unnerving and when he finally reached out to take my hand, it burned, matching the fire of the mezcal in my throat.

"You look luminous." Not pretty. Not beautiful. *Luminous*.

Edison's words were meant for me and yet his voice carried across the crowd and, hearing it, people fell quiet.

"I can't tell you how good it is to see you." He leaned in and kissed my neck. It was such an intimate gesture, I suddenly felt naked in front all those people. But as Edison's lips brushed against my skin, he whispered, "No one else will bother you now. I'm sorry that happened."

Then he gave me a steadying smile—like we were in this together. We might be playing a game, but we were on the same team. He squeezed my hand. "Let me introduce you."

There was a blur of names and faces as Edison ushered me around his immediate circle. I nodded my head in greeting a few times, before I realized that no one else followed that custom. After that, I just plastered on a smile. This was probably not what Lotus and the Indignos had imagined when they'd asked me to infiltrate the Dome and investigate the Citizens' deaths—parties and formal introductions.

And I suddenly felt lost. What was I supposed to do now? Search for sinister glares? Vials of poison? The Curadores might be lustful and drunk—but none of them looked like killers.

The only two names I remembered out of the bunch were the Curadores I'd met at the Exchange with Edison: Planck and Sagan.

Like everyone else, they treated Edison with a kind of fawning respect.

Everyone except Jenner.

I knew who the man was even before Edison introduced me to him. Jenner was talking boisterously with a group of young Curadores, his wide jowls jiggling as he pontificated. But as we got closer, I could see that Jenner was talking *at* them, not with them. The men around him were full of nods and plastic smiles, but there was fear behind their eyes. And whenever Jenner stopped to take a swig from his glass—which was often—the conversation went silent.

Edison seemed to make himself smaller as he led me over to the much shorter man and, in a deferential voice, said, "Leica, this is Jenner. He keeps this whole place running smoothly."

"Now, now." Jenner beamed with false modesty, reaching up to thump Edison on the back. "I couldn't do it without my protégé!"

Jenner was old—older than any person I'd ever met. Thick tufts of hair sprouted out of his ears and nose. On the other hand, the hair on his head was thin—his parchment skin shining through. I wanted to back away from him. Not because he was ugly, which he was, but because there was something off about his horrible cheerfulness.

But Jenner was the only lead I had—even the other Curadores were wary of him. *He* was my place to start. So I smiled sweetly and said, "Nice to meet you."

"The pleasure is all mine." He took my hand in his pudgy one—raising my fingers to his sticky lips. "You're much more lively now that you're awake."

It took every ounce of self-control not to rip my hand away. I hated to think of this man being anywhere near me while I'd been unconscious in isolation.

Then Edison said, "And you know Marisol, of course."

She'd practically materialized at Edison's side and he touched her chin in a careless but familiar way that made me a little prickly. Marisol didn't look very happy about it either.

Then, finally, Edison addressed the whole group, hundreds of faces turning toward us. "Thank you, friends, for coming out to welcome Leica. I, for one, am very grateful she chose to join us in the Dome."

Faces beamed at me from all around the tent. The reception was so different from what I was used to in Pleiades. It was a heady experience. But not an unpleasant one.

Then Marisol wheedled her way into the moment. She handed me a tall, thin glass, then raised her own. "To Leica! May my old friend become yours!"

"To Leica!" People all over the tent raised their glasses and drank. I followed suit and took a swallow of the clear liquid, almost choking with surprise. It was bubbly, cool, and a little fruity, with the subtle warmth of alcohol under it. The effect swirled my head.

Edison bent slightly, pressing his mouth to my ear. "Sorry about all this. Custom demanded it."

His voice was low and soft, and a shiver ran down my spine. Then more people started closing in around me—laughing and asking questions. Kisaengs touched my dress admiringly. Men kissed my hands. Everyone was too loud, speaking at once. I barely had room to breathe.

The panic must've shown on my face, because Edison drew me out of the crowd, saying, "We must give Leica a chance to eat."

But as he escorted me toward the food table, he whispered, "I can't stand this. Being close to you, but not being close." He ran a finger along the inside of my palm and down the length of my extra finger. "Let's sneak out. They can have their party without us."

My smile was back, but this time it was real.

"You go first. Slip out that way." He nodded to an opening in the tent—a haven of shadows waited just beyond the glare of lights. "I'll wait a few minutes, then tell people I'm going to check on you."

His voice grew louder for the benefit of the others around us, saying, "Don't be too long." He kissed my hand and, out of nowhere, produced a round orange fruit and slipped it into my palm.

I rubbed a finger over the fruit, eyeing the gap in the tent. I walked toward the opening like I knew exactly where I was going, keeping my focus on the fruit instead of the crowd. Its skin felt a lot like a lime or a lemon. I held it to my nose and inhaled. It had the same citrusy smell and my mouth watered, thinking of sour lime juice.

Then I was out in the dark. But it was different from being outside in Tierra Muerta or even Pleiades. The air was warm, but not hot. And aside from an occasional burst of laughter from the pavilion, it was completely silent here. There wasn't even any wind. I looked up, trying to fix myself by the stars, but the glass Dome was too thick and I couldn't make them out.

Instead, I saw a pair of rustling wings outlined against the glow of the tent. A curve of a beak. Blue eyes in the dark. My heart pounded as my bird—that's how I thought of him—landed on a nearby branch. Almost close enough to touch.

Fingertips of light brushed his feathers and I could finally see that his wings were a deep blue. Brilliant yellow-gold feathers accented his face and decorated his breast. Up close like this, he reminded me of one of the fairy tales: "The Owl." He looked almost like the picture in my book, but not quite. He was more colorful and his hooked beak was comically huge in his round face.

"So this is where you come from," I whispered. "Or maybe you're a stranger to this place, like me?"

Then the owl-bird opened his wings and slipped off the branch. He drifted down to me, swooping back and forth in the air, like a leaf on the breeze. Until he stopped right in front of me, hovering so close that his wings brushed against my face.

Before, when I'd seen him out in Pleiades or Tierra Muerta, the appearance of the bird had been unsettling. But here, inside the Dome, he fit. I smiled. "Well, hello. I'm Leica."

His blue eyes pulsed softly, echoing my greeting.

"If you're going to keep showing up, I'll need something to call you." And again, I thought of the fairy tale. "How about Grimm?"

"Who are you talking to?" Edison's voice cut through the dark trees and the owl-bird took off, one of his wings grazing my face in his hurry.

"Just myself." The words came out without thinking—protecting this one thing, amid all the newness, that was familiar and mine. Perhaps a lie wasn't the best way to start with Edison, but I reminded myself that I was now a Kisaeng with secrets.

"What's that?" I asked, pointing to the basket hanging from his arm.

"You don't think I'd make you go hungry, do you?"

"I thought that's what this was for." I held up the orange fruit.

"That's dessert." Edison gave a sly smile that made my stomach flutter. Then his face went serious. "I meant what I said back there. I'm so grateful you're here."

He moved in so we were just centimeters away from each other, face-to-face. Edison slipped his hand under my hood, laying it on the back of my neck, and I closed my eyes. Standing there with him, in the quiet darkness of the trees, I relaxed. And that was the last thing I'd expected.

"Leica, I will be whatever you want me to be. Friend, lover, protector . . . all of those things if you'll let me. But the decision is yours."

I couldn't think for the nearness of him, but it didn't matter. Neither did hidden agendas or carefully sculpted fantasies. Because I knew what I wanted. I'd known it as soon I'd seen him standing there in the magnificent chaos of the tent.

I climbed up onto a nearby clump of roots so that I could look Edison straight in the eyes. Putting a hand to either side of his face, I pulled him to me. His lips seared against mine and hunger rose up inside me again.

It was all still there—my uneasiness in this new world. Marisol's warning. The Indignos' questions. Even so, I wanted Edison. I wanted this night. And it was incredible to realize that, for the first time in my life, I could *have* exactly what I wanted.

CHAPTER 16

"WHERE ARE WE GOING?" I peered out the window of the magfly as it glided through the darkness. All I could tell was we were heading away from the party. Away from the house I'd woken up in. "I can't see anything."

"Hold on." Edison got up and fiddled with some buttons on a panel and we slowed down a little. Then he dimmed the lights inside the magfly so I could see the streets around us better.

We were passing by a beautiful glass building, all lit up. It was shorter than the Pleiades towers but much wider. A few blurred figures moved here and there behind the glass, but it was mostly empty. "What is it?"

"The Genetics Lab." Edison peered over my shoulder and his voice thrummed in my ears, so much less clipped now that it wasn't funneled through the suit's microphone. And there was a textured warmth to it. "That's where I work."

"You have a job?" I don't know why I was surprised.

"Well, we don't lounge about feasting *all* day. Every Curador has some duties—manning the labs, supervising the Salvage Hall, going out to trade with the Citizens. But for the most part, the

Dome takes care of itself, so we have a little more . . . *recreational* freedom."

"Does Jenner work there too?" A Genetics Lab seemed like a promising lead.

"Yeah, he oversees the whole place. It's mostly just a glorified nursery. Like I told you before, with our small population, we've had to—" Then Edison clamped his mouth tight and waggled his finger at me. "Nah-ah-ah. You almost got me going. No work tonight. Only play."

He kissed my cheek and the faint reflection of his face was superimposed over the streets outside the window. We slid past more huge, important-looking buildings. It was strange to see. Aside from Pleiades—which had been protected by the foothills of the mountains—every structure I'd ever encountered had been crushed by God's fist. Eaten away by time and sand.

But time had made its mark here as well. As larger structures gave way to houses, and then to boring, blocklike apartments, the trees grew wilder. The streets had buckled under their roots and their sprawling limbs blocked the view.

"It's like Briar Rose," I said in a hush.

"Like what?"

"There's a story in my book about a princess who's cursed by a witch. On her fifteenth birthday, she pricks her finger on a needle and falls asleep. And the whole castle falls asleep around her."

"Everyone?" Edison asked.

"The king and queen, the servants, even the hounds. Everyone. And thorny rose bushes grow up all around the place, every year growing higher and thicker until the entire castle is nothing but an impenetrable thicket."

We were silent, staring out the window at the fairy tale come to life. Branches stretched up through broken windows like massive hands. Saplings perched on mossy, caved-in rooftops. Whole rooms hidden behind streamers of vines instead of walls.

Edison broke the spell, "What happens?"

"A prince rescues her." I remembered how disappointed I'd been by that ending when I was little.

Edison grinned. "There's always a prince."

Amid the maelstrom of green decay, the magfly slowed and stopped, its doors sliding open.

"Careful," Edison said, helping me step over a root that'd grown up through the shattered pavement.

"What happened to this place?"

"A curse?" Edison looked sideways at me, but I wasn't buying it. "Well, it's as good an answer as any. Before the plague there were thousands in the Dome, now there's only about four hundred Curadores. We don't need the whole Dome and we don't have the resources to keep it all running anymore either. So it's falling apart."

Alejo had said that the Curadores had been demanding more salvage for less food. It looked like the Indignos were right—the Dome did have limited resources. Almost against my will, I probed at the idea. "What about all the scrap we trade with you?"

Edison kissed the top of my head. "I promise, I'll answer anything you ask me. I'll give you a tour of the Salvage Hall myself. Anything." Then his voice dropped to a whisper, as if the trees were listening. "As long as it's tomorrow."

"Anything?" I raised an eyebrow, giving a devious smile.

"Anything. But tonight, I want to show you something."

There wasn't much of a street here. Scattered pools of light from the occasional working streetlamp revealed more weeds than concrete. I wasn't used to wearing such a long dress, or any dress, and I had to hold up the skirt to keep it from catching. Edison took my arm, guiding me through the maze of encroaching tree roots.

I breathed him in . . . a deep musk that spoke of wild things in the night. It was a scent I knew well. One that told of gathering sandstorms and hidden pockets of water beneath the sand. And of shadows who made their homes inside the dark places. My whole body came awake with it.

We stopped in front of an immense building—its thick stone looked out of place in this city of glass and metal. But its tower reached proudly into the air, taller than any of the other buildings. Taller than the trees.

We walked up the steps and my delicate shoes rang out as I climbed. Huge wooden doors greeted us at the top, but only one of them was still on its hinges. The other one was propped against the frame and Edison had to heave it out of the way. It was a testament to its bulk that he grunted as he hauled it to the side.

Then we stepped into a dark hallway. Small panels of purpley-red glass were laid into the walls and a threadbare red carpet covered the floor.

"This is my favorite place in the Dome. No one else ever comes here, but I thought you might understand."

His voice was still hushed, but it echoed against the stone—making Edison sound solemn and grand. It made me want to tip-toe, like a child trying not to wake up her parents. Edison ducked under a rounded doorway and reached back for my hand, pulling me with him.

The whole place opened up and we were standing in a long room with great arching ceilings and intricately carved pillars. The only word for it was vast. The whole thing was made of grey stone and dark wood, except the series of tall, mottled windows. Muted light from the streetlamps filtered in through the intricate colored glass.

Here, too, the trees and plants had tried to take over. Branches had smashed windows and clawed their way inside. Roots had pushed up through the tile on the floor. Moss hung in patches on the stone walls. But this place was too strong for them to destroy. I walked into the center of the room, trying to take it all in.

"Stop right there," Edison said. And I froze, my eyes searching for signs of danger.

But Edison just stared at me, his face breaking into a smile that managed to be wistful and satisfied at the same time.

"Yes. You look like a vision," he said. Like he'd been picturing this moment and it was exactly the way he'd imagined.

And, watching him, I *did* understand about this place. Before this, I'd seen Edison masked by isolation suits or fighting for his life in the desert or in the center of a crowd. But this was the first time I had truly seen him.

He *fit* here. His height was perfect inside the arched building— not diminished by it, but in perfect proportion. The whole room was balanced and beautifully crafted, just like him. The columns of stone echoed in his shoulders, his great hands. Soft light glowed around him, illuminating him with power.

A greedy fire stormed my body. I wanted him—here in this place. I wanted all of it.

I turned away, startled by my sudden need. "I've never seen anything like this."

I was staring hard at the windows, but I was talking about him and the building and even myself. And I suspected he heard the current of tension in my voice.

He followed me as I click-click-clicked my way across the stone floor to get a closer look at the windows.

"I never get tired of looking at them, though some are fairly brutal," he said.

I saw what he meant immediately. The small pieces of colored glass were put together so they made pictures. And though the glass *was* beautiful, the scenes were not. Men hung, bleeding, from some sort of torture device. A woman wept over a dead body. Somber figures paraded in heavy robes and strange hats.

"Was this a place for punishment?" I asked Edison.

He shook his head. "It's a church. From what I understand, they held big meetings here . . . something like your Rememberings."

Edison took my hand. He kissed the tips of my fingers— lingering on my extra pinkie—then led me to the front of the church. We passed through a low wooden fence and climbed up two steps so we were on a stretch of marble slightly higher than the rest of the room.

The only other thing up there was a statue of a woman in a robe and head covering. Edison unpacked the basket, spreading out a blanket on the cool floor in front of her. I touched my own hood, which mimicked the same look. The statue's face had an infinite kindness that reminded me of my mother.

"Your picnic, my princess." Grinning, Edison gave a low bow and gestured grandly to the food spread out over the blanket. I hardly recognized any of it. He poured a bloodred liquid into two glasses and, once I'd settled on the floor, handed me one.

"This is one of the best bottles of wine left in existence. Not like that machine-simulated bubbly we had earlier. *This*"—and he held the wine up to catch the gentle light coming in through the window, making it gleam—"was made on Earth. By hand, with real grapes growing in real dirt."

"Earth?" And reverently, I reached for the bottle, wanting to touch it. I wiped the dust off the paper label and it crackled under my touch. There was a faded painting of mountains and I traced the ridges with my finger. Below them, rows of winding green vines led down to a rustic house. The bottle read: *Les Montagne des Agnes*. And in smaller letters underneath: *California, 2082*.

Something about the painting felt familiar and I realized that this was the sort of world the Indignos dreamed of creating. But was that even possible? I angled the bottle toward the candlelight— trying to imagine our own valley that green and lush. Then I spotted something that wiped the picture from my mind. Stamped across the label was the flower emblem I recognized. And the word *LOTUS*. And around it, in a circle, were the words *Ad Astra Research Colony*.

"This is the same as the shuttle." I looked up at Edison, trying to keep my voice even.

"What?" And Edison took the bottle from me, then nodded. "Yeah. It's stamped on the supply crates down in the old storerooms. That's why I was so surprised when we found those necklaces."

"What else is down there?" The idea of Earth was becoming more real—this bottle had come from there. Not just a broken, rusty Find, but something whole.

"The storeroom?" Edison shrugged. "There's not much left,

just a few almost-empty crates of wine." He picked up his glass again and smiled. "To the last of the last."

I raised my glass and Edison touched his to mine, making a rich gonging noise that resounded off the stone walls. The liquid was bitter and sweet at the same time. Instead of the burn of mezcal, this shivered down my throat with a delicious warmth. "It's amazing."

Edison grinned. "I know."

And he held out his glass to me again, this time saying, "To us."

The wine was only the first of a thousand new tastes. Edison fed me crumbs of rich cheese, salty on my tongue. Thick bread dipped in bowls of fruity olive oil. Sweet and creamy pieces of chocolate, which I stole from him and gobbled up, refusing to share. But my favorite was the orange.

As soon as he pressed his fingernail into the peel, a sharp smell hit my nose. Edison slipped a wedge into my mouth, and it was like morning light pouring though a window. The acid tartness teased my tongue, but unlike our limes and lemons, there was a bright sweetness that trickled down my throat.

"More, more!" I grabbed at the half orange still in his hand. The juice squirted everywhere.

"That's what you get for being so greedy. Now, hold still." And he pinned my hands in my lap while he ever-so-gently kissed the sticky juice off my cheeks and the base of my neck, his lips drifting lower.

"I don't think any of it got down there." I tried to keep my voice steady. I was glad he held my hands because the same tension tremored through them.

"Well, we'll have to do something about that, then." Edison

pulled off my hooded cape, leaving me in my plunging bodice. He kissed the newly exposed skin, leaning into me so that we both eased back onto the blanket.

He started to tug at the bodice strings, but I pushed his hand away. I wanted to untie it myself. If I was going to do this, I was going to do it my way. But it was awkward, lying down, and my extra fingers were never good at knots.

"Let me." Edison pulled my hands away.

"No," I snapped, shaking my hands free from his grip. Surprised at the irritation in my own voice.

So far tonight I'd had no need for any of Marisol's lessons. Being with Edison had been easy—I'd forgotten all about her sexy strawberry and my shimmering hands. Now, for the first time all night, I felt uncertain and her words came back to me: *All that matters is the fantasy. From this point forward, you are only what a Curador wants you to be.*

Edison started unlacing my dress again, and this time I let him. It was such a little thing, after all. "Your body is nothing to be ashamed of, Leica. You're beautiful."

"Ashamed?" I sat up and my bodice fell away. I'd never once felt ashamed about my body—angry maybe, or awkward, but not ashamed.

"Just relax." He dipped his fingers in the bowl of olive oil and then rubbed it on my shoulders. Then breasts. Then lower. My whole body waking up at his touch.

And I *tried* to relax. I tried to let him in as his hand, warm with oil, crept between my legs. Heat tingled through my core and I wanted to let myself surrender to the sensation. But I couldn't.

I *wasn't* a fantasy, I was a fighter. I pushed his hand away. "I don't want to relax."

"What *do* you want, then?"

My heart pounded in my chest. My fists clenched and un-clenched. I knew the answer—what I always did when I was too agitated to be civil—but my throat squeezed around the words. "I want to fight."

And he laughed. Big booming guffaws that echoed around the colossal room. The statue of the woman looked disapproving now. Frowning her stone frown at me. "I should've known that wine and pretty dresses wouldn't work on you. Okay, then."

He stood up and started clearing the food and blankets away.

"What?"

"Let's see what you can do," he said.

I looked down. I was bare from the waist up and my long train drifted out behind me. Not the best fighting gear. But fighting was when I'd always felt the strongest, the most in control, and I badly needed some of that now.

Dad had always said that sparring was about harnessing the wild-ness inside you and not letting it win. That is what I would do.

"I'll even the playing field." And Edison pulled off his shirt as well. His body was beautiful too. Unreal. One of the silver neck-laces from the shuttle gleamed against his dark chest. And one word kept coming back to me: *perfect*. Seeing him in front of me, blood pumped through my body with a fierceness I'd always con-nected to the fight.

I was on my feet—ripping the train off my dress and wrapping it around my chest like a tattered ribbon.

LOTUS and THORN · 159

He goaded me. "Ready?"

And I was. Ready to punch. To lay him out flat on the ground. To roar. Anything to feel in control again.

I was best when fighting with sticks, but my hands would have to do. I curled them into fists. "Yes."

He grinned. Not the sharp, confident smile I was used to—but Edison's own secret smile. I knew it was, because it looked just like mine. The one I save for private things. The cinnamony first bite of a sweet tamale. The smell of Sarika's garden when the rain comes. Scouting deep in the Reclamation Fields and catching the tick-tick-tick of a clock whose heart's still beating. Things that made me deeply happy.

We spiraled around each other. Circling. Circling. And I threw the first punch. It missed him. He literally skipped out of way, playing with me. And a growl rose up inside. In a flash, I jetted out my other fist and caught him on the arm.

Edison grabbed me and spun me away from him and I used the momentum, throwing out my leg as I went. Kicking him in the stomach.

We were both flung away from each other. But Edison sprang right back, seizing me around the middle. Pulling me closer.

Instinct took the place of control, a ferocious strength surging into me. I knocked his feet out from under him. Edison fell and took me with him. I landed on top of him—breathing hard. And now, my fingers clutched at him.

I was an animal awakened. And the hunger that had gnawed at me before consumed me.

I kissed him and could feel his desperate, insatiable need. It was echoed in me and I was ravenous with it. Everything that I was disappeared into that all-powerful wanting. I wanted his mouth, his hands on me. Mine on him.

My fingernails cut into his skin. Pulling him closerclosercloser. Until I couldn't bear *not* being part of him. Couldn't bear not being one single body.

We melted and burned and fused together. One devouring wildfire of *us*.

CHAPTER 17

"SO?" MARISOL FLOUNCED on the bed, thrusting a cup of coffee at me. She wore a dazzling red dress that hurt my gritty eyes.

Bright light streamed through the window and made my head ache. Edison had brought me home very late last night. Or was it very early this morning? Hard to tell. Either way, the effects of too little sleep and too much wine had left me feeling dazed.

I accepted the coffee and sipped, letting it clear away the cobwebs. After a few sips I felt more human, but there was Marisol, still looking at me expectantly.

"So . . . what?" I tried for nonchalance, but my voice had a rasp to it.

"So! How did it go?" Marisol's tone was bright and excited, but her eyes had that dangerous glint. I was instantly on guard.

"We had a picnic." And there was Edison in my mind, shirtless and grinning, *Let's see what you can do.*

She snorted. "Well, that's a new word for it."

I was *not* going to have this conversation. Last night had been like spun sugar—delicious and lovely—and I had no intention of handing it over to Marisol to smash. But she was sitting on the edge of the blanket, trapping me. I tugged the other side of the covers free and escaped.

I went straight for the closet, hugging the evening close to me. It wasn't just the cascade of new sensations that'd danced and sang and sizzled through my body . . . though that had been lovely too. There was a giddy sense of power ringing out deep inside me that I didn't quite understand yet. An exhilaration.

Searching the racks, I tried to find something that was worthy of this Leica I'd become. Kisaeng. Spy. And part of me—a part I wasn't quite sure I liked—congratulated me on securing Edison's affections so profoundly.

I pulled out a silky thing and held it up against me. But it was clear in the mirrors that it was too long for my short body and too tight for my curves. I suddenly longed for my own clothes, worn-in pants and a loose shirt. But I didn't know where any of the things I'd brought here were. I could only hope my book had made it through the Curadores' decontamination procedures. I'd have to remember to ask Edison.

Marisol leaned on the doorway of the closet, smirking at my obviously ill-fitting choice. I shoved the dress back on the rack, wishing I could punch that arrogance off her face.

But I wasn't going to let her squash me. I made my voice light. "What are we doing today?"

"Going to the Kisaengs' Sanctum, of course." She said it as if I should know this already—a little dig to remind me that this was her home, not mine. "I'll introduce you to the others."

Others. The last thing I wanted was to spend the day becoming one of the flock of chirpy girls. What I *wanted* was a closer look at the Genetics Lab. To know more about Jenner. I wanted the answers Edison had promised me.

But I had to trust that that would come. I scanned the closet, evaluating the hundreds of bright colors. But I didn't feel bright or sparkly—especially not with Marisol hovering, her smugness masquerading as kindness. I felt strong. Defiant.

A defiant Kisaeng—the idea of it made me smile and my eyes caught on a loose dress the pale blue-grey color of the dunes. And I knew it was right. Last night's tryst-turned-battle had proven that I couldn't play dress-up as well as Marisol. A smile slipped onto my face without my permission.

Perhaps fairy tales were overrated.

This morning, I wouldn't try to disguise myself with capes and layers of fabric. While Marisol watched, I stripped off my night-gown and slipped the simple dress over my head, letting the light fabric swish down around me.

"A bit rustic, but it has a certain . . . something," Marisol admitted, and I realized that next to her, that was probably exactly the right description for me too.

Well, I can work with that.

Inspired, I sat down in front of the mirror and pulled my fingers through my hair. Bits of it were down to my shoulders now, but it still had the rough cut I'd kept in Tierra Muerta. Though, now that it wasn't being beaten into submission by the brutal desert, there was a sheen and slight wave that hadn't been there before. Marisol came at me with clips and creams, but I snatched them from her.

"I don't think it wants to be tamed." Then seeing her tight frown, I added, "Thanks for all your help. This would've been so much harder without a familiar face."

I met her eyes in the mirror. For a moment, Marisol looked as lost as I'd felt. More surprising was that I meant what I'd said. Having her here—no matter how smug—had made everything less overwhelming.

I tested the tubes of cream. One of them was sticky on my fingers and I ran them through my hair, giving it a wilder, storm-blown look. Perfect. I used the shimmery lotion again, but this time, I put streaks of it around my eyes too. Making them shine even darker against the gold. I smiled at the whole effect.

Still me. Just more so.

Feeling a little smug myself, I offered my arm to Marisol. "Shall we?"

Outside, Marisol hit the call button at the magfly stop where Edison had left me just a few hours ago. With a press of the button, a map lit up showing the whole Dome. At the top of the screen it read **Ad Astra Laboratories: Bringing Tomorrow to Today.** Here and there on the map blinked little green lights—moving around large circular tracks with little offshoots connecting them.

I studied the map as a few girls joined us, waiting for the magfly. One of the dots was moving in our direction now, and I already recognized some of the places it passed. The Promenade, the Reservoir, and the Genetics Lab. Other places, were less familiar: the Recreation Center, the Education Complex. The entire center of the Dome was taken up by something called the Gardens. As the dot moved toward Village A, the humming noise of the tracks grew louder.

Then there was a horrible shrill screeching and the tracks near our feet sparked and crackled. One of the girls yelped in pain and we all backed away as the whole map went dark.

"What was that?"

"Our ride." Marisol sounded frustrated.

"I meant . . . what happened?" I followed Marisol and the others as they started walking.

"I know what you meant." Marisol sighed. "Probably just another power surge."

So the Dome *was* having problems, and not just little ones.

More Kisaengs joined us as we walked. I spotted a few familiar faces, some from last night, others I was sure had lived in Building Nine. A bunch of them, including Oksun—the woman who'd glared at me the night before—came out of a large, squat building.

Marisol saw me looking, and in a fake whisper, she said, "They have to share rooms and supplies. Each girl is invited into the Dome by one Curador, of course, but once she's here, she can pick and choose as she pleases. Or more like, as she is able. It's all a matter of whose attention she can catch and whose she can keep hold of. The more important the Curador, the more important the Kisaeng."

Suddenly, my pretty yellow house felt more impressive. Then the bigger truth hit me. If Edison was the prince of the Curadores, what did that make me? His princess? If so, I finally had an answer for why Marisol was being so helpful.

We turned the corner and saw the magfly. It must have been *some* power surge. The thing had flipped on its side, skidded across the pavement, and plowed into a tree. Oksun was already running—tucking her skirts up and climbing on top of the crashed magfly.

I ran after her. "How can I help?"

Oksun peered down into the windows and was clearly surprised as I climbed up next to her. "There's two girls inside. We have to get them out, but the door's on the other side."

I was already climbing down through one of the windows. The glass was broken, and as I dropped through the frame, the remaining shards scraped my arm like jagged teeth.

The metal groaned and shuttered around me. "It's okay," I said as much to myself as to the Kisaengs inside.

One girl had been thrown out of her seat and was now lying against the curve of the roof—unconscious or dead, I wasn't sure. The second Kisaeng was curled up against one of the seats, whimpering. I repeated myself: "It's okay. Take my hand."

Her black hair glistened with crushed glass. She looked at me, but I don't think she really saw me. Her hand was pressed against her cheek, blood welling up between her fingers, and she was saying something under her breath.

I leaned closer so I could catch the words.

"My face," she said. "Myfacemyfacemyfacemyface."

"I think she's in shock," I called up to Oksun.

"Olivia? Is that you?" Oksun's voice was steady and quiet. "Olivia, I need you to take Leica's hand, okay? She's gonna help you."

The girl blinked up at Oksun. Her hair was cut very short—unusual for the Kisaengs—and it stuck out maniacally around her face. Her expression was still blank, but she reached out for me anyway. I helped her stand up and I was grateful when her legs held.

Then she looked at me and said, "My face."

"Your face is going to be fine. It's just a cut. And we're gonna get you out of here. Ready?"

Olivia shook her head but I ignored her. "Ready, Oksun? On three, I'll boost her up . . . I think she'll fit."

"Wait a sec. Cover your heads." Oksun kicked the remaining fragments out of the window frame. Accompanied by the sound of smashing glass, Olivia kept up her chant of *myfacemyfacemyface*. "Okay. Ready."

The girl was oblivious to what was happening as I positioned her under the window. "One, two . . ."

On three, I hoisted her up and Oksun grabbed her, hauling her out of the magfly. A second later, a horde of insects buzzed over Oksun's and Olivia's heads and poured in through the windows.

"*Kya bakchodi hai!*" I yelled in surprise and ducked, but the creatures ignored me. More and more of them swarmed to the magfly until there were black bugs crawling over every centimeter. Making the whole place vibrate with their insistent droning.

"What are they?" Their roar crowded out my thoughts, but they were fascinating to watch. As they crawled over and under each other, I swore I saw dents in the side of the magfly melting and reforming.

"Flys!" Marisol shouted over the din. "They're evaluating the damage. We need to get you guys out. Now!"

"Why?" But even as I asked the question, a cluster of flys began repairing the crumpled roof near the unconscious Kisaeng. Before I had a chance to do anything the whole roof melted into a silvery liquid. Beneath the flys' feet, the molten metal shimmered, lapping the edges of the girl's body. Then it instantly hardened again— outlining her limp form in the recast metal.

"Oh my God!" I crawled over to the girl, trying to pry her

loose, but the metal had molded perfectly to the edges of her body, trapping her there.

"Leave her! Get out!" Oksun said, and she started banging on the outside of the magfly, trying to bat away the flys.

Glass rained down on me as I headed back to the window and flys swarmed into vortexes around me. They must have seen Oksun as a threat because they flew to the nearest window and created a thick net of flys over the opening. Then their eerie droning grew louder, and the flys melted together—forming a solid wall of black metal. More flys sealed the next one. And the next.

"Hurry!" Oksun was waving frantically at the final open window, trying to keep it free of flys.

I scrambled through the magfly, crawling over seats, racing the flys. Despite Oksun's efforts, they'd already managed to create a mesh of bodies inside the frame. I forced my hands through, pulling myself up and out—my face plastered with flys as I shot through the window. Oksun hauled me the rest of the way up and the three of us jumped off the magfly.

Marisol rushed over to me and pulled me away from the debris. "Are you okay?"

Curadores were running down the street toward us now and a second later the entire swarm of flys burst out of the magfly, leaving it a twisted, half-melted hunk.

I nodded, brushing at my face—still feeling thousands of prickly insect legs all over my skin. I was shaken up, but aside from the scrape on my arm, I was fine. Marisol took my hand and was already dragging me back into the group of waiting Kisaengs.

Near the magfly, Oksun was busy shooing Curadores off her, insisting she was okay. Olivia was almost hysterical as the

Curadores tried to help her, yelling, "I don't want to go. Please! My cheek is fine!"

Oksun tried to stop the Curadores from taking Olivia, but more of them stepped in, blocking her path. She looked furious as they carried the girl away.

"What's going to happen to Olivia? And the other Kisaeng?" I asked.

Marisol smiled brightly. "They'll be fine! The Curadores are here now!" But I noticed she was pulling us farther into the crowd and down the sidewalk even as she spoke.

The rest of the walk was a blur to me—more houses, more buildings. I was vaguely aware of passing a huge compound, the shouts of playing children carrying over the wall. But I couldn't get the image of the girl out of my head—trapped there. A piece of the magfly. Or Olivia babbling in panic. What had happened? Why had the magfly crashed? How could I have saved that Kisaeng? I went over and over the events in my mind.

And then we were back where we'd been last night. A lawn. A lake. And trees.

It was the trees that pulled me out of my stupor. Dense, towering woods crowded the shore of the Reservoir. The map had called them the Gardens, but those trees were nothing like Pleiades' small patches of vegetables. The forest looked wild and dark—making me want to run into it and away from it at the same time.

"What's in there?" I asked, pointing to the trees.

"Nothing . . . and don't even think about it. The Gardens are off-limits."

I wanted to ask why, but it seemed better not to. Instead, I added it to my mental list of things to investigate. I followed

Marisol across the grass toward a magnificent circular building not too far from Edison's lab. As I got closer, I could see that it was actually less of a circle and more of a spiral—a wall of thick blue glass wrapping in around itself like a snail shell. I paused outside, reading the words engraved over the entryway: **RECREATION CENTER**.

Marisol waited for me to catch up. I got the feeling it wasn't so much out of consideration, but so we would enter together. Side by side.

We stepped into the opening of the snail shell—not really a hallway since there was no ceiling—more like a walkway between two curved walls of glass. The walkway pulled us deeper into the spiral; the light was cool and blue as it filtered through the transparent walls. And even though I could see the blurry, scurrying shapes of people on the other side of the glass, it was blissfully quiet on this side.

Marisol and I walked two full circles before the spiral opened up and we arrived at the center of the building. And then the spell was broken. The noise of the vast courtyard washed over us. Women were everywhere. Blanketing the benches and grass. Running along a black rubbery path that bordered the courtyard. Talking in the shade of the trees. About seventy-five of them in all.

Marisol beamed and spread her arms wide. "Welcome to the Sanctum."

Then she took me on a sweeping tour of the courtyard. Clearly the story of what had happened with the magfly preceded us. There was a preoccupied, manic energy electrifying the place. Everyone *looked* busy—little clusters of Kisaengs strummed instruments or painted or stretched their bodies into complicated poses—but their heads swiveled toward me as we passed. And they all wore pasted-on smiles.

Marisol paraded me along a narrow stream that ran through the courtyard—crossing the lawn, and becoming a rippling waterfall on the far side. We strode across an ornamental bridge to get to a small circle of girls sitting on elaborate pillows next to the creek. The six girls fell silent, ready to lavish us with their full attention.

"Girls!" Marisol beamed. "Edison has brought us another sister."

They made tiny hand clapping motions as Marisol pulled me down onto a pillow next to her. All smiles and welcomes. It was surreal. No one said a word about the accident or the injured Kisaengs. They just laughed and nodded and chatted to each other.

Marisol rattled off names and I tried to pay attention. The girl next to me was Gabriella. Or had Marisol said Isabella? I recognized her vaguely from the party. She was pretty, but her dark hair and brown eyes were nothing special. Not much different from the girl next to her. Not different *at all*, in fact. And the girl next to them looked *exactly* the same too.

"Triplets. You can just call us the Ellas," they said all together. They were wearing identical pink dresses too. "We're pleased to meet you."

They inclined their heads in a slight bow, not so much smiling at me as looking amused. I was so distracted by seeing the same snub nose turned up on all three faces, I completely missed the name of the next Kisaeng. But she had dark eyeliner that made her eyes pop: one of them was pale green, the other a light brown. The fifth girl in the circle, Aaliyah, had no hair at all. No trace of eyebrows or eyelashes either. She'd painted her naked head with intricate swirls and patterns of color that spiraled down her neck and down her equally bare arms, making her look otherworldly.

I glanced down at my own six-fingered hands and at Marisol's distinctive bright red hair. I was starting to get what this circle had in common. Some anomalies, like my fingers, or Marisol's hair, were spoken of in the Rememberings. They disappeared from Pleiades for generations only to suddenly spring up again—a fresh rebuke from God. Others were simply unusual. But any aberration made the Abuelos nervous. We were all Corrupted.

"And this is June."

I couldn't see anything that made this last girl unusual, except that she was incredibly glamorous and the only one to give me a real smile. And instead of a pillow she sat on a flat, metal seat that curved up slightly at her back. Before she looked up, she nervously brushed grass off her wide, velvety blue skirt.

"We're so happy you've joined us!" June beamed at me, tucking away a loose strand of her black hair, which fell in graceful waves to her waist.

"Yes!" said Aaliyah. "You left dinner so early last night, we didn't get a chance to introduce ourselves."

"Not that we blame you!" June grinned. Her round face seemed to be made to smile—her lips permanently turned up at the corners. Unlike the others, June seemed genuinely unaware of how beautiful she was. "Edison is quite enough to satisfy any girl's appetite."

One of the Ellas gave me a coy non-smile and said, "Or three girls'." And the triplets laughed and nodded their heads.

And I suddenly understood the real link between these Kisaengs. Evidently, our Corruptions weren't the only thing we had in common.

CHAPTER 18

SISTERS.

Edison has brought us another sister. That's what Marisol had said. And now I knew what she'd really meant. This circle of Kisaengs wasn't just joined by what made us different. We were connected by something that made us the same. Someone. Edison.

The "sisters" were all watching me, waiting for my reaction. As a Kisaeng, should I be angry? Did I have a right to be? I honestly didn't know. I didn't even know all the rules here yet. Clearly they were hoping for drama, but I couldn't bring myself to give it to them.

Instead, I made myself smile back at the Kisaengs around the circle, sharing the Ellas' joke.

But figuring out my own feelings was so much trickier. I was mad. Of course I was. All that time together and Edison didn't bother mentioning this one little detail.

Out in the Indigno camp he'd said, *This time I came to find you.* Now my face flamed. Was this why? So he could add me to his collection? And suddenly everything that'd happened since I'd met Edison became suspect. Had he been scheming to get me here ever since we'd met at the Exchange? Is that why he'd been kind to me?

Then again, I had my own agenda . . . Should I really be surprised that Edison had one too? And it was painfully clear to me that you could use someone and fall for them at same time. Hell, you could hate them and fall for them at the same time—I saw it all the time in Pleiades. The real question was, if emotions overlapped and crisscrossed and contradicted each other like this, how were you ever really sure about anyone?

But there was *one* certainty in all this: Edison *knew* he was sending me into the lion's den today. He knew and he'd said nothing.

I looked away from the group of Kisaengs, blinking hard, and my eyes fell on a girl who was sitting by herself in the grass about five meters away. The girl was sewing a complicated-looking dress, but every few seconds, her eyes flicked up from the needle and landed on me.

And I noticed that the girl on the grass wasn't the only one in the Sanctum staring at us. It dawned on me that the "sisters" might look relaxed—lounging on pillows, absorbed in their gossip—but it was an act put on for the benefit of the entire courtyard. Because just as Edison was the center of the room, so were his Kisaengs. They looked so natural, chattering and smiling, but it was hard to get comfortable with all those eyes on me.

It didn't help that I had no context for anything or anyone they were talking about. I'd expected the Kisaengs to grill me about their families and friends. But no one so much as *said* the word Pleiades. As if nothing outside this Dome even existed. I could understand why—we'd made our choice and it couldn't be undone. Once you entered the Dome, you weren't allowed to leave again. After the amount of food at last night's feast, I could see that the

Curadores had secrets they'd like to keep that had nothing to do with diseases or death. That information would not do much to alleviate the mounting suspicion surrounding the Curadores.

But even if the Curadores allowed Kisaengs to leave, we would not be welcomed back. Kisaengs weren't demonized in the eyes of the Citizens. It was worse than that. They were forgotten. Erased from conversations, from family stories. Because stepping inside the Dome took you outside of God's salvation. You would not see your family again in this life, or the next. And that was not a comforting thought.

So instead of speaking about anything that mattered, the Kisaengs jabbered about parties and dresses and Curadores. And I tried to make the appropriate responses. But there was the girl on the grass. Still watching me.

Finally, I couldn't stand it any longer. I was not going to be an object of curiosity or ridicule. I stormed over, planting myself in front of her.

"Would you like a closer look?" I thrust my hands in her face. She cringed away, hugging her sewing to her chest.

Now that I was closer, I realized she was the Kisaeng who'd been singing at the party. I hadn't recognized her before because her dark hair—which had been long last night—was now very short and messy like mine. But instead of going spiky and wild, hers had feathered out around her face. What was also painfully obvious now was that she wasn't recoiling in disgust, but in fear. Not of my hands. Of me.

I felt the eyes of the courtyard on me again—eager to see what I would do. Under the beautiful dresses and friendly smiles, there was a pack mentality within the Kisaengs. The sisters . . . they were clearly the alpha dogs of the whole group. And Marisol was the alphaest.

No, that wasn't quite right. *We* were the alpha dogs. I was one of them now.

My face burned again, this time with real shame. I took a step back, giving the girl room. When I spoke again, my voice was gentle. "I'm Leica. I don't think we've met."

I nodded a greeting and she returned it automatically. Then I stood there, quiet—a trick I'd learned with Lotus a long time ago. Some people simply need the space to speak . . . especially if you've just terrorized them.

The girl nodded again, as if making up her mind about something, then shoved her sewing aside and unfolded her long legs. Her tawny-colored tunic and pants blended with her skin, obscuring her. And yet when she moved, the cloth rippled around her, drawing attention to the girl anyway. She was like a moth, strange and fluttering.

Marisol was at my shoulder now, glaring at the girl. "What do you want? It's rude to—"

"I want to speak to Leica." The Kisaeng's voice was quiet, but not weak. Her face held that same balance—straight nose, small, rounded mouth, pointed chin—strong, but subdued. And her eyes had steel in them. The effect was echoed in her clothes—a crisscrossing sash made from tarnished belt buckles laid heavy over her soft tunic. It should've looked cumbersome, but it suited her.

"How dare you interrupt me!" Marisol said.

"What's your name?" I stepped in front of Marisol, trying to limit the damage. After all, I'd started this.

"Riya."

Every ear was listening. Waiting to see what would happen. "What do you want to talk about, Riya?"

"How did you do that last night?" She swiveled her wrist back and forth in the air. "With the Curador and the arm twisting and the . . ." She made a whistling noise and let her arm drop.

It was the last thing I expected her to ask. "It was a move my dad taught me. It's simple, really. You just use your opponent's hold against him. Or her."

I only had to show Riya once and she repeated the movements flawlessly.

"This is ridiculous!" Marisol tried to insert herself again. "This is the Sanctum, not a fighting ring."

I started to snap at Marisol, but then June was at our side—defusing the situation with her easy tone. "Could you do it again? Looks like a good trick. I've put up with one too many pairs of groping hands."

I smiled gratefully at June. I didn't want my first morning to deteriorate into a shouting match between me and Marisol. But when I turned to June, I was speechless. She was looking straight in my eyes—but she wasn't standing. Instead, her torso was perched, midair, on a floating metal seat. Her velvety skirts draped over the front of the hovering board, but she had no legs dangling under the cloth folds. No legs at all, in fact.

A soft hum, similar to the magflys, filled the awkward silence. As I gaped at June, it dawned on me that I was on the wrong side of all the rude stares I'd ever endured in my life.

"I'm sorry, I—" But then I stammered, afraid that apologizing would just make it worse.

June generously pretended that she didn't notice my unforgivable behavior. The permanent half smile still on her face, she busied herself with smoothing out her skirt so it cascaded dramatically into the empty air between her torso and the ground. Waiting until I managed to find something coherent to say.

This time I was saved by Riya. "But what if the move doesn't work? What if he manages to keep hold?" Riya's gaze was intense and I could tell this was something she'd had experience with.

Suddenly I wondered how many other Kisaengs had found themselves in situations like I had last night—or worse. Edison had been clear that our relationship was my call, but was that always the case with Kisaengs and Curadores?

"Well, if they're too strong, then you have to find a way to weaken them first."

By now, five or six other Kisaengs had wandered over to join us and right there on the grass of the Sanctum, I gave an impromptu lesson. We moved to an open stretch of grass, leaving Marisol and her circle by the creek. June didn't follow us, but she swiveled a little on her seat so she could watch.

The Kisaengs worked together in pairs, going through the motions of the arm twist, as well as attacks on some the most vulnerable points. Groin, shins, knees. I decided to save throat punches and eye gouges for another day.

"Okay, Riya. Show me what you've got." I grabbed her wrist, and with surprising force, she twisted my arm behind me and continued the momentum, flipping me over her back and onto the ground.

"Well done!" Edison suddenly towered over me, laughing as he offered me a hand up. "I see we'll be in for more of the entertainment we got last night."

"Entertainment?" I pushed myself off the ground, refusing his help. When I looked at Riya and the other Kisaengs around me, their faces—which seconds ago had been fierce with concentration—were now embarrassed. He had no right to treat me—to treat us—like that.

"Kisaengs, I want you to remember that these are more than just party tricks. Let them laugh. Let them underestimate you . . ." Anger over meeting my new "sisters" caught up to me as I put a hand on Edison's chest, and I was surprised by the intensity of it. Feeling his heart beating though his shirt, our eyes met—in that split second, he saw what I was about to do. "Then take them down."

I pushed his chest and, at the same time, hooked my foot around his legs—yanking them out from under him. I won't deny that it felt good.

Everyone gasped as Edison crashed to the ground. Only *I* knew that I hadn't used nearly that much force.

He lay there, eyes closed. Unmoving. Whispers went through the crowd. I nudged him with my foot. Still nothing. Finally I knelt down next to him. "I know you're fak—"

But I couldn't finish, because Edison grabbed me and drew me to him in a consuming kiss. And heat flared up inside me. Embers still glowing from last night. I was back in the church, his fingers in my hair. Breath in my ear. The hunger calling out to me.

And when he let me go, I felt seventy-five pairs of eyes on us.

Edison threw up his hands. "I relent! Please stop! Forgive me!"

I pulled away and got to my feet. But Edison was up on his

knees now, still making a spectacle of himself. "Please, my sweet lady," he begged. "Forgive my foolish ways."

I tried to put on a smile—acting the part—but I hated the spotlight. Hated being player in his spectacle. "Yes. Okay. I forgive you! Anything to make you stop."

"Good!" Edison said, leaping to his feet, used to getting his way. He held his hand out to me. "I've come to fetch you for your checkup."

I was happy to do whatever would make this uncomfortable scene end. But as I reached for his hand, Marisol casually insinuated herself between Edison and me. Smiling like nothing unpleasant had passed between the two of us. "Surely, you're not going to steal Leica from us so quickly. The girls were just getting to know her."

I hated her tone. Like she'd arranged the whole fighting demonstration herself. To help me make friends. And I was struck by a sudden memory from childhood. I couldn't have been more than eight and the four of us, Marisol, Taschen, Lotus, and I, got up early to weed Sarika's garden.

It'd been Taschen's idea actually—a surprise for Sarika, who had been absorbed with tending the giant pitfire for days, smoking agave for the latest batch of mezcal. We'd worked hard as the sun came up. And when we were almost done, Marisol had suggested the three of us take a break and get a drink.

I'll finish up, she'd said, *as long as you guys bring me back some water.*

I'd thought it was so nice of her. We'd gathered around the spigot, taking turns sipping at the dripping tap. Then I noticed Sarika walking across the Commons, smiling at her daughter working diligently in the garden. They were talking and I could tell that Sarika was impressed by the work. And I understood why Marisol had offered to finish up. She'd wanted the credit.

Clearly Marisol hadn't changed in the decade since.

"Sorry, Marisol." Edison barely glanced at her, putting an arm around me.

Marisol's face went rigid. And her look of shock showed me what should've been obvious from the beginning. Marisol was not just *one* of Edison's Kisaengs; she'd been Edison's favorite. And now I was.

My arrival in the Dome had displaced Marisol and she was desperate to cling to whatever power she could. I wasn't fond of Marisol, but I had no interest in fighting a war with her. And no interest in hurting her.

"I'll bring her back to you after she gets the okay from Jenner," Edison said.

"Jenner?" And when Marisol said the name, fear rippled out from her, infecting me. It was the first confirmation that I was right to suspect him and I pushed.

I grinned at them both, trying out my Kisaeng role and said, "Oh no! Should I be scared? Am I in trouble?"

Aaliyah and the Ellas managed a nervous titter, but Marisol looked at me with a warning. A small shake of her head told me this was *not* something to joke about. And there was real concern in her eyes.

Maybe I was wrong. Maybe there was a piece of Marisol that didn't fit into her own flighty Kisaeng fantasy.

Maybe Marisol *had* changed.

CHAPTER 19

"A CHECKUP?" I hesitated in the filtered sunshine of the Promenade. I'd wanted to get a closer look at Jenner but this wasn't exactly what I'd had in mind. And Edison wasn't exactly my favorite person right now either.

"It's routine. And painless, I promise. I know I haven't given you a very good impression of Jenner, but his intentions are good. He just wants to make sure you're acclimating to the Dome." We stood looking up at the huge glass building we'd seen the night before.

Cold, vague memories from isolation still floated at the edges of my mind. Chilling me in a way I didn't fully understand. I tried to push them away. To be brave. But I'd seen the fear in Marisol's eyes at the mention of Jenner's name.

Still. If Lotus was right and the Curadores had killed Tasch, there had to be *some* sign of it somewhere. Some evidence that they were connected to the recent outbreaks. And if this was my way to get inside the Genetics Labs to look for it—to see what Jenner was doing in there—I had to take it. "Okay."

"Good. Because afterward, I have a surprise for you in the Lab." Edison took my hand, and this time it wasn't a show. He punched a series of buttons on a panel next to the entrance to the Lab—like a smaller version of the ones at the magfly stops—and the glass door slid open. The door code had been too fast for me to catch, but now I knew to keep an eye out. There was a rush of frigid air as Edison pulled me into a huge lobby.

The light was dazzling. It rainbowed through the glass ceiling several stories above. But it also flashed and flickered on wide screens around us—a constant flow of numbers and images pouring across them.

Flys buzzed in every direction. Swarming high into the air. Crawling across the thousands of blue glass bricks that made up the walls. But I was drawn toward the center of the room—to a mass of buzzing machines. Fans whirled and lights blinked. "What is this thing?"

"The main computer makes up the heart of the Lab, controlling all the experiments from here. And monitoring the entire Dome."

"Experiments? I thought you said this place was a glorified nursery?" I walked up behind one of the Curadores, watching numbers stream across the monitor. Trying to see what he was doing.

The Curador seemed surprised to see me, but as soon as he caught sight of Edison, he gave us space. The man reached up and touched something on a screen, reciting instructions into thin air—like he was having a conversation with himself.

A swarm of flys burst into action. I flinched as they buzzed over me and up toward the ceiling.

"They won't hurt you." Edison squeezed my hand.

"Tell that to the Kisaeng I saw this morning. What are they doing anyway?"

A shadow passed over Edison's face as he checked the screen.

184 • Sara Wilson Etienne

"Well, it looks like that swarm is headed to the Meat Brewery to fix the chiken vat. When they're working correctly, this whole Dome is self-regulating. The flys monitor and repair everything . . . food synthesizers, reprocessors in the Salvage Hall—"

"Magflys," I filled in.

He nodded. "Magflys. They're all controlled from here."

My brain churned away at the new information—seeing all the implications this had for the Dome, for the magfly accident. If I was going to find out anything about what the Curadores were really up to, I needed to know how this place worked. Or didn't work. "But this morning, those flys . . . they . . ." And I saw it happening all over again, too fast for me to do anything about. "They embedded that girl in metal."

"Yes, like I said, *when* they're working correctly." Edison tried to leave it at that. But as I stood there, arms crossed, he realized that half answer wasn't going to satisfy me. "If something breaks, the flys alert the computer, or we do, and the computer tells the flys how to fix the problem. But a while ago, before I was born, the whole system started getting buggy—pardon the pun. Here or there, a fly would develop a glitch. And either the computer *couldn't* fix the glitch or the glitch got integrated into the learning systems . . . and then into the copies. And into the copies of the copies. So whenever the computer shuts them down and orders the reprocessors to make a new fly, the problem just gets worse."

"If the computer can't fix them, then why don't you do it?"

"We don't know how. The Curadores are great at interpreting data and making decisions based on it—choosing which egg is the best genetic match for which sperm or what parts of the Dome to shut down in order to be more efficient. But we don't actually know how to *do* those things anymore. That knowledge was lost hundreds of years ago.

"We instruct the computer and *it* splices genes and cables and wires. It's an imperfect system, but no one ever anticipated that the plague would kill off most of our scientists. Or that we'd lose our link with Earth's databases. Like I said last night, the Dome is falling apart. No one——"

Edison cut off as Jenner came in from a side entrance. The man practically bellowed his greeting. "Hello, my boy! So this is where you're hiding our lovely new addition."

In Jenner's presence, Edison's whole manner transformed. He became more tentative. More formal. I'd noticed the same thing the night before. "Sorry for the delay. Leica was fascinated by the computer."

"As she should be! This lady's the only reason we're all here." Jenner fondly patted the whirring machine. "I doubt the Colonists who built her had any idea she'd still be keeping us alive half a millennium later."

"What was she supposed to do, then?" I stepped closer, injecting a little awe and confusion into my voice.

Jenner took the bait. "Well, long before the plague, Ad Astra Colony was intended to be a place of research and development. Planetary exploration. Robotics and computers. Food production. Recycling resources. Next-generation technology. Biotech." He slipped an arm around me—leading me toward one of the monitors—and I let him. I concentrated on smiling and nodding at what Jenner was saying, instead of his hand . . . inching down my waist. If there was ever a time for Marisol's be-whatever-they-want-you-to-be advice, this was it.

"They provided the Colonists with anything and everything that was needed to keep a civilization like this self-sustaining. But it was only meant to be a jumping-off place. Still, when the plague hit Gabriel, the Dome was exceptionally well-equipped to survive."

I nodded encouragingly, not saying anything. I didn't need to. Some people loved to fill up the room with their endless streams of words. As if they were waging war on silence.

"Perhaps a demonstration of her abilities can be arranged as part of your checkup," Jenner said. "What do you think, Edison?"

Edison nodded deferentially, almost cringing. And Jenner, who was over a head shorter than Edison, reached up and clapped him on the shoulder. "Let's put on a show for our girl."

Jenner punched a code into the monitor. I tried to see it—in case it might come in handy at some point—but his hand blocked my view. Then he said, "Kisaeng, Leica. Blood sample."

A long list of names scrolled across the screen and for a second I thought I caught Olivia's name in the list. Then a picture of my face, eyes closed, flashed up on the screen and next to it: **Sample number 2789: Two Pints**.

It was unsettling to see the unconscious Leica lying there. I wanted to shake her awake.

"You see, this whole Dome functions like a giant insect colony. You could think of us, perhaps, as a beehive. This room would be the center of the hive and our computer here would be the queen bee. She makes all the decisions and sends out messages to her workers." Then, illustrating his point, Jenner said, "Computer, retrieve sample."

Immediately, a swarm of flys took flight, but this time I didn't flinch. My eyes followed them as they traveled up toward the high ceiling.

"Of course, if they were truly bees, they'd use chemicals and movement to communicate. Cryptic dances spelling out the answers to the cosmos. But Ad Astra is much more sophisticated than any of that. Within the Dome, our computer—our queen, if you will—can send data through the air, communicating with her children. For they are, in essence, tiny infinitely useful computers."

The cloud of flys finally stopped several stories up and hovered along the left wall. Then one of the blue blocks popped forward and pushed out—revealing a little drawer. A cloud of fog spilled from it, and for the moment, the flys were lost in the mist.

"Are all of those drawers?" I marveled at the upper stories, which were made out of what I'd assumed were small glass bricks.

Jenner nodded. "The Colonists were sent here with hundreds of thousands of samples of DNA . . . and not just human, but animal and plants as well."

I tried to comprehend the mass of life this room represented, but it was impossible.

Then the drawer shut itself again, immediately disappearing back into the wall. One square among thousands. As the fog cleared, I saw the swarm had disappeared. In its place was a small black metal cylinder, descending toward us.

"Put out your hand," Jenner said.

I hesitated, nervous, and suddenly Jenner grabbed my wrist, yanking it up. He was still smiling and his voice still had its swagger, but there was danger there too. "Put. Out. Your. Hand."

Edison took a step toward us, his face thunderous. I gave a little shake of my head—calling him off. Jenner's grip was painful, and

I was unnerved by the man who wore this plastic smile even as he hurt me. But what I needed now was to see the rest of Jenner's little demonstration. Edison nodded, though his jaw was clenched tight.

I opened my upturned hand.

The cylinder landed precisely in the center of my palm. Then the black metal coating liquefied, trickling away, exposing a clear vial, filled with red blood. The glass was icy, and I almost dropped it when the pooling metal suddenly congealed and reformed into flys—their feet scritch-scratching over my skin.

Then Jenner, still crushing my wrist, said, "Verify match."

One of the flys crawled along the length of my index finger. There was a sharp prick as it stuck a proboscis into my flesh. The fly stayed there, its tiny wire embedded in my fingertip—the pain traveling down my finger, becoming a throbbing ache in my hand. I fought the urge to smack it *and* Jenner away, gritting my teeth and forcing myself to stay put. Finally, the nearby monitor beeped and the computer said, "Match verified."

Jenner released my wrist with a little laugh—leaving pale fingerprints on my skin. I took a step back, putting space between us, though I suspected the whole Dome wouldn't be enough distance. But then the screen behind him was flooded with diagnostics. Blood type. Levels of nutrients and chemicals. Blood pressure.

"Well done. Looks like you're healthy and adapting to life inside the Dome," Jenner said.

I didn't know what most of the information meant, but my eyes honed in on one detail—making sure my excitement didn't show in my voice. "What does that mean, 'Disease Resistance Markers Detected'? Does that mean you tested it against Red Death?"

"We don't use the disease itself . . . that would be too danger-ous," Jenner said. "We merely check the blood for genetic mark-ers. We've known for decades that a few of your kind carry an immunity to Red Death. In fact, we wasted a lot of time trying to replicate it. But it turns out it's not just one gene. Immunity results from a slough of complex, tiny variations across many genes . . . probably one of the reasons it's so rare even within your own peo-ple. We probably haven't even identified all the pertinent factors. And to be honest, we haven't invested any more resources into it either. Let me show you what we're doing instead."

Jenner slipped his arm around my waist again and guided me out of the main room and down a long hallway. *Your kind.* That's what Jenner had called the Citizens. As if they were just some spe-cies of animal to be studied. Who cared that *my people* were still dying by the hundreds of Red Death? It was like the glut of food at the party last night, when people in Pleiades were barely getting enough—if it wasn't affecting the Dome, then it didn't matter.

"As Edison has probably explained to you, the Curadores have been isolated for so long, we are without resistance to many, many diseases. That's why we're so strict about who goes in and out of the Dome. And it's why it would be impossible for us to leave without losing a vast percentage of our population. So it's essential that we find a way to access the computer and fix the pieces that are wearing out."

We arrived outside a busy-looking room. Like so much of the building, this wall was made of glass, letting us see into the lab. Metal tables were lined with trays of test tubes and clear plas-tic dishes. Flys clouded the air and Curadores in isolation suits monitored computer screens. Robot arms descended from the ceilings, siphoning droplets of liquid from the test tubes into complicated-looking machines.

"This area is really Edison's domain," Jenner said, deferring to the younger Curador.

But Edison looked uncomfortable, like he wished he was anywhere but here. Finally Edison said, "Let me introduce you to my children." Edison gestured to the lab. "Well, they're really the Dome's children. When Red Death infected Gabriel five centuries ago, only the scientists that happened to be in one of these sealed-off 'clean labs' survived. With only a handful of Curadores left, they decided to use the genetic bank to repopulate the Dome."

Jenner cut in. "And now we're using that same bank to make smarter, stronger Curadores. Aren't we, my boy?"

And when he said *my boy*, I heard it. The disdain disguised as pride. And I realized that Jenner meant smarter and stronger than *Edison*. I'd heard the same veiled tone somewhere before without registering it . . . the condescension masquerading as kindness. And I was shocked to discover that it was in my memories of Sarika.

All her words to me, her actions, had been kind—loving even. But still, there had been a thread of revulsion there. I remembered her eyes flicking toward my hands as she said, *I blame myself for not being vigilant. For not seeing what was right there in front of me.*

Now I realized that Sarika had forgiven my betrayal not because she thought of me like a daughter, but because she thought me as Corrupt—incapable of doing better. Sarika *might* have loved me, but in her heart of hearts, she believed God had damned me. She believed I was *wrong*.

I could only recognize it now that I saw that same wrongness reflected in Jenner's interactions with Edison. All the fatherly affectations—all the shoulder claps and *my boys*—were simply Jenner's way of underscoring that Edison had failed him. A sort of inverted hatred. I wondered how Edison could stand it.

Then I thought about myself and Sarika—and I wondered if Edison could even see it.

CHAPTER 20

"DO YOU REALLY RUN that whole lab?" I asked when Jenner was called away. Edison was preoccupied as he watched Jenner's receding figure—the older man's hands animated as he discussed something with another Curador—and I tried to summon Edison back to me.

"Yeah," Edison finally answered, turning to lead me down a different hallway. "I do."

"You don't sound too happy about it." And honestly, I wasn't either. I wasn't happy about anything I'd seen here.

Because one thing was clear: the Curadores certainly had the technology to manipulate Red Death and to infect Pleiades. But if that's what was happening, then why would Jenner allow me to see all this? Or did he think I was so insignificant that it wouldn't matter if I figured it out? And the fact that I had no real read on what Jenner's motives were worried me. Marisol seemed terrified of him. Edison was cowed by him. All the other Curadores were intimidated . . . a perfect setup for Jenner's authority to go unchecked and unquestioned.

But authority to do what? And why? This wasn't just about retribution for Tasch's death—this was about the thousands of Citizens out in Pleiades who were still at risk from whatever was going on. Suspicions would not help me protect my people.

"It's important work, don't get me wrong," Edison continued. "It's just when I was a kid, that place used to give me nightmares. Nikola too."

And I wondered when I might meet this brother of Edison's. We turned a corner and now the floors slanted downward a little. The lighting was dimmer here and there were no more glass walls. Only windowless doors.

"What I don't understand is, after the plague, if there were so few Curadores left, why didn't they just let in the rest of the survivors from Pleiades?"

"They couldn't . . . not without dying," Edison said. "It wasn't until much later that they figured out a way to bring Kisaengs into the Dome using the isolation rooms and intensive blood filters and tests. The people outside—your ancestors—survived because they had some natural resistance to the disease, but they could still be carriers. And the remaining Curadores had no resistance at all. They were only alive because they hadn't been exposed in the first place. The Curadores had to think of the big picture."

"I think you mean they had to think of themselves." I imagined what it would've been like to grow up inside this Dome instead of the desert of Pleiades. Taschen, my parents, Suji . . . they'd all still be alive.

"Think of it this way. What if the Curadores *had* let your ancestors in? And what if, because of that, the only remaining people who knew how to run this place had been infected with Red Death and died? There'd be no uncontaminated food. No power. No clean water. Then nobody would've survived."

"I can play the 'what if' game too. *What if* there'd been engineers and scientists in that group of Citizens? *What if* the Curadores had let them in and those Citizens had known how the main computer functioned? And *what if* the understanding of this technology had never been lost?" All I could think about was Lotus and the Indignos' accusations—that the Curadores had been deliberately keeping the Citizens of Pleiades weak. "The Curadores have no right to make the decisions about who lives and who dies."

When Edison finally spoke, his voice had a frantic edge to it. "What do you want me to say? That you're right and I'm wrong? Even if you *are* right, I can't undo the past. And it's not only Citizens who suffered from that decision."

We stopped in front of a sealed door, but Edison didn't open it. Instead he looked like he was getting up the courage to say something.

"At first, the Curadores used the egg and sperm banks simply as a way to maintain diversity. Your immunity is passed down over the generations, but so are other things. Genetic anomalies that stay hidden for decades only to pop up again." He kissed my extra fingers. "The DNA bank solved that problem. But then, the Curadores started getting picky . . . deliberately cultivating the population by only using the best samples.

"Mostly size and intelligence. When a particularly good pairing was made, that person's DNA samples were added to the banks. And with every new match, the computer made sure there were no issues of interbreeding. Over time, we became taller, stronger, smarter. But none of that mattered, because our world was still disintegrating around us.

"Finally, twenty-two years ago, Jenner decided selective breeding wasn't enough. That if we were going to find a way to save ourselves, we'd need someone who had talents beyond the ordinary. Not just combining choice specimens, but cutting out all the best pieces of DNA from the whole genetic bank and stitching them together."

Edison had said he was *different*, like me. I thought about how everyone looked at him as if he were a god. About Jenner calling him *my boy*.

"You."

"Yes. Me. Nikola and I are the first generation of Jenner's grand experiment. All the best genes spliced together and tweaked and tinkered with *just so*. A DNA cocktail served up inside an unfertilized ovum. The Dome's hope for the future!" His voice had a manic edge to it.

"As children, we spent hours shut inside one of these rooms. Being prodded and tested and analyzed, all for the good of Ad Astra. I *hated* this place . . . couldn't wait to get out. And yet here I am, doing the same thing." Edison wore a hard, closed-off look. I reached out to him and his anger fell away, leaving behind a kind of desperation. It looked wrong on his usually confident face.

"I'm sorry. I didn't mean to dump all this on you, it's just . . . when Jenner asked me to bring you here, I was glad. I knew I'd have to take you past all of this, and I hoped if you saw the place, if I told you about how I was *manufactured* . . . then maybe you'd understand me."

And he was right. I *did* understand him, because in many ways, we *were* the same. I pulled him to me so I could kiss him.

He put his hand on the back of my neck, threading his fingers through my hair. "It's just that everyone inside this Dome wants to *use* me for something. Power. Influence. Salvation. A few years ago, I got it into my head that maybe if I found someone different enough, someone who knew what it was like to be separate from everyone else, then that person would know me."

"Your Kisaengs." The knot of anger still sat tight in my chest.

"Yes. I know I should have told you. I'm *so sorry*." And I was surprised to see the shame on his face. He wouldn't even meet my eye. "I didn't know how to say the words to you . . . I couldn't." Now he forced himself to look at me. "I was a coward."

The truth of it was in his eyes. And I remembered not being able to face Sarika—how I'd had to wait almost two years to get another chance to say I was sorry. I understood what it meant to regret your silence.

"I hope that you can forgive me. Because I know something now . . . I know that I was right. That what I was searching for . . . that *whole time* . . . was you."

Edison pressed a button on the panel and the door in front of us slid open. He pulled me inside and the lights flickered on. The room was crammed full of shuttle parts and in the middle sat a table covered with wires and speakers and other various components.

"The radio." That voice from Earth seemed so long ago. That I thought it would be the key to getting back home to Pleiades seemed impossible—impossible that I'd ever believed there was a home to go back to.

Edison smiled. "My way of saying thank you."

But I couldn't return his smile. In my head, I saw Lotus standing in the shadows that night in the Indigno camp. I thought about my real reason for coming here. And I realized I was a coward in my own right—Edison just hadn't found out about my secret yet.

I was a trap Edison didn't even know he'd walked into.

So I decided not to wait until he inevitably stumbled over the truth. "The Indignos wanted me to come here with you. They *wanted* you to steal the radio."

"What?" Edison looked confused. "Why?"

I didn't need to be specific in order to be honest—there was no need for me to put other people at risk. "They think something wrong is going on inside the Dome, that somehow the Curadores are making the Citizens sick, and they wanted me to use you to get inside. To spy on the Curadores." I didn't mention Tasch or Lotus.

"And what did *you* want?" Edison's words were careful. Cold. His eyes staring at the floor.

I knew that whatever I said next would determine whether I had just made an enemy or an ally. "I wanted to come with you. I've wanted to know what was inside the Dome my whole life. And I wanted to start a new life . . . to look for a new world." I gestured to the radio. And now Edison was looking at me again, his eyes searching mine, wanting to see the whole truth there. So I showed it to him. "And I also wanted to know if their suspicions were right."

"And? Do you think they are?"

"I think the Dome is in trouble. And I think that Jenner has the capacity and the technology to hurt Pleiades."

"If you think the Indignos are right, then why even risk telling me?"

I locked onto his eyes. "Because I refuse to be one more person using you to get what they want."

Edison held my gaze and whatever he saw there must have been enough. "What will you do if you find something?"

Neither Lotus nor Jaesun had spoken about what I should do if I discovered evidence that the Curadores were infecting the Citizens. But the understanding had been clear. The steel of my knife was in my words. "When I find out who is hurting the Citizens and how, I will *stop them*."

Edison nodded again, understanding my full meaning, and said, "What can I do to help?"

CHAPTER 21

WE CAME UP with a plan. Edison would look for evidence inside the Genetics Lab that pointed toward Citizen sabotage, while I kept a lookout around the Dome. We'd meet back in the radio room the next day and report anything we'd found. On the off chance he might get a peek at Jenner's files, Edison skipped dinner. And I wished I'd thought to do the same.

I was mobbed the second I entered the Pavilion—smiling Kisaengs and solicitous Curadores asking me how my day was. The Ellas insisted I try the cream puffs. Sagan handed me a glass of champagne, nervously running his fingers through his curly hair. I braved the crowd in order to grab some fruit and cheese from the mounds of food, and Marisol spotted me.

She had a determined smile on her face as she headed toward me, and I pretended not to see her, dodging around Sagan and losing myself in the crowd. I finally found a tall stool in the corner, slightly hidden behind the singing Riya. Safe in the shadows, I munched on a slab of cheese, thinking through what it was going to take to fix the radio.

The equipment was a little worse for wear after its trip across the desert. Wires had frayed and come loose. Dozens of chips had fallen out of their sockets and needed to be replaced who knows where. Plus there was about a kilogram of sand everywhere. When I'd asked Edison why he hadn't started work while I was in isolation, he'd said, "It didn't seem right . . . working on it without you. After all, you're the one that found it."

Even if it meant contacting Earth? Even if it saved us? Edison must've seen on my face that I wasn't convinced.

Then he threw up his hands. "Okay, you got me. I didn't have the benefit of seeing how all this was originally put together in the shuttle. I had no idea where to even start with the thing. I needed your help."

I smiled a little now, thinking about it. It felt good to be needed. And, after the last couple days, it felt good to be working again too, splicing wires and testing circuits. I was thankful my dress was the same color as the sand, because I was covered with dust. Edison and I had opened everything up in order to clear it out and make sense of it. The table had been strewn with chips—looking like a horde of black rectangular bugs standing up on two rows of straight metal legs. The tiny codes stamped on their backs meant nothing to us and we had no way of know where any of them were supposed to go. So we'd cleaned off the chips' delicate legs—making sure not to bend or break off the connector pins—and tried plugging them into sockets. But we hadn't gotten so much as a power light. It was going to take a long time to find just the right combination.

Still, I felt more like myself with tools in my hands. And the Curadores had *tools*—not just dull knives and rusty screwdrivers, but wire strippers, pliers of every shape and size, insulated gloves.

I missed my calluses, though. My fingertips were red and sore as I tried to peel an orange.

"Here. Let me." And Oksun was beside me, taking the fruit out of my hand, planting herself on a neighboring stool. She dug her nails in and pulled the rind from the flesh, as if she blamed it for something.

"Do they do this every night?" After seeing the magfly accident this morning and the work they were trying to do in the Lab, it seemed incongruous to see everyone flirting and laughing.

"What? Eat and drink and screw like the Dome isn't falling apart around them?"

I choked on the champagne I was holding, bubbles stinging my nose as they went up instead of down.

"That's *exactly* why they're doing it." Oksun pulled the orange apart and handed me half. "They can't fix it, so they just try not to look too closely. Like today with the accident, most of the Curadores and Kisaengs will just wait around till someone tells them what to do."

I thought of Jenner's description of the beehive . . . the workers and the queen bee.

"Thank you, by the way, for helping." Oksun looked at me, and the guarded look was gone from her face. She seemed almost friendly.

"Do you know if Olivia is okay? Or the other girl?" I didn't even want to think about what they'd have to do to get her out.

The distant look came back to Oksun's face. "I don't know. I haven't seen them."

"Surely Olivia's injury wasn't that bad? I thought maybe she'd be here tonight."

"Don't expect to see her anytime soon." Oksun's mouth made a thin, tight line across her face. The conversation was over.

For a moment the two of us sat there, listening to the music. The song was intricate, Riya's fingers picking out a complex, melancholy tune, her muscular arm tense as she gripped the neck of her guitar.

"Why is Riya so intent on learning to fight?"

Oksun was quiet for a moment, then she said, "They see something in her . . ."

"Who does? The Curadores?"

"The Curadores, the Kisaengs, they see something unique and enigmatic. You'd think they'd want to understand it, but no. They either want to own it or crush it."

Oksun's face was calm, but there was rage under the surface. It ran through every muscle of her body. Without saying another word, she walked away.

June drifted up beside me. "Don't take it personally. It's impressive that she even spoke to you in the first place."

"I won't." As I watched Oksun leave the tent, something caught my eye. Something I'd been watching for without even knowing it—a bird landing on a branch just outside the opening.

"Sorry." I handed my glass of champagne to June. "Will you hold this? I'll be right back."

"Sure you will." June raised her eyebrow, but her smile was friendly—like we were coconspirators. Did she think I was going to meet Edison again? Fine by me.

I dodged the last of the well-wishers and slipped out of the tent into the dark. The bird fluttered down to a lower branch so we were face-to-face.

"Well, Grimm," I said, trying out the name I'd given him. "We have to stop meeting like this."

He simply stared at me with his glowing eyes. But he made the vaguest humming noise—a noise that I'd started to associate with the flys.

"Do you talk to the main computer too?" I was half thinking out loud, half asking. "But if you're just a more complicated version of a fly, why in the world are you following me?"

By way of an answer, the bird flew to a branch a few feet away, then looked back at me, expectant like a little kid. I tried to step closer to him again, but he flew to the edge of the Gardens—waiting just inside the line of trees. The glow of his eyes made him stand out against the dark.

"Fine." I was eager for an excuse to venture into the woods. After all, there had to be a reason it was off-limits and I had yet to find much of anything to explain Taschen's death. "It's only fair I follow you for a change."

Grimm ruffled his feathers importantly and flew to the next branch, then the next. I followed him deeper into the Gardens and it was just like I'd imagined it—the forest from the fairy tale. Branches crisscrossed in an arc above my head. Layers upon layers of leaves blocked out the sky and I could almost pretend I wasn't inside a glass bubble. It was like discovering that a hidden place inside of you actually existed.

Grimm never went too far ahead of me, but he was hard to keep track of in the monotony of trees. Every so often I'd think I'd lost him, but he would always come circling back.

Those moments alone were off-putting, though. Not because I was afraid of getting lost—even without mountains or stars, I still knew which way I'd come from. Besides, if these "gardens" really were a circle, I'd eventually come out the other side. No, it was my book that was bothering me.

Practically every single fairy tale ever had a girl going off into the woods and getting eaten by a wolf or a witch. Or getting cursed. Or hunted. The woods are where stupid, helpless girls went to die. Well, I wasn't helpless. But I was afraid I was being a little stupid.

I looked around for low-hanging branches. Grimm circled back and landed a few meters off and his eyes cast just enough light for me to see what I was doing.

I spotted a perfect branch and broke it off—making it about as long as my forearm. When Grimm saw what I was doing, he blinked and his eyes got brighter. I almost dropped the branch in surprise. He blinked again and they got brighter still. Now I was standing in a little circle of light.

"You couldn't have done that in the first place?" I said, breaking off another branch—arming myself with a pair of makeshift fighting sticks. And when the bird looked strangely chastised, I added, "Thanks."

From then on, Grimm flew ahead and lit up my path while he waited for me to catch up.

The trees got bigger the farther I went in. Trunks so huge I wouldn't have been able to get my arms all the way around them. Big enough that all three Ellas wouldn't have been able to either. I touched the orangey-red bark of one of the giants—it was shaggy and rough in places, in others, worn smooth. How old was it? Was it brought from Earth as a seed when the Colony was first built? That would mean that it'd seen the very first settlers, the plague, the destruction of the city, and the survival of Pleiades. And watched over everything that'd happened in Ad Astra.

I followed Grimm farther into the forest until I was sure I must be close to the middle of the Dome. Then he flew ahead and landed again, but this time it wasn't on a branch. Grimm perched on top of a roof. At least I think it was a roof.

There was a house shape to the thing, but there was no house. Instead, curtains of tree roots tangled and knitted together, draping themselves in the rectangular shape of a building. And up high, where the peak of a roof should be, the roots all gathered together and became a vast, leafy canopy that stretched wide over the clearing. The whole thing was strange and beautiful, like a waterfall of tree.

The only sign that there had once been a real structure here was the porch. Two columns were embraced by a mesh of roots, spiraling around and around the concrete pillars.

Grimm swooped off his perch and in through what looked like an open door. I climbed the steps to the porch, then hesitated.

"Hello?"

I swore I heard something inside, but there was no answer.

"Hello?"

Nothing. A prickle of irritation grazed my skin. Grimm had clearly brought me to this place for a reason, but there was no way I was walking into an enclosed space blind with who knows what waiting for me.

"The least you could do is show yourself." I waited another moment. "Fine. I'm exhausted anyway. I'd love some sleep."

I turned and left the porch.

"Please. Stay." The voice was scratchy and hesitant, like it wasn't accustomed to being used.

A shadow appeared in the doorway—too tall to stand up straight inside the frame. And as Grimm came and landed on his shoulder, illuminating the figure, I recognized him with a fierce intimacy.

There was no doubt about it. *This was Nikola.*

I stepped closer. "Edison didn't tell me you were twins."

CHAPTER 22

IT WAS UNCANNY, this replica of Edison. Same broad shoulders. Same height. Same perfect face. And yet, not the same, at all.

"Technically, we're clones," Nikola said, and I was stunned by how different their voices were. Nikola had none of the bold certainty that reverberated from Edison. More wind and grit than Edison's thunder.

Their hair was different too. Where Edison's head was cleanly shaven, making each feature of his face stand out, Nikola had long dreadlocks obscuring his.

I finally managed to speak. "Clones?"

But Nikola ignored my question, giving me a small bow of his head. "I'm Nik."

"I know."

"Yes. And I know you're Leica. But some rituals are important anyway. They remind us of who we are and where we come from." And there was wariness in the lines of his face—a narrowing of his eyes. A tautness of the skin across his cheekbones. Clenched jaw. Like he was bracing himself against the elements.

"Of course, you're right." Looking at this broken version of

Edison caught me off balance. All of that intensity was still there, but it had turned in on itself. Like the funnel of a dust devil. I bowed my head too. "I'm Leica. Pleased to meet you, Nikola."

"Nik." He corrected me. "Only Edison calls me Nikola." And mentioning his brother brought a bitter twist to his mouth.

"Come. I have something to give you." Nik turned and ducked back under the door frame. He carried his size like it was a burden. Like he wasn't sure what to do with so much person.

I followed him inside, stepping around a large plant practically blocking the entrance. Then around a pile of ancient computer parts. The place was a little like the Indignos' workshop—a maze of scavenged tech. Circuit boards, copper wires, half-assembled machines. Grimm landed on one of the piles, nesting inside an empty computer case.

There were more plants in jars and bottles on the floor. And as Nik dug around for something on a long table, I picked one of them up. Inside, tiny seedlings poked through mounds of moss and rocks—like a miniature forest encased in glass.

"Aha," Nik said, moving aside hard drives and processors. "Here we are." And he turned, thrusting a knife at me.

I jumped back, knocking over a collection of bottles with a deafening clatter. Grimm shot into the air, crying *Awwrawk! Awwrawk!* and swooping around both our heads.

"Sorry!" Nik said, ducking to protect himself from Grimm. "Sorry!"

He flipped the knife around so it was handle first. "I'm not really used to being around people . . . I forget how sometimes." He offered me the knife again. "Here. This is yours."

"Where did you get this?" I took it from him and turned it over in my hands. Just holding my knife made me feel stronger. More myself.

"It was with you when you came in. I just had my bird . . . I think you called him Grimm?" Nik smiled for the first time and it was like a revelation. His whole face rebalanced, the sadness slipping away, leaving an open curiosity in its place. "I had Grimm . . . um . . . liberate it. And these."

And he handed me my book of fairy tales. Balanced on top was the scope with the camera lenses and Lotus's necklace. Nik was careful with them—like they were something precious. The same way I'd handle them.

"Thank you." These were even better than the knife, like having a piece of home with me. "How do you know what I call him?"

"Well, you may have noticed he's not a normal bird."

"The glowing eyes did give me a clue," I said.

"Yeah . . . that might've been overkill. But it does come in handy." Grimm was perched on a tower of computer cases and Nik reached up and stroked Grimm's forehead. The bird closed his eyes, pushing into Nik's hand—clearly fond of him.

"I can see and hear whatever he does, as long as I have this thing in." And Nik pulled back his curtain of dreads and I got a glimpse of something in his ear. "Grimm's something I've been working on for a long time."

Nik hesitated, as if he was evaluating how much to tell me.

"I'm not going anywhere until you tell me why Grimm keeps turning up and what this place is." I crouched down, clearing a space on the floor. Then I curled my legs under me, leaned against a stack of computers, and I looked back up at Nik, ready to listen.

"Fair," Nik said, and he sat down too. He had the same way

that Edison had of locking onto you with his eyes. But when I *really* looked, Nik's eyes were different too. They were amber, like Edison's. But instead of the unrelenting fire, Nik's were mottled with pale yellow specks—like stars in an orange sky.

It was as if someone had taken all the pieces of Edison, and rerolled them, like dice. It was heady, this mixture of strangeness and intimacy. Nik's hands sat centimeters from mine, resting on the floor—vast, huge hands that I recognized. They'd touched me, and yet . . . they hadn't. And like a sudden craving, I wanted them to.

I tried to shake off the disorientation and focus on what Nik was saying.

"Grimm started out as an idea that Edison and I came up with. We were stuck in the Lab a lot when we were little . . . mostly away from all the other kids . . . and we started dreaming up a way to find out what was going on outside. Something like the flys—running off the Dome's electromagnetic field—but better. Something that would be *ours*.

"We built our first model of Grimm when we were just six. He couldn't go far at first, just tiny trips around the Dome."

"You built him when you were six years old?" I'd seen a lot of machines scouting the Reclamation Fields but nothing as complicated as Grimm. "How?"

"Well, he was just a basic machine then, all wires and clunky circuits we'd snagged from the Salvage Hall. Over the years we improved him: better cameras so he could see at night, better microphones so we could hear what was going on. We made him smarter, programming him so he had his own artificial intelligence . . . essentially his own mind. But we could still give him instructions. The last thing we did was integrate his system with a living body so he'd blend in." Then Nik's face suddenly went blank, as if lost for a moment.

Grimm seemed to sense the change in mood, flying down and landing on Nik's shoulder. It worked, bringing Nik back from wherever he was, shaking his head. "We were thirteen when we decided to send him out into Pleiades . . . at night so no one would see him." And Nik's eyes darted away from mine.

"Except . . . *I* saw him. When I was training," I said. And he nodded.

"The first time Edison and I saw you, we were captivated. Even at eight, you were everything we were not: strong, a fighter, your own person. And yet you were the same as us too." Nik wiggled his fingers.

"You . . . and Edison . . . have been watching me?" I stood up, alarmed, as I put the facts of the story together. The idea that I had just met Nik and Edison, but that they had known me *for years* was . . . disturbing.

Nik looked uncomfortable. "Not just you. Pleiades. Everything."

"That doesn't really make me feel better." And I had my answer—about how Edison had known I had sisters. About the mezcal. Of course he'd given me a bottle from Sarika's batch, he'd probably *watched* me distilling it.

I wish, growing up, that Nikola and I had known you and your sisters.

But *why* had Edison had kept that part a secret? Was he afraid I wouldn't come with him to the Dome if I knew the whole truth? Was he just waiting for the right time to tell me? And with an uneasy lurch in my stomach, I thought of my confession early that afternoon. Had Edison already known about the Indignos' suspicions? Had he been watching me that night in the camp through Grimm?

"Why was Grimm out in Tierra Muerta? Was Edison watching me there?"

"Edison? No . . . we made a pact to stop watching you and Pleiades almost three years ago." A shadow crossed Nik's face. "Edison hasn't been near Grimm or me since."

"If you weren't watching me, what was Grimm doing out there?"

Nik looked uncomfortable again, shifting on the floor next to me. "Nowadays I usually just send Grimm out to collect soil and plant samples. But I'd heard Edison had gone looking for that radio transmission. I only had rough coordinates. But then with the storm . . . I sent Grimm to search for him." And it was clear that whatever distance was between Nik and Edison, Nik still cared about his brother.

"But you found me instead."

"Yes. I barely recognized you at first. I hadn't seen you in so long."

"And you followed me to the camp."

"I was worried." Nik rubbed his forehead, seeming tired. "Look, I know it was wrong to spy on you. That's why we stopped, but you have to understand. Growing up, Edison and I were trapped in that lab, with endless tests and experiments and trials. Grimm was our escape without escaping. Our way out."

"And me? What did that make me?"

"You?" Nik held my eyes, like he was trying to figure that out for himself. "You were the closest thing we had to a friend."

In the fighting ring you learned how to size up your opponent. And my instincts said that Nik was without deception. When he fought it would be head on, without feigning or tricks.

The truth was, I was appalled and a little bit flattered that Grimm had been spying on me. But more than that, I was fascinated by him. "How does he work?"

Sitting on Nik's shoulder, Grimm moved and acted like a real bird. Even if he was like no other bird I'd ever seen.

"Do you want to give him try?" Nik smiled—the small, contagious smile of someone who's passionate about the same thing you are. He pulled the tiny bean-shaped gadget out of his ear. "We used to have to use a monitor, but a couple years ago I modified this combud."

I wiped the combud off on my dress, examining it. The whole thing was no bigger than my pinkie fingernail—little metal bumps dotting red rubber. I slipped it in my ear, and suddenly, I was seeing double—the dark room overlaid with bright colors and lights. That was disorienting enough, but what made it worse was that I was seeing the room from two different perspectives.

"Close your eyes; it'll help."

I did what he said and was relieved when I was left with only one image. Though it was still disconcerting, since I was looking straight at myself.

"The combud interfaces directly with your brain so you can see and hear everything Grimm does."

But Nik's voice was doubled too. As if there was two of him, standing on either side of me. The effect made me dizzy and I teetered a little—grateful I was already sitting down.

"That'll go away soon. It's amazing what your brain can adapt to." And by the time he'd finished his sentence, the echoes had merged into a single source.

"How do I tell him to do something?"

"You don't so much *tell* him as *think* about something in an entreating way."

"How do you . . ." I said, but Grimm suddenly darted forward and bit Nik's nose. Well, it was more of a teasing nip than a bite, but there it was.

Nik let out a bark of surprised laughter and I cleared my throat, embarrassed. "Ah. That's how you do it."

Then I thought *trees*. And even though I was still sitting inside the house, I was also lifting off, talons tucking. Squeezing through the framework of roots that made up the house and out into the forest. And though it was night, the forest was almost as bright as daylight—with a hundred gradients of shadow. I was soaring, feeling the rush of air under my wings and Grimm's excited heartbeat, just as real as my own.

His mind was there too, a strange mix of logical analysis and animal instinct. We circled the area above Nik's house, and it was strange to think that my body was still down there.

Higher, please.

We flapped harder, the trees falling away until we looped in the air—upside down—skimming the glass curve of the Dome. But when I thought about visiting the Promenade and the Genetics Lab, I felt Grimm push back. Instead, we spiraled downward, flying lower and lower over the trees. Finally swooping into the clearing around Nik's house.

Nik was standing on the porch watching us with a look of delight on his face and I felt a sudden rush of affection for him that was physical—the equivalent of the pup's wagging tail. Alarmed, I realized that Grimm's emotions were mixing with my own. Grimm's were brighter, more concentrated, and it was like a sugar rush—delicious and dizzying, as they washed over me. As we hovered and landed on Nik's outstretched arm, there was a feeling from Grimm that I could only describe as homecoming. And the feeling rang through me, resonating, so I wasn't sure what was Grimm and what was me.

Nik was smiling at us now, with a look of such kindness and returned affection that it almost hurt. The experience was overwhelming and confusing, and when Nik reached out and smoothed Grimm's wings, the sensation traveled across each individual feather, through the interface, and into me. Tremoring through my real body.

I yanked the combud out of my ear. Goose bumps played across my skin and I could still feel Nik's spontaneous gesture—his hand on me, strong and warm and so intensely *there*. I sat there for a moment, the intoxicating realness of it ricocheting through my nerves.

When I finally went out to the porch, Nik must've realized what happened. He had a sheepish, startled look on his face. "I'm sorry. I didn't even think . . . I didn't realize . . ." And he trailed off in embarrassment.

I shrugged, as if it hadn't been a frighteningly intimate moment.

Then I changed the subject. "When I came to the Dome, why did you send Grimm? If you wanted to meet me, why not come yourself . . . to one of the dinners?"

Nik was quiet for a moment—so long I thought he might not answer. Then he said, "I was seven the first time I ran away. I was eight when I found this place." He reached out and traced the intricate network of roots.

"I think it used to be a greenhouse . . . maybe some kind of laboratory. But over the years this tree took over. The strangler fig's an epiphyte . . . it kinda grows backward . . . from the sky to the ground. Its seeds nestle themselves in the canopies of other trees or in the crevices on a roof or wherever, and its roots search for the ground.

"At first, I imagine it spread out across the roof and down around the building . . ." Nik's hands traced the outline of the structure. "Its shoots and vines and roots weaving a kind of frame around place. But eventually, the fig would've squeezed too hard—breaking the glass—until there was no greenhouse left. Only tree."

"It's beautiful." I looked at the cascade of roots, propping themselves up in the shape of a nonexistent building.

Nik nodded. "It's so quiet here . . . it got harder and harder to leave. Now I just don't."

"Don't what?"

"Don't leave. Not anymore."

It was late when I got home and I was overwhelmed with the day. I wished more than anything that I could talk to Lotus about everything. Instead, I turned on the bathtub taps, feeling the water warm as it ran over my hand. Hot water was a luxury that still stunned me—one of a thousand things I hadn't gotten used to yet. I lay, floating in the scented water, thinking.

I'd been inside the Dome—or at least awake here—for two days. What had I found so far? Jenner and his plan for creating the perfect Curador. Edison and his radio. A hybrid bird. Haywire flys. A Dome that was falling apart and a whole community trying their best to ignore it. And Nik.

I felt his hand running across my body again and the same tremor ran through me. I told myself it was just the water getting cold.

Nik was right, it *was* quiet under all those trees. And knowing that tomorrow I'd have to go back to the Sanctum and play Kisaeng, I'd wanted to stay there too. But I was sure there was more to it than that—Nik was hiding from something under all those branches.

I pulled myself out of the bath. I was loath to, but I did it anyway—stepping out onto the chilly tile. There weren't many mirrors in Pleiades and I still wasn't used to them. Infinite Leicas from infinite angles. *Everywhere.*

Droplets of water spiked with juniper oil drew lines down my curvy, compact body. I didn't recognize it anymore. The months in isolation had softened it. My muscles were still strong, but my ribs no longer jutted out at painful angles. My cheeks were no longer rough from the brutal winds of the desert. Even my skin had gone from bronze to brown without the intense sun.

I stepped closer to the mirror, searching for some sign that I was me. Only my hands were the same, twelve fingers so distinctively Leica. But as I ran my fingers over my skin, I knew that wasn't quite true either. They were smooth now, unmarked by work or the brutal desert. Then my eyes caught on a spot right below my belly button. A tiny pale line marring the surface of my skin. It didn't feel any different—the skin wasn't ridged or puckered. But it was there nevertheless.

A scar.

Scars were nothing new . . . I had a whole collection of them. A brown, almost invisible line on my leg from seven years ago—I was ten, training with my dad, and fell on my own knife. A stretched, pinkish burn on my arm from a boilover in Sarika's brewery. A stripe on my shoulder from the chafe of the slideboard harness. Those scars were a map to my life and I remembered where I got each and every one of them.

But not this one. Despite the fact it looked healed and faded, this one was *new*. And I had no idea how I'd gotten it.

CHAPTER 23

THE NEXT MORNING, I was up and dressed before Marisol came for me. I chose a dress that was long enough to cover the hilt of the knife stuck in my boot. There were layers of secrets inside this Dome, and everyone seemed to be keeping some.

Still, as long as I was constantly escorted—by the Kisaengs, by Edison, by Grimm—I had little hope of uncovering the one I was really looking for. Was Jenner playing with Red Death like he was playing with the Curadores' genetics? Had Tasch been just another of his victims? How many more lives did he plan on taking?

And now, I had a new question . . . a more personal one. What had been done to me while I'd been sedated in isolation? I thought about Jenner's checkup yesterday, the fly taking my blood, the files flashing up on the screen. There were answers inside this Dome and I was going to find them, before anything else was taken from me. I touched my hidden knife for reassurance as Marisol came through the front door without knocking.

"This morning we're going hunting!" Marisol announced cheerfully.

"Hunting?" We walked outside and the sisters were there, waiting for us.

Marisol said, "Sure. We want a go at yesterday's Finds before they break them all down."

The Salvage Hall was on the opposite side of the Gardens, so we risked taking a magfly. The whole line had been slowed down—in case of any future malfunctions—so I got a good view of the Dome this time. And, because the magfly tracks ran in concentric circles around the Dome with spokes connecting the different rings, I got to see a lot of it. We passed the old church where Edison and I had gone that first night—it looked even more impressive in the daylight.

Statues perched high on the stone spires and I wished I was flying with Grimm again so I could get a closer look at them. The rush of last night's flight was still buzzing inside me. And like the betrayer my mind was, it flickered back to the feel of Nik's hand across my body. I reminded myself, *Focus. Eyes open. Knife ready.*

The magfly passed a double line of women walking through the streets near the church. They all wore the same long cream tunic dress and every single one of them was pregnant. A line of children walked single file between the rows of women.

"The Mothers," I said. Edison had talked about this . . . children being raised by the group, not the individual. Now I remembered the huge compound we'd passed the day before, filled with shouting, playing children. And I remembered the tall wall enclosing the whole place. I'd barely noticed it at the time because *all* the apartment buildings in Pleiades were surrounded by walls. But those were to isolate the populations, keep them separate so outbreaks wouldn't spread.

So in a city with no disease, what were the walls protecting?

"Yeah. They're always out parading around. Noses up, looking down at us." Marisol said it with a shrug, but her voice was bitter. "I try my best to avoid them and their little brats."

But her eyes followed them as our magfly glided away.

Soon we entered a totally different section of the Dome. Old magflys and machinery littered the ground alongside the track. There was a long windowless building, labeled the Meat Brewery, where, according to the Ellas, the chiken and beeph was grown in huge vats.

Then, finally, we arrived at the Salvage Hall. We got out and descended down a steep moving staircase into a huge underground room. It was like being in a vast reclamation pit. Only louder.

Flys buzzed in massive swarms, descending on stacks of old appliances and corroded metal scraps, assessing their worth. Giant machines sorted the scrap into more stacks and more piles while simultaneously Kisaengs picked over them—snagging tendrils of bright, plastic-coated wire or bits of pretty glass, checking them against the colors of their dresses. As we descended into the room, I looked for Olivia again, hoping she'd recovered from the magfly accident. I wished I'd gotten more than a glimpse at her file yesterday in the Lab.

Marisol swept into the room like she owned it. As we walked, Kisaengs stepped out of the way for her. Curadores bowed and smiled. Actually, they did the same for me too. It was a strange feeling—the world making way for me—but one I could get used to.

"Exquisite!" Marisol gushed over a trinket another girl had found.

"Thank you." The girl looked unsure whether to be flattered or cautious.

"Just look at how it catches the light, will you, Aaliyah?" Marisol said.

Aaliyah knew her part well. She raised a painted eyebrow, which swirled up to join the rest of the spirals on her head, perfect in its enigmatic amusement. "Marisol! It would look spectacular against your hair."

No one spoke for a moment, and there was an awkward silence before the girl realized she'd missed her cue. The Kisaeng scrambled to catch up with the scene unfolding around her. "Oh! I'd be honored to give it to you."

Marisol took the item, scrutinized it for a moment and then said, "On second thought, maybe it's not quite as special as I thought." And Marisol threw it back on the pile. Her aim was perfect, so the treasure spun around for a moment before falling down into a crack—lost among the salvage again.

I hung back, watching Marisol and the sisters repeat the performance again and again. Sometimes Marisol took the gift. Sometimes she handed it over to June or the Ellas or one the others in her circle. I didn't know what her system was, but it wasn't random. It was clear to me that *everything* Marisol did was deliberate.

I cringed as Marisol zeroed in on Riya. The Kisaeng had been absorbed in the salvage piles, collecting a basket full of bright toys—tiny cars, dolls' legs, plastic bracelets. I couldn't hear what was being said, but I watched the sisters cluster around Riya like circling vultures. Marisol began admiring Riya's Finds, carefully picking up and examining every object, before plucking the whole basket from her grip.

In a final insult, Marisol reached up and snagged a beautiful ornament from Riya's hair—an intricate creation made of plastic gears and brass screws. Riya started to take it back, half reaching out a hand before dropping it again. With a smug smile, Marisol put the decoration in her own hair, punishment for Riya's boldness the day before.

Riya's face was thunderous and I was afraid, after our lesson yesterday, that she might punch Marisol. But instead, Riya calmly unfastened the necklace of bright plastic knitting needles from around her own throat. Then her bracelet. She surprised both Marisol and myself by dropping them in the basket as well—castoffs for Marisol.

And I was reminded of what Oksun had said. That the others see something unique in Riya. *You'd think they'd want to understand it, but no. They either want to own it or crush it.* Clearly Marisol wanted to do both. I smiled at Riya's perfect revenge—no one can steal something if you're willing to simply give it away.

Then a loaded magfly pulled into the Hall, blocking my view. Flys descended on the fresh scrap, till it was completely covered with twitching black bodies.

"The trick is to get to it before they do."

I practically jumped at the sudden voice in my ear. June hovered next to me up on her silver seat.

"Sorry, sometimes I forget to make noise. Let me try again." And straight-faced she said, "Clomp-clomp-clomp-clomp. Ahem!"

"Much better," I said, matching her faux seriousness, and I was surprised to find I was glad to see her. But it was impossible to imagine her doing anything as gauche as clomping. June commanded a certain grace, her torso balanced on her board, her skirts flowing as she moved. "What happens to all these Finds?"

"Reprocessing."

And I remembered Edison talking about the reprocessors making new flys when the old ones broke.

June elaborated. "Most stuff gets shredded or melted down into raw materials and reformed into things we need. There's a whole complex of machinery farther underground that deals with that."

"Machines underground?"

"Sure. Or perhaps you think this place runs off pure love?" June made ridiculous kissing noises.

It was amazing to think there was a whole level to the Dome I wasn't even seeing. As it was, the piles of scrap and machines and noise went on and on. Clusters of flys were everywhere. They carried items off the magflys, over the Kisaengs' heads, and to the conveyor belts along the walls. Or to one of the many piles. And sometimes they seemed to be doing the whole maneuver in reverse—loading things back onto the magflys.

The smash of breaking glass cut across the din. One of the clusters of flys had literally dropped out of the air along with a pane of solar glass they'd been carrying. There was shrill scream and I saw the three Ellas standing, terrified but unharmed, in a puddle of blue shards.

I had flashbacks of the magfly accident the day before, wondering if we were all about to get "fixed" by the flys. But there was another clatter as more flys dropped—sending spools of copper wire rolling in every direction. Then another *crash*. And another.

Kisaengs were screaming and running for cover as flys went dead, midair and midjob. June was on the floor now too, her board having inexplicably dropped to the ground like dead weight. She tried to maneuver herself out of the way, heavy skirts dragging behind her. But between falling debris and trampling feet there was nowhere to go.

I reached down to help just as her board mysteriously came back to life. June pulled herself onto it and shot out of the room. I was right behind her when I caught a flash of white out of the corner of my eye.

One of the Mothers was crouched behind a pile of old computers, her hand reaching for a fallen circuit board. The Curadores often had unusual looks, but this Mother was a study in contrasts. Her freckle-dusted brown skin was set off by white-blond hair that was twisted into a bun. Her face was long and elegant, but her nose had a slight bump to the bridge. And in the middle of it was a pair of immense, wide-set eyes. The whole combination should've looked odd, but instead, it was breathtaking.

While the other Kisaengs ran back up the stairs to safety, I dodged behind a pile of styrofoam insulation, watching her. What was even more unusual than the Mother's appearance was that she was perfectly calm—we were the only two people not running away from the chaos. She moved low and stealthy, despite her very pregnant belly, and I moved with her, slipping from scrap heap to scrap heap. Watching.

She picked up a shiny data storage drive and fiddled with her tunic—tucking the drive into her dress in such a way that it completely disappeared behind the bulge of her stomach. Then just as a conveyor belt on the other side of the room went haywire, speeding up, flinging metal scraps in every direction, she darted out of her hiding place and grabbed a spool of copper.

I darted too, trying to get closer, and my foot sideswiped a pile of aluminum cans. They went clanging in her direction and the woman's head snapped up. I was surprised to see that she was just a few years older than me, and we stared at each other across the deserted Salvage Hall, still going mad around us. What was the protocol was for this situation?

I settled on "Hello?"

She looked startled by my voice. Maybe she was stunned that I would dare to talk to her. Maybe there were rules against that sort of thing. She glared at me, freckles popping dark against her tawny skin. Vivid against her white-blond hair.

The Mother did not scurry away. She stood tall . . . almost defiant. Slipping the spool into the pocket of her white dress. Then I noticed a small device, half hidden in her other hand. She pressed a blinking button and a cluster of nearby flys jettisoned their haul. A collection of plastic bottles rained down on me. I ducked, shielding my head.

When I looked up again, she was gone.

CHAPTER 24

"I DIDN'T SEE anything strange in Jenner's files, nothing about Red Death or the Citizens, but I'll try again tonight. Did you find anything on your mission?" Edison's voice was light—like this was some kind of game—and it irritated me.

We were working on the radio again, without much success. Since my visit with Nik, I wasn't sure how to act around Edison. There'd always been question marks surrounding Edison, but before they'd been an intriguing mystery waiting to be solved. Now I realized I'd let my attraction to him blot out my uneasiness. I'd justified his secrets with my own.

But the omission of Grimm—that he and Nik had been *watching* me for most of my life— felt like a much bigger transgression. Even more than his collection of Kisaengs. Because in asking me to tell him about my sisters, about my family, Edison convinced me to hand over pieces of myself that he'd already taken.

No. I'd told myself that I didn't *need* to trust Edison, that we were using each other for our own agendas—but that had been a fantasy of my own making. I'd trusted him, because I'd believed his original lie. *We were the same.*

We might both be exceptions, but Edison had been crafted and created, while I was merely a Corruption. Edison's differences made him a prince among his people. Mine made me an exile. It would be like saying an eagle and a moth were the same because they both had wings.

Now I glanced at Edison. He was splicing a damaged wire as he waited for me to answer to his question. If I stopped telling him things, he'd know something was wrong. And just because I couldn't trust someone didn't mean I couldn't still get information from them. Wasn't that the whole point of coming to the Dome? Of being a Kisaeng?

So, for the moment, I stopped thinking of the bigness and the noise, stopped thinking of the huge question I was after, and started shuffling through the pieces of information I already had. The Mother in the Salvage Hall. Olivia still missing. The scar on my belly. And this radio, tucked away in a locked room in the Lab. Suddenly I could see the gaps—all the pieces I was still missing— and I start digging for them.

"How come no one else is here, helping with this?" I kept my eyes fixed on the radio's main board, inspecting each chip and card—carefully prodding a pin here or double-checking a connector there. "Is the radio a secret?"

"No. People know about it . . . they just don't care."

That surprised me, but then I guessed why. "No one believes I really heard a voice, do they?"

"I believe you." Edison put down his soldering iron and met my eyes. But they didn't have their absolute pull on me anymore. He was still handsome and dazzling. But after meeting Nik, there was something a little too perfect about Edison—all smooth edges and confidence, until the moment when he was soulful confessions and apologies. And suddenly I wondered, what did Edison look like when there was no one else around? When he had no Kisaengs or Curadores to perform for? And I couldn't imagine it.

"And it's not that they don't believe you," he continued. "It's that the whole thing seems unbelievable to them. Coded messages bouncing across satellites from worlds away? No. They want to stick with what they know."

"Even if what they know is falling apart?" It was like the Indignos—they were too busy making a garden out of a desert to imagine something as revolutionary as Earth.

Then I thought about something Edison had said. "Why is the message coded anyway? I mean, you said you've been picking up garbled transmissions on this channel since forever . . . so if Earth was trying to contact Gabriel all these years, why code the message?"

Edison nodded, reconnecting the wiring inside the speakers. "I've been thinking about that too. And all I can come up with is that whoever you spoke to on the radio, whoever's been broadcasting that message, knows something we don't about the plague . . . about what happened here five hundred years ago. And they want to make sure their message only gets to the *right* people."

"And who are the right people?"

Edison looked sideways at me, a hint of a smile on his face. "*Now* you're asking the right question."

He reached over me, attaching the speaker cable to the main board. Then he plugged in the radio and switched it on. One of us must have done something useful, because this time the power light glowed orange, though nothing came through the speakers. He messed with the buttons, trying to get sound.

That was the trick wasn't it? Asking the right question. But it wasn't as simple as that. You also had to know what answer you were looking for. And answers didn't have to be *true* to be *telling*.

Reaching into my pocket and pulling out an orange I'd saved from lunch, I thought about Marisol's lesson the first night in the Dome. And I thought about Suji's rule and the importance of details. Then I pushed my fingernail into the peel. A scent of giddy brightness welled up out of it, the smell perfuming the air with memories of Edison's and my picnic.

It worked. Edison's body changed as the scent of the peeled orange hit his nose. He was still busily tweaking buttons and knobs, but his shoulders dropped. And his hands relaxed. His eyes met mine as I placed a slice into my mouth. And I knew he was thinking about that night.

"The girls took me down to the Salvage Hall today."

"Oh? Nikola and I used to escape down there when we were kids." Then suddenly, Edison's face split into a grin and he actually started laughing to himself. "One day, when we were about thirteen or fourteen, one of Jenner's assistants—a horrible, tedious man—was escorting us to the Lab for testing and stopped to flirt with his favorite Kisaeng. The moment he turned his back, we ran off. I'm sure the Kisaeng saw us, but she must have liked us more than him because she didn't say anything."

I could almost imagine the miniature versions of the two of them. Maybe a Nik who was not quite so sad and an Edison who wasn't so charismatic. "And you ended up in the Salvage Hall?"

"Yep. We found an intake conduit near the Meat Brewery lead-ing down into the tunnels. We were happily scrounging for parts when the flys spotted us. So we just picked a direction and ran. Ten minutes later, we were completely lost in a maze of passageways."

It sounded a little like scouting in the Reclamation Fields. "Were you scared?"

Edison thought for a moment. "Mostly I remember feeling elated . . . knowing that if we couldn't find ourselves, then proba-bly no one else could either. That was the day we found the crate of wine. I was sick for two days."

I let myself crack a smile. "You didn't drink the whole crate!"

Edison smiled ruefully. "Nah . . . but a couple bottles at least. Though if I remember right, a lot of it got spilled. I don't think we even liked the stuff, but we drank it anyway."

"Why?"

"'Cause we weren't supposed to, of course!" Edison's amber eyes glowed with the memory. "It wasn't long after, that Nikola . . ." Then Edison paused, looking a little lost. "He changed, Leica. He became a stranger. Hiding away with his experiments. Some of the things he did . . . well, they scared me."

I wanted to ask more about Nik, but I didn't dare. After all, to bring up Nik would be to bring up Grimm and the fact that Edison had pretended that he knew nothing about me when we first met. This was not a conversation I wanted to have right now. Not until I was sure if I could trust either brother. Just one more shadow in this dark Dome—and it wasn't the one I was after.

What I wanted to know about was the Mothers. If I was going to ask about what had happened in the Salvage Hall, I wanted Edison relaxed. I needed to see his reaction.

Edison took another slice of orange and this time he fed it to me. But as his fingers brushed against my lips, my body betrayed me. My skin transformed into a network of nerves—all singing out at once.

Before I even knew what was happening, Edison's lips were on mine. And I was pulled under—my mind awash with wanting.

His hands. His closeness. The taste of him filling me as I pressed my body against his.

But Edison was already pulling away, turning back to the radio—as if his world hadn't just spun out of control. Then Edison must've found the right setting, because static crackled through the speakers.

"Finally!" he grinned.

But I was still locked inside that moment, trying catch up. Trying to breathe. Trying to figure out what'd just happened.

I'd thought I was so clever—playing the game, like Marisol had said. But it was obvious that I had just lost. Now I tried to get a grip on myself again. On that treacherous hunger. I concentrated on the simple—the ordinary—around me.

The shush of static on the radio.

The flicker of power lights.

The fruit cool in my hand.

I ate another slice of orange and cleared my throat. Trying to refocus on the information I'd been after. "All the stuff from the reclamation pits comes in through the Salvage Hall, right?"

"Sure." He scanned through the channels, but there was still no signal. Then he picked up the microphone, testing it—interrupting the static as he switched it on and off. On and off.

"Is any of it of particular value?"

He glanced over at me. "You found something, didn't you?" Then he grinned again. "I knew you would!"

"The Mothers," I said, keeping my voice even. I didn't want it to sound like I was blaming anyone. "One of them was looking through the scrap piles and she . . ."

"The Mothers were down in the Salvage Hall?" His tone was relaxed, but his shoulders tensed again. "I heard about the incident . . . but *nothing* about the Mothers."

"I think I was the only one who noticed her. She seemed to have some sort of device in her hand and . . ." Then I hesitated, not sure how to phrase my question without making it an accusation. "Could they be responsible for the other things going wrong?"

Edison didn't say anything. The lights of the radio outlined the stark angles of his face—all deep purples and yellows—making it unreadable.

After a moment, he answered. And there was a blade of anger running though his words. "I don't know. But I'm going to find out."

He turned back to the radio, killing the power. I'd missed something—something left unsaid—but it was clear the discussion was over. And as I watched him pry a tiny circuit board out of the microphone, I had a very disconcerting thought.

Edison claimed that he hadn't worked on the radio while I'd been in quarantine because he'd needed my help. But if Edison helped build Grimm—inventing new technology and figuring out how to embed it in a living organism—then surely he could fix a radio.

So then, why didn't he? And Edison's earlier comment echoed back to me. *Now you're asking the right question.*

• • •

So the next morning, I woke early. I carefully picked out a purple dress, spiked my hair, shimmered my hands, and made my own way through the streets of the Dome. The magflys were running, but I walked.

After Edison's reaction to my question yesterday, I wanted to get a closer look at the Mothers' compound. I heard children's voices, but couldn't see them over the stone wall. I strolled around the whole perimeter, but didn't glimpse anything beyond a gravel path on the other side of a tall gate—the words *Education Complex* spelled out in wrought iron in an arch above it.

When I got to the Sanctum, Riya was waiting for me. As soon as she saw me enter the courtyard, she stood up with that flutter of hers. Oksun came to stand beside her and there was a group of fifteen Kisaengs at their backs. Several of them had hacked off their hair since yesterday's trip to the Salvage Hall so their uneven manes barely covered their ears. Evidently, I was quite the trendsetter.

And I remembered Olivia's hair had been painfully short too. Had she cut hers that first night, like Riya?

"I've been teaching the others . . ." And Riya made the arm-twisting maneuver, letting that movement finish her sentence. "But they have a few questions."

I spotted June by the creek, pretending she wasn't watching us. She was plucking little white flowers out of the grass and dropping them into the current, one by one. They made a little parade of blossoms, meandering along, until they dropped over a tiny waterfall and were swallowed down the drain.

Marisol must have been watching too because there she was, crossing the bridge to join us. And I could sense the storm coming.

Riya must've felt it too, because she spoke fast. "Can you show us the move again?"

Marisol casually swept in between us—a trick she was good at. "Don't be ridiculous. Leica has better things to do with her time."

"That's right." Oksun stepped up, provoking Marisol. Either she was hoping to protect Riya or she was a glutton for punishment. "Keep pretending you're still ruling this place . . . like you have *any* say in what's going on."

"Leica, you don't have to listen to this drudge. The only way she gets a man into her bed is if she bores him to sleep. Come on, sisters." Marisol flicked her head at her fellow Kisaengs who'd followed her over the bridge and offered me her arm. I didn't move and Marisol made the mistake of grabbing me anyway and pulling me along with her.

That was the moment—the one I'd hoped I could avoid, but knew I couldn't.

Technically, as Edison's favorite I was now the de facto leader of the Kisaengs, but I hadn't really been acting like it. Up until then, I'd been trying to figure out whether Marisol was less dangerous as an ally or an enemy. But when Marisol grabbed me, I had my answer.

One of the most important things my dad had taught me was what kind of damage to inflict in any confrontation. If someone was truly dangerous, you went for lasting pain—a reminder of what you could do. Bruised ribs that hurt every time you took a breath. A dislocated shoulder.

But most of the time, you wanted to go for drama rather than injury. A bloody nose. A kick to the crotch. Shaking up your opponent was more important that hurting them. Whatever I did to Marisol didn't have to be painful, but it did have to be public. I had to make it clear that she no longer called the shots.

So I settled on another quick-twist maneuver—jerking my wrist in, flicking my elbow out. Instantly breaking her grip on my arm. Marisol was jostled by the movement and she stumbled back against her group of Kisaengs.

"I am *not* your sister." I let my voice carry across the Sanctum. My words ringing out in the silence. "Do not make that mistake again."

Marisol's face was unreadable. She said nothing, simply stood there surrounded by her Kisaengs, but I doubted this was over. Marisol was a fighter. A schemer. Even as I turned my back on her—letting everyone see I didn't view her as a threat—I worried what her next move would be.

But I made my face confident as I looked to Riya, Oksun, and their friends. "Now. Who thinks they can replicate the move I just demonstrated?"

CHAPTER 25

WHEN RIYA FOUGHT, she became a different person. She had an untethered quality about her that reminded me of Lotus. As she faced off with a much sturdier Oksun, Riya repeated my techniques—but in her hands, they became something new. She moved differently than anyone I'd ever known—like she was hearing a rhythm that no one else could. And it made her fun to watch, unskilled but innovative. You had no idea where she'd come from next.

She finally got the best of Oksun, with a surprise dodge followed by a mimed kick to the knees.

"Excellent!" I applauded and the girls around me joined in.

"Will you show us more?" Riya's dark eyes gleamed as she landed a kick high in the air. As if she was trying out her body for the first time.

"Of course. This sort of thing is best when you practice consistently." As I said the words I realized how much I'd missed my own daily ritual—that focused space during the day that returned you to yourself. "I'd get up before dawn in Tierra Muerta and watch the sun rise while I went through my practice. Sometimes it was the only bit of peace I'd get . . ." But everyone was suddenly staring at me and I realized that I'd slipped up.

"You're an exile?" Oksun leaned in and her severe, shoulder-length hair fell across her face.

I nodded, looking around at the group of uncertain faces. We weren't Citizens anymore, but the lessons of the Remember-ings seeped into your bones—it took more than a pretty dress to change what you believed. Maybe Marisol wasn't the only Kisaeng I needed to worry about hating me.

"And you survived," Riya said.

I nodded, even though it'd been a statement rather than a ques-tion. I wasn't sure what else to do.

"Impressive. Knocking Salk on his ass your very first night makes a little more sense now." Oksun barked out a laugh.

Relief washed over me. Marisol had *said* this wasn't the same as Pleiades, but I wasn't sure a criminal would be welcome.

And Riya had a different expression on her face. Not just re-spectful anymore, but almost protective. "That settles it, then. We'll meet here tomorrow, at dawn."

As the morning wore on, I watched the girls spar and laugh and show off. It was strange to see them fighting in dresses—it made it harder to move, but also harder to see what your opponent was about to do. A different kind of challenge. And as I watched, I noticed something else as well.

Every single one of them was young and strong and energetic. In fact, now that I thought about it, all the Kisaengs were. Though the Curadores were a mix of old and young—from Edison's age to Jenner's—there couldn't have been a Kisaeng over thirty. Not a single grey hair or crow's-feet among them.

I managed to get Oksun alone, sparring with her as an excuse to talk. "Where are the older Kisaengs? Do they live in a different part of the Dome?"

Oksun was only a few inches taller than me, but she was much bigger. Her shoulders were broad, her arms and legs thick with muscles. And she didn't hold back as she threw a punch. "When they're no longer desirable, Kisaengs just disappear."

I blocked her blow, but the force of it still rang through my forearm. "Like Olivia has?"

Oksun nodded, throwing another. "One day they're just gone. And no one knows what happens. Why do you think we spend so much time making ourselves beautiful? Why do you think we want to learn to defend ourselves?"

I dodged and threw a punch of my own, but it was clumsy. I was barely paying attention anymore. "What do the Curadores say when you ask what's happened to the others?"

Oksun caught my arm, gripping hard as she jerked upward— her black eyes holding mine. "No one asks."

"Why?"

"Because we don't want to disappear too."

I made sure no one was watching as I slipped into the forest that afternoon. I had an idea about the Kisaengs and the computer system and Grimm. As if my thought had summoned him, Grimm glided down from the trees. He let out a soft *awwrawk*, and we made our way to Nik's house together.

It looked completely different under the bright sun. The walls were simply a web of tree roots, which meant light poured into the house. More that than, Nik had hung bits of tinted plastic and glass from the living framework, scattering the floor with colored sunlight.

"Hello?" If it was possible, it seemed even more crowded in the daylight. Plants were everywhere. Blooming under glass jars. Hanging from pots on the walls. Vining across the ceilings. And everywhere there weren't plants, there were gadgets that performed complicated, unimaginable tasks. Bits of motors. Bright green circuit boards. Tangles of wire.

"Back here," Nik called.

Grimm flew around me in dizzying circles as we navigated our way through the house. Until I finally thought to offer him my arm. "Did you program Grimm to like me?"

I stroked Grimm as he settled on my wrist—brilliant blue wings, mottled with grey. But a closer look showed not grey feathers, but silver strands of wire—each one thinner than a single hair. They glistened as Grimm moved, making his plumage beautiful and intricate.

"It's not like that." Nik looked up from a jar he was packing with dirt. The curtain of thin dreadlocks that hid him from the world was tied back in a thick ponytail, leaving Nik's face exposed and open as he talked about his friend. "Grimm was programmed with his own personality. He likes you because you're you and he's him."

"How does it work? The other night, one second I was wishing we could fly higher and next we were skimming the Dome. Did *I* make him do that?"

"Sort of. If I have the combud in, I can think, 'I want to find Leica,' and if he wants to, Grimm will go find you. But I don't tell him *where* to find you. Or how to act when he gets there."

"So how does he do it, then?"

"He might use the filaments in his feathers to intercept signals from the flys' visual feed and find you that way. Or, if their feed is on the fritz . . . as it is more often than not these days, he might go somewhere he's found you before. He learns your behavior patterns as he gets to know you. And he's known you for a long time."

I thought again of the strange history I had with Grimm and these brothers. And it felt a little like the scar on my belly—a piece of me that wasn't fully my own. "The reason I'm asking is . . . I had an idea about Grimm and the Kisaengs who are missing."

Nik gave me a confused look and I wondered how isolated he really was. How much did he know about what was going in the rest of the Dome? To be safe, I started with the disappearing Kisaengs. Then I told him about the magfly accident and Olivia being taken away. But I stopped there. There was no reason for Nik to know that I was afraid that Jenner was harming the Citizens as well.

"I'm sorry about your friend, I'll do whatever I can to help . . ." Nik's face was rigid with anger. "But what's any of this got to do with Grimm?" Nik's voice was wary—rightfully protective of *his* friend.

"Well, when I was in the Genetics Lab, I saw that Jenner had files on all the Kisaengs, dating back to when we were brought in from Pleiades. And I thought maybe Olivia's file might give us a clue about what's happened to her. And the others." *And me.* But I didn't say that part out loud. "It occurred to me that maybe Grimm could talk with the main computer or the flys or whatever and get us a look at the files?"

But Nik was already shaking his head. "Grimm works on an entirely different system. It was much easier to invent a whole new communication protocol than to reverse engineer the Dome's technology. The flys, the magflys, the Lab, they're all part of the Colony's integrated computer system, which is hugely complex. Over the years, we figured out a way to let Grimm listen in or even jam some of the signals broadcast between the components, but he can't control any of them."

I thought I understood what Nik was saying. "So basically, Grimm can eavesdrop on the flys, but he can't 'talk' to them."

"Right, he speaks a totally different language. Actually *no one* can really talk to the computer or flys. Not only can we not speak their language, we don't even know what language they speak. Everything's locked up and coded. The Curadores can *use* the computer, ask it to do stuff for us, but we can't *change* anything about the way the computer does those things.

"That's what's so insane about Jenner's plan to fix the Dome. He just keeps trying to make smarter and smarter versions of Edison and me—hoping that eventually one of them will magically beat the system. It's like Jenner keeps making copies of the wrong key, but still expects one of them to open the door."

Locked doors seemed an apt metaphor for most of the Dome. Ancient inaccessible computer programs. Children behind tall walls. Women who simply vanished.

"But," Nik added, seeing my frustration, "that just means Grimm isn't the right man for the job." And he stopped to think for a moment. "You said Jenner brought the files up on the central computer in the Genetics Lab?"

I nodded.

"Then I have a friend who might be able get us a copy."

"Really?" I tried not to sound surprised. It was just that I'd gotten the feeling that life in the Dome hadn't been kind to Nik—after all, he'd chosen to hide away the middle of a forest. So, who in this place would Nik consider a friend?

But I didn't pry. I simply said, "Thanks. That would mean a lot to me."

Grimm started combing his beak through my spiky hair. Making his ridiculous *awwraaaaawk* noise. I reached up to pet him. "Maybe Grimm could still be a help. I'd like to get a better idea of Jenner's movements. Or really, any sort of activity around the Lab." Edison said he was keeping an eye on Jenner, but I wasn't really sure anymore if he and I had the same motives.

Nik studied Grimm for a moment—that protective look on his face again—then finally nodded. "We'll have to be careful, though. Jenner knows about Grimm and he's easy to spot . . . that's why I don't let him leave the woods or the Dome till after dark."

"Then I'll come back again. Late tonight." I thought about what Edison had said about Nik. Hiding away with his experiments. I tried to sound casual as I asked, "Why *does* Grimm leave the Dome?"

"I told you, to collect soil samples and vegetation." Nik gently tucked a seedling into the jar. His fingers barely fit inside the narrow mouth and he struggled with it. "I only work with plants now."

"Here, let me do that." I took the jar from him. Despite my extra fingers, my small hands were a much better fit. I packed dirt down around the roots. "What I meant was, *why* do you collect plants?"

"Oh, sorry. I'm . . . I'm trying to create crops that can withstand the conditions of Gabriel's desert."

"Like sandstorms and drought?"

"That too. But there's also five hundred years worth of humanity decaying under that sand . . . leaking oil and battery acid and who knows what into that soil. It's not really even soil. Half of it is shattered solar glass from the old city."

Nik made a note on the side of the jar and went on to the next plant. He measured out a precise mix of dirt and sand into the jar and then handed it to me to add the plant.

I thought of the Indignos' crops dying off. "So you're trying to create plants strong enough to live in polluted soil?"

"Yeah. I tried that for a while, but they kept dying. The last few months I've been trying to create plants that will clean the soil itself. Actually, I'm not even trying to alter the plants anymore."

"Then what are all these?" I spun around the room, gesturing to the plethora of green. Grimm squawked at my sudden movement and flapped off to a safer perch.

"They're test subjects. I'm trying to create a system of nanites who'll live inside the plants and help filter out anything harmful . . . poisons or mold or anything that attacks it."

"Like the flys inside the Dome?"

"Kind of . . . but for defense. And microscopic."

"Is it working?"

"I don't know." Nik's face was bleak as he looked at the glass jars full of sprouts. "I test them in these mini biomes, and if they look promising, I take them outside."

"Into the woods?"

"Not quite. Here . . . let me show you." And he took my hand. His was enormous and rough, with calluses on every finger. I liked the feel of it. It was the kind of hand that made you feel confident.

We walked a few meters through the wall of trees, then the forest opened up into a spectacular garden. But *garden* wasn't even the right word for it. It was a riot of plants. Thick vines dripping with berries. Vast towers of tomatoes. Forests of orange trees and lemons and limes. Rows of pungent but unrecognizable herbs. And suspended above us, a constellation of mechanical arms reaching down to pick, prune, and weed the magnificent feast.

I was speechless.

"All of the Garden used to look like this. At least, that's what I understand from the few historical records we have access to."

"Then why haven't I seen that thing anywhere else in the woods?" I pointed to the giant metal grid hanging about seven meters above us. Thousands of robotic arms slid and maneuvered along the rails in an intricate, mechanical dance.

"The computer's only concerned about generating enough fresh food for the current population. As soon as it deemed the rest of the Gardens unnecessary, the grid and arms would've been dismantled and reprocessed by the flys. Then the trees must've taken over."

It was the most beautiful place I'd ever seen. A waterfall roared nearby and the mist drifted across us making the air cool and wet. I filled my lungs with the scent of flowers and fruit and plenty. I could understand why Nik stayed here.

"Is this all part of your experiments?"

"Oh no, most of this is tended by the computer. I had to make some space for myself over here where I replicated the soil contamination levels found out Tierra Muerta." And he showed me an irregularly shaped clearing where corn, adzuki beans, and kabocha pumpkins grew in rows. The Citizen's main crops.

Some of the plants were enormous, swollen past the point of believability. Others were dead and dying. And still others looked perfectly normal. "For a while I had to battle it out with the flys . . . trying to get them to leave my plants alone. I finally had to suppress the electromagnetic field in this whole area, like an invisible fence."

I was amazed and a little confused at how much work Nik had put into this. "But if the Curadores can't even leave the Dome without isolation suits, and the Dome is breaking down, I don't understand how crops out in Tierra Muerta are going to help you."

"About five or six years ago, Edison and I realized we couldn't repair the Dome's systems like Jenner had hoped. Even if we somehow figured out the computer's architecture, we still wouldn't have access to modify it. When we told Jenner, he went quiet. I'd seen him angry before, but never like this." And Nik seemed to cringe away from the words even as he said them. His huge body drawing in on itself. "He said he couldn't believe that he'd made such weak, stupid creatures. That in surrendering so readily to failure, we'd also surrendered our reason to exist. You can't imagine what it was like."

But of course, I *could* imagine. I squeezed Nik's hand, wishing I could communicate my shared pain. Jenner was Nik and Edison's "God." He'd created them only to deem them *Indigno*. Only Jenner hadn't needed to exile Nik; he'd done it to himself.

"After that, we were desperate to prove ourselves. So we stopped looking for ways to fix the system and started looking for ways to escape it. And that's where we disagreed. Edison wants to create a Curador that can live beyond the walls of the Dome. But from what I've seen, I'm not really sure the Curadores *deserve* to leave this place."

"Then how do you intend on saving your people?"

"I don't. I'm not really convinced it can even be done . . . at least not in Edison's 'nursery.' We've been isolated from the world for too long. *But* . . . if I can find a way for your people to be self-sufficient before this whole Dome falls apart, then at least someone on Gabriel will survive."

As Nik talked, the scraps and bits and pieces I'd learned about him came into focus. He was like the Indignos—dreaming a beautiful dream. Saving what he could. Trying to bring a desert back to life.

For the first time since I'd got here, I really let myself think about my sister, who was still out in that desert, and the home I'd almost had. If the Indignos were lucky, the corn in the fields would be harvested by now. The tree cuttings they planted would have rooted and sprouted leaves and probably lost them again.

What would Lotus make of my long absence? Would she think I was lost to the Dome? Would she think I was sick? Or dead like Tasch? And my chest ached thinking of her. It had been different when I'd been an exile. I'd had no hope—no real expectation to see my sisters again—and I'd managed to lock that part of myself away.

But now Lotus was waiting for me. The Indignos were counting on me to stop whatever was going on here. And all I had to show for my time were questions and forgotten months. More than anything, I just *missed* Lotus. "I wish my sister could see this."

"Maybe she will someday. Maybe all of Gabriel will look like this," he said.

I stood next to him looking at all the green around us, looking at the vision of it playing across Nik's passionate face. A cascade of yellow glittering in his eyes. Nik had already created such extraordinary things . . . maybe he could do this too. Maybe Gabriel *could* be the home I'd dreamed of. And a tiny hope sparked in my heart.

Nik's voice was low when he spoke again, like he was afraid to break the spell. "I wish I'd been born a Citizen . . . I wish I'd met you at one of your Festivals."

"If you were a Citizen, you'd hate me. You'd hate my Corruption." And the idea of that hurt me.

"No. I don't think I would." Nik took my wrong-fingered hand in his and faced me. "I wish I'd seen you fight in that ring and gotten up the courage to talk to you afterward."

"I never fought at the Festivals. They wouldn't allow—"

But Nik didn't let me finish. "More than anything, I wish you didn't belong to Edison."

"I don't belong to Edison." The truth of my words rang through me. I was not Edison's Kisaeng. Or the Abuelos' Corruption. Or the Indignos' spy. I was only Leica.

A crease cut across his forehead like it was splitting him apart. And I thought of last night, the feeling of his hand on my body. It had shaken me, not just because of the unexpected intimacy of the moment, but because of the pure spontaneity of the gesture. The unthinking kindness of it.

Echoing his gesture, I reached up, smoothing his forehead. Resting my hand against his cheek. Nik was shaking under my touch, the feel of him tremoring through me.

"I don't belong to anyone." And I kissed Nik—not because there was some kind of secret sameness about us. In fact, I wasn't sure I really understood who Nik was yet. But I *wanted* to understand him.

And the kiss was not a dizzying, devouring fire.

It was the morning sunlight stroking my body. It was roasting agave and cinnamon. It was solid ground under my feet.

But when I opened my eyes again, it all disappeared. Because there she was. Watching from the trees.

Marisol.

CHAPTER 26

MARISOL HELD MY EYES, letting the smile spread across her face. Only then did she turn and run.

I didn't think, I just went after her. Racing through the trees. Branches tearing at my dress.

Nik shouted something, but I couldn't hear what it was. God knows what I'd do when I caught Marisol. All I knew was I needed to stop her. I needed to know why she'd followed me. What she'd heard. And what she was planning on doing about it.

She'd gotten a good head start. But I was stronger. And more appropriately dressed. I gained ground as her sculpted red hair tangled in the low-hanging branches and her heels sank into the soft leaves. Halfway to the Promenade, I managed to catch up, bringing my foot down on the train of her dress—sending her sprawling.

"Whhhhy are you—" I dropped to my knees next to her, gasping, clutching a cramp in my side. "Why are you following me?"

I was ready for Marisol to bully and mock me. I was ready for her to threaten to tell Edison about Nik. I was *not* ready for what she said.

"You should let the Dome keep its secrets, Leica. You won't like what you find." Marisol wasn't smiling anymore.

"What do you mean?" I was still catching my breath. Trying to understand what was happening.

Marisol leapt to her feet, quicker than I'd imagined possible. "I kept my eyes open when I first came here too. Looking for opportunities, ways to get the upper hand. And I learned the hard way that it's better to keep your eyes closed when it comes to the Dome. And to Edison."

I got to my feet to face her. Marisol's retribution for this morning had come swifter than I'd anticipated and I wondered exactly how far she was willing to go to stay alpha dog. "Come on, you know me better than that. Ominous warnings aren't going to scare me off."

The color drained from her face and she spit the words at me. "You might amuse him. You might be intriguing enough to keep his bed warm. But nothing more. Nothing real."

"And I suppose Edison *loves* you?" We were circling each other—like at the beginning of a fight—our words jabbing, testing the air between us.

"You think this is about love?" She laughed, a kind of high-pitched shriek. "You think he believes you're special? How *could* he? You're nothing but a Citizen." Marisol smiled, but it was full of poison. "A Corruption!"

"Is this your strategy to win back the Sanctum? Ugly words?" Then I saw something in her face, pain tucked behind her hatred. Clearly, this wasn't *all* about power. This wasn't even all about me.

Marisol was still looking at me, but I got the sense that she was talking to herself now. "Deep down, you already know something isn't right. Have you noticed none of the Kisaengs are pregnant? Doesn't that seem strange to you? Considering our role here?"

"What are you saying?" My voice was hard, as if its edge could protect me against whatever weapons Marisol had in her arsenal.

"Come on. You're a smart girl. You *know* what I'm saying. I know you've already found the scar . . . we *all* find it. It just takes a while for us to admit what it means."

All her posing and bravado dropped away, and the forest's shadows turned her face gaunt. This was *not* the same Marisol I'd grown up with. *This* Marisol still had a bold glint in her eyes, but it was only a trick of the light. Beneath it, her hazel eyes were dead. The Curadores had cut out her core.

"No." But my hand drifted to my stomach. Covering the scar.

The worst part is that Marisol was right. I *had* known. I'd seen it in Marisol's eyes that morning as she'd watched the children— children she would never have.

I'd never really thought about kids one way or another—never imagined I'd find anyone in Pleiades willing to risk my Corruption. I mean, who wants children cursed by God? But still . . . it had always been there. This future piece of me still unknown and unrealized.

"Is it permanent?" My voice was a whisper.

Marisol didn't answer. Brushing a dead leaves off her dress, she turned and headed back toward the Promenade. After a few steps, she called back to me, "Why don't you go ask Edison?"

But I didn't ask Edison about the scar. I didn't ask him anything. He was quiet during dinner in the Pavillion and I was too. Being careful. I didn't know if Marisol had told him about this kiss. I wasn't even completely sure of her motives anymore. As I watched him chew his curry in silence—his face stony—I realized I was scared.

The feeling caught me off guard. I'd been cautious of Edison before, but I'd never truly believed we were on different sides. But the secrets were piling up between us. Edison had watched me *for years* through Grimm's eyes, and the longer he went without telling me, the more disturbing that idea became. Now there was the scar. Marisol was right, you couldn't live in the Dome long without noticing that none of the Kisaengs were pregnant. Edison must at least be aware of whatever they'd done to me. And then there was Nik . . . and the kiss.

Was I truly capable of playing the Kisaeng with Edison any longer?

Marisol's words came back to me: *You'd better figure out what you want and who's going to get that for you.*

Well, the idea that the Curadores were willing to sterilize Kisaengs because we were unfit made the idea of them infecting Citizens quite convincing. The sooner I discovered what'd happened to Tasch, the sooner I could keep it from happening to anyone else. And for that, I still needed Edison. For now, at least.

I wiped my mouth with my napkin for the hundredth time, feeling like he must be able to see Nik's kiss there.

My movement caught Edison's eye and he smiled sheepishly. "Sorry! I'm terrible company tonight. I was just thinking about the damn radio. I've been triple-checking everything, all afternoon . . . everything seems clean and undamaged and in the right place. But all I get is static! It's like we're missing a piece. Like someone doesn't want us to succeed. So I was thinking that tonight we should—"

But I cut him off, remembering my late-night appointment with Grimm. "Actually, I think I should go to bed early. I'm exhausted."

"I bet!" Edison said. "Sounds like you had a full day."

I squeezed my balled-up napkin. *Does he know about my trip into Nik's woods? About the kiss?*

But Edison smiled indulgently. "I heard you and the Kisaengs were fighting again."

"Sparring," I corrected, and I ordered myself to relax.

"Well, whatever you call it, you and the girls are causing quite the stir among the Curadores." His amused tone made me bristle. He misread my irritation for tiredness and, pushing away his bowl, he said, "Let me walk you home."

I allowed him to take my arm as we set off across the grassy Promenade. I racked my brain for something to say. "Did you find out anything about the Mothers?"

"Huh?" Clearly Edison was still lost in thoughts of the radio.

"The accident . . . down in the Salvage Hall?"

"Oh, it was nothing." He hit the button to call the magfly. "Jenner tracked the problem to the main computer . . . another power fluctuation in the magnetic field."

"But I saw her—"

"Must've been just coincidence." The drone of the arriving magfly competed with his words. "Probably just a case of her being in the wrong place at the wrong time."

That didn't explain the device the Mother had been holding. What if Jenner was lying to Edison about the power fluctuations? What if Edison was lying to me?

I had so many questions and they all came back to the endless chorus of: *Why?* What did the Mother in the Salvage Hall, Olivia going missing, my scar, and Taschen's death all have to do with each other?

What if it was nothing? What if these weren't even pieces to the same puzzle? My head hurt and I rubbed it as I stepped onto the magfly. "But I thought the Mothers didn't usually go . . ."

Then I noticed that Edison hadn't moved, hadn't gotten onto the magfly with me. And there was a strange look on his face. "I just thought of something! With the radio . . . I've got to . . . I'm gonna go back . . ."

Before he could finish, the doors were sliding shut—cutting off his words. And then the magfly was on its way, gliding through the streets of the Dome without him.

I fell asleep wondering about Edison's sudden inspiration. Had he really had an idea, or had he just been avoiding my questions? Then again, did it matter? Either way, it had allowed me to go home on my own.

Now, as I woke, deep in the night, I hoped that Grimm might be able to help me see something in the Dome I was missing. I slipped on my clothes and looked out the balcony window. The backyard was quiet and empty, stretching back to the trees.

I'd gotten used to the fact that everything in the Dome was circular—the streets, the magfly tracks, the Garden—and that meant those trees were also the edge of Nik's woods. As I headed into them, I kept expecting Grimm to show up. But when he didn't, I found my own way easily enough—though the woods felt less friendly without him.

I heard the shouting long before I could see the house. Angry voices traveling though the forest.

"*That's* why you asked me to come? Do you know what I risked to get here?" It was a woman's voice.

I hurried as fast as I could without making noise. When I got to the edge of the clearing, I recognized her. In the glow of Nik's house, I could see that it was the Mother I'd seen in the Salvage Hall—her white-blond hair pulled into same high bun, and the same tunic dress. But tonight the fabric was stretched over a much smaller bump. And I remembered how the data drive had disappeared into the vast folds of her tunic. Clever—using her pregnancy to disguise her smuggling.

The Mother's freckles popped dark against her angry face. "We've just been raided. Edison found out about me sneaking into the Salvage Hall to test our device and brought the wrath of the Dome down on us. Equipment seized. Surveillance raised. And now you ask me to risk everything we've been working on so I can help a Kisaeng?"

"Ada, I didn't know. I'm sorry." Nik looked miserable and Grimm flew in desperate circles around their heads.

"Of course you didn't. You just stay in your little bubble. Leave the danger to us." The Mother—Ada—spit the words at him. She looked terrifying and beautiful even in her scorn.

"You know I can't leave—" Nik's voice broke and her face crumpled. Her rage disintegrating into weariness.

"I know. I'm sorry." And she took Nik's hand, leading him into his house.

I turned as quietly as I could and melted back into the woods.

That woman—Ada—*had* been responsible for what happened in the Salvage Hall. And despite what he'd told me, Edison had known that. In fact, he'd raided the Mother's Complex.

And Nik. Nik was somehow involved with this Ada and her sabotage.

I walked back through the woods, heading toward the Genetics Lab. Turns out, sometimes the only person who can get you what you want is you.

CHAPTER 27

I WOULD FIND A WAY to get a look at Jenner's files myself.
I crept out of the woods and past the Pavilion. This late at night
there were only a few couples left in the tent—taking refuge in the
dim corners or spinning slowly on the dance floor, drinks in hand.

But the Genetics Lab was still lit bright, and I could see Curadores moving around in the main room. They were busy monitoring the main computer, screens blinking with a thousand bits
of data—even so, it'd be impossible to sneak in the front door
without being seen. A Curador came up the path to the Lab and I
pulled back into the shadow of a nearby tree. He punched a code
into the panel by the door and it slid open and closed again. I'd
forgotten that part.

I circled the building trying other entrances. Each one had a
panel. Each one was locked. But as I came around the front of the
building again, I caught a glimpse of Edison leaving the Lab. He
was a ways ahead of me and walking fast, looking agitated. I practically had to run to stay with him, keeping a block between us as
he walked through the streets of the sleeping Dome. I thought he

might turn off and go to the church, but instead, he headed toward the Kisaengs' neighborhood.

I wondered if he was going to Marisol's and a tiny bit of panic shot through me. Then, as I traced his path through the streets, I suddenly realized where Edison was headed. *To my house.*

We were only a few blocks away now and there was no one else out in the wide open streets—it wasn't like I could simply slip past him and hope he didn't see me. The panic surged into my feet and I ducked between a pair of houses. Cutting through their backyards. Dodging trees and bushes.

I didn't know what Edison wanted with me. But I didn't think he'd be very happy if I wasn't home when he got there.

I ran, leaping over a low hedge, in through my back door and up the stairs. I was barely at the top when I heard the front door creak open. Breathing hard, I ripped off my dress, tossed it on the floor, and dove under the covers. My bedroom door swung open and I forced my breathing to slow. Forced my whole body to be still.

Edison knelt by my bed. His face close to mine.

"Leica," Edison whispered. "Wake up."

I fluttered my eyes open, trying to look groggy. "What time is it?"

"It's late. Well . . . maybe it's early . . . it doesn't matter. You have to come. I fixed it! It works . . . the radio works!"

The walk back to the Lab seemed to take no time. The whole thing was like a dream. And when we got there, it was already playing—the message from Earth.

"Lotus Colony, this is Homebase. You are under temporary quarantine. Enter verification and transmit on priority frequency so emergency evacuations can be coordinated."

Edison grabbed the microphone, his face one big grin. "Hello! Hello? We can hear you! We're transmitting! Is anyone there?"

A flutter of excitement quivered in my chest. It hadn't just been a ploy—he *did* figure out what was wrong. Edison had managed to get the radio working.

"Hello?" I gave it a try, but the message simply repeated itself again. And again.

"When you got it working, did anyone answer?"

"No, but I didn't really try. I just heard the message and ran to get you."

"It says something about transmitting on a priority frequency . . . What if we're still missing something?"

"I don't know . . ." Edison was thinking it through. Excitement and concern fighting for control. "It worked for you in the shuttle. Then again, it's possible that the shuttle was already transmitting the code. Or more likely, this radio is. There's a lot of variables, but the important thing is that we just took the first step. Do you know what this means?" His eyes were so vibrantly orange, they were practically glowing. And I was reminded of that first day out in Tierra Muerta, when he saw the shuttle hatch.

I couldn't keep the smile off my face. "Earth."

"Earth!" His voice was full of awe and he laughed, pulling me into a hug as he spun me around.

The hugeness of it made everything that'd happened over the last few days fade. I imagined myself making contact. Ships and supplies coming to Gabriel. My people lifted out of ritual and penance. Lifted out of disease. And I imagined Lotus and I, traveling together. Going home for the very first time.

Edison said exactly what I was thinking. "This could change everything."

We tried for hours, taking turns at the microphone. Talking about what it might be like. About what might happen when we told people. Curadores and Citizens joining forces. Becoming a new community.

But there was still no reply. Only the message playing over and over and over again. I stared at the radio, wondering if we'd ever hear anyone on it again. Wondering if it was really working. So many wires and switches and circuits connecting me to this tenuous thread of hope.

Then I spotted it.

One wire. Shredded near its connection to the main circuit board. It hadn't been damaged when I'd left—I'd double-checked everything myself.

I didn't say anything. Hoping it was nothing—something unimportant. I silently traced the wire with my eyes to where it connected to a jack in the front panel of the radio. I already knew what plugged into that socket, but I checked the path of the cord just to make sure, following each twist and coil. All the way to the microphone in my hand.

A chill crept through me, but I didn't change my expression. Didn't move. Didn't even stop speaking into the mic.

Except now, of course, I knew we weren't really transmitting. No matter many times I said "Hello!" Earth would never respond, because it couldn't even hear us.

I glanced at Edison, chatting passionately about humanity's innate ability to adapt and thrive and it occurred to me that Edison never mentioned *how* he got this thing working. Never told me what his big idea was that made everything suddenly start functioning. Because the thing is, I'd been the one working on the main board. On those wires. And the last time I'd seen them, they'd been intact.

Wasn't it possible that someone had sabotaged the microphone at the same time they fixed the radio? Wasn't it possible that someone would want it to only *look* like we were transmitting? And wasn't it possible that someone was Edison?

Edison finally fell asleep midafternoon, slumped over the microphone. He'd been up all night, so it was bound to happen sometime. It'd been horrible trying to pretend I hadn't seen the wire. Our calls going unheard and therefore unanswered. Waiting for him to give up. I wasn't sure what kind of game Edison was playing, but I knew enough to play along.

Luckily the doors inside the Genetics Lab were only locked on the outside. As I slipped out of the building, it occurred to me that if Edison *was* playing some kind of game with me, then the radio was the *perfect prize*. Thanks to Grimm, Edison knew a lot more about me than I did about him. He knew I loved machines and electronics. And he knew that I was fascinated with Earth. The lure of the broken radio was too much for me to resist—that's why Edison hadn't fixed it while I was in isolation.

So why fix it now?

I thought about Edison's most recent lie about the Mothers. Had I stumbled onto something that'd provoked this distraction?

Still. How long did he think I'd chatter into the radio before I noticed?

I didn't get very far from the Lab before Grimm appeared. He dove, grabbing my shirt, tugging me toward the forest. In full view of everyone on the Promenade.

"You shouldn't be here!" I swatted him away as Kisaengs and Curadores started glancing in our direction, but Grimm dove again. Refusing to leave me alone. I'd never seen him like this. A needle of worry pushed into me and I followed him into the woods before we managed to attract the attention of the whole Dome.

Grimm swooped around me, calling out in agitation, as we traveled toward Nik's house. When I got there, Nik was standing at one of the long tables, but he didn't look up. He was cramming a new radish sprout into a jar, and he wasn't his usual, deliberate self. Bits of soil were spilling out over the rim and his rough fingers were smashing the green shoots.

"What did that poor plant ever do to you?" I said, trying to break the tension with a stupid joke.

He ignored me, starting on another pot.

"What's wrong?" I asked.

Nik didn't speak, but every muscle in his body seemed strung taut. Like any second he would snap. Nik started stacking the re-potted jars in the corner of the table. Banging them on the counter as he went. *Slam. Slam. Slam.*

Behind him on the wall, a computer screen glowed and I spotted my name.

I read the entry out loud, "Leica. Age 17. Processed: July 2592."

Nik grabbed another jar. *Slam.*

I went on. "Blood filtration. Bacteria cultivation. Body scan. Ova harvested. Cycle simulated." *Slam.*

"What does this mean? Ova harvested?" I pointed at the screen, asking the question I was afraid I already had the answer to.

A jar tipped over. *Smash.*

"Dammit!" Nik bashed his hand down. Dirt and glass went everywhere. Strewn across the table. Carpeting the cracked concrete. Embedded in his skin. Blood blossomed up—red mixing with the shimmering wreck.

He barely seemed to notice the cluster of cuts that decorated his palm. Or the great slice that cut across the center.

"Let me see that." I hurried to him, stumbling over a bag of dirt. As I fell, Grimm tried to help, diving for me, catching my hand with his talons.

I clutched at my palm, wincing.

"Leica!" My pain finally pulled Nik out of his rage. He blinked like he was waking up from a dream.

"I'm sorry." He reached out as if to touch the deep ribbon of red that spanned my knuckles, then stopped himself. He looked me straight in the eyes, his jaw tight. And I could see the words were hard for him to say. "I'm so sorry."

A horrible idea rose up inside me and I touched the scar on my belly. "Did you know about this?"

"Not about your scar, not about the missing Kisaengs . . . not until Ada snuck into the Lab and copied Jenner's files."

I shook my head. "Ada? That's the woman who was here? Why would she help me? She clearly hates Kisaengs."

"So you *did* come last night," Nik said quietly. And some of the hurt cleared from his face. "Ada doesn't hate them. And she helped because I asked her too."

I was struggling to put everything together. To understand what was happening. "But she's the one sabotaging the Dome. I saw her."

"No." Then Nik hesitated. "Well . . . yes. But she has her reasons. You'll have to take my word for it. I've known Ada my whole life. I trust her."

Trust. The word was meaningless now.

Grimm came and perched on my shoulder, burying his beak in my hair for comfort. I ran my hand over the gold feathers on his breast. Reassuring him.

I pointed at the screen again. "Tell me, what does it mean?"

"They cut you open," he said. I nodded, knowing that part. "And they took your eggs."

"My eggs?"

"They removed your ovaries and replaced them with a device that synthesized the same chemicals so—"

"Don't tell me how they did it." I cut him off. Needing to hear him say the words. Needing to know for sure. "Tell me what it *means*."

Nik knew what I was asking and there was grief on his face. "It's impossible for you to have children now."

His words made my chest ache—my heart struggling to grasp his words. To make them real. It wasn't like I suddenly longed to hold a baby. Or imagined little girls running around with my same nose or eyes or hands. No. It was that yesterday, there had been all these paths I could've taken. All the people I could've become. And now—where there'd been noise and chaos and color—there was just blankness. And there was just me.

"Taken, but not destroyed?" Making sure I understood what they'd done to me. "It says *ova harvested* . . . like I'm some kind of crop?"

"Not destroyed . . . they're used to make clones. They need unfertilized eggs . . . like blank canvases. They remove the nucleus from your cell—take out your DNA—and insert the cloned one."

More Edisons. More Niks.

But *not* more Leicas. And somehow that was a relief. My eggs were merely the empty receptacle—incubators. At least there weren't scraps of my soul being twisted and manipulated without me even knowing.

There were other files on the screen too. Other names I recognized: Riya, Marisol, Aaliyah. They all said the same thing: **Ova Harvested. Cycle Simulated.** But when I got to Oksun's entry, it was different.

Oksun. Age 29. Processed: November 2585. Pending.

"Pending? What does pending mean?" And I thought about the fact that Oksun was a little older than most of the Kisaengs.

Nik shook his head. "I have no idea."

I scanned the list, but none of the others were labeled pending. Then I got to another file that was different. Cold dread squeezed my chest. **Olivia. Age 22. Processed: May 2583. Infected: October 2592. Red Death. Isolation Ward C.**

So Lotus had been right. The Curadores *were* infecting people with Red Death. They were infecting the *Kisaengs*. And according to this, Olivia was still somewhere in this Dome.

"Where's Isolation Ward C?" I demanded.

"I'm not sure."

"But you know something, don't you?"

The haunted look came back into Nik's eyes and his shoulders hunched—like he was trying to fold in on himself.

"Nik." I said the word in a low, calm voice. "I didn't come to the Dome to be with Edison . . . he was only my way inside. I came because we suspected the Curadores were doing something horrible to Pleiades. So if you care about me at all, then tell me what you know. *Please* . . . my people are dying."

He was quiet for so long, I thought he was lost. Then he started speaking. "Grimm was one of my *good* ideas. A friend. Someone to keep Edison and me from going crazy locked inside that lab."

He hesitated and I jostled Grimm off my own shoulder and onto Nik's. He absently petted Grimm's feathers and it seemed to give him the courage to continue. "Once we got Grimm's personality and mechanics working, Edison thought it would be an interesting experiment to give him a real animal body so he'd blend in outside the Dome.

"And I wanted to see the sky so badly, Leica. The real blue . . . not this thin, faded color. The *real* stars—even if it was just through Grimm's eyes. So we snuck through the underground tunnels and into a network of abandonned laboratories we'd found. No one else knew the LOTUS facility was even down there—it'd been locked up and forgotten about years and years ago—but we'd used those tunnels as our playground.

"We set up in one of the old isolation rooms, but Edison and I started fighting over Ad Astra's DNA files. I wanted Grimm to be an owl, but Edison said that parrots were more intelligent. So in the end, we used both." Nik shuddered. "A chimera."

My mind was ringing with the word LOTUS. The word from the shuttle and the necklaces. "What happened?"

"The first attempt was horrible. When the bird emerged from the egg, it had too many wings—four half-formed monstrosities—and his beak was fused and twisted. It was grotesque, but something even worse had gone wrong. The bird wasn't supposed to have its own functional brain . . . it was only supposed to be an empty body for Grimm's computer. But it wasn't." And Nik was stock-still, staring into nothing. Like if he moved, if he blinked, the memory would hurt too much.

"When he saw it, Edison just started cracking up . . . this wild, hysterical howl of laughter. Then he started flapping his arms, imitating the thing while it tried to cry out in agony."

My stomach turned. There was no sparkle in Nik's eyes now—the yellow embers had all died out. "Edison was still laughing when he snapped the bird's neck."

The worst part was, I believed Nik. I could almost picture Edison myself.

"I begged him not to try again. I should have stopped him, but I didn't." Nik looked ashamed. He reached up and stroked Grimm's feathers. "I never do."

Then as if I wasn't even there, Nik turned away and started cleaning up the broken glass and spilled dirt. Sweeping it all into a neat, little pile.

CHAPTER 28

NIK HAD GIVEN ME enough to go on. Both he and Edison (and June for that matter) had all talked about tunnels and facilities running beneath this Dome. I was sure that's where I would find Olivia and hopefully the other missing Kisaengs.

As I emerged from the forest, the sun was setting, flooding the Dome with purple shadows. I couldn't go to the Salvage Hall—even at this time of day it would be swarming with Curadores and flys. But Edison had said something about using an intake conduit near the brewery. That was just a complicated term for a drain, and I knew where to find one of those—and close to the Genetics Labs at that. If there was one thing I'd learned in the Reclamation Fields, it was that *getting* underground was the easy part.

The Kisaengs were already at dinner and the Sanctum was silent—except for the constant babble of the stream. I followed the creek across the courtyard to where it ended—shivering as I stepped into the icy current and peered down through the decorative grate. The water didn't drop straight down, but angled gently, becoming an underground river. The metal drain was rusty and old. Easy to pry off.

It was much harder to make myself get down on my hands and knees and crawl into the wet darkness—the pipe was barely bigger than I was. But the water was only a few centimeters deep. Not enough to drown in. Still, I didn't know where it went, other than down.

My hands went numb almost instantly, which was convenient, since one of them still hurt from Grimm's talons. The roar of the water echoed in the cramped tunnel, deafening me as I crawled through the dark. I could feel myself going deeper, the weight of the ground above pressing down on me.

The pipe grew wider and steeper as more water dumped in from somewhere else. The current was stronger here—but there was no way to turn around or go backward. I was half crawling, half being sucked forward.

When a sudden gush waterfalled in from a third pipe, there was no longer even the pretense of crawling. I was swept down through the angled pipe—on my belly one minute, flipped onto my back, then pulled under.

My hands managed to push off the bottom, shoving my head above the surface. As I gasped for breath, I banged my head against the top of the pipe. There was only a few centimeters of air left.

My lungs ached and I sucked in what little air there was. Water roared in my ears. Burned my nose. Pressed in on me from every direction.

Then I was flung into space. And I was falling, reaching out, tumbling, grabbing onto nothing. I landed with a smack—pain blossoming across my skin and reaching deep into my bones. My boots and dress weighed me down, dragging me under. As I flailed in the deep river, my hand knocked against a rusty ladder bolted to the side and I grabbed on.

Sputtering and shaking, my feet treaded water as I looked around. I was in a huge tunnel. Orangey dim lights lined the ceiling, glowing eerily against the surface. Two meters up, I could see the smaller tunnel I'd been jettisoned from. A permanent waterfall thundering in the dark.

The water was deep here, but slow. And it ran through a channel in the middle of the tunnel. Gripping the rungs, I heaved myself out of the underground river and collapsed, dripping, on the cement bank.

After a few minutes, I managed to get my shaking legs to hold me and started walking. Up ahead, the tunnel split, one fork taking the river deeper into the bowels of the Dome. But I took the other fork, a small, dry tunnel.

I had to crouch a little so my head didn't hit the ancient pipes and cables running along the ceiling. Lamps came on as I passed, then switched off again—keeping me in a finite bubble of light. But I was grateful for them anyway. I drew courage from the fact that at least there was power here. And it was a tunnel. It had to lead somewhere.

As best as I could tell, the river was heading away from the Reservoir and toward the Kisaengs' houses. But *this* tunnel veered back toward the Sanctum. Soon the electric thrum of a magfly vibrated through the walls and I was sure I was close to the Genetics Lab and the Promenade.

Then there it was. A metal door in the wall of the tunnel, reading

LOTUS. It had a rusty lock but I made short work of it with my knife. A scout picks up all kinds of skills out in the Fields.

My teeth chattered as I stepped through the door into a glare of white. The hallway was immaculately clean and the lights radiated a bluish glow, illuminating every square of pristine tile. Every corner. Every doorway.

The hall was lined with blank white doors—each one with a tiny reinforced window at the top. A memory swam up to my consciousness. There'd been a window like that in my isolation room, crisscrosses of wire running through the glass. And for a moment I was frozen there again, cocooned in that horrible sling—the plastic mesh hammock constricting my body while wires and tubes spidered out in every direction.

The windows here were too high up for me to see through. And the doors were locked. But I could hear movement and voices coming from behind them.

I shuddered, my wet shoes clammy on my feet. Nik had described abandoned, forgotten laboratories. But whatever LOTUS was now, it was no longer some underground relic.

I hurried on down the hall. I didn't want one of the Curadores to find me and take me to . . . who? Jenner? Edison? I wasn't even sure who I was afraid of anymore. I just knew I didn't want to end up behind any of these locked doors.

I lost my bearings in the maze of identical hallways. I stopped every once in a while to listen for voices or try a door. Looking for any signs for Ward C. Looking for signs for *anything*. Then at the end of one hallway, there was a pair of double doors. The LOTUS flower that I'd seen in the shuttle and on Lotus's necklace was etched into the foggy glass and there was a sign reading:

WARD A DECONTAMINATION PORTAL. And nearby, a long rack of isolation suits.

I grabbed a suit and stepped into it. It was baggy, but the moment I zipped it up, the thing cinched in around me—shortening the sleeves and legs. It also heated up, blowing dry air across my damp, frozen skin, and for a moment, I savored the sensation of being warm.

Then I stepped forward and the doors slid open, letting me into a tiny room. They sealed again behind me, and a fine mist sprayed from the ceiling and walls, coating the suit. There was another set of clear double doors in front of me, but I could barely see through the fog. Then there was a hiss of air—clearing the room—and when the second set of doors slid open, I could barely force myself to step through them.

The smell reached me, even through the filters of the suit— astringent chemicals and death. My stomach twisted as a chorus of cries and groans crackled through my speakers. It was like walking into a wall of suffering.

There were hundreds of them. Sick, dying people—each one cradled in a mesh sling suspended from the ceiling. They stretched out in front me, hanging like rows of terrible cocoons—five people high and four wide and I had no idea how many deep. A vast web of tubes and wires spanned the enormous room.

Fighting back nausea, I made myself go deeper into the nightmare. Made myself *look* at the people trapped there. The lowest tier of slings was at eye level and as I moved down the narrow aisles between them, I could make out faces and bodies through the clear mesh—flys swarming over blotchy, seeping skin. But listening to them was almost worse: murmuring, pleading, in their half-comatose state.

All I wanted was to run away. But then I pictured Olivia and the other missing Kisaengs, immobilized and in pain, somewhere among the hundreds. And I made myself go on.

I skirted past a hulking, blinking machine that sat in the middle of the aisle. It looked a little like the main computer, except for the thousands of tubes and wires that spiderwebbed out from it, connecting the machine to each of the slings. Liquids flowed through the vast network of tubes—deep reds and bright yellows funneling in and out. Medicating and filtering and hydrating the layers of hanging bodies.

The machine started buzzing and I jumped as an engine somewhere above me whirred to life. Metal claws descended from the ceiling, like the robotic arms in Nik's gardens. They closed gently around the top layer of cocoons and turned them slightly, so the bodies were rotated a bit inside their slings. Then the whole top row descended down a level and the slings on the bottom revolved up to take their place—like a giant pinwheel. The tubes and wires doing a delicate dance around each other so they wouldn't tangle as the bodies moved.

What the hell *was* this place?

I walked through the rows, looking for answers—the people had dark hair, brown skin, and seemed tiny against the Curadores I'd grown used to. Clearly they were Citizens. Some of them might've been Kisaengs, but there were men here too. Some of the faces almost looked familiar and my heart ached with the certainty that these people were from Pleiades.

They were *my people.*

Moans went up from the patients as I passed, as though they could sense my presence. And now I saw that their symptoms were all different. Some had blood tinting their eyes, dripping from their noses—like Red Death. But others had strange sores or rashes I didn't recognize. And still others looked as if nothing was wrong with them, aside from being a little pale and weak.

A few had their eyes open, staring at me in a kind of frozen horror. Others were able to actually focus on me, tracking me as I moved. Their hands twitching as if trying to reach out—despite the constricting slings. I remembered the half sleep I'd endured in the isolation room. Keeping me in a kind of drugged stasis while the Curadores filtered and tested and removed bits of me. Then I understood.

They're keeping them like this on purpose. Killing them in slow motion. In that moment I yearned to reach for my knife. To slash through the perverse web of tubes. To destroy the industrious machines keeping these people in suspended agony.

But then I recognized her. Despite the cracked and bleeding skin. Despite the sores and the blood. A face I loved.

It was impossible. If there was a God, if there was any mercy in this world, I never would've seen her again. She would've died. Her bones rendered into ash.

But there was no God. There was only this pitiable creature in front of me. There was only my sister.

Only Taschen.

CHAPTER 29

"TASCH?" MY VOICE BLARED through the room, amplified by the speakers in the suit. I knelt by her sling. "No."

And the word rippled through the ward—low moans repeating my protest.

My sister's eyelids struggled to open. She looked at my isolation suit and fear flashed in her dazed eyes.

"It's okay," I whispered this time. "It's just me. It's Leica."

"Leica . . ." Taschen's voice was no louder than a sigh. A pink tear leaked out the corner of her eye.

I was fighting to stay calm, my breath fogging up the window of my suit. I wanted to take her hand, but the sling was in the way. And the wires and tubes were too thick to negotiate with my clumsy, too-few fingered gloves.

"I've dreamed . . . you're never real . . ." she said.

"I am this time. And I'm going to get you out."

But then the machine buzzed again and the mechanical arms at the ceiling sprung to life. Turning and rotating the top slings before all the rows shifted places again. And Tasch was being pulled away from me. Up to the top of the pinwheel.

276 • Sara Wilson Etienne

"Stop! Tasch!" I raced to the hub of machines and tubes, searching for some kind of button or lever or screen that would stop the cycle, but there was nothing I could make sense of. And when I looked back, I'd lost track of her amid the rows and columns of identical cocoons. I ran back to where I thought I'd been standing, trying to figure out which one was hers. But she was gone.

Then there was a different noise—a hiss of air. And I spotted a cloud of mist filling the decontamination portal between the two sets of doors. Someone else was coming.

"I'll come back for you, I swear."

I ran through the rows of bodies. Trying to put as much space as possible between me and whoever was coming. I spotted a second set of doors on this side of the ward and I jammed on the button—slipping between the sliding doors and into my own cloud of mist.

My vision fogged, but when it cleared, I saw a group of Curadores step through the entrance of the vast room. One was bigger than the others. Holding himself tall and proud. Walking with a confident stride I'd gotten used to. I didn't need to see any more to know it was Edison.

I shed the isolation suit and ran. Not looking where I was going. Only caring that I was heading away from that place.

I pushed my way through another ancient, half-open set of decontamination doors. After that, the hallways turned into stone tunnels. And still I ran.

Then the stone floor turned to dirt and I stumbled. Sprawling across the ground, sobbing.

Even after the tears were gone, I let myself stay there, curled in a ball. Breathing in the dusty desert smell. Letting the vaguest trace of sagebrush comfort me.

And it was the scent of sagebrush that finally got my attention. That forced me to unfold myself and stand up and really breathe.

It was not the stale, constant atmosphere of the Dome. And running my hand along the wall, I stepped carefully through the dark, following a trickle of cool, fresh air. Which became a waft. Which became a breeze. Which became the desert and sky and stars.

So many stars.

I climbed out of a dusty pit and found myself in the middle of the Reclamation Fields. And in the distance was a semicircle of shining lights.

Home.

THE MIDDLE SISTER *was glad she was not carrying the egg, for surely she would have dropped it. Inside the forbidden room was a basin filled with blood and bones. Beside it sat a chopping block and ax that dripped red. And, by her feet, hundreds of eggs lay smashed and broken upon the floor.*

Alas, what more did she behold? Her beautiful sisters lay in the basin, murdered and chopped into pieces. The brave girl gathered the parts of her sisters together, and laid them on the floor: feet, legs, torsos, arms, and heads. The middle sister knelt beside them, weeping for what she had lost. And as her tears mingled with the blood, the pieces of her sisters knitted together and began to move.

Fingers twitched and eyelashes fluttered, until they looked up at her with wondering eyes.

"What has happened to us?" the sisters asked.

The middle sister hugged them close, but before she could answer, she heard the sorcerer call out for her.

"Wait here and I will return for you." She kissed their cheeks and locked them inside the room. Then she hurried to retrieve the egg.

When the sorcerer saw the middle sister, he said, "Give me the egg so I know it is still safe."

And he was surprised to see the shell was white as snow, without a drop of blood to mark it.

"You have proven yourself worthy. You shall be my bride." And as he uttered those words, his power over her was lost.

"FITCHER'S BIRD,"

FROM *FAIRY TALES OF THE BROTHERS GRIMM*

BY JACOB AND WILHELM GRIMM,

EARTH TEXT, 27TH EDITION, 2084.

PART THREE

CHAPTER 30

IT HURT . . . looking at the dazzling lights of Pleiades. Sarika was out there. And somewhere on the other side of the desert was Lotus. I wanted to go to them. I wanted to walk across the sand and the stars and forget what I'd seen.

But that was impossible. Taschen was still inside the Dome. And Riya. And Oksun. And Nik. And hundreds of other Citizens down in that ward.

And Edison.

I doubled over, retching on the ground. I had to go back. If I stayed out here tonight, I'd be missed. And if I was going to save Tasch, it would have to be from the inside. The Indignos had known that when they sent me there, even if they hadn't known what I'd find.

I had to go back in. I had to come up with a plan. I had to save my sister.

Because only a Kisaeng could smile and plot and move around the Dome. Only a Kisaeng could destroy it.

CHAPTER 31

IT TOOK ME HOURS to find my way back through the tunnels, back through the decontamination portal, and back up to the surface of the Dome. Even with my good sense of direction, I was still lost half the time. At least I didn't have to go back through the Sanctum. Thankfully, I found an exit that came up through the street near the old church.

Even though it was the middle of the night, I traveled by foot so I wouldn't run into anyone. As I reached the edge of the Kisaengs' neighborhood, a cloud of flys passed overhead. I ducked into the doorway of a nearby house, hiding. Barely breathing.

When Nik mentioned that Grimm could "pick up" the flys' feed, I hadn't thought twice about it. Now it hit me that with the flys, there were eyes everywhere.

I was stumbling with exhaustion. But when I turned onto my street, exhaustion was replaced with panic. Through the balcony curtains, I could see a light in my bedroom. A light I hadn't left on.

I reached down into my boot and pulled out my knife. Then, thinking it through, I slid it back in—leaving it hidden. I was pretty sure Edison hadn't seen me down in the ward with Taschen. Even if he'd glimpsed someone in an isolation suit through the mist, it was unlikely he'd known it was me. The only reason I recognized him tonight was because I was used to seeing him wearing the suit out in Tierra Muerta.

I didn't have a plan yet for rescuing Tasch, and until I did, there could be no suspicion. I'd have to play my role as Kisaeng to perfection. So when I finally pushed open the door to my bedroom, there was a smile on my face.

Edison was standing by my bed and he said, "So nice of you to stop by."

His tone was pleasant, but his eyes were cold and distant. I tried to say something clever—to say anything—but I couldn't. This Edison was a stranger to me. His forehead was smooth and untroubled. His jaw slack.

In fact, Edison was completely calm up until the moment he smacked me across the face and sent me flying. Slamming me against the wall.

I was so surprised I didn't even cry out. Blood trickled into my mouth from a split lip. My cheek throbbed, already swelling. I curled into a ball and a groan seeped out of my mouth.

"No! This is *not* how it happens." Edison shouted the words and I wasn't sure if he was talking to himself or me. Then he walked over, his face crumpling, his hand outstretched. Like a little boy begging for answers. "How could you?"

I stared at the hand reaching out to me, but I didn't take it. Panic hissed like static in my head. Fear was an animal burrowing through my thoughts. I wrapped my arms around myself—my hands digging into my shoulders. *If I hold on tight enough, I can protect myself.*

Then I heard Dad's voice in my ear, counseling me to be calm. *Loosen your grip. Loosen your breath. Loosen the knot.*

I could be brave. I steadied myself—breathing in—and unwound my body. I took Edison's hand, letting him help me stand up. Not allowing the ripple of pain to show on my face.

"I was worried when you didn't come back to work on the radio." Edison's grip tightened, the ache shooting up my arm. "So I came by to make sure you were okay."

His tone was wheedling, but by now his huge hand was crushing mine. My finger bones ground together—the blinding pain making me go limp. "And do you know who was waiting for you in your room?"

"No . . . please—" And now *I* was the stranger, my desperate pleas foreign in my own ears. But at least my brain was working again, and somewhere behind the agony, I marveled at how much Edison must've been holding back the first time we'd fought.

Edison released my hand and I dropped to the floor. When he spoke again, the other Edison was back. Cold, his voice playful as he said, "Three guesses."

I held his eyes, but I didn't speak. Words were not going to save me. I knew the Dome's secret. I knew what Edison was capable of. Right now, I was a crumpled heap on the floor, but I slipped my hand under my skirt. Concentrating on wriggling my knife free from my boot without Edison noticing.

"Time's up!" He hunkered down, so close that flecks of spit sprayed my check. "It was your little bird friend! Nikola's spy."

Edison's nasty grin echoed Nik's bitter smile and the similarity was unnerving. My hand was on my knife now, but I hesitated again. *What did this have to do with Nik?*

"Did you think you were clever? Were the two of you laughing at me?" And he kicked me where I huddled on the ground—a sharp, stunning blow to my hip. "After everything I've done for you. After I came across the desert, into the grit and the filth to find you and bring you here."

My thoughts moved slowly, trying to crest the throbbing waves of pain. *Nikola's spy.* I wasn't completely sure what Edison was talking about, but this wasn't about the LOTUS or the wards. *He's angry about me visiting Nik.*

I just didn't know whether that meant I was in less danger, or more.

It took every bit of strength I had—every bit of courage—but for the second time, I left my knife where it was. If I pulled it on Edison now, I'd lose my place in the Dome. Or worse. And as far as I knew, I was the only one that knew about the Citizens down in that ward.

I *would* use my knife. Just not tonight.

Instead, I gently pulled at the string of Edison's words, hoping if I was careful, this knot would unravel. "I'm grateful you came for me."

"After all those years. There was your voice again, on the radio, calling out to Earth. And I thought, 'Of course.' Nikola and I had *known* you were special. *Of course* you would be the one to save us."

"And so you came out to Tierra Muerta for me."

"Yes, I had to be patient. But on the third day . . . there you were, walking along the tracks," he said, his eyes wide. "But I should've known Nik wouldn't stay in that hole he crawled into. I should've realized he'd recognize your voice too and try to turn you against me."

Then Edison's face hardened—his words a belted accusation. "But *you*. I never imagined that *you* would demean yourself. Can't you see what he is?"

I shook my head—anything I said now would be the wrong thing.

"Nothing more than a bad copy of me. Twisted." His eyes flamed with disgust. But there was hurt there too. "Cringing away in the dark."

Edison's voice rose now until it was almost a scream. *"He is a mistake!"*

It was like his humanity was stripped away and stripped raw at the same time. And I had my answer—*this* is what Edison was like when he had no one to perform for. I reached out and touched his shoulder. "I'm sorry."

"Sorry?" And Edison yanked me up by my arm and flung me onto the bed, like I was nothing. My head slammed into one of the posts and the whole world roared and spun around me.

I pushed myself up, wanting to retch again. I wouldn't pull my knife, but I wouldn't stay put and let him kill me either. I tried to steady myself while I estimated the distance between the bed and the porch. Between the bed and the door. Getting ready for my moment.

"Marisol was right. You aren't worth my time." Edison noticed my gaze on the door, and I leapt up, running in the opposite direction toward the back balcony.

In two steps he was on me. His giant hands bruising my arms in his grip. I scratched and spit and clawed and bit. But he barely flinched. After all my training, after all my sparring and lessons with the Kisaengs, I was defenseless. I gave up and stopped fighting.

He held me there—in midair—for another second. His face blank. Fingers digging into my bones. Then he dropped me. I slammed onto the floor, watching his feet move farther and farther away from me. Fighting back the sob that clawed at my throat.

He paused at the door. And when Edison spoke again, he sounded almost friendly. Almost happy. "I left you a present on the dresser. Hope you like it."

CHAPTER 32

I DON'T KNOW if it was minutes or hours until I could move again. All I knew was that it was still dark. I'd never felt this way after a fight before. Not after sparring. Not even after skirmishes in Tierra Muerta. My soul had been scooped out to make room for the pain.

But Edison's words kept repeating in my mind—taunting me. *A present.*

Finally, I crawled over to the bed. Using the post, I pulled myself to my feet. Then I hobbled to the dresser.

A silk scarf had been draped across something—red splotches seeping through the bright fabric. My empty stomach churned again as I forced myself to pull it away. And there he was. Grimm. His wings sprawled at a horrible, unnatural angle. His head was smashed in, wires fused with blood.

I let the hurt of it saturate my own body, propping myself up against the dresser as my whole body sagged with it. Visions of Tasch, wires and tubes stretching from her body, transposed themselves over Grimm's broken corpse. Magnifying the impossibility of what Edison had done. And the question rang out in my mind—asking itself over and over:

How could he?

Edison had killed Grimm—a creature he'd brought to life. A friend.

"I'm so sorry." I stroked his lovely golden breast feathers. "He did it to hurt me. Not you."

I took Grimm in my arms and the light caught his wings—shimmering blue and silver. He was beautiful, even now. I carried him over to the fireplace and tucked him between the lengths of wood. My hands shook as I struck the match. Another funeral pyre.

The room filled with the stench of burned flesh and the sting of smoke. I let them choke me for a minute before flinging open the doors to both balconies.

Then I turned the water on in the tub, as hot as it would go. When it was full, I lowered my body into the steaming, scalding water. I bit my already split lip, refusing to scream. Refusing to cry.

I would burn it off of me. Whatever I'd been to Edison, whatever he'd been to me, I would burn it away. Then I would burn him.

CHAPTER 33

I WOKE UP aching and cold. My right eye was almost swollen shut, and my mouth was mushy and sore. I felt around for blankets—pain searing through my arm—and pulled them over me. Then I went back to sleep.

The next time I woke, a door slammed downstairs and there were footsteps. I fumbled under my pillow for my knife and forced myself to sit up.

But it was only Riya. "You missed morning practice and we were afraid something—"

Then she *really* saw me and, from the shock on her face, I got a pretty good idea what I must've looked like.

"Oh, Leica." Riya said my name in a hushed whisper.

"I don't want your pity." I couldn't take it from her. Not the same girl who'd chopped her hair so she could be like me.

"Never pity." And Riya crawled onto the bed with me—her long legs curling under her as she faced me. "Not for you."

She reached up to stroke my hair. I held myself stiff, anticipating pain, but she was careful of my bruises and cuts. "This doesn't make you weak. You know that, right?"

I squeezed my eyes shut. That was exactly what it made me. Weak and stupid. I had trusted Edison. Worse than that, I had *fallen* for him.

"Let me tell you a story. There was a girl who lived in Pleiades and an older boy there who fancied her. But there was something wrong with him . . . a violence behind his eyes. For a while, the girl felt safe because, by law, the boy couldn't touch her, since they were born in the same building. But sometimes he caught her alone, in the garden or the stairwell, and he whispered things in her ear. She was a quiet person . . . shy . . . and she didn't tell anyone.

"When he was twenty, he became one of the Abuelos' guards and then I didn't *dare* tell." Riya got a glint in her eyes as she took ownership of the story. "I knew that I had two choices. I could stay and live in fear of the day when he did more than whisper. Or I could marry someone I didn't love and flee my building.

"But I knew there'd be no happiness in either choice . . . so I made a third one. *If* I was going to give myself to someone, then I was going to do it on my own terms. So, one day in the Reclamation Fields, I smiled at a Curador. And that was that.

"Now. Do you think I'm weak?" And her chin stuck out stubbornly, daring me to say so. When I shook my head, she said, "No. There's the courage it takes to fight—you're good at that. A natural. But there's also the courage to endure."

Then she gathered me up like Taschen had so many times before, laying my head in her lap. And the image of Tasch's face, half conscious, contorted in pain, blazed against my closed eyelids. A tear rolled down my cheek and soaked into the blanket.

Then I was truly crying—great choking sobs that made my sore ribs sorer. The sound was more animal than human, and I despised myself. In the midst of it, the words that had been chasing themselves in my mind broke through like a wail. "How could I have gotten it so wrong?"

All that time we'd spent talking about my sisters . . . and Edison had *known* Tasch was sick and sedated in that ward. How could I not have seen the monster that he was?

How do you move forward after this? How do you trust anything again? I looked up at Riya, hoping for answers.

"You want me to tell you it's all your fault." She wiped my tears with the heel of her hand. "Or maybe you want me to grant you absolution. But those are not mine to give. Sadly, *this* is the best I've got to give." And Riya handed me a tissue, a little smile on her face as I blew my nose.

"And this." She kissed my forehead, careful to avoid a nasty bruise.

"Now, come on," Riya said, easing me off her lap and going to the closet. "I'll help you get ready."

"For what?" I hurt everywhere. I pulled the blankets up to my chin. I was in no condition to go anywhere.

She kept her voice light as she rummaged through my clothes—studying skirts and dresses with an evaluating eye. "Then you're going to hide here? Let him win?"

Like Nik in his trees. It sounded nice to just disappear. "Can't I stay? For a little while?" I was like a kid, begging her mother for permission.

"You can. But know this, if you make room for the fear, it will build a home inside you. It'll get comfortable in there, making up a bed for itself. Pushing other parts of you aside so it can stretch out. You don't want that."

And for an instant, I saw the war that raged inside Riya. Not just now, but always. Each day, a battle against her fear.

Still I couldn't force myself out of the bed. My face burned as the words spilled out. "I don't want them to see me like this."

"Leica, the Kisaengs admire you because you're a survivor. We're under no illusion that you're some kind of invincible god."

She didn't mean for her words to hurt, but they did. *Invincible.* It stung because that's exactly what I'd thought. That I was too clever and too strong to be hurt like this. That I was *better* than this.

Riya pulled a dress out of the closet. "In practice, when you knocked me down, what did you do next?"

I didn't want to answer. I already knew where she was going with this. "I asked if you were okay . . . then I told you to get back up."

"Yes. And that's what I'm telling you to do now."

"But what if I'm not okay?"

"Sometimes, the only way to find out is to get on your feet."

The Sanctum courtyard went silent when I limped in. I had no energy for a stoic entrance.

"Rough night?" Marisol sneered as she passed, the Ellas tittering around her. But I heard the tension in her voice. A flash of fear beneath her taunt.

And Edison's words echoed in my head: *Marisol was right. You aren't worth my time.*

Maybe it wasn't just Grimm who gave me away. Ignoring my bruised muscles, my hand shot out and grabbed hers. Stopping her. Forcing her to face me. But I couldn't make her meet my eyes.

And her avoidance spoke the truth: Marisol had gotten her revenge. She'd told Edison about the kiss.

"Thank you for letting me know where we stand." I spoke in a calm voice, empty of emotion. "For showing me what my friendship means to you."

Shame burned on her face and I knew Marisol was truly seeing the bruises on my body. She blinked hard and pulled her hand out of my grip.

I let her go.

Riya helped me sit down on the grass and I sucked in air as my bruised hip hit the ground. Then Oksun came over and had a whispered conversation with Riya. I lay down—letting the cool grass soothe my muscles—and turned my back to them. But I could feel Oksun standing over me.

"I got dressed. I dragged myself here," I said without opening my eyes. "What else do you want from me?"

"I want you to get up. I want you to fight!" Steel ran through Oksun's voice.

Then, more gently, Riya said, "Leica, people are waiting for you."

"For what?" I squinted up at her.

"For training," Riya said.

I sat up slowly, looking at my two friends, Oksun's fierce square face untouched by sympathy, Riya's hopeful but determined. Behind the pair of them, the Kisaengs were gathering. Not ten or fifteen—but sixty-some of them, arranged in four neat rows. Everyone, except Marisol's circle. Then June glided into the lineup as well.

I actually laughed. "You've got to be kidding. I'm living proof that those moves are worthless."

"No." Oksun's jaw was clenched, her compact frame braced for confrontation. She shoved a strand of hair behind her ear. "What you've proven is that all Kisaengs are vulnerable. And we must do whatever we can to make ourselves strong."

"And what about when it still isn't enough?" I pushed myself to my feet, pointing to my face. Pulling up my shirt to show the red welts on my ribs. "How can I help them if I can't even help myself?"

"Fine." A chord of anger shook Oksun's voice. "Go ahead. Explain to them that it's fun to *pretend* we're fighters, but when someone beats the crap out of us, we just lie down and give up."

"Leave me alone." My hands balled into fists. My legs were shaking, but at least they still held me. "You know nothing about this!"

"Oh yeah? You think you're broken? You think you're pathetic? Well, I'm starting to think you're right!" Oksun shouted the words at me, but it was *Edison's* voice I heard. *Edison's* words screaming accusations in my head.

How could you?

Rage numbed my body and I went for her. I punched—one, two—and lashed out with my foot.

Oksun blocked it all. I swept my leg out again and she hooked it with her own. I fell backward and Oksun grabbed me. I thought she was catching me, but instead she yanked me forward and flipped me over her shoulder.

But she didn't slam me to the ground. She just held me there.

Then Oksun lowered me gently to my feet, her eyes glinting with a savage anger. "You started something here. I won't let you tell these girls it was all a lie."

Then I saw what I hadn't before: This had happened to every Kisaeng. If not in violence, then in words. In groping hands. In the threat of disappearing.

Riya squeezed my fingers, lending me her courage. "Come on. They're waiting."

Then I was in front of them, every eye fixed on me. But there was no pity there. No disappointment. They stood with their chins up. Eyes somber. Waiting for my instructions.

"Okay. Today is about truth. Sometimes your opponent is stronger than you. And no matter how fast you are, or how smart you fight, you still can't win. But you still fight, in whatever way you can. So. Let's talk about how to anticipate an attack . . ."

By the time practice was over, I felt stronger. Not to say that my sore muscles didn't hurt more, because they did. But I was ready to figure out what came next.

And the conclusion my mind kept coming back to was, be-fore I did anything else—before I even came up with a plan or started surveillance or made a move against Edison—I needed to tell someone about what I'd found. In case something happened to me, someone else needed to know about LOTUS. After Edi-son . . . and Marisol . . . I hated the idea of trusting anyone else, but I couldn't risk Taschen getting abandoned down there.

Oksun and Riya were getting bowls of soondubu stew from the Sanctum food synthesizer. The spicy, homey scent made my mouth water as I pulled them aside. "We have to talk."

We carried our bowls to a quiet spot on the grass. While I tried chewing with just one side of my mouth, I figured out where to start. Finally, I looked at the pair of them and said, "I know where the missing Kisaengs are."

CHAPTER 34

RIYA FROZE, chopsticks halfway to her mouth. Oksun put her spoon down. I had their full attention.

I started with Lotus and the Indignos' theory that the Curadores were infecting people as a form of population control. "When Jenner showed me the Genetics Lab, it was clear the Curadores had that kind of technology, but I still had no clue *how* they might be doing it. *Or* how to stop it. Then Oksun told me about the missing Kisaengs and I did some more digging."

I wondered if I'd have to explain about Nik, but apparently it was common knowledge that Edison had a brother living in the Gardens. The forest might be officially off-limits, but that simply made it an irresistible place to sneak off to for a rendezvous. So I told them about my visit and the files Nik had showed me. About the Kisaengs' harvested ova and Olivia's infected status. I hesitated when I got to the part about Oksun's own pending status, but now seemed like the time for complete honesty.

Oksun took it in stride, like it didn't surprise her—and maybe it didn't. Though I wouldn't expect anything less from her. Finally, I got to the part with Tasch and finding the isolation rooms hidden behind the LOTUS door.

I watched my own emotions play out across their faces as I described it. Suspicion. Horror. And in the end, outrage. Talking about the underground ward made its existence more awful and more bearable at the same time—at least I was no longer alone in this.

"But wasn't Taschen dead?" Riya said, trying to understand.

"Lotus thought so, but obviously not," I said.

"Do you think Edison's trying to find a cure for Red Death? Using Citizens and Kisaengs as test subjects?" Oksun asked.

"Maybe. But here's the thing . . . the Curadores don't simply need a cure for Red Death." My brain had been mulling this over for hours. I thought back to what Edison and Jenner had told me that first morning while the flys tested my blood. "They've been isolated for too long . . . they have no resistance to anything out-side the Dome. Jenner as much as said they weren't even both-ering with Red Death anymore. Instead Jenner's been trying to build some kind of uber-Curador who'll be smart enough to fix the Dome."

"So what the hell's happening down there, then?" Oksun asked.

"Well, Nik told me that he and Edison gave up trying to fix things and were looking for ways to escape them instead. So the only answer I can come up with is that Edison is trying to create an uber-Curador as well. One that has all the right genes to make him immune to . . . well . . . everything."

"Is that even possible?" Riya twisted a bracelet made out of tiny plastic animals as she talked.

"I have no idea," I said.

"We're still sidestepping a huge issue here. *If* Edison is infecting the Citizens and *if* he is killing them off . . ." Oksun jabbed her spoon in the air for emphasis. "How is he also experimenting on them?"

I shook my head. "Lotus said that Taschen's symptoms had been strange. Like Red Death, but not. It's what made them so suspicious about the outbreak in the first place. That's gotta have something to do with it."

"Well, if I'm 'pending' I'm not about to wait around to learn the details firsthand," Oksun said.

"Agreed," Riya said, nodding. Then they both turned to me. "So. What's the plan?"

That afternoon, I could barely make myself step inside my bedroom. I'd been fine in the bright open of the Sanctum, conjuring up plans and strategies. But in here, the brutality of last night was still hanging in the air. Waiting for me.

I threw open the doors of the front and back balconies, trying to purge the place while I started putting the room back together. Untangling blankets. Righting chairs. Sweeping ash back into the fireplace.

Something glinted in the grate. I knelt down, groaning as pain shot through my hip, and I dug through the soot.

It was a long, fringed filament. One of Grimm's feathers. I pulled it out, feeling through the soft ash. Grimm's body had burned and the thing that had been his brain had melted, but an array of thin metal wing feathers remained. I collected them all and took them out to the porch to brush them off.

A movement in the woods caught my eye. Nik was standing there—just inside the tree line. Barely even bothering to stay hidden. Did he know what Edison had done to me? My heart clutched in my chest. Did he know that Grimm was dead?

I held up a hand for him to stay put. Then, tucking all but one of the feathers in the bottom drawer of my dresser—where I'd stashed the book of fairy tales, Lotus's necklace, and the scope—I went down to face him.

The first thing he said when he saw me was "Thank God." Immediately followed by "I'm going to kill him."

And he meant it. Nik's eyes flashed and it was disturbing to see the same buried rage there that'd exploded from Edison. I took a step back, reminding myself that they didn't just *look* alike. They were essentially the same person. *Clones.*

"No. There's been enough death." And gently, I handed him Grimm's feather.

Nik's head bowed as his ran his thumb across the feather, wiping soot from the silvery filament. But before his dreadlocks shrouded his face, I'd seen the tears there. And I knew I was wrong. Edison and Nik may have started out the same, but life had forged them into very different people.

"I'm sorry." I pulled Nik deeper into the trees so there was no chance of us being seen together.

"He can't do this and get away with it." Nik glared at me. At the world.

"He won't. But things are going to get worse before they get better. If you want to help me get retribution, then I need to trust you. And I can't do that until you answer some questions."

"Okay." Nik held himself impossibly still—like he was afraid if he made the wrong move, I might send him away.

"Yesterday, you told me about the laboratories down in the tunnels where you and Edison made Grimm." Nik nodded again, and I went on. "Did you know he was still doing experiments down there?"

Nik looked like he was summoning his courage. "I suspected. And yesterday, when I saw the files on the Kisaengs, I was afraid he might be using the place again."

"I found more than just Kisaengs down there." I kept my voice neutral, my eyes on his face. I couldn't help but hear Edison's warning about Nik in my mind. *A bad copy of me. Twisted.*

But there was real fear in Nik's eyes. The yellow flecks burning bright. "Please . . . you have to tell me what he's done."

I was convinced Nik had no idea about the captive Citizens, but there was still a shadow in Nik's eyes—something he was holding back. For the second time that day, I relived the nightmare. Telling him about finding Taschen in the spiderweb of tubes and wires.

"Oh God." Nik's whole body shook, but he wasn't crying. It was more like the grief was quaking through him. And suddenly I wished I could hold him. Wished I could hold his pain for him.

"This is my fault. This is *all my fault*. Edison's experiments . . ." He touched the blackened feather in his hand. "Grimm. Even you."

He put his hand against my swollen cheek, barely brushing my skin with his fingertips—as if it hurt him to touch me. "This is why I stay in there!"

"*Edison* infected the Citizens. *Edison* killed Grimm and attacked me. This is not *your* fault." And I leaned into his hand where it cradled my cheek, turning my face to kiss his palm.

He jerked away like I'd burned him. Stepping back. "You don't know! You don't know me."

"Nik!"

But Nik was gone. Fleeing back into his trees. Leaving me alone.

CHAPTER 35

SLEEP DIDN'T COME that night. I held my knife close as I lay unblinking on the bed. Then on a blanket on the floor. Then the chair downstairs. Every noise, every imagined shadow held me hostage. And of all the things Edison had done to me, that was what I resented most.

That he'd made me afraid.

Dawn finally came, bringing the relief of light. I stumbled back upstairs and drew a bath—slipping down into the warm weight of it. Letting myself sink below the surface until the whole world was muffled and far away. But the comfort was short-lived. As I got out of the tub, I pulled the towel tight around me, careful to hide my battered body from the mirrors. But I couldn't cover my face.

Swollen and grotesque, my lip bulged out. A cut ran across my cheek. A bruise was purpling just under my eye.

Edison had done this to me. This man who'd saved me in the flood in Tierra Muerta. This person who I'd let touch me. Who I'd touched in return. Who I'd told my most important stories to. He had turned and done *this* to me.

And what about me? What had I done? I'd *known* something

was wrong inside the Dome, I'd known that Edison had lied and kept secrets and still I let him distract me with his radio and his smile.

No. I would not let Edison win. I would not hate *myself* for the things he had done.

I made myself think about Tasch, waiting for me to come back for her. About all those Citizens lying in the LOTUS ward under the ground. About the missing Kisaengs, stolen before they'd barely had a chance to live.

Anger seared through me, cauterizing the shame. I curled my six-fingered hands into fists. Dad had taught me long ago: *Shame is like putting a weapon in your enemy's hand and asking them to beat you with it.*

I would not give Edison any more weapons to use against me.

CHAPTER 36

IN THE SANCTUM, we stepped up to training with fighting sticks. A few at a time, the Kisaengs scoured the Salvage Hall for old chair legs, metal rods, anything that would work. We shared them out until they'd gathered enough weapons for everyone—working with sticks early in the morning when Curadores were least likely to wander by. Luckily, no one paid much attention to how Kisaengs passed the time.

Within the walls of the Sanctum, though, I didn't need to give an explanation for the added intensity or the added stealth. As far as the Kisaengs were concerned, my bruises were reason enough. There would come a time when I had to tell them the whole terrible story, but first I wanted them to have the tools to do something about it.

Once June had weapons in her hands, she was a natural. Her arms were already incredibly powerful—since she used them for, well, *everything*—and her board allowed her to be unpredictable.

After she knocked three girls off their feet, I stepped up. "Okay, then. Let's see what you got."

June gave me an evil grin that didn't quite match her glamorous appearance. She tucked her skirts into the straps that kept her secured to her board and said, "Let's go!"

We circled around each other, and I saw her immediate advantage. While I had to watch the uneven ground, June glided seamlessly. Trying to get a feel for her, I made my first move—swinging out with my right stick. She instantly dropped half a meter, letting the blow breeze right over her head.

"Oh, you think you're clever!" I grinned. I hadn't had a challenge like this since sparring with Jaesun and it felt good to think on my feet.

"No. I *know* I'm clever." She was floating at waist height now and I jabbed down at her. Her board swung sideways, and she landed a blow in my ribs.

June laughed, a deep hoot of pleasure. And I wondered if her usual calm softness was simply her own version of armor against the world.

We continued to circle around each other dizzyingly. I jabbed here and there, only occasionally making contact. But June was relentless, her board zipping everywhere, driving me backward. Tension pulled tight around us, like the excitement of the Festival ring. And though I didn't take my eyes off June, I knew everyone was watching us. They couldn't help it.

June was faster, but I had years of training and it didn't take me long to learn her tricks. I lunged forward with my left stick, and like I expected, June dodged to the right. I let my weight carry me as I spun my left foot up, landing the full force of my kick right in her stomach.

Her board flew backward, flipping over, and her straps came loose. I cringed as June was thrown off the board, her body hitting the ground with a thud. It was awful.

"June! I'm so sorry! Are you okay?" I dropped my sticks and rushed over to her.

But to my astonishment, she was almost as quick across the ground—moving on her hands. Before I could even change my momentum, June was back on her board, sticks in hand, flying toward me in a retaliatory attack. A keening war cry flooded from her.

Surprised and weaponless, I stumbled backward. But the ground was nowhere to be found. Flailing midair, I landed unceremoniously with an enormous splash in the creek.

A huge cheer went up from the watching Kisaengs.

"Surrender!" June cried, hovering above the water, grinning down at me. And sitting in the stream, sopping wet, I grinned too. Maybe the Kisaengs *could* be a force to be reckoned with.

Oksun was suspicious of the accelerated training regime. "It looks like you're training an army. You've come up with a plan, haven't you? Just when exactly are you going to share with the other children?" She was smiling, but it was clear she didn't appreciate being kept in the dark.

"All I know for sure is . . . whatever happens, it'll come down to what it always does. A fight," I said. "And to win that fight, we're going to need more than the Kisaengs."

The group I was training had swollen from the original dozen to a consistent sixty or so. And with the new lessons, the atmosphere in the Sanctum had changed overnight. Marisol and her sisters no longer judged who should be able to keep what from the Salvage Hall. At dinner, Marisol's disapproval no longer kept Curadores from seeking out certain Kisaengs. Marisol was back at Edison's side—who thankfully had been keeping his distance—but she didn't try to wield her power. At least not publicly. She had lost the support of the Kisaengs.

Now I looked around us, at the sparring women filling the courtyard with the clack of fighting sticks and staccato shouts. It had been less than a week since we'd stepped up training, but the Kisaengs had already been strong, and they were getting stronger. They were eager students, but I had to admit that wouldn't be enough.

Still, Oksun was right—my sleepless nights had resulted in one benefit. I did have a plan. Or at least the seed of one.

"Do the Curadores ever celebrate any of the Pleiades' festivals? Any loud, boisterous ones?" I asked.

Oksun understood instantly what I was getting at. "Folks distracted on both sides of the glass? Something noisy enough to cover up an invasion, maybe?" She tucked her hair behind both ears and made what I'd started to think of as her "calculating face." "The Kisaengs don't celebrate the traditional holidays, but maybe it's time to get back to our roots. Would Dia de los Muertos give us enough time?"

There were less than two weeks before the celebration of the dead. "It's not a lot of time to prepare, but it'd be perfect. Masks. Bonfires. Fireworks!"

"Did you know that a few of the girls are familiar with explosives?" Oksun raised an eyebrow. "Used to be blasters out in the Reclamation Fields. Me too, actually."

"That I *did not* know." And just like that, the seeds took root.

• • •

After almost a week of barely sleeping, I was delirious and desperate. Every day had been the same. During the day I was myself, strong and powerful. But at night, fear would creep in to sit beside my bed, holding my hand. Riya had said not to make room for fear, but I didn't know how to make it leave. That night, I walked into the trees—the only place I'd ever felt safe inside the Dome.

I hadn't gotten so much as a glimpse of Nik—not since he'd run—and I worried I wouldn't be welcome. Even so, as I entered the shelter of the branches, something loosened in me. The rich smell of moss and green coaxed a sigh from my strangled lungs. And deep in the night, I crept into Nik's garden and collapsed next to the little waterfall that sang of comfort in the dark.

I woke with a blanket lying heavy across me and the sun bright in the sky. And a few meters away—weeding the garden—was Nik.

"Sorry. Was I being too loud?" He dusted off his hands on his pants and came over. "I didn't want you to wake up alone . . . in case you forgot where you were."

He seemed reserved, almost shy. As if we didn't know each other. And maybe Nik had been right about that—maybe we didn't.

Nik's outburst in the forest still hung in the air between us. Feeling awkward, I stood up and folded the soft blue cover. "Thank you for the blanket. I didn't mean to . . . I just . . . I haven't been sleeping."

"No! I'm glad you came." Nik waved the blanket away, leaving me hugging it. "Sit down. Let me get you something."

I climbed up on a boulder near the waterfall and took a deep breath, trying to let the burble of the stream calm my jitters. Nik came back a few minutes later, carrying coffee and croissants. As he handed them to me, he said, "I really am glad you came." And his eyes had genuine relief in them. "I'm glad you feel safe here."

He took a seat next to me on the rock and we sipped our coffee together. The silence was still full of unsaid words, but it was no longer awkward. Our hands lay almost touching on the stone, just centimeters apart. They were so different: his vast and callused, mine small and strange. But I liked the way they looked together, his purpley-black skin against my light brown. They looked right. The only thing ruining it was the scabs on my knuckles from Grimm's talons. A painful reminder of him.

Then Nik tore off a piece of croissant and I noticed something. I grabbed Nik's hand, turning it over in my own.

"What?" Alarm tinged Nik's voice. But I didn't answer.

Nik's palm was unblemished. His calluses were still there, but there were no scabs or scratches from the broken glass. No blood. Not even any scars. I checked his other one, in case I'd gotten them confused. It'd been barely a week since he'd cut his hand. Same as me.

"Must be nice to heal so fast," I said, showing him my own scabbed knuckles. "I suppose that's a perk of being genetically engineered?"

Nik looked perplexed for a second, flexing his hand. Then he checked it too, as if expecting to find traces of the wound. "Hmm . . . that's new. I wonder—"

The buzz of flys cut across his words. Instinctively, I scrambled off the boulder, crouching as a huge swarm flew over the clearing.

"Did they see me?" I asked when the noise died away. Clearly, without my permission, fear had still made a home inside me.

"Probably not." There was sadness in Nik's eyes as he helped me out of my hiding spot—like it hurt him to see me cower. "Even if they did, I doubt anyone was paying attention to their visual feed."

But I could see Nik's own fears about my safety making him second-guess his answer.

I returned to my place on the rock, but the calm had evaporated. My thoughts came back to the same problem I'd been turning over in my mind for days. "How good of an eye *do* the flys keep on things inside the Dome?"

"Well, they're not like Grimm." And Nik's forehead creased as he remembered Grimm was dead. "They can't see much in the dark. And Ada and the Mothers have been systematically interrupting their video signals for a while now. Fuzzing what the Curadores can see and hear with static so the Mothers have some semblance of privacy and freedom. Edison and the others think it's simply a result of the flys breaking down . . . and a lot of it is . . . but Ada's definitely helping the process along." Nik paused. "I guess what I'm saying is . . . it depends."

Then he went quiet. I took a sip of coffee, filling the pause, but I could feel Nik's eyes on me. "You've come up with a plan, then?" he said. "To save your sister?"

I nodded, but I wondered how much to say. Nik might not love what Edison or the Curadores had done, but that didn't mean he wanted to be an active participant in the destruction of his own home.

"Well, I'd like to get back out to Pleiades through the tunnel I found. If we were only trying to save Tasch, we could do it from inside the Dome, no problem. But if we want to save everyone, then . . ."

"You'll need outside help," Nik finished.

"Oksun mentioned Dia de los Muertos, and it seems like too good of an opportunity to pass up." I kept my voice purposely light, tearing off a bit of croissant and popping it in my mouth.

"What kind of opportunity?" Nik's voice was cautious.

I kept my answer vague. I wasn't ready to risk Nik knowing the extent of our plan. And until I talked to Sarika, nothing was certain. "An opportunity for the Citizens to get our people and our power back."

"Well, if you're going out there again, we should talk to Ada. She's the expert at getting around this place unnoticed."

"But Ada hates me. I heard the two of you fighting."

"No. Ada hates *Edison*. She didn't trust you because you were his Kisaeng. Your circumstances are different now. She'll help."

"How do you know?"

"'Cause I've known Ada for a long time . . . pretty much forever."

"I thought you and Edison were mostly alone growing up."

"When we were younger, we got sent back to the Complex for a few weeks at a time . . . to 'socialize' us. Most of the other kids stayed away. But Ada was fascinated by us. She loves all things gadgety and when she found out about Grimm, she helped us with his control systems. Edison and I were great at creating artificial muscles or lightweight wings, after all we'd been basically *raised* in a biotech lab, but Grimm's electronic hardware was a mess. Luckily, Ada's genius with that sort of thing . . . taught us a ton."

"The three of you were friends?" After the venom in her voice, it was hard to imagine. "Then why does she hate Edison so much?"

Nik didn't answer. He put down his coffee and turned to face me on the boulder. "Listen, I have to tell you something. All I ask is that you stay and hear me out. Then you can decide if you still want me to be part of this."

His tone made me nervous and I wrapped my hands around my coffee cup as if it could give me strength.

"I didn't know Edison was experimenting on your people, but I wasn't surprised . . . because I experimented on them first."

"What?" I stood up fast, my coffee cup smashing on the rocky ground.

"I was trying to help. Jenner had stopped trying to treat Red Death years ago and, intellectually, we *knew* Citizens were still dying from it. But when we sent Grimm out to Pleiades, we *saw* it. I'd spent my whole life hearing about Red Death, knowing it was why we were trapped inside the Dome, but seeing it . . . it was horrible.

"I thought if we could just get near enough . . . if we could study the disease up close, then maybe we could find a cure for it. So I talked Edison into sneaking out with me in one of the mag-flys. We put on isolation suits, went into Pleiades, and collected one of the bodies for cremation. But instead of burning it, we took it to our lab to study."

"You stole a body?" And I was horrified, imagining the body left unburned, its soul locked away inside its bones. Nik and Edison slicing open the decaying flesh.

"Yes. But its systems were already deteriorating . . . too badly damaged to teach us anything. We tried again, this time taking someone from quarantine who was alive but unconscious . . . the disease advanced enough for our deception.

"Then we had the reprocessors replicate the equipment from

Jenner's isolation rooms, the ones he used with incoming Kisaengs, and hooked the patient up to it. The Citizen was already near death, and I told myself that we were merely prolonging his life. I became obsessed, chronicling the symptoms through Grimm's observations in Pleiades, then studying them in the actual Citizen. And I studied the DNA of Red Death, discovering that the reason it was so deadly, the reason we couldn't find a cure, is that it's a hybrid. A mutant like Edison and me."

"You mean someone *made* Red Death?"

"I'm sure of it . . . two different diseases spliced together. And when I understood that, I knew how to create the vaccine. For the first time in my life, I felt like the genius Jenner had created me to be! Godlike! My destiny wasn't to save the Dome, but to save all of Gabriel. To bring an end to suffering.

"I couldn't wait to see Jenner's face when he understood what his prodigy had accomplished. So the very next day I doctored a vat of chiken with the antigens and sent Grimm out into Pleiades to witness the miracle." Nik's face went stony.

I had lived the next part of the story. I knew what happened. "But they died instead." A numb horror crept over my body. "Hundreds of us died. My father . . ."

"Yes." The fear had left Nik's eyes now. He had stopped hiding. "And your mother. I watched your mother die."

And a memory emerged—one I'd kept locked away—of that nightmare of a day. People had been getting sick all morning, but no one would tell me and my sisters anything. Sarika ordered us to stay inside the apartment, but I was determined to find out what was going on. I snuck out to the courtyard and waited for my mother to come home from the Reclamation Fields.

I screamed when I saw her. She came staggering in through the gates, her eyes red. Face rashy and impossibly swollen. And I ran away from her, like a coward, leaving her to collapse in the dirt. And as I ran, Grimm was there. His shadow hovering over me. I remembered thinking he was protecting me. That *he* was the one that'd kept me from dying too.

"No."

"It turned out there was a protein in the vaccine that was *so similar* to one inside the human body that it confused the immune system . . . it couldn't figure out what it was supposed to be attacking. Like a massive allergic reaction, the vaccine turned the body against itself . . . *and* left its systems defenseless to Red Death as well. The response was immediate and lethal." There was such sorrow in Nik's face as he spoke, but he was unflinching as he faced me. "I killed your mother. I killed all of them.

"That was the day I walked into the forest and stayed. I hid away in here working on my plants. Trying to forget. Trying in some small way to make up for what I'd done. But I can never atone for that."

Grief was a tangible weight sitting on my chest and I reminded myself to breathe. It was like watching my parents die all over again. And in some ways Nik's betrayal was worse than Edison's. Because it was not complete. Because I could not hate him.

"I stayed. I listened. Is that everything?" I asked.

Nik nodded.

Without a word, I turned my back on him and walked away.

CHAPTER 37

EARLY THE NEXT MORNING, the Sanctum was filled with the rhythm of cracking sticks and shouting Kisaengs, but I wasn't registering any of it.

"What's wrong with you?" Oksun asked after she knocked me off my feet for the second time.

"Sorry," I mumbled, brushing dirt off my tunic. "Let's take a break. I don't know where my mind is today."

In fact, I knew exactly where it was. It was frozen in that moment by the waterfall—Nik telling me he killed my parents. The blade of it still cut into me. Not just because he was responsible for so much of my hurt. But because I'd convinced myself that somehow Nik was a refuge from all of this.

"Good. I wanna talk to you about the explosives anyway."

"Explosives?" I tossed my fighting sticks onto the grass. Oksun had my full attention.

"Right. I talked to the other blasters and we don't think it'll be hard to get our hands on the right ingredients. The reprocessors synthesize all kinds of chemicals for the labs and none of them are tracked very closely."

My mind was whirling to catch up. "You talked to the other Kisaengs? Do you think you can trust them?"

"I thought we agreed." Oksun seemed taken aback by my questions. "Yesterday, we said we'd plan the attack for Dia de los Muertos. I haven't told anyone about the LOTUS wards yet . . . I was just feeling people out. And, of course, I only spoke to girls I trust."

"Infiltration and rescue," I corrected. "Not *attack*."

"Leica, the Curadores have been infecting, kidnapping, and experimenting on our fellow Citizens. On our families. On your sister. They aren't just gonna to let us grab our people and walk out of here. Either we do whatever it takes to get back what is ours, or we stay silent and do nothing. There is no in-between. If we do this, people are going to get hurt and no amount of semantics is going to change that."

While the Kisaengs punched and shouted and practiced maneuvers around us, my mind spun. "This is going to change everything, isn't it? All I've been thinking about is the details. How do we distract the Curadores? How do we get Tasch and everyone out of the wards? I hadn't thought at all about what happens after. It's going to turn this place upside down."

Oksun nodded. "Not just inside the Dome. If we bring these Citizens back, if we fight the Curadores, the whole Pleiades system of reclamation and trading will fall apart."

"Can we really do that to our own people?"

"Let me ask you something . . . the Abuelos called you Corrupted, they forced you to spend your life scouting in the Reclamation Fields; then they exiled you. What exactly about our way of life do you want to save?"

I blinked hard. I had no answer for her.

Oksun put her hand on my shoulder. "Let's put it back together better this time."

"I'd like that." And I imagined the grove in the Indigno camp, thick with trees. Fruit heavy on the branches. But the only way to make that happen was to get to work. I focused on the explosives. "The way I see it, we need to limit movement in three key locations. The party will be the main distraction, but we'll need a way to trap people *inside* the Sanctum once we get them there."

"Small detonations along the outer arm of the spiral should do the trick."

"Good. Next, we'll need a way to shut down movement through the streets of the Dome so the Curadores have difficulty sending reinforcements."

Oksun grinned. "Easy. We'll hit the magfly lines."

"And third, we'll need to collapse the underground tunnels once the wards have been infiltrated and we've rescued the Citizens. We don't want anyone trying to follow them out," I said.

"If *we* are going to be the ones distracting the Curadores at Dia de los Muertos, who's doing the infiltrating?" Oksun asked.

And I smiled. "Now, *that* would be my other sister."

If only I could get out of the Dome again to let her know about it.

It would've been naive to think Edison wasn't keeping an eye on me—after all, he had flys, Kisaengs, and Curadores at his disposal. So even though the idea of sneaking out to Pleiades seemed like a huge risk, I could see no other option. For this plan to work, I needed to get to Sarika.

But when I got back to my room that night, there was a note waiting for me.

I don't blame you. But please let me help. Ada is expecting you
at the Complex at ten.

Riya and I walked arm in arm, chatting, trying to look casual. The Mothers' Complex was impressive and a little ominous. There were at least ten buildings inside the walled compound and all of them were dark.

"Tell me why *I'm* here again?" Riya asked. She'd started picking up habits from Oksun and now she gave me a wry eyebrow raise.

"Moral support."

Suddenly, the gate leading into the Complex swung open. In spite of the lights that lined the sidewalk, I couldn't see anyone inside.

"Come in if you're coming," Ada's voice hissed, "before someone sees you."

We hurried through the gate and it swung shut behind us. But there was still no one. Then I heard the voice again and spotted a speaker on the wall. "Walk straight up the path. Third building on your left."

I tried to peek inside the windows as we passed the other buildings, but I only saw my and Riya's reflections in the dark glass. Were there children sleeping inside? Classrooms?

We knocked at the door to the third building and it was answered by a pregnant woman in a cream dress. Despite the late hour, a few children were playing a dice game on the floor behind her and a little girl glanced up at me as I came in. She had no hair, like Aaliyah. Another boy stared at me with serious, mismatched eyes—one bright blue, one green. If Curadores didn't want Kisaengs to pollute the DNA, then why these Corruptions?

Then a cold, treacherous idea crept into my heart. When I'd learned about my scar, about what the unfertilized ova were used for, I'd taken comfort in one thought alone. That they wouldn't be turned into more Leicas. That my DNA wouldn't be used for some terrible purpose.

But how did I know that for certain? After all, hadn't Edison told me that Gabriel had made me better? More evolved?

"Come with me," the woman said. Feeling sick, I watched the children for another second before I forced myself to turn away— the rattle of dice following me down the dim flight of stairs into a brightly lit basement. *First, let's just make sure they all live through this. Let's make sure we all do.*

"Who's that?" Ada looked up from a panel of blinking lights and pointed at Riya. It was the first time Ada and I had actually met, and she was even more intimidating up close. "I was only expecting one of you."

"We come in pairs." Riya's voice was hard. The training had done more than teach her moves.

"You can trust Riya," I added.

"I don't even trust you, why would I trust her?"

"Because you don't have a choice," I said. "We're already here."

Ada looked at us both. Then she shook her head—as if it was against her better judgment—and said, "Suit yourself."

"I will. Thanks." And I gave her my most dazzling smile.

Riya gazed around the room. "What is all this?"

It looked a bit like the main computer room in the Genetics Lab. Except there were no flys here and everything was cobbled together with bare wires. Ancient monitors covered the walls, showing fuzzy snapshots of the Dome: The gate outside the Complex. The Promenade. The Villages.

"This is where we keep track of what happens in the Dome," Ada said.

"Why?" I asked. There were about ten other Mothers down in the basement, cream dresses swishing efficiently as they checked monitors or dismantled old computers or soldered circuit boards.

"Because *it's* keeping track of us," Ada said matter-of-factly. "The women of Ad Astra are practically prisoners of the Dome. We serve only one purpose, to carry and bear children. For centuries, we've had no choice in the matter. The Curadores have always made sure there were enough of us to sustain the population, but not enough to fight back."

It sounded eerily familiar to the Indigno theories about controlling the Citizen populations.

"But things have changed." Ada gestured at the screens around us. "The Dome is breaking down. There are gaps and holes in the system now and we plan to take advantage of them. To take control of them . . . first the flys, then the reprocessors, then the whole damn computer."

I was confused. "But Nik said that no one could fix the computer because no one knew how to reprogram it."

"True. Even if we seize control from the Curadores, the Dome will still be doomed. That's the only reason we're talking to you."

"And the Curadores have no clue?" Blue computer light reflected in Riya's eyes as she gazed around the room.

"Well, thanks to Leica here, they know some of what we're up to. She so kindly told her boyfriend that I was doing a little browsing down in the Salvage Hall."

My face burned. "I had no idea—"

"Yes, yes, so Nik said. Luckily, we have decoy stashes set up. They found a few things, but nothing important."

"It's hard to believe that *no one* besides me has noticed," I said.

"You have to understand," Ada said. "The Curadores are conditioned to ignore us as much as possible. In their minds, Mothers are merely incubators. Why else do you think they have Kisaengs? If they really looked at us . . . if they remembered we were women with thoughts and desires and ambitions . . . they'd risk remembering they're holding their own people hostage. And until we're ready, we're more than happy being ignored."

"Let them underestimate you." I repeated one of my core training lessons. Despite all our differences, Ada and I were the same kind of fighter. "These gaps and holes you mentioned . . . I'm hoping you can help me take advantage of them."

"Of course you are. But first, I want something from you." Ada flipped a switch and there was a squealing noise punctuated by scraps of distorted radio transmissions. It poured through every speaker, filling the room, until I covered my ears. I'd never heard the sound before, but it was exactly how Edison had described the scrambled transmission from Earth.

She shut it off and looked at me. "Well, what is it?"

"Why are you asking me?" I watched her carefully, trying to figure out how much Ada already knew about the radio—information was one of my few assets at the moment. I sympathized with the Mothers, but I had no idea what their ultimate agenda was. If they did have the ability to commandeer the computer system, that made them hugely powerful allies. But until I knew what they intended to *do* with that power, I wanted to hold on to whatever leverage I had.

"Because about four months ago, we picked up a transmission from you from out in Tierra Muerta. Your voice squawked across all the Curador frequencies, saying 'Hello? This is Ad Astra. We're alive!' We'd never picked up an outside transmission before, but since then we've been monitoring all frequencies. So I ask you again. What is it?"

Ada was testing me—I could hear it in her voice. I couldn't risk the Mothers deciding not to help me, so I told the truth.

"It's a coded message. My crew picked it up in a shuttle we found buried beneath the sand dunes. If you had a descrambler, you'd know that it said, 'Lotus Colony, this is Homebase. You are under temporary quarantine. Enter verification and transmit on priority frequency so emergency evacuations can be coordinated.'"

Riya stared at me. I hadn't told her or Oksun about the message. In the last week, I'd been too busy with happenings inside the Dome to give much thought to the outside.

"Homebase?" Even Riya's round mouth became pointed as she repeated the word.

"Then it *is* Earth," Ada answered. "And that is what you and Edison have been doing in that lab of yours. Trying to make contact."

I tried to hide my surprise. And this time, Ada couldn't keep the smile from slipping onto her face.

"You *are* keeping tabs on the Dome." I was impressed. "Edison heard my transmission too and followed it out to Tierra Muerta." I told them about the voice that'd answered. "I thought he was after the shuttle and radio, but as it turned out, he was more interested in *me*. He knew the radio was important to me and he used it to lure me here. And to keep me distracted."

"Thank you for not lying. Honestly, nothing would give me greater pleasure than to hitch my little rebellion up to yours. But I had to make sure I trusted you first."

"And do you?"

"Enough for now." And the smile became a wide grin that broke up her flawless face. It gave her a mischievous look that made me realize I liked her.

"Well then," I said, my grin matching her own. "Where should we start?"

So Ada, Riya, and I came up with a plan for my journey the next night. It felt good to be taking action. And I could tell that it was satisfying for Ada too.

When it was time for us to leave, Ada walked us out to the gate. Then she pulled me aside.

"I'm sorry about what Edison did to you. And I'm sorry about Grimm too. Did you know I helped build him?" Ada's face wore its haughty mask again, but her voice was softer. "I loved working on him; it was the only time in my life that I was really useful . . . that I felt challenged."

Then she smoothed her hair, touching up her tight bun, and her voice got its bite back. "That was my mistake . . . letting Edison see how much I loved it, how *good* I was at it."

And she wasn't bragging or exaggerating—simply stating a fact.

"But then, he wasn't always the way he is now. At least, I don't think he was. I like to think that once, when we were all kids, that he was my friend."

I wasn't sure where she was going with this.

"Listen, Nik is a good man," she said.

My voice came out hoarse. "This has *nothing* to do with you."

"But it does. Nik is my friend. He was stupid and reckless and people paid the price."

"*My* people." My voice was a growl. "*My* parents. He had no right."

"And you? You have the right to put this Dome in jeopardy? To risk *my* children? They won't survive if the Dome is breached. *I* won't survive. Is that *your* risk to take?"

I was stunned into silence.

"You hadn't thought of that had you? You were too busy thinking of how to save your sister. Jenner raised Nik and Edison as if they were soldiers of the Dome. And when Jenner realized he'd failed, that his prodigies couldn't win the war, he passed that failure on to them. By the time he was done with them, Nik and Edison would've done anything to prove themselves. The difference between the two of them is that Edison *still* would."

Her words rung in my ears, but I shook my head. "You don't know what it's like to lose the people around you. To find out they've been part of some experiment gone wrong."

"I don't know?" Ada's face was incandescent. She grabbed my hand and held it against her rounded stomach. "I have *no idea* what I'm carrying. A clone? Some sort of engineered monster? Edison has pulled us all into his experiments. Every child born in the last year has some kind of anomaly. That is *if* they managed to survive. Some births have not been so lucky." A band of anger pulled her words tight. "For Mother or child."

As I looked at Ada, my own fear about what was done to me—about what was done to Tasch—was split wide. Ada, Nik, Tasch,

Suji, Olivia, me. Even Edison. The same blade had cut us all. "I didn't know. I'm—"

"I don't want your pity." Ada's blue eyes glittered with defiance. "I'm only telling you this so you understand. *This is personal.* So we're happy to help you make your trip out to Pleiades—that sort of thing's right up our alley. But there's a catch."

"What?"

"Whatever you're planning next—and don't even pretend that you don't have some sort of revolution in mind. Whatever you're planning, the Mothers want in."

The idea of more allies was tempting, but I didn't want to be responsible for more people risking their lives. "No . . . I can't drag you into my mess."

"Sweetie," Ada said, adding an eyelash flutter. "It was our mess first."

CHAPTER 38

THE NEXT NIGHT, I dressed in dark pants and a lightweight long-sleeve shirt Riya had whipped up for me. It was going to be cold out there in the desert, but I was also going to be moving fast. I would leave by the same entrance I'd come back up through. Near the old church.

But this time, Ada would be redirecting any flys that were headed toward my trajectory. She'd also found a route that bypassed the LOTUS wards—I'd have to go through some ventilation shafts, but there was less chance of being seen. I was grateful; I didn't want to have to see Tasch only to leave her again.

Ada knew an impressive amount about the underground tunnels and the Dome's security. But as I slipped into the backyard, I was thinking about what else she'd had to say to me. Nik had done terrible things, but his purpose hadn't been terrible. And I felt the blade of my knife slicing through the thin skin at Suji's throat. I had killed too. And I thought of the bombs Oksun was already building. I would kill again.

I turned away from the street and headed into the trees.

Nik's head jerked up when he heard me coming and he set aside the plant he was pruning. "Leica . . ."

"Hating you will not bring my parents back."

He was quiet, waiting for me to continue. His eyes held a tentative hope.

"Thank you for setting up the meeting with Ada. I'm going out to Pleiades to tell Sarika about Taschen. I'd like you to come with me. You know your way though those tunnels."

Nik tensed. Almost like I'd hit him. "You know I can't."

"We can find you an isolation suit."

"It's not that."

"You've hidden in here for long enough. You say you're sorry for what you did to my parents, but you're unwilling to take responsibility and make it right."

"Responsibility? Why else do you think I've shut myself away . . . so I won't do any more harm."

"You didn't mean to infect anyone. You thought you were helping."

"That's exactly the point! I wanted to save your people and I *murdered* them. Worse than that, Edison perverted my idea, using it to infect *more* Citizens. If I don't even know I'm doing the wrong thing, how do I stop myself?" Nik's eyes shone in the lights of the garden. "Jenner *never* should've made us. We're a twisted version of humanity and what we touch becomes twisted in the process."

Edison's enraged words came back to me. "That's exactly the word Edison used . . . 'twisted.' Then he said you were nothing more than a bad copy."

Nik frowned. "That doesn't make sense. *I* was born first. Jenner made sure I was born healthy, then cloned Edison from my cells. Edison *knows* that."

But it made sense to me and I couldn't believe I hadn't seen it before. Edison hated himself. Despite his arrogance and despite his schemes, he was still nothing more than Jenner's failed experiment. This was the truth he spent his life trying to hide from the world, and more importantly, from himself. I remembered the cold hatred in Edison's voice when he said, *He is a mistake.*

I looked at Nik now. His beautiful face full of regret. He hated himself too. But unlike Edison, Nik wore it like a coat around his shoulder. Sewed into every line in his body.

And I found a cold rage in my heart—a malicious hatred I'd never felt for anyone before. Not even the Abuelos who'd exiled me. *Jenner.* His cruelty had forged every joist and girder and bolt of this terrible mess.

"Maybe Jenner *shouldn't* have made you. But he *did*. And yes, like all of us, you have the capacity to do great evil. But you also have the capacity for greatness. You can hide in here, planting a forest of blame and fear around yourself. Or you can come with me and believe you've learned from your mistakes . . . exceed your limitations.

"Now," I said. "Which is it going to be?"

Nik looked stunned by my speech. He blinked and almost laughed. And his answer seemed to surprise even him. "I guess I'm coming with you."

We took the miles through the Reclamation Fields at a slow jog. It was as fast as we could manage with Nik in an isolation suit and me watching out for digsites. It was wonderful to see the lights of the Pleiades towers growing bigger. Nine glowing blue towers standing in a semicircle. Home.

By the time we got to Pleiades, it was long past curfew, so the gates were guarded. We skirted the seven-foot wall until we were right behind Building Nine. Nik boosted me up and I perched on top of the concrete barrier, reaching back down for him. But he was already pulling himself over.

When I dropped down into the Commons, I didn't recognize where I was for a second. There should've only been the compost shed and the quarantine shed back here. But instead we were surrounded by a cluster of six squat buildings.

I peered in the window of one. Rows of beds lined the walls and each of them was filled. Rashes. Bloody eyes. Weeping open wounds as the body broke down.

I peeked in another shed. More beds. More people.

And another. They were *all* quarantine sheds.

"This is Edison's work," I said. Before, I'd been worried about what Sarika would say when she saw us. But now I knew I'd convince her to help us. I had to.

Nik slipped his gloved hand into mine and together we climbed the five flights of stairs, knocking quietly at my family's door.

Sarika opened it, and—despite my revelation about her—homesickness rushed at me. She took one look at me and Nik in his suit, and pulled us inside without a word.

"Who did that to you?" Sarika was looking at my face, anger tight in her voice.

My hands went to my cheek—my bruises had almost faded, but Sarika's eagle eyes had spotted them anyway.

"I'm taking care of it," I told her. She nodded, her long braid pulling her face into an unapologetic ferocity.

Once we'd gotten that out of the way, she moved on to Nik. "What are you thinking? Bringing a Curador here?"

"Sarika, this is Nik. He's going to help us."

She glanced at my fingers, involuntarily, as if I had brought their curse down on us all. And when she spoke, there was a trembling vibrato to her voice, like she used when she spoke at the Rememberings. "What is so terrible that we need help from a Curador?"

"Sarika." I took her hand in mine. "Taschen is alive."

We sat at my family's scrubbed wooden table, and over mugs of strong tea, I told Sarika about the Dome and the LOTUS wards. But it was hard, being in this place that was mine, but not mine. Everything was still in its proper place. The kettle, sitting on its worn pot holder. Dad's fighting sticks crisscrossed on their shelf. Boots lined up by the door. But it didn't smell like home. It was all Sarika now—stringent alcohol and burnt agave.

I pulled my mind away from memories and my eyes from the closed door of the room I'd shared with my sisters, focusing on explaining everything I'd discovered. I tried to tell it all in order so it would make sense, but I was hurrying. It was already past midnight and I could feel the countdown to dawn ticking away.

But Sarika couldn't get past the idea that Taschen was alive. "Then Alejo is right. The disease has changed."

I hesitated. I didn't have any real answers for her, but Nik stepped in.

"I think Edison's infecting people with something mimicking the symptoms of Red Death. Maybe via the food supply? Or the

Curadores who come to collect the dead? Whatever this new virus is, it's shutting down the body with minimal damage . . . sending the person into a coma. It's even possible that they're clinically dead for a short while and he's reviving them. But my guess is that Curadores are the only ones who risk getting close enough to quarantined patients anymore to tell the difference. Once the Citizen appears dead, Edison brings them into the Dome and experiments on them."

"To what end?" Sarika asked.

"The Indignos were right," I said. "The Curadores need us more than we need them . . . that's why the Curadores have been demanding more Finds. They're trying to repair things faster than they break down."

Nik jumped in again. "Edison's trying to create a Curador who can survive outside the Dome. Who's resistant to all possible strains of disease."

Sarika was shaken. I was so used to seeing complete calm on her face—her shrewd eyes seeing and understanding all. But now she looked like a hawk unsure where to strike. "What's your plan, then?"

"Well, if we manage to break into the wards and get our Citizens out, secrecy will not be an option. The ward where I found Tasch isn't the only one on record . . . we won't be able to hide a sudden influx of hundreds of people," I said.

"The Abuelos will never accept them." Sarika's certainty was absolute. "A return of the sick? A questioning of the Curadores motives? No, that'd be tantamount to questioning the Abuelos' authority." I could see she was weighing things out in her mind, as if she was preparing a new recipe. "So it'll have to be a simultaneous attack. Yes, that could work."

"I've been training the Kisaengs inside, and the Mothers—the women from Ad Astra—want to fight as well. We'll need to take control of the Dome at the same time you take control of the Abuelos' council. But Taschen and the other Citizens are our primary concern. They need to be rescued before any fighting starts so they don't get trapped down there." Or so Edison doesn't try to simply destroy the evidence. "That's where Lotus and all the Indignos come in. Everyone else is being watched, so they're the perfect infiltrating force. They can sneak into the wards through the tunnels, same way I got here, and get the Citizens out before anyone knows what happened."

"I'll go out to Tierra Muerta tomorrow," Sarika said.

"Thank you."

"Our people have cooperated with the Curadores long enough and it's kept us from finding redemption. It's time for that to end."

Then Sarika addressed Nik directly for the first time. "Tell me honestly, even if we get our people out, will they survive? And if they do, will they infect the rest of us?"

"Honestly?" Nik took his time, thinking through his answer. "Many of them won't make it, but it's likely some of them will. From what Leica tells me, not everyone appears to be suffering from Red Death. I suspect some are only as sick as Edison has made them. We'll be as careful as we can with the Citizens we rescue. We'll put them in quarantine. We'll treat their symptoms. And we'll keep a close watch on them."

"You mean . . ." And Sarika smiled for the first time that night. "We'll pray."

"That's one way to put it," Nik said, a half smile on his own face.

Then Sarika looked at me across the sand-scrubbed table.

"You know once we put this in motion, it can't be stopped. The Abuelos will have to fall . . . it'll tear apart Pleiades. And it won't easily go back together again. Are you sure that's what you want?"

Taschen's agonized face haunted me. And sitting here in my old apartment, I could almost see her spinning in her purple dress, grinning. But this was about more than just wanting to see my sister again, wasn't it?

And I thought of the other Citizens whose lives had already been destroyed—infected by Edison or exiled by the Abuelos. Of the word *pending* stamped on Oksun's file. Of Ada's pregnant belly. And all the Kisaengs lined up that morning after Edison's attack—ready to fight. A swift anger surged through me, lifting my voice. "Yes. I'm sure."

"Okay, then," Sarika said. "There's only question left. When?"

"Dia de los Muertos. The masks will disguise the Indignos if they need to move among you. And the fireworks will cover the sound of any fighting."

"Yes." And Sarika smiled again. A real smile this time. "What better day to bring our dead back home?"

We spent another hour strategizing, before Nik and I headed back out into the darkness. We traveled in silence, each lost in our own thoughts as we retraced our path to the Dome. I hadn't been able to bring myself to step into my old room. Had Sarika left our things where they were? Or had she gotten rid of them? The closed door loomed in my mind. Asking all the questions I hadn't dared to.

Despite knowing me my whole life, despite being a second

mother to me, some part of Sarika only saw me as a reminder that the Citizens had failed their God. Was it possible that someone could love you and hate you at the same time?

And looking over at Nik, I thought of Jenner. Did any part of him love the pair of boys he had created? Could any part of him see the greatness that he'd wrought? But Jenner *did* have the grace to leave Nik alone to his forest and his plants . . . maybe that's the closest thing to love a man like Jenner could manage.

I looked up, searching the sky. But it held the kind of vastness that only made way for more questions. What had brought the Colonists so far out into that blackness? What had pulled them away from everything they knew? And I thought again of that coded signal—following them out here, reaching across the stars, trying to tell us . . . what?

Nik seemed to pick up on my thoughts. As we climbed down into the pit, he took one last look around the desert. "It's hard to believe there was ever a city here."

I gripped the rusty metal scaffolding that served as our route back down into the tunnels and tried to see what he saw. Tried to see the Reclamation Fields, and Tierra Muerta beyond them, with new eyes. "In the Rememberings they say God smashed the Colony with his fist."

"Do you believe that?" There was no challenge in Nik's question—the face peering at me from inside the suit only showed an earnest curiosity.

"No." And then I thought of all the Rememberings—all the stories that still flowed through my veins, whether I wanted them to or not. "And yes."

Then he gave me a hint of a smile. A crinkling at the corner of his eyes. "What do you think the fist of God even looks like?"

I shook my head. "When I was a kid, all I could think about was how much noise it would've made. All that shattering glass. Buildings popping and crunching under the weight." And I realized, like my Corruption, the idea of God's fist was something I'd never truly abandoned. "What do *you* think happened?"

Nik looked around at the empty desert, silver in the moonlight. "All I know is that someone set out to destroy this city. And they succeeded."

I glanced behind us, "Why save Pleiades and the Dome, then?"

"Your guess is as good as mine." And he dropped into the dark reclamation pit, his long limbs deftly navigating the scaffolding.

We made it back without seeing a single fly—or Curador for that matter—arriving at the waterfall in the Gardens as the sky turned grey with dawn. But my thoughts were still out in Pleiades with Sarika. And with Lotus and Alejo and Jaesun in the camp. Almost all the pieces were in play now and nightmare scenarios ran themselves through my mind. "If the Dome is damaged in the attack, the Mothers, the children, you . . . you'll all be lost."

"The Dome is *already* damaged. We are *already* lost. Your rebellion changes none of that. The Citizens, the Mothers, the Kisaengs, me . . . *all* of us know the risk. You have to respect us enough to let us take our fates in our own hands."

"Of course I respect you!"

"Then you have to stop thinking of us as children you have to save. Or you'll make the same mistake I did. If you trust us, then what happens will not be your responsibility . . . it will be *all* of ours."

I expected to see fear in his eyes, but instead there was hope.

I pressed my forehead into his chest. I wanted to hide there. To rest in this moment before everything started. But I couldn't. I wouldn't let myself.

I wasn't safe. Not here. Not anywhere in this Dome.

But Nik folded me into his arms anyway, his hair falling down around me like willow branches. And from inside that cadence of breath and blood and breath, I realized that I'd been searching for the wrong thing. No one can keep you safe.

Not my parents, not Suji, not Nik.

But the people who love you can keep you strong. They were like Nik's tree—roots twining around and between and through each other until they built something new. Until they made a house of light and air.

I didn't know what would happen to us tomorrow. Or on Dia de los Muertos. Or after. But whatever was coming for us could not change *this* moment. It could not steal this away.

Standing there in the Gardens, I knew what I wanted *this* moment to be. I tilted my head up, and when I kissed Nik, I saw my way into the future. Everything I was, everything I dreamed of, everything I dared to hope, was echoed back to me. Like voices in a canyon.

But that was for later. Right now I had one more piece of the plan to take care of. And I made myself say the words.

"I have to go back. I have to go back to Edison."

Nik took a long breath and let it back out again. Then he rested his forehead against mine, and said, "I know."

CHAPTER 39

THE SKY BEYOND the Dome brightened as I walked through the forest. The flys were still absent and I silently thanked Ada for the scrap of time I'd stolen with Nik. I placed the quiet, tree-covered moment in my center. It wasn't much, but it gave me courage to do what I had to do next. And that would have to be enough.

The pale yellow sky became a watered-down blue as I climbed the steps to my house. And up to my room, where I found Riya and Oksun waiting for me.

"Have you been here all night?"

"Did you think we'd be able to sleep?" Riya sat cross-legged on my bed sewing—her fingers a blur of speed as she whipped the needle in and out.

"How'd it go?" Oksun looked up at me from where she sat on the floor, back propped against the bed frame. Spools of thread, thimbles, and bits of fabric were strewn across the floor in front of her. But she didn't seem to be doing any sewing.

"Good. No one but Sarika saw us."

"Us?" Riya looked up from her sewing.

"I took Nik with me."

340 • Sara Wilson Etienne

"Do you think that was wise?" Oksun said.

"It doesn't matter if it was wise or not. We need all the allies we can get." I heard the irritation in my voice and realized I was angry that I'd had to leave Nik. Angry that I had to go back to Edison in order for our plan to work. By way of apology and explanation, I said, "I trust him."

"Then that's good enough for me," Oksun said.

"And me," Riya added, without looking up from her sewing.

I got us all mugs of coffee from the food synthesizer, gulping mine down as I tried to shake off my exhaustion. There would be no sleep today. "Sarika's traveling out to Tierra Muerta to talk to Lotus and the Indignos. I imagine they'll be more than happy to liberate the LOTUS wards. And she likes your idea of using fireworks as signals, Oksun."

"Good. I've been going over the plan all night, and I think it's a good one. As soon as it gets dark on Dia de los Muertos, the Indignos will cross the Reclamation Fields and come down through the tunnels to evacuate Taschen and the others." Oksun moved a blue spool of thread near her left knee that'd been sitting on a fat pin cushion—so it marched its way toward a larger red spool.

And suddenly, I saw it. This was not simply remnants from sewing, this was a map. From left to right, the pin cushion was the Reclamation Fields. The thimbles represented Pleiades. And the large circle of thread was clearly the Dome. Inside it, clusters of purple, yellow, and white spools sat in seemingly strategic positions.

"The night before the evacuation, bombs will be planted along the magfly lines, here, here, and here." She pointed to spots along a circled measuring tape running through the "Dome."

"By the time the Indignos infiltrate the tunnels, the Kisaengs

will be distracting Edison and the Curadores inside the Sanctum."
Oksun moved the yellow "Curador" spools into place along with
the bright purple "Kisaeng" ones. Then she added a pair of tiny
dagger-sharp scissors which I presumed were Edison.

Oksun then turned to the semicircle of thimbles that was Pleiades. "When the fireworks start, Sarika and her sympathizers will
use the noise and distraction to grab the Abuelos and disarm their
guards. Once she and her sympathizers have control of the Abuelos and Pleiades, they'll set off . . ." Oksun looked at me.

"Sarika said they'd use red."

"They'll set off red fireworks so we'll know Pleiades is secure
and we can work on getting the Dome's magfly tunnel open in
case we need backup."

Oksun shifted her attention back to the Dome. "Once the Indignos have rescued all the Citizens and the wards are clear"—she
marched the blue and red spools back out toward Pleiades—"the Indignos will blow up the whole LOTUS facility and the Mothers and
Kisaengs will know that it's time to begin our own coup in earnest.

"Kisaengs will trap Edison and most of the Curadores in the
Sanctum. While the Mothers"—she gestured to the white spools—
"take out the magfly lines to slow down anyone else. Hopefully,
that'll give Ada enough time to take control of the main computer."

With a flourish, Oksun triumphantly placed the largest white
spool in the center of the Dome. "And then . . ."

"Then happily ever after!" I finished glibly.

Oksun was right, it was a good and detailed plan. What was
less clear was what the aftermath looked like. What would happen
once the Mothers and the Kisaengs had control of the Dome? All
I could do was trust that we would make it work.

I didn't like the nebulousness, but there was something even less pleasant still missing from the plan.

"There's one more factor to account for: Edison." My stomach twisted at the idea of crawling back to the man who attacked me.

"We've been talking about that." Riya looked at Oksun, a little nervous. And Oksun nodded her encouragement. "And we think . . . I think . . . what you need is a really phenomenal dress."

She stood up on the bed, showing off what she'd been working on—a cascade of shimmering gilt fabric unfurled all the way to the floor.

"Try it on!" said Riya, practically dancing with impatience. "So you can get the full effect."

I slipped off my dusty clothes and pulled the dress over my head. The almost-transparent fabric shivered down my body.

It *was* phenomenal. The long, sleeveless dress was a warm, gleaming gold with a hint of rose—almost the same shade as my skin. The neckline was steep, inching down between my breasts. And the back of the gown draped low as well. The whole thing gave the effect of wearing nothing, but being intensely elegant while doing so.

"Don't forget the gloves," Riya said, handing me a swath of gossamer fabric.

But gloves weren't quite the right description. The thing was all one piece—like a wrap with sheer, lustrous sleeves and with gloves that finished in golden rings instead of fingers. Riya helped me thread my fingers through the six rings attached to the end of each glove—the sleeve stretching up one arm, across the back of my shoulders, and down the other arm.

The best effect of the wrap-gloves was something I could only glimpse in the wall of mirrors behind me—it also had a hood that draped gracefully down my back. I marveled at Riya's genius. "Like the one on my first dress."

"Yep . . . a nod to your first night together."

"Thank you." I hugged Riya. "For this and for everything."

I looked at myself in the mirrors. The dress was a triumph. In one outfit, Riya had laid me bare, yet kept me hidden. I marveled at the beauty of it. "I can't believe you managed all this in one night. It's incredible!"

"Oksun helped too . . . no surprise that she's impeccable at detail work." Riya leaned down and kissed Oksun's cheek.

Oksun shrugged off the compliment, but was clearly pleased. "We wanted you to have to grovel as little as possible."

If you'd asked me a month ago if a dress could be a weapon, I'd have said no. But this one was. It was a subservient apology perfectly mixed with seduction. And wearing it, I felt ready to face Edison.

That night, I showed up late to dinner. There was a buzzy, relaxed atmosphere by the time I walked into the tent and everyone already had drinks in their hands.

Riya noticed me first, switching to a dreamy, a cappella ballad to match my entrance. She tapped her hand against the guitar—an intricate cadence playing counterpoint to my heartbeat. Her naked voice soared, its eerie high notes stretching thin across the air.

It's what the prince must've felt like as he walked through Briar Rose's paralyzed city—Kisaengs and Curadores all mesmerized. Their eyes followed me as I cut through the crowd. Until, finally, I was standing in front of Edison.

He was with Marisol, her arm looped through his. For a second,

I met her gaze and what I saw there disturbed me—resignation and a deep sadness. But there was no time to worry about Marisol. I lifted my eyes to Edison, facing him for the first time in two weeks. Trying not to flinch as I remembered the white-hot pain of my body slamming into the wall.

He took in every inch of me, and though I felt the heat of his eyes as they raked across my body, they no longer burned me.

"Dance with me?" I stretched out a sparkling hand and Edison took it.

Riya transitioned into a different song, a quicker one that soared and flitted. People stepped back, making an instant dance floor for us. Marisol was swallowed up by the crowd as Edison glided me around the room. My feet barely touched the floor as he led completely, his arms propping me up, moving me where I should go.

"You're radiant tonight," said Edison with a satisfied smile. "I'm glad you decided to join us again."

There was something breathtaking about basking in that smile—being someone's dress-up doll. Being the very reflection of what someone craved. And I realized that *this* was the Leica that Edison had wanted all along. The fighter, yes . . . but broken.

Lying in bed later that night, I let myself wonder *when* Edison first decided he would have me. Was it while he watched me training out in Pleiades? Or when he heard my voice over the radio? Or when he came back for me in the Indigno camp?

Then I silenced the questions. I would no longer try to guess Edison's mind. Instead, I closed myself to it. And like Marisol had counseled that first night, I made myself into the Leica that Edison dreamed of.

"We should do something to celebrate our reunion." I kept my voice light, kissing his cheek.

Edison's arm was flung around me—heavy, anchoring me to the mattress.

"What sort of celebration did you have in mind?" Edison ran his hand along my arm, across my fingers.

"In the fairy tales they always have parties with masks and elaborate dresses." I knew it was a risk to ask him so soon, but Dia de los Muertos was about a week away. So it was now or never.

"I always imagined you hated that kind of thing." There was an indulgent amusement in his voice. I froze, thinking I'd blown it.

What would this new Leica do? I stuck my lip out a little, making my eyes wide, and said, "It's just that Dia de los Muertos is coming up and I can't stand the thought of hearing all those fireworks and not having any fun myself."

I was sure the pouting was too much—that he wouldn't buy it.

Edison stared at me. Taking in my whole face. And then he smiled. Accepting my lie as the truth he so profoundly wanted to believe.

"Of course, you shall have your festival. You shall have whatever you want, sweet Leica." Edison cupped his hand under my chin. "I hadn't realized how much you missed your home. Anything to make you happy again."

When I opened my eyes the next morning, Edison was still in my room—but he was staring at me from a nearby chair. I instinctively pulled the covers up to my throat. *How long had he been sitting there, watching me?*

"I missed you, Leica." He was in a much different mood from

the night before. He leaned over, tucking my hair behind my ear. "We're the same, you and I. We were *meant* to be together."

I saw the truth of it in his eyes as he came and sat on the edge of my bed, folding his hand into mine. Our fingers intertwining. He *believed* what he was saying. I forced myself not to pull away as he kissed my forehead. "I have something for you," he said.

"What?" My attempt at excitement came out as a squeak, as I remembered the last "present" he gave me.

He handed me a long, thin box with a ribbon around it. Inside, lying on a satin cushion, was a syringe with a thick needle. Fear pumped through my veins. *Was I about to join Taschen down in the ward?*

"This is Grimm's tracker," Edison said. "I want you to have it."

"Thank you?" I didn't mean it to come out as a question, but the image of Grimm's body lying crushed on my table flooded my mind. Wires and microchips covered with blood. Had Edison killed him for *this*?

Riya's words came back to me: *There's the courage it takes to fight . . . But there's also the courage to endure.* It didn't matter what happened next. It didn't matter what was in that needle, I'd do whatever it took to save my sister.

"Come here. I'll help you," Edison said, patting his knees. I got out of bed and obeyed, sitting on his lap. He threaded one arm around my waist, and in the mirrors, I watched him bring the needle up, so it was hovering behind my right shoulder. "Hold still."

There was a flash of pain just above my shoulder blade and an ache deep in my neck muscles. Then it was over and Edison was kissing the wound on my back, my blood red on his lips.

"There now. I'll never lose you again."

CHAPTER 40

"SURELY MY KNIFE has better things to do than make calaveras." I sat on the grass cutting strips of gauzy fabric to make papier-mâché skull masks.

Two days had passed since Edison had inserted the tracker and it was already driving me crazy.

"But you do it so well!" Oksun gave me her best deadpan look.

I flung a strip at her. We'd called a meeting of the Kisaeng fighters just before dawn and I'd told them everything. About the missing Kisaengs. The infected Citizens. And the experimentation. Then Oksun told them the plan.

Now I looked around at the laughing, smiling Kisaengs in the courtyard—it was hard to believe it was the same group of women. There had been a fire to their rage when we told them. Fighting sticks gripped in their fists. Stony faces incised with righteous indignation. And here they were hours later, stringing together bright orange and pink paper flowers. Showing off bits of half-made dresses. I reminded myself that these women specialized in creating fantasy.

And that was why this was going to work. The courtyard was

being transformed into a festival grounds. Kisaengs were already stringing up banners of colorful flags—turquoise, pink, and yellow filling the open space. The reprocessors had been set to synthesize multitudes of twinkle lights. Cheerful orange and yellow marigolds were being constructed from intricately folded fabric, plastic explosives artfully tucked into the pleats of bright cloth.

June soundlessly glided up to us and started cutting lengths of cloth next to me on the grass. I looked over at Marisol just in time to see her glance away. The sisters had sequestered themselves on the far side of the courtyard.

I hadn't even attempted to invite June to the meeting this morning. She was harder to contact because, unlike most of the Kisaeng fighters, who lived in dorms, June had her own small house. And I wasn't sure how close an eye Marisol or Edison kept on her.

But it was more than that. I didn't want to force June's hand. She'd risked a lot to support me the day after Edison's attack—regardless of the political fallout—and for that reason, I trusted her. But if she joined the fight, I wanted it to be of her own free will.

June was the kind of person who noticed *everything*. I had no doubt that she would see for herself that this was more than a festival. And, as she had done now, would come to us if she wished.

She worked beside me in silence for a few minutes, making a neat stack of cotton strips. When she finally spoke, it was as if we were in the middle of an ongoing conversation. "Did you know they wanted to kill me when I was born?"

"The Abuelos?" I'd heard rumors of babies "disappearing," but I hadn't believed it. There was a sick twist in my stomach as I looked at my friend. And then at my own hands.

"Yeah. When I was a week old, the Abuelos brought my mother

in front of the council and told her to take me out to Tierra Muerta and return me to God. To assure him that we had heard his judgment and vowed to do better."

"What did she say?"

"My mom . . ." June shook her head in disbelieving admiration. "She walked over to one of the guards, who was a friend of the family, and said, 'Hold June for a minute, will you?' Then stood in front of the council and said, 'Do what you want to me, but if God wants my baby, he can come here and take her.'"

I imagined the scene. A guard cooing at baby June, her mother defiant in front of the council. "They must've been . . . uncomfortable."

"I would've given anything to see it!" June's eyes shone with a fierce pride. "The Abuelos explained to her that in my Corrupted form, I wouldn't be able to 'contribute to Pleiades' salvation.' But my mom simply told them I would work in the gardens.

"And for as long as I can remember, that's where I was . . . right by her side, weeding and harvesting. In fact, I was particularly well suited for it, being just the right height and all. But no matter how hard I worked, the Citizens never let me forget what I was . . . Corrupted." There was an undercurrent of rage in June's voice and I wondered what it had cost her to temper it with sweetness all these years.

"The Dome is better, but I've still never felt like my own person." June ran her finger around the rim of her ornate seat. "What I'm saying is . . . I can be *more* than just a novelty."

"Can I see it?" I asked, and June scooted herself off the metal seat and handed it to me. "How does it work?"

"Works on the same magnetized system as the magflys and the flys. While I was sedated in isolation, they inserted a tiny chip into my brain and synced it up with the seat. I think *left* and it goes *left*. I think *up* and it goes *up* . . . though not very far."

"I wonder if that particular limitation could be adjusted." I looked at her sideways. "How do you feel about reconnaissance?"

June gave me a slow smile. "Like I was born for it."

So Riya smuggled the chair into the Complex, and overnight, the Mothers fixed up June's board so it would go much higher than it was supposed to. I didn't say so, but I was relieved to have a way to get eyes on what was happening that wasn't dependent on Ada and the Dome's systems.

Riya had more to report from Ada that day as well. "They've decided that the most obviously pregnant women will evacuate the children into the tunnels in case things get violent."

I nodded. "As long as the wards remain sealed off by the decontamination portals, they should be fine."

"The rest of them will dress like Kisaengs in costumes and calavera masks and get into position to detonate the charges around the Dome."

Ada herself would be focused on getting control of the Dome's systems—first from the Mothers' Complex, then ultimately from the main computer room in the Genetics Lab. The hope was, if we could seize control of its vital functions—power, communications, transportation—then we wouldn't have to take the Dome by physical force.

"And you told them, right? Maximum effect . . ."

Riya finished my mantra with me: "Minimum casualties."

I'd repeated the phrase over and over the last few days. Because I'd seen the rage on Ada's face as she talked about their dead children. I'd seen it on the Kisaengs' faces after Edison had beat me. On Sarika's when I told her about Tasch. On Lotus's, even before she understood the depth of the Curadores' treachery. And the same rage kindled my own heart.

But if there was any hope at building a new world, then this had to be a rescue. *Not* a massacre.

Reminding people of this was the most I could do. Because even though everyone reported in to me, I could do nothing practical myself. Sometimes I swore I could feel the tracker choking me, like a cord around my neck.

It didn't help that Edison was everywhere that week. He stopped by the Sanctum several times a day with his wide smile and his loud voice. And at night, he came to my room. At those times I wasn't sure if I hated him or myself more.

But most unnerving was when I took a walk by the lake or around the Promenade—just so I wouldn't go crazy with waiting—and he came to meet me. Like he wanted to remind me he was watching. At least he'd dropped the ruse of the radio. I was sure I couldn't focus on circuits and wires with him looming over me.

On the evening before the attack, I convinced Edison that I needed time to finish up my dress. Channeling Marisol, I smiled coyly. "I want you to be surprised!"

The rebellion was to have one final meeting at my house. And that night, even Ada risked coming. She sat on the floor of my bedroom, next to Riya, putting the finishing touches on a calavera that had been molded from her own face. The wide grin and painted black eye sockets made the skeleton gaunt and manic at the same time.

Ada idly added purple petals to the vivid flowers decorating the forehead while we waited for June to come back from the tunnels. It'd been a risk, but we were hoping for some sign of Lotus and the Indignos. Without them, the rest of the plan was moot.

"Ada, I'm putting in hidden dagger pockets for all the Mothers." Riya was busy making last-minute alterations, her needle whipping in and out of the fabric. "And I've made them all hoopskirts like Leica's, so no one will notice they're pregnant. At least . . . not so much."

"It'll be dark, so that'll help too," Ada said. "And they've all got their masks ready so they can blend in with the Kisaengs."

"Should fool people at a distance," Oksun said from her spot on the bed. The whole mattress was covered with spools and thimbles and tiny props as she ran the scenario again and again. Preparing for different contingencies.

I felt untethered. In the midst of my friends, I felt completely alone. Longing to hear news that Lotus was safe. Wishing I could see Nik. Just for a second.

I stood up, heading to the front porch to see if I could spot June coming back. Then changing my mind, I headed out to the back balcony.

The dark pressed in on me as I peered up, wishing I could see the stars through the hazy glass of the Dome. Ada came out, putting her hands on the railing and stretching her back. "He's not coming."

"I know." And I did know, but part of me still hoped.

"But he's not hiding anymore either." There was a note of pride in her voice. "He just doesn't want to take any chances. He understands how important tomorrow is."

"What's he going to be doing? Do you know?" I wanted to

be able to picture Nik as he moved through the night. As if that would keep him safe.

"He'll go down to LOTUS to see if he can help with the evacuation. He's come up with something he's hoping will reduce the shock of taking people off the machines. And he's the only one that knows anything about that equipment." Her voice was cautious, tiptoeing around unpleasant realities. Tiptoeing around Taschen.

"Well, tomorrow I'll be the same as Nik and Edison. Blood on my hands."

"Blood on *all* our hands. But I'd rather die fighting than live like some kind of livestock. I won't have whoever's in here"—she touched her pregnant belly—"grow up to be another Edison."

And I realized that Ada had changed since the last time I'd seen her. She'd said *who*, not *what*. That was the effect hope had.

"I'm ba-aaaa-ack!" June's voice drifted through the door and we hurried in to join the others. "I found the Indignos holed up just inside the entrance from the Reclamation Fields. And I brought back a bit more than news."

Lotus walked into the room, combing her fingers through her shoulder-length black hair—looking extremely self-conscious in a low-cut Kisaeng dress. I wasn't sure whether to laugh or cry, so I settled for tackling her.

"You're here!" I said, hugging my sister as tight as possible. "How are you here?"

June looked pleased with herself, swaying a little so her skirt swished in the air beneath her, her long black hair swinging with it. "I brought an extra dress with me and snuck her in through one of the decontamination portals. Figured we could use a firsthand report on the Indignos' activity."

I couldn't come up with the words, so I just said, "Thank you," to June. Then to Lotus, checking her over. "Are you okay? Is everything okay?"

Lotus had grown another inch or so and was officially tall, like Tasch—though I saw now that some of the other similarities between the two of them had been lost. Lotus's face was narrower. Dominated by dark eyebrows and fierce eyes. As if the sheer force of Tasch's death had reshaped Lotus's countenance. At least she wasn't quite as thin as last time I'd seen her.

"I'd be better if I wasn't wearing this contraption." Lotus tugged at her dress, trying to get it to cover more of her cleavage.

I laughed. I couldn't get over how good it was to see her and I realized that I'd prepared myself for the possibility that I might not ever get to again. I grabbed her close, saying, "I found Tasch."

And this time, Lotus stopped messing with her dress and hung on. There were tears in her voice when she spoke. "I know . . . I still can't believe she's alive. I can't even believe *you* are! All those months and no sign of you. I thought you were . . . I thought it was my—"

I stopped her. "No, it was *my choice*. And it was the right one. *You* were right. And now we're going to get her back." And I let myself imagine it. The three of us, a family again.

She nodded her head, her eyebrows knitting together, clearly trying not to lose it in a room full of strangers. Everyone suddenly got very busy with sewing and masks and anything but Lotus. And when Lotus finally spoke, her voice was calm.

"Everything's set for tomorrow. Sarika and our people inside Pleiades have planted bombs in the Reclamation Fields, at all the gates, and along the walls between buildings. They'll detonate them simultaneously in a show of strength—taking the Abuelos by surprise. June's explained *very thoroughly*"—and I could tell by Lotus's tone that June must've been insistent on the point—"that the idea is to gain control without loss of life. And that's the plan. The explosions will be synchronized with the first round of gold fireworks so no one in the Dome knows anything's going on. Then, once Pleiades is secure, Sarika will send up red."

Oksun said, "And you'll start evacuating the underground wards at the same time?"

"Right. As soon as we hear the first fireworks." It was impressive watching Lotus. She'd forgotten about the revealing dress and she stood tall, like she owned her body. Like she owned the room. "Once we've pulled everyone who can be saved from the wards, we'll blow the whole facility so no one can follow us out."

"Everyone who can be saved." Riya put down her needle, as if the stark reality of what we were talking about was sinking in for the first time. "Still, I suppose it's better than a half-life in the wards."

"Not even a half-life." Oksun put her arm around Riya. "They're trapped in a perpetual death down there . . . the explosions will be a quick mercy." Her voice left no room for doubt.

Then Oksun picked up the plan. "Up until the moment the wards are blown, the Curadores won't know anything's up. But the LOTUS facility will be practically under our feet. Once we feel the explosion, it'll be our show. We'll need—"

And we went over the plan that everybody already knew by heart. And then we went over it again.

Around midnight, Riya put down her needle and asked, "And what happens after?"

"After what?" Oksun said.

"After tomorrow. After we run out of plan." There was no challenge in Riya's open face. Only curiosity and concern.

"I don't know," Lotus said, as if she'd been thinking about this very question. "The Indignos have been dreaming and planning for this future, but our time frame's always been in years, not days."

But Ada'd had a whole lifetime to think about this. She stood now, towering over us all. "Well, the Mothers have some ideas . . . things we'd like to do. Ways we'd like to raise our children. We've talked about it a lot, but the one thing we all agree on is, we won't let anyone else govern us. And rest assured, we have little interest in governing the Citizens either.

"But the thing is, *if* the Dome is breached . . . *if* we have to leave . . . it's going to be like the original plague half a millennium ago. A few of us will survive through sheer luck and genetic rolls of the dice, but more will die. And it's a risk every Mother is willing to take. Because maybe *this time* we'll find a way to make Gabriel work. Maybe we can make it the home our ancestors dreamed of when they first came here."

I could see the dream reflected in every pair of eyes around the room. Some with skepticism, some with fear—but they could see it. A Gabriel thriving again with people and cities and *life*. This time, I could see it too.

"Well, there's not much sleep left to be had, so we better grab what we can get." Oksun cleared up her mock battle and Riya left with her, slipping her hand into Oksun's. Ada and June hurried to collect their things as well and I could tell they were trying to give Lotus and me a little space before June led my sister back through the Dome.

It was hard to say good-bye . . . after all, I'd barely gotten a chance to talk to her. When the room was clear, Lotus hugged me, her face softening so she looked, just for a second, like my little sister again.

"Sarika said you *saw* Tasch. How . . ." And she trailed off, as if she wasn't sure exactly what question to ask.

"She didn't look good." There was no room for lies tonight. "I don't know if she'll make it."

"I wish I'd killed him when I had a chance." And Lotus meant it. "That bastard Curador was standing *right there* . . . in *our* camp. It wouldn't have been hard."

"But then we never would've found Tasch. And we wouldn't be here . . . on the verge of this new world."

"Leica, I know what you said about 'maximum effect, minimum casualties,' but tomorrow if I get the chance, I swear . . ." And she gripped the knife at her belt. Intensity reverberated through every line of her long, straight body.

I took her arm, walking downstairs with her. "Let's worry about keeping everyone alive before we start thinking about killing."

But I didn't meet Lotus's eyes as I said it. Because I remembered my *own* promise to myself, the night Edison attacked me. That night, my knife had remained unstained, hidden in my boot. But that isn't what knives are for. And tomorrow, it would find blood.

CHAPTER 41

IN THE MORNING half-light, I slipped on my clothes and went to my closet. I rooted through the beautiful fabrics and pulled out a bundle of orange cloth I'd hidden there. I was glad it was still early; there was something I had to do.

My shoes echoed on the spiraling sidewalk into the Sanctum. It was strange seeing the festive courtyard so empty. Like a party that'd been forgotten. Strings of lights zigzagged their way across the yard. Banners of bright paper flags—pink, orange, turquoise, red—hung high, gloriously clashing above me. Marigolds festooned the entryway and bridge. And spreading out along the curving wall was the altar.

It'd just appeared there a few days ago. No one saw who put it up, but I suspected Oksun—she'd lost the last of her family to Red Death before coming here. It'd started out simple. A table facing north. Two white candles on either side. A glass of water. A bowl of salt and another one brimming with raspberries. An invitation to absent loved ones.

By that afternoon, there'd been bowls of fruit lining the edge of the altar. Cherries and strawberries and limes. Orange and yellow paper flowers had been strewn between the bowls. And someone had left a small sketch in the middle of the table—a man with a crooked smile and crinkle lines around his eyes.

Now, three days later, the altar had taken over the northern half of the Sanctum wall—curving around the courtyard in a riot of color. And what had started out as distraction meant for the Curadores had grown into a genuine celebration.

Hand-drawn portraits and mementos peppered the brigade of tables. Scraps of faded cloth. Carved toys. The Kisaengs rarely talked about Pleiades—but they had evidently not forgotten the home they'd left behind. Or the people who'd left *them* behind. Beautifully decorated papier-mâché skulls squeezed in between bowls of kimchi and plates of tamales filled with sweet red bean paste.

I went to the food synthesizer and got a bowl of beeph curry. The warm, spicy scent made me yearn for home. To stand in our crowded kitchen, window fogged from the pot that'd been simmering all day. Dad singing as he chopped peppers. Tasch sitting up on the counter swinging her legs in time. Lotus stealing the stirring spoon when Mom wasn't looking—burning her tongue as she snuck a bite.

"I know it's a little early in the morning for curry, Mom, but it's your favorite." I slipped my pair of whittled chopsticks into the bowl and found a spot for it on a table. I bowed to the altar. Then I put a glass of mezcal next to the curry for my dad. And another one for Suji.

"I hope you'll all be with me today. I'm scared . . . I don't really know what I'm doing and so many people are counting on me. I just want to thank the three of you for making me strong."

Behind me, the first of the Kisaengs filtered into the Sanctum. I hid the cloth bundle with my body as I unwrapped it. Inside lay the book of fairy tales. I kissed the faded binding and made a place for it on the table. Then I covered it with orange flowers—it felt too precious, too private, to leave exposed.

I bowed one more time. "Thank you for believing there was more."

The Sanctum was filling up with Kisaengs, but a hush stayed over the courtyard. Part of it was that no one had gotten much sleep. Even Marisol and her circle—who didn't know what was about to happen—had stayed up late making the final alterations to their dresses and masks. But mainly it was the sense of everyone holding their breath. Waiting for what was coming.

Riya, Oksun, June, and I spent most of the day surreptitiously drugging bottles of wine and decorating the Sanctum entrance with chains of cloth flowers and explosives. When it was time, the Kisaengs would abandon the Sanctum and the exit would be blown—trapping the lethargic Curadores inside. Maximum effect, minimum casualties.

An hour before the party, we all went home to change. Oksun stopped me on my way out, her body tense, her hair securely tucked behind her ears. She handed me a package tied with a beautiful bow. "Riya made you a mask to match your dress. There's a present in there from me too."

"Thank you."

Oksun wasn't a huggy person, but she put her arms around me anyway, pulling me close and whispering, "They each have a three-minute timer. Simply connect the detonator to the explosives, then hit the button. That's all there is to it. Oh . . . and don't forget the running."

"Thanks." I wrapped my arms around the package, shielding it.

Back in my bedroom, I untied the ribbon and lifted the lid. The skull mask was stunning—perfectly color-coordinated to go with my red dress. The skeleton's wide eye holes were each encircled by a fiery crimson sunflower. And they hadn't simply been painted on. They were a mosaic of glittering glass, flashing around the eyes.

Around the flowers, green vines twisted and swirled into intricate patterns across the forehead and down the cheekbones. They edged the gaunt lines of the skull and gathered at the chin where, when I looked closely, I saw Riya had painted the silhouette of the LOTUS flower—tucked under slightly so it was just out of sight.

The finishing touch was the crown of orange and red marigolds that clustered and draped along the top—looking both playful and regal at the same time. The mask was a masterpiece. I pulled it out carefully and placed it on the dresser. Then I gently lifted the layers of decorative paper. Underneath lay two bundles of explosives and their detonators—made to fit perfectly inside my skirt.

The golden dress Riya designed might've been a psychological weapon, but *this* was a real one. The Festival gown was the perfect mix of shimmering silk and deadly architecture. Ornate red blossoms clustered across the bust and climbed up the shoulder straps—hiding a pair of daggers and a tiny radio. Crimson chiffon cascaded over my hips, and the night-black bodice cinched in along my waist.

The corset itself was made from a black, impenetrable cloth with lengths of electrical wire threaded along its framework, accessible by a false seam. Tiny flashlights, wire strippers, pliers, and cutters were pleated into the folds of the dress. Disguised in the embroidery of the bodice. Sewn into the hems. Even the hoop of the skirt could be pulled out, deconstructed, and used as fighting sticks.

But the most ingenious part was that the wide hips contained two pouches for explosives. I slid the bombs and detonators into the hidden pockets and pulled the elaborate dress on. The large skirt was cumbersome, but at least my legs would have plenty of room for running. And I would need it.

Once Ada got my tracker offline and Pleiades was secured, it would be my job to get through the main magfly tunnel and open the sealed door that led out to Pleiades. I was chosen not only because of my previous excursions through the tunnels, but because no one knew how the door would be controlled. If I was lucky, there would be an access panel and I could fool the circuits into thinking a magfly was coming. Or figure out a way to rewire them. On the other hand, I might need the explosives. And the running.

Because no matter how hard the Kisaengs and Mothers fought, we would still be outnumbered by Curadores. We would need reinforcements from Pleiades and they couldn't get in through the LOTUS wards without risking infection. The Indignos could use isolation suits, but there wouldn't be enough for everyone.

A nervous dread formed in the pit of my stomach as I walked across the Promenade. The cold steel of my knives pressed against my chest. Rubbed against my boot. The weight of the explosives tethered me to the ground. This was not a game. People might get killed tonight. Maybe people I cared about. Maybe me.

I stood on the grass for a moment, watching the parade of beautiful Kisaeng skeletons heading toward the gilded Sanctum. Actually, some of them were probably Mothers, using the crowd to hide in plain sight as they made their way to the magfly lines—ready to blow the charges. We couldn't use remote detonators because Ada was about to wreak havoc on all communication systems.

Sarika had been right—even if I wanted to stop this now, there was no way I could. There were too many people involved. Too many plans already in motion. This was not just *my* fight anymore.

For the hundredth time that day, I wondered how things were going on the other side of the glass and I hoped for all our sakes the answer was *very well*. It was almost dark enough for fireworks and my heart went out to Sarika in Pleiades. I pictured her standing in the middle of the jubilant Festival Grounds, knowing it would soon be marred by fear and explosions.

Then I imagined Lotus and Alejo and Jaesun, creeping their way across the Reclamation Fields and through the tunnels to the sleeping Tasch, deep under my feet. And I clung to the thought that by the end of this long night we would be a family again.

"Focus, Leica," I commanded myself. And as I crossed the lawn to the Sanctum, I went over what I needed to do.

Keep Edison close. Get him a drink. Incapacitate him as soon as the attack starts.

Get to the main magfly tunnel. Wait for Ada's radio confirmation that red fireworks have been spotted. Get the entrance open.

Garlands of bright orange and yellow flowers lined the spiral entry to the Sanctum—each blossom a tiny, beautiful bomb. On the other side of the glass walls, the blurred silhouettes of costumed Kisaengs flitted through the glow of party lights. It was lovely and I put my hand to the glass, wishing just for a moment that we weren't about to smash all of this.

I reached for my mask, but decided to leave it where it was for now—loosely fastened to the curving hips of my dress with a ribbon. I wanted to make sure Edison could find me. Then I stepped inside.

The Sanctum was packed with Curadores and Kisaengs— hundreds of decorated calaveras flashed in the twinkle lights that filled the sky like stars. I went over to get a drink, in the hopes I could offer some to Edison, if I could find him. A few days ago, I'd made him show me his costume. But now I saw that it would be close to impossible to pick him out in this crowd of skeletons.

A masked Kisaeng in a delicate mahogany dress poured me a shot of mezcal. I was about to take a sip when Marisol's voice came from behind the calavera.

"Please forgive me." We hadn't spoken since I'd taken Edison back and now her slurred words made me prickle.

"For what?" I kept my voice light. "Pretending to be my friend? Tracking me through the forest? Telling Edison I'd kissed Nik?"

"No. For tonight." The skull's wide eyeholes were edged by dark brown thorns and Marisol's hazel eyes looked grim in their center.

"Tonight?" I couldn't help the alarm that tinged my question. Marisol grabbed the shot of mezcal from me and downed it.

"I told him you were planning something . . . I wasn't sure what. Then last night, they caught Lotus down in the tunnels."

"Lotus?" I grabbed Marisol's shoulders, blood roaring in my ears. "Marisol, listen to me. Where's Lotus? What's happened to her?"

"We mean nothing to them. Less than Mothers." Marisol swayed a little—clearly she'd started drinking long before the party started. "You can't build your life on someone else's. You can't! I know you can't . . . but I couldn't let him leave either . . ."

"Let him leave?" I was trying to make sense out of her babbling.

She started swaying again and clutched at my hand. "Please . . . don't leave me alone."

"Easy there." Edison came up behind Marisol, steadying her. He wasn't wearing a mask, or any kind of costume. Instead he wore a loose black shirt, silver buttons glinting in the lights, echoing the silver chain from the shuttle around his neck. He laid his hand on the back of Marisol's neck and leaned in. "Darling, it's almost time for me to go."

"Go?" I asked. My mind was sorting through the scraps of what Marisol had just said. Edison knew we were planning something. Lotus had been caught. But my brain just kept rattling off my to-do list. *Find Edison. Get him a drink.*

I blurted out, "But you haven't had any wine. Let me get you a glass!"

Edison shook his head. "No time for a drink, but I suppose I could squeeze in one final dance."

Marisol offered him her hand, but Edison was already taking mine. He wrapped his arm around my waist, spinning me onto the dance floor. But he looked back over his shoulder at her. "I'm afraid I might have broken Marisol . . . I forget she's not as strong as you."

I had to get away. I had to warn Oksun and the others that things were going wrong. I tried to pull free. "I'm sorry, I have to—"

"All of that can wait. We have a long night ahead of us, you and I." Edison cinched his arm tighter around me and his voice had that cool distance I remembered from the night of his attack.

I stopped struggling and studied his face. Quieting my mind, I worked on anticipating his next move.

"I want to tell you a few things before we part." He gave me his most charming smile.

"Before we part?"

"Yes, I'm afraid I have places to be. But I want you to know, I truly believed . . . I *still* believe that we are one and the same." He folded our fingers together, crushing me to him as we swept around the dance floor—so tight I could barely breathe. The corset didn't help either. The sky above the Dome lit up with the first flashes of fireworks. Red spiderwebs blurring through the solar glass. But that was wrong too—it should be gold first, *then* red. It was too early.

"You and I are visionaries. This plan you hatched . . . all those secret meetings, sneaking out of the Dome, bringing in Ada even! It's truly incredible."

"If you knew . . . if you know . . . then—"

"Because a little chaos was exactly what I needed. So thank you. And remember through everything that happens tonight . . . I love you." The current of excitement in his voice scared me and one thought repeated itself, screaming in my head.

Lotus. He has Lotus.

"If you've hurt Lotus, I'll—"

Somewhere close by, an explosion shook the ground and I stumbled.

"It begins," Edison said. My ribs ached as he squeezed the last of the air out of my corseted lungs and smashed his mouth against mine.

Then he was gone and I collapsed on the ground, wheezing. June materialized by my side, helping me to stand up.

"There shouldn't be any bombs yet. It's too soon," she said. "And Sarika's fireworks—"

And I managed to force the words out. "Edison knows."

Her eyes went wide. "How?"

"Marisol. And Lotus . . . he's got Lotus."

"Oh, Leica, I'm sorry," June said. "We'll figure out what's happened and we'll get her back. I promise."

There was another little quake and June steadied me. I looked around the Sanctum; the Curadores were starting to look a little nervous, but the Kisaengs were laughing and teasing and chattering . . . valiantly distracting the Curadores. June said, "I don't think those explosions are coming from the tunnels. The Indignos couldn't have evacuated the wards already, could they?"

"No. There hasn't been enough time. Maybe the magfly lines? But the Mothers aren't supposed to set anything off until after we'd drugged the Curadores and trapped them in here. I think the only thing it's safe to assume is that we need a new plan." It was like a nightmare.

Then the world exploded around me. Glass sprayed through the air, glistening in the colored party lights. The ground rocked beneath my feet. I was down again and time went wrong.

People were screaming, but I couldn't hear anything. June was thrown up into the air away from me. Oksun's face came into focus in the crowd, a trickle of blood streaking her cheek. She was yelling something at me, but I couldn't make sense of it.

I closed my eyes and tried to breathe. Tasch and Lotus needed me. I shook my head, and when I opened my eyes, time caught up with itself and sound came roaring back.

"Where's Edison?" Oksun screamed. Her usually subdued hair was singed and wild around her face.

"Gone. And he knows everything. And he's got Lotus."

"Bad start." She reached down and pulled me to my feet—wiping blood from the small cut on her face.

"Not great." I checked my dress. Knives. Tools. Bombs. All safe. Then I realized what was missing. "Where's June?"

I scanned the crowd, but the place was a madhouse. Half the people still had their masks on and the emaciated skulls grinned in the flickering party lights. The bombs had collapsed the doorway of the Sanctum and there was glass everywhere. No one could get out, so they settled for panicking. Oksun and I focused on not getting run over.

Suddenly, June descended on us—her board easing down from above. "I got high enough to see over the walls of the Sanctum. Looks like someone beat us to the punch, and I'm guessing they used our own flower garlands to do it too. The whole outer arm of the spiral is blown, blocking the main exit as well. There's definitely injuries, but since the bombs were planted high enough, no one's been killed . . . as far as I can tell. Bad news is that there's also smoke coming from the magfly lines. And near the Genetics Lab."

"*That's* the bad news?" And Oksun let out a hysterical laugh that sounded all wrong coming from her.

How had everything gone so terribly *wrong*? "We've got to get out of here and figure out what the hell's going on."

There was the hiss of static and I looked around for the source.

"I believe it's coming from your cleavage." June smirked, the edge of hysteria playing with her as well. I ripped a handful of flowers off my bodice and pulled out the radio.

"I thought you were going to signal me before you blew the Sanctum!" Ada sounded furious.

"It wasn't us! None of it was us. Edison knows everything . . . Lotus was caught heading back last night." I had to yell to be heard over all the shouting Kisaengs and Curadores. "He must've found a way to trigger the bombs."

"Do you need me to send help?" Ada asked.

I glanced at Oksun, who'd pulled herself together by now and shook her head.

"I don't think so. But we've got to get back in control of the situation." I rubbed my ears—everything still sounded muffled from the blast. "I want flys everywhere. I *know* Edison's behind this but I don't know why. I mean, if he knew we were planning this, then why not just stop us? Why blow up the Dome?"

"Tell me exactly what you need from me," Ada said.

"We need to know if he's sabotaged the evacuation and Pleiades as well. And we need to know if he's coming after us with more than just our own weapons. Whatever he's up to we need to get ahead of him, so obviously, the sooner you can get control of the Dome's systems, the better."

"Okay," Ada said. "I'll send some flys into the tunnels . . . get an idea of where things stand. And I'll have the Mothers keep a close eye out for Edison."

"And Marisol. Even if they're not together, she might know where he is," I said.

"And Marisol," she confirmed. "Heads up—according to my monitors, it looks like you've already got some action . . .

Curadores on their way to the Sanctum. Should I hold the rest of the detonations?"

I hesitated—looking to Oksun again—and she grabbed the radio. "Blow whatever's left of the magfly lines to slow everyone down. Then we're gonna need new targets, far from the Promenade. Pick a few of them—scattered, but in the general vicinity of each other—and detonate them all within five minutes. We need to draw as many Curadores away from the Genetics Lab as possible so you have an open route to the main computer when you're ready. The Kisaengs will focus on getting out of here and regrouping."

"Right," said Ada. "Just so you know, Leica, your tracker is still working. I can't isolate the signal and I can't block it. And while I was looking, I noticed something else strange. That coded radio signal? The one from Earth?"

"What about it?"

"It's changed."

CHAPTER 42

"THE SIGNAL'S CHANGED? How?" In the midst of this mess, I tried to focus on what Ada was telling me. Tried to understand its significance.

"Well, I still can't decipher what's on it. But it's not constant anymore, more like bursts of static. And there's another coded signal now too, coming from somewhere on Gabriel. As if—"

"As if someone's having a conversation." I finished her thought. Whatever that meant, it was *not* good. "Okay. Keep listening in and let me know if anything changes. Oh, and Ada?"

"Yes?"

"Can you shut off the water to the Sanctum? It'd be nice to get out of here."

I was no longer having to shout to be heard over the chaos. And when I turned around, I was amazed. Riya and our Kisaengs had the Curadores and Marisol's sisters lined up against the wall at knifepoint. Riya looked to me for instructions, her cropped, dark hair spiked with sweat. Her small mouth was drawn in a grim line, but there was something ecstatically defiant about her as well. Suji would've said Riya had been gripped by *the euphoria*. And it suited her well.

There were about a hundred and fifty Curadores in all. Some were slumped and moaning, having already indulged in the drugged wine. Others looking around, bewildered, as if their favorite toy had just bit them. A few even wore stupid, amused grins, convinced this was all part of tonight's entertainment.

"Impressive," I said to Riya. She gave me a curt nod—and in spite of her elaborate silk gown, there was nothing fluttery about her now.

"Everyone take off your masks," I ordered. I scanned the faces of both friend and foe. I knew Edison and Marisol wouldn't be among them, but I *had* to check anyway.

"As you can tell, things have not gone as we planned. I won't pretend that this night hasn't just gotten a hell of a lot more dangerous for us." I looked at my Kisaengs. Soot and makeup and blood smudged their faces. The glass had been brutal. And while no one had been killed, most were adorned with makeshift bandages, torn from skirts and capes. They were not the frivolous, flirty girls I'd met only a few weeks ago—though in truth, they'd probably never really been those girls.

But Edison's attack had galvanized them. They were fighters now.

"We've lost the element of surprise, but our goals are the same. Evacuate the Citizens in the underground wards. Take control of the Genetics Lab and the main computer. Get the Dome open to Pleiades. But first we need to get out of here. Lucky for you, I know the way." I pointed to the Sanctum's waterfall and gave them a cocky grin.

Being friends with Suji had taught me that you might not always know what you're doing, but you sure as hell better *look* like you do.

We surfaced near a pump house at the edge of the Reservoir. Thick smoke hung over the Promenade and the air tasted like ash. Fireworks continued to explode outside the Dome, lighting up the street in reds and yellows—a blitz of confusion. Damp Kisaengs stood clustered on the grass as we watched the Sanctum's glass walls flash bright, then go dark, as June caved in the waterway behind us. Then we were moving again. Putting distance between ourselves and the Sanctum.

And I was glad, because moving meant being one step closer to finding out what happened to Lotus. To rescuing Tasch. And more than anything, getting moving meant finding Edison and making him pay. Plus, there were still a couple hundred Curadores loose in the Dome, and from the look of it, they were *all* on their way to the Promenade.

"Okay, masks back on." Oksun barked the order and I was happy for her to take charge. Like Riya had said, Oksun was impeccable with the details.

June had barely caught up with us before Oksun sent her off again. "Take a team of five. We don't know what Edison's agenda is or if he has explosives of his own. But if any of us want breakfast and clean water tomorrow morning, or ever again for that matter, then we'd better make sure the Meat Brewery and the water pumps aren't rigged to blow. Now get—"

But fresh explosions interrupted Oksun's instructions. We could see flashes on the far side of the Dome and we held our breath, watching to see if our trick would work. Then Kisaengs were smiling—a couple even cheered—as the Curadores who'd been converging on the Promenade took the bait, heading off in the direction of Ada's new detonations at a run.

"Okay, now that our path's clear, everyone else break into twos or threes and start moving toward Leica's house. You'll get your new orders there. Edison's still tracking Leica, so until we can fix that, we'll minimize that advantage by meeting somewhere obvious. Have your knives at the ready, but choose evasion over attack. The longer we can keep the Curadores guessing, the better. If you get caught, shout and someone will try to come for you. But from this point forward, assume you're on your own."

The Kisaengs took off, scattering into the night, and Oksun turned to me. "Leica, please tell me you have a theory about what Edison's up to."

"Well, there's definitely more going on tonight than our rebellion," I said. "Back there in the Sanctum, Edison *thanked* me. Said a little chaos was what he needed. So whatever he has planned is bigger than our little war."

"I don't like the sound of that."

"Me either. Whatever he's doing, I swear, I'll stop him. But we need you to keep our people safe. Take my radio—find out if the Indignos have managed to rescue the Citizens. Find out what's going on outside the Dome. Get Ada to the main computer."

"I don't need—"

I pressed the radio into Oksun's hand. "I'll get another when I get back to the house. Right now, they need you."

I saw on her face that she wanted to stop me. But instead, Oksun gripped my hand. "Wherever you're going, be careful."

"If you can't be safe, be smart." And I ripped a dagger from a hidden pocket in my bodice. Oksun gave me a grim smile before slipping on her mask and disappearing into the dark.

I left my mask tethered to my waist. I was worried more about visibility than being visible. Running low, I headed back into the center of things. Jenner hadn't been in the Sanctum and I needed to talk to him. Whatever was happening here tonight had more to do with Edison's plans than with mine. Edison clearly had many secrets, but I didn't believe Jenner was so blind he hadn't guessed most of them.

But by the time I got to the Genetics Lab, I was too late. Blood streaked the door—red fingerprints smearing the glass. I followed the trail with my eyes and spotted Jenner staggering across the Promenade. Breathing hard. Stringy white hair falling in his eyes.

When I reached him, Jenner slumped onto me—the weight of him almost taking me down. His hand pressed against his flabby belly and his white lab coat was soaked with blood. "Forgive me . . . I tried to stop him."

Jenner's eyelids drooped as I lowered him onto the grass. I shook him, not bothering to be gentle. "You tried to stop Edison? From what?"

Jenner nodded, then grimaced—even that tiny movement hurting him.

Of course. This stupid, horrible man couldn't even die right. Couldn't even hang on long enough to be useful. "What's he planning?"

"He's been talking to them . . . on the radio." His fat lips were wet—blood frothing at the corners—and he started choking.

"Breathe," I said in my best Taschen voice, trying to soothe him. I needed more information from him. "Just breathe."

His coughing eased, but his eyes drifted shut again and I shook him by the shoulders. "Tell me about the radio."

Jenner's eyes rolled until they found mine. ". . . thinks he's talking to Earth."

"If it's not Earth, *who* is Edison talking to?" My voice was high-pitched with frustration. "What do they want?"

"They destroyed . . ." His voice dwindled to an inaudible hiss. Then he whispered, "Forgive me."

But I couldn't bring myself to lessen Jenner's guilt, even in death. His eyes lost focus and he was gone. I wasn't sorry. This man had sliced me open and taken not only who I was, but who I *could* have been. In the name of survival he'd made unthinkable choices and they'd brought him here. Murdered by his son, left to bleed to death in the dark. It wasn't the computer or some mutated gene that'd brought Edison and Nik to opposite edges of the brink. *Jenner* had done that. This Dome had done that.

Wiping my bloody hands on my dress, I took off across the grass, cursing the fact I'd given Oksun my radio. If I cut around the Reservoir, I could make it to my house faster than the Complex. I needed to talk to Ada. I needed to know more about these signals she was monitoring.

I ran along the dark path, my hoopskirt banging against my shins and snagging on branches, trying to make sense of it all. I had the pieces, I just wasn't seeing the picture yet. Edison had gotten the shuttle's radio to work—or maybe it'd worked all along—and now he was talking to Earth.

Or at least what he thought was Earth.

But why? What did he hope to accomplish? As new explosions rang out in the night, it was clear he wasn't coordinating some kind of rescue mission for Gabriel.

I broke through the trees on the other side of the Reservoir, zigzagging my way through the neighborhood. Curadores were everywhere—examining what was left of the magfly lines, heading toward the explosions, huddling in small groups talking. I dodged in and out of houses, cutting through backyards to avoid them. At least none of them seemed menacing so far, just confused.

Then a terrible wailing pierced the night.

"Dammit." I froze, clutching a cramp in my side as I listened, trying to figure out what to do. I was only a few blocks from my house, only minutes from a radio and talking to Ada.

More screams. I changed directions—running toward the desperate noise.

I turned a corner and ran straight into a mob of crazed Citizens. They were armed with knives and fighting sticks, and when they saw me, a greedy rage swept onto their faces.

"This place shall be cleansed!" a man shouted, holding up a Kisaeng's mask smeared with blood. His patched clothes and gaunt face looked out of place in the streets of the Dome.

Another man grabbed at me and I struck out with my knife. More arms seized me from behind, and voices screamed in my ear. "This place shall be cleansed!"

Then there was a *crack-crack-crack* of wood against wood, and a command cut through the shouting.

"Stop!" And there was Sarika, pushing the crowd aside. Relief washed over me as they reluctantly let me go.

"Has everyone gone mad? How did you even get in?" My words were whispered, meant only for her.

But Sarika's answer carried across the whole crowd. "God opened the tunnel for us."

"God?"

"We prayed for the gates to open and they did." Sarika played to the crowd, as if she was in the middle of a Remembering.

I didn't have time for this. But at least Sarika could tell us what'd been going on outside. "Did the Indignos make it into the wards? Is Taschen okay? Do you know what happened to Lotus?"

"Lotus was taken." And I hated her for the drama she injected into her voice. "She was—"

I grabbed Sarika's arm, forcing the words through gritted teeth. "That's my sister you're preaching about. Where is she?"

A glimmer of the woman I knew surfaced through the facade. "She never came back last night. And, today, someone in Pleiades already knew our plan. They knew where and when the bombs would be going off. Someone disarmed the explosives before we could detonate them and we had to take the Abuelos by force, instead of surprise."

Then her voice regained its theatrical tremor. "The Festival Grounds are soaked with the blood of our Citizens. It never should've been this way! Many lives were lost this night. Now we will have our vengeance!"

Sarika wasn't speaking to me anymore, but to the mob gathered around her. "For too long, the Curadores have kept us bound to our ancestors' sins. They believe themselves Gods, holding themselves above us. But no more! We shall pull down this abomination. Render sin into glass and ash. God will smile on us tonight!"

Crack-crack-crack! The crowd pounded their fighting sticks together and raised their voices: "God will smile!"

"No!" I shouted over the din. It was my turn for a speech. "There are innocent people in here . . . God will not smile on the killing of children! And if you destroy this Dome, that is *exactly* what will happen . . . we will *all* starve. Even the Indignos know that we're not ready to support ourselves."

"Then God will have no choice but to show us his fist or grant us his mercy." Sarika had already been a mighty voice back in Pleiades, but now she held an otherworldly power. The crowd was mesmerized by her, willing to follow her into any battle.

"This is insanity!" I cried.

"No! It's faith!" Sarika raised her arms and the crowd echoed her, thrusting their knives and sticks up toward the sky. "God will finally see, without a doubt, that we are humble and righteous before him. And he will reach down and reward us for our courage."

As if she herself was God, Sarika reached down and picked up a chunk of loose concrete. She lobbed it through the air and shattered a nearby window. The crowd went crazy, following her, throwing anything they could find. Hungry for violence.

I'd counted on Sarika—and the Citizens—to be our allies. But these were not Citizens anymore. They were a sandstorm devouring the desert. They would strip anything they came across, until there was nothing left but bone.

Hands grabbed me, pulling at me. Tearing my dress. Sarika vanished into the crowd again, leaving me at their mercy. I lashed out with my knife but they were all around me. Their chants and slurs crowding out my thoughts. Pulsing through me. Vibrating in my bones.

Only seconds before it happened, I realized that it was not simply *voices*. The air went dark. Streetlamps blotted out by throngs of flies. They choked the sky—a swarming, swirling mass descending on the Citizens.

People tried to shake off the metal insects. Tried to smack them out of the air. But there were too many of them. Too many to breathe. The shouts of triumph turned to screams.

I stood among them, an island untouched. Then I dodged through the panicked mob. Sprinting through the streets. Until finally, I stumbled up the stairs to own my house.

I burst in the front door. "The Citizens! They're tearing the place apart!"

Dozens of faces turned to look at me, but no one spoke. Silent Kisaengs were crammed into the hallway and kitchen. The house was a vigil, listening to Oksun's voice as it crackled across the radio.

"Looks like someone bombed the tunnels around the wards before anyone could be evacuated. The Indignos are still managing to get our people out, but it's slow going. Good news is Ada and the Mothers made it to the main computer in the Genetics Lab and they've started sending flys down into the tunnels to help clear the way."

The crowd of Kisaengs parted for me as I followed the sound of Oksun's voice, squeezing my way into the kitchen. Riya was sitting on the edge of the counter holding a handheld radio mic. She gave me a relieved smile. "I have good news too. Leica just showed."

"Thank God," Oksun said, and the relief was obvious in her voice. "Put her on."

I took the mic from Riya. "The Citizens are already inside the

Dome and Sarika has them bent on destroying the place in the name of redemption."

But it was Ada's voice that answered me. "I know. About a half hour ago, the computer registered a magfly leaving through the main tunnels. It had to be Edison. That's how the mob got in, somehow managing to jam the door mechanism as he left. I sent the flys in when I saw you show up, but it's not going to stop them for . . . hold on—"

There was the faint sound of urgent voices and the radio was handed back to Oksun. "You have to send Kisaengs out to protect vital areas. We need to save as much of the Dome as we can, for our own sake as well as the Mothers'."

Riya was already counting out teams, sending them to defend their home. That was all well and good, but I had a horrible feeling that none of this would matter if we didn't figure out what Edison was up to. The radio signals. The magfly. Earth. "Oksun, can you ask Ada if she's been picking up any more outside transmissions? Jenner said something about—"

An enormous squeal blasted through the radio. The lights flickered and the whole house went dark.

One of the girls ran out onto the porch, reporting back, "It's just this street. The others still have power."

"Oksun?" I tried the radio again, but there was nothing. Not even static.

Riya lit a candle and we made our way to the front porch to see for ourselves. The whole street was dead, though we could still see a little in the glow of the streets behind ours.

I expected my own terror to be reflected in Riya's eyes. But hers were calm and steely. "Well, we already knew Edison was *watching* you. Now we know that he's listening to you too. If you go after him, he'll be waiting."

"*Listening to me,*" I repeated. Wherever Edison was going, he'd want a strong signal, and if he *was* talking to Earth or whoever, he'd need power for the radio. Something clicked in my mind. "I think I know where he's heading. Get to the Genetics Lab and tell—"

But I broke off as someone in a white isolation suit came barreling down the street—a swarm of flys following him. He veered toward us and staggered up the porch steps, clutching a limp body in his arms.

CHAPTER 43

"NIK!" I COULDN'T BELIEVE he was here. My heart lifted for a second; then my eyes drifted to the girl he was carrying.

Taschen.

Her skin was a horrible grey, eyes bloodshot, chest barely moving. A swarm of flys buzzed around them.

"The tunnels are barely passable." Nik's eyes were frenzied, blazing violently. "I wasn't sure where to go . . . wasn't sure where you were. Then the flys came and made a path for us."

I silently thanked Ada again, tearing my eyes from my sister. Pushing down the wail that was surging up inside of me, I said, "Go around back. I'll meet you in two minutes."

Nik nodded and disappeared into the dark. Without looking at me, Riya went inside and addressed the remaining Kisaengs.

"Listen up. You all heard the situation over the radio . . . we're under attack. I've given you your assignments. I know they're our people, but if we don't find a way to stop the Citizens from destroying our power generators and food supplies, it's gonna be a rough, hungry year." She was magnificent. Learning to fight had just been the first step—tonight had transformed Riya into someone new. I just hoped that tomorrow morning something of the old Riya still remained intact.

I hugged her. "Thank you."

"Go take care of your sister. Then send him to hell . . . just make sure you don't follow." Riya handed me the candle. She looked at the room of frozen Kisaengs and said, "Let's move, folks!"

The room burst into activity, Kisaengs spilling out the front door and into the night.

Then I was alone in the house. Taking a deep breath, I tried to find my center as I walked through the now-empty kitchen, but there was only the liquid ache of grief seeping into me. I opened the back door and there was Nik—an illuminated face in the dense darkness.

"Upstairs." I could barely get the words out. "Put her in my bed."

Nik took the stairs two at a time, bounding up into my bedroom. I followed, slower—my mind pleading with every step: No. No. No. Not Tasch.

Nik was tucking the blanket around Taschen when I came in. He turned to me, a deep sadness on his face. "I tried, Leica. I tried to save her, but her organs were too badly damaged. She's too weak."

I sat on the bed, smoothing the hair away from Taschen's burning forehead. It was creased with pain and I ached for her as I wiped a trickle of blood from her mouth. She didn't open her eyes. They didn't even flutter.

"I'm so sorry. I thought you should at least be able to say goodbye." Nik sat across from me, on the other edge of the bed.

"Thank you." I didn't know what else to say. My mind was filled with a collapsing dream. Edges tearing off. Sand eating away at the foundations. Me, Taschen, and Lotus together again. A home.

"Lotus?" I forced myself to ask the question. "Did you find her down in the wards too?"

Nik nodded. "But Edison didn't get a chance to do much to her. Lotus is *strong* and the thing is . . ." And Nik grabbed my hand, his voice tense with excitement. "I think I found something . . . something that might help her . . . help all of us. I wouldn't have even thought about it except for what you said about my hand." And he opened his palm. "No scar."

I couldn't follow what Nik was saying. My mind filled with smoke and the whispers of hungry flames. My rage screaming like vultures, calling for death.

Edison had taken it from me. He'd taken my home—the only thing I'd wanted.

And suddenly, I understood something, the pieces clicking into place. Nik was still talking, but I interrupted him. "What does Edison want? More than anything?"

Nik simply stared at me, confused.

"Answer me! What does Edison want more than anything else in the world?" I thought of the hundreds of Citizens sacrificed on the altar of his singular objective.

Nik's voice was quiet as he said, "To leave the Dome . . . for good."

"I think he's found a way." I was nodding to myself. And my voice was calm, silencing the shrieking in my head as I thought of Edison's room in the Genetics Lab—cluttered not just with radio parts, but with pieces of the shuttle. "But not *just* a way to get out of the Dome, but off of Gabriel . . . maybe even to get to Earth. And now he's headed out to Tierra Muerta. That's why he let us have our rebellion . . . he wanted us to clear out the Indigno camp for him."

"Why?"

"Think about it." And I could hear the impatience in my voice. I could feel it prickling across my skin. "It's got power for the radio. Tools, supplies, clean water. And most of all, no one to stop him."

Nik was on his feet. "I'll go after him—"

"No! This is for me to do," I said. Nik started to argue, but I cut him off. "You don't even know where the camp *is*."

Now that I understood what Edison was doing—understood what I'd have to do to stop him—I realized I had to get Nik to leave. I had to say all the right things. Whatever it took.

Because I knew what came next and I couldn't have Nik here, trying to stop me. "You said you found something that might help Lotus. If you can do anything for her . . . for the people in the wards . . ." And I let some of the hurt pooling in my chest escape, tears tripping down my cheek.

"I will. I promise." His eyes met mine—embers of yellow glimmering in the orange. "Will you be okay?"

He touched the glove of his isolation suit to my face. And I leaned into it. Letting myself have that one tiny moment.

"I'll be fine," I lied.

I followed him down the stairs, locking the doors behind him. Then, from my balcony window, I watched the beam of his head-lamp get smaller and smaller. Until I was sure he was gone.

"Tasch?" I knelt by the bed, taking her hand, but she just lay there. Limp. Even the lines of pain had faded. Only the faintest pulse in her wrist told me she was still hanging on. "I'm sorry I didn't tell you what I was going to do that day. I'm so sorry I wasn't there for you and Lotus. And I'm sorry I couldn't save you this time either."

Indigno. A sob caught in my throat as that single word ricocheted through my mind, the chorus of it threatening to destroy everything in its path.

Sarika is right. The Abuelos are right. God is punishing me.

No. I looked down at my strong hands, twelve wonderful fingers curling into fists. If there was a God, then he would not hate a thing he so carefully made. And he would not punish my beautiful sister for my mistakes. *Those* are the games of humans.

I kissed Tasch's forehead, my tears mixing with her blood, and said, "I love you. I know you know that, but I'm gonna say it anyway. I would take your place if I could. But I can't. The thing I *can* do—what I'm good at—is fight. I'll make Edison pay for what he's done to Pleiades and the Kisaengs and the Mothers. *Then* I'll make him pay for doing this to you."

I'd lost my first dagger in the mob, so I ripped the second one from my bodice and got the candle. Then I walked over to the wall of mirrors and stripped off my costume, carefully laying it at the end of the bed, alongside my mask. My cheeks were smeared with Tasch's blood from where I'd dried my eyes. I stood there for a moment, staring at my naked, wrong-handed body. I could see myself at every angle—my large breasts, round hips, extra fingers, stubborn face. This powerful, mutated, lovely place I'd inhabited for almost eighteen years.

I knelt down, in case I fainted. In the mirror, I could see the *thrum-thrum-thrum* of my pulse racing just below the skin at my throat. Breathing deep, I tried to calm down, trying to slow my heart rate so I didn't make things worse.

Then I reached back, so the point of the knife rested just above my right shoulder blade. I meant to kill Edison. Wherever he was.

Whatever he was planning. And I couldn't do that if he saw me coming.

I shifted the blade up a bit, so it was digging into the skin just under the ropy muscle that ran across my shoulders—estimating where Edison had injected the tracker. Then I made the incision.

The pain was a blanking-out, dizzying sharpness that eviscerated all my other thoughts. I fought against it with everything I had. Pushing the hurt from my mind.

I'd only get one shot at this.

Still, when I stuck my fingers into the wound, I almost passed out. I forced myself to focus on the multitudes of mirrors, but there was so much blood: leaking down my neck, over my breasts, dripping onto the floor.

My fingers were slippery as they dug around inside my own skin. The edges of my vision lit up with stars, a whole sky of them—the darkness kindly offering to swallow me whole. And I wanted it to.

Edison had put the chip in too deep. There was already too much blood. But I kept digging anyway—even as I knew it was too late. I couldn't hold myself together long enough to staunch the flow.

Then, among the stringy muscles and pain, my fingers hit something. Something hard and thin. The tracker.

Fighting against the dizziness . . . trying to stay conscious . . . I grabbed onto it and pulled. Then I gave in to the stars.

CHAPTER 44

DARKNESS.

I closed my eyes and opened them again. Still dark. But I heard voices. Faint ones. And screaming. Somewhere in the distance.

Then a pale rectangular glow on the floor. Light coming in through the curtain.

I tried to sit up, but my body was too heavy. I lifted a finger. Then another. The tracker was still clutched in my fist. I willed my hand to open and it slid out, dropping into a pool of blood.

It'd worked. And I was alive. How?

I flexed my whole hand, but it didn't hurt. I shifted my arm—there was no sharp twinge of pain. Not even a dull one.

I rolled over. The floor was sticky and the room stunk of death and sickness.

I touched my shoulder. It was crusted with blood, but there was no gaping wound. I couldn't even feel a scar. And suddenly, what Nik said came back to me.

I found something . . . something that might help her . . . help all of us. I wouldn't have even thought about it except for what you said about my hand. No scar.

And I remembered how quickly he'd healed after he cut himself on the glass. I'd assumed it'd just been part of what made him special. But maybe not. And a small hope flared inside me.

"Get up," I ordered myself, and my voice came out in a croak. I sat up, using the bed to pull myself into a crouch. I fumbled for the candle on the floor next to me, searching for matches with shaky hands. When I finally managed to get it relit, the dim glow cast shadows over Tasch's frozen face. Her mouth was slightly agape, her eyes open. I shut them and kissed her forehead.

"'*Wait here and I will return for you.*'" My voice shook as I repeated the words of the fairy tale. "*She kissed her sisters' cheeks and locked them inside the forbidden room.*"

"*When the sorcerer returned, he said to the middle sister, 'Give me the egg so I know it is safe.'*

"*And he was surprised to see the shell was white as snow, without a drop of blood to mark it.*

"'*You have proven yourself worthy. You shall be my bride.' And as he uttered those words, his power over her was lost.*"

A streak of light flashed by my windows and from downstairs there came the sound of someone rattling the locked doors. Careful to stay hidden, I eased myself off the bed and crawled over to the balcony door—pushing back the curtains a few centimeters to look.

Outside, four Curadores wearing isolation suits stood in the street. The Dome was dark except for the beams of their flashlights scanning past the house. I cracked the porch door open and listened.

"Nope . . . doors are locked. Tracker says she's in there, but we haven't seen any movement. Not out back either. Decontamination must have gotten her."

Pause. Static.

"On foot. The magfly tracks are a wreck."

Pause.

Static. Then a squeal of feedback.

"Repeat that last part, Edison."

Short pause.

"Of course . . . I'll report back if there's movement anywhere on the street."

I eased the door shut again. At least I knew that Edison was still close enough to make contact with the Curadores and I didn't intend to let him get any farther. More importantly, I knew Edison was afraid I was coming after him. And he was right to be.

But first I had to find a way to get out of this house. I was too drained to fight my way through Edison's Curadores, and even if I could, Edison would hear about it. It would defeat the whole point of removing the tracker.

There was another problem too. Everyone had seen me in my Dia de los Muertos outfit. And I would be easy to pick out in the streets of the Dome if I had no costume at all. That had been the whole point of the Festival—the ability to hide in plain sight.

I needed to make something new. And quick.

I rummaged through my closet, picking up the fairy tale again—trying to steady myself.

"The middle sister agreed to marry the sorcerer. But she said, 'Give me a day, for I must make myself beautiful for the wedding.'

"And she sent him away to invite all his friends and relations to the celebration."

I grabbed the first thing I found with pockets, a short blue dress. Then I pulled the bottom drawer out of the dresser. Grimm's feathers lay inside it, catching the candlelight. Leaning against the bed, I sewed Grimm's feathers onto the fabric—tacking them down with quick stitches on either side of the shaft. Every so often I heard a distant explosion and my fingers worked faster and faster. Until the skirt was covered with them.

Then the mask. I covered the eyes, the cheeks, the chin with smaller feathers—hiding Riya's designs. Tall plumes fanned out around the top, concealing the crown of flowers.

Finally, I removed one of the pouches of explosives from my old dress and sewed it into the hem of my new one. Leaving the other for Tasch.

I picked up the tracker from the floor. Rolling Tasch onto her side on the bed, I made a small cut above her shoulder blade. I knew she was dead, but I still flinched as a trickle of blood leaked from the wound. Carefully, I slipped the tracker under the skin.

My cheeks were wet and my throat tightened against my voice. But I forced the words of the story out, as if they could take away the horror.

"As soon as the sorcerer had gone, the middle sister crept into the gruesome basement to free her sisters. She sent them home and promised to follow soon after. Then she pulled a skull from the basin of blood and took it with her."

I pulled the blankets off of Taschen and slit her gown with my knife—letting the ragged fabric fall away. Her body was covered with sores and bruises, and a whimper rose up inside me.

"This isn't her," I reminded myself. "This is only a body."

Carefully, I fit Taschen into my corseted dress and arranged her in a chair facing the porch door—her now-pale face stark and terrible against the bright marigolds.

"She decorated the skull with flowers and a wedding veil and carried it to her bedroom. Then carefully, she placed it on the windowsill.

"One by one, guests began to arrive at the house for the wedding. They waved to the grinning bride sitting by the upstairs window. Even the sorcerer was fooled when he returned home. Looking up, he delighted in his bride's wide smile and blew her a kiss."

Stripping the bed, I balled up the sheets and pulled down the gauzy canopy, piling them on the mattress. Then I slipped on the feathered dress and tied the mask. One knife in my pocket. One in my boot. Almost ready now.

"Finally, the sister sliced open the feather bed. She covered herself in honey and rolled in the white feathers. When she was done she looked, not a bit like herself, but like a magnificent bird."

Below the window, there were more Curadores now—their isolation suits standing out against the dark street. The perfect audience.

"Taschen . . ." I looked at the girl propped up and decorated in the chair—that was not my sister. Taschen had finally been given leave from this world and I was not going to keep her here any longer. I kissed the top of her head. "Thank you for . . ."

But how do you thank someone for being a piece of your soul? So I said, "I'll look after Lotus for you. I promise."

I pulled Lotus's necklace from the drawer and hung it around my neck. Then tucked the scope with the glass lenses in my pocket. There were still two sisters left.

I was ready now. Standing off to the side of the balcony window, I yanked down the curtains and added them to the bundle on the bed. Finally, I nested the candle in the middle of it—wax and flames spilling across the cloth.

The fire caught immediately, flaring up behind Taschen, bright and dramatic. Shouts came from outside. I imagined what Tasch must look like in that gorgeous gown. She would be perfectly framed by the door, the room ablaze around her. Illuminating her in the black night.

As I fled down the stairs, I heard someone pounding on the front door. "Leica? Are you in there? Quick! Sagan, help me get this door open!"

Panicked shouting rose up from the front of the house and then they were trying to force their way through the door and the rhythm of their blows matched my heart. *Whomp! Whomp! Whomp!*

I raced through the kitchen to the back door. How long till the flames reached Taschen? Minutes? Seconds?

Like I'd hoped, the back of the house was empty. Any Curadores who'd been standing guard had run to the front at the first cries of alarm.

I made it out the back door, just as Curadores rushed in the front. I sprinted around the house and into the street—trying to get clear as fast as I could. In the chaos, no one noticed me as I ran.

As the sorcerer came into the house, he walked passed the middle sister without even recognizing her.

"Little Bird," he said. "Won't you stay for my wedding?"

"I cannot," the sister said. "It is time for me to fly away."

When I got to the end of the street, I glanced back. Just for a fraction of a second, I saw her. Taschen's body blazing white hot. A silhouette of flame.

Then she erupted into ball of fire and the vast explosion shattered the air. Glass shards and splinters rained down into the night—the house consumed by a magnificent burst of light.

CHAPTER 45

I RAN THROUGH the network of streets, my lungs choked with smoke and grief. But I felt strong too—like Tasch's fire sizzled through my veins as well. I no longer had my tracker, so I was free to follow Edison now. But that was easier said than done. Even if I was right and he'd taken a magfly out to the Indigno camp, we'd just spent the last few hours bombing the hell out of tracks and taking down the Dome's systems. I just hoped when I found Ada she'd have a better answer than walking.

And finding Ada in this wreck was going to be its own challenge. When I got to the Complex, the whole place was crackling like an enormous bonfire, and it wasn't the only building burning. Water misted from the Dome ceiling—trying unsuccessfully to contain the blazes. I had to hope—I had to assume—that Ada and the Mothers made it safely to the Genetics Lab.

There were no streetlamps on anywhere, but I could see by the flicker of flames as I ran through the neighborhood toward the Lab and the Promenade. And what was worse than the fires was the silence. The emptiness. Other than the Curadores outside my house, I'd seen *no one*.

Then I heard the hiss. I followed the static, tracking it down one street, then another. Until there, sprawled on the dark asphalt, was Riya—a small radio gripped in her hand.

I dropped to my knees, scanning for a knife wound. For blood. There was nothing . . . but her body was *so still* and my voice shook as I called her name. Her eyes stayed closed, her face slack, but I swore her hand twitched.

Then she started seizing—terrible, violent convulsions. I pried the radio out of her hand, shouting into it, "Hello? I need help!"

Static roared its blank answer while I pulled Riya onto my lap, trying to keep her from hurting herself.

My voice sounded so tiny in the empty night. "Please! Anyone!"

But no one was coming. Adrenaline surged through me and I scooped Riya up, cradling her as I ran through the village toward the Genetics Lab. "You can't have her too. I won't let you!"

I turned down another street, following the magfly lines, and I saw them. My eyes didn't register what they were at first. Piles of cloth. Heaps of salvage. I slowed to a walk, not wanting them to come into focus. There must have been thirty of them. Limp in the street.

Riya's seizure had slowed to a quiver and I laid her gently on a stoop. Then I crept closer. They were gauzy bundles of fabric-draped women. Knives and fighting sticks still gripped in their hands. Some wore masks. Others were barefaced, eyes closed. But like Riya, there was no blood. No obvious injuries.

And there were Curadores too—dressed in their party finery. They were unmoving, but visibly unhurt as well. Like they had been fighting one minute, then dropped to the ground the next. It made no sense.

"Edison, what have you done?" my voice was a whisper. Then I felt the burning in my own lungs. More than grief or fear.

I hoisted Riya over my shoulder and I ran.

I was wheezing by the time I got to the Promenade. The grass was muddied and strewn with more bodies. Whatever had happened to theses people was clearly happening to me too. I dodged and leapt over them, my back aching from carrying my friend. Breath fighting its way in and out of my body. A movement caught my eye, and I ducked behind a bench just as a Curador in an isolation suit walked out of the ruins of the Sanctum.

He barely glanced around him as he crunched across the broken glass. He obviously wasn't expecting any surprises. As I watched him cross the lawn—ground blue glass glittering in the path of his headlamp—something bothered me about the scene. I pulled off my mask to get a better look.

It was too dark.

The Promenade behind the Curador should have been lit up by the Genetics Lab. Had it been destroyed as well? But then surely there'd be fires or at least ruins. I saw nothing but blackness. Maybe the main computer had been destroyed and none of the systems were working anymore. Maybe that's why I couldn't breathe.

But as the Curador got close to where the Lab should be, his light strobed across the building, reflecting a dull sheen. As if someone had replaced the glass walls with a burnished black metal. Like the walls the flys had made when they'd sealed off the magfly accident.

The Curador was headed away from the Promenade now, and as he disappeared down a street, I ran—air clawing down my throat. I didn't bother hiding anymore. My head was spinning, and if Riya and I couldn't get inside the Lab, then it didn't matter *who* found us. But maybe if the flys had sealed this whole building up, the air inside might still be good. Ada and the Mothers might still be safe.

I readjusted my hold on Riya, and with the last of my energy pounded on the metal shell that encapsulated the entire Genetics Lab.

"Ada! Let me in!" There was no answer. I pounded again, sliding down the slick surface as my legs gave way. I braced myself with my free hand, trying to keep myself upright, and my fingers caught on a ridge.

I traced it, hoping it might be a crack—the edge of some sort of door. And in the dim light of the burning magfly, I saw it. An emblem formed into the metal, right where the door should be. The LOTUS flower.

I fumbled with Lotus's necklace—my hands shaking so hard I could barely make them grip—pulling it off over my head. The same emblem glimmering in the same metal. And the number.

I flipped it over, trying to keep it in focus as my vision fuzzed around the edges. *A code.* Edison had used a code to get in the Labs.

But, of course, the keypad was unreachable too—on the other side of the seal. My throat and chest, my head, my muscles, my heart—all ached. Begging for oxygen. *Sometimes your opponent is stronger than you. And no matter how fast you are, or how smart you fight, you still can't win.*

"Dammit!" I hit the black metal barrier with all the strength I had left.

And the necklace in my fist quivered—the pendant pulling on its chain. Straining to close the distance between it and the other LOTUS. *But you still fight . . . in whatever way you can.*

With a last shred of hope, I slammed my necklace into the LO-TUS flower and the barrier began to hum—my body pulsing with the chorus of a thousand flys. The necklace was vibrating now too. The edges of the pendant melted, then fused with the wall, sending a ripple through the surrounding metal. Then the whole barrier was liquefying—a shimmering, living wall.

The metal began to ooze up and around my fingers, and remembering the Kisaeng who'd been trapped inside the magfly, I pulled away. But it was too late. The metal was already creeping up my arm. My shoulder. Cinching around my throat. And I could taste it now too. Metallic and bitter. I managed one last gasp before Riya and I were sucked into molten blackness.

CHAPTER 46

THE LIGHT WAS BLINDING. I squinted, trying to shield my eyes—it didn't help. But I could breathe again and that was something. I sat up and checked on Riya, still unconscious on the floor next to me.

"Don't move."

I blinked, trying to get my eyes to adjust to the light. I was on the floor of the main room in the Genetics Lab. Screens flashed and flys flew in manic circles around the high ceiling. A woman I didn't recognize pointed a long iron and wood rod at me. By the way she was holding it, I was sure it was a weapon.

"Can I at least see if she's okay?" I motioned to Riya. The woman nodded, but I was already feeling for the faint pulse on Riya's wrist. "She's still alive, but I don't know for how long. What happened out there?"

"I don't think I'll be the one answering questions right now." The pale, stone-faced woman did something to her weapon and it made a *shick-shick* noise. She was wearing a hooped dress and I recognized Riya's handiwork—she must be a Mother. "*No one* can get through that door . . . but you did. Who the hell are you?"

"I'm Leica, I need to speak to Ada *right now*."

"Wrong answer." She pointed the weapon just over my shoulder and fired, the glass behind me blowing apart. I threw my arms over my head, my ears ringing with the noise. "Don't play games with me. Leica's dead! Everyone out there is dead . . . except you. So you have one more chance before I shoot your head off. Who are you?"

After everything, I was going to die *here*, *now*, killed by allies. I put my hands in the air. "Please, look! Six fingers! I'm a friend!"

"Emmy, what the hell's going on in here?" Ada ran into the room, addressing the Mother, who by now was already lowering her weapon. "We heard—"

"Leica!" June flew past Ada, descending on me. Hugging me tight. "We saw the fire and then your tracker stopped transmitting . . . we were sure you . . ." Her voice died out as she saw Riya.

"I found her like that. She's stopped seizing, but I don't know if that's good or bad. Will someone please tell me what's happening?"

"Edison initiated some kind of fail-safe and the flys sealed us inside here." And Ada pointed to the screens, which all read: **Quarantine Established. Decontamination Protocol Reinitiated.** "It locked down all communications too. Judging by readouts from the filtration system, we think it's flooding the rest of Dome with something intended to kill, well, anything and everything. We can't stop it and we can't get out." The frustration was clear on her face. Then it turned to confusion. "Wait. How did you get in here?"

I held up Lotus's necklace. "This tag. Edison has one too."

Ada snatched it from my hand, glanced at it, then immediately punched the code into the computer. All of the screens went black for a second. There was a melodic *bwong* and they were back up, white words scrolling endlessly down a black screen. Finally, when the new screen loaded, there was the LOTUS flower emblazoned on a grey background. Then a warning flashed onto every monitor simultaneously, in giant letters.

Decontamination Protocol initiated: 2084. 06. 20. 07:23

Decontamination Protocol complete: 2084. 06. 20. 12:47

Decontamination Protocol reinitiated 2592. 11. 01. 21:05

"Whoa," June said.

And the computer responded in a friendly, efficient voice, "LOTUS admin access granted."

Ada didn't waste any time. "Shut down Decontamination Protocol!"

But the computer simply said, "Decontamination Protocol has not been completed."

Ada repeated her command, "Computer, shut down Decontamination Protocol."

"Decontamination is at eighty-five percent, not sufficient to terminate all viral and bacterial life-forms. Are you sure you wish to—"

"Shut down the fucking Decontamination Protocol!"

"Protocol terminated." The computer answered. "Seal will be lifted when atmosphere has returned to viable levels."

Ada looked at me. "Eighty-five percent. You should be dead."

"I nearly was. Then your Mother over there almost finished the job."

The Mother, who Ada had called Emmy, made no apologies. "We're the only ones left and I'll be damned if I let someone walk in here and wipe out the rest of us."

The Mothers had courage, even if I didn't agree with their methods. "What the hell kind of weapon *is* that?"

"Shotgun. We ransacked the place once we were locked in. There's a stockpile of them in the basement . . . along with a lot of other crazy stuff. Thought they might be able to break through the seal, but no luck. But let's not change the subject. I mean, I'm glad and everything, but why aren't you dead?"

"Nik did something to me. Or actually, to Tasch." I looked at my hands, still smeared with blood—mine and hers. "Whatever it is, I think it saved me."

"Computer, sample Leica's blood."

A fly buzzed down from the ceiling and landed on the back of my hand. Its sharp metal legs crawled over to a blue vein; then there was a sharp sting and it took off again.

"Display results."

Percentages and data scrolled across the screen. Ada followed the stream of information carefully, nodding, but it was meaningless to me. "Now show me the blood on a cellular level."

The screen filled with hundreds of red, puffy discs.

"That clever little clone." Ada had admiration in her voice. "Those round thingys are red blood cells, but see these ones?" She pointed to a shape on the screen that was smaller and sleeker. Once I knew what I was looking for, I spotted more of them floating among the blood cells. "Those are the nanites Nik's been working on—so his plants could filter out toxins. Evidently, he's figured out how to use them on people."

And I remembered Nik's fist, slamming into the broken glass and dirt . . . and nanites. They must have gotten into his bloodstream and *that's* why his hand healed. And when Tasch's blood mixed with mine, they must've gotten into my bloodstream too. That must be why I healed so well.

"Computer, can you replicate the artificial elements in this sample?" Ada asked.

"Yes."

"Good. Prepare a sample and distribute it to Riya—the one in need of medical attention."

"Task complete in thirteen minutes, forty-nine seconds."

"Do you think it'll work?" I asked, looking at Riya's motionless grey face. It reminded me too much of Taschen for comfort.

"I'm not sure. I'll have to figure out what kind of toxins were used, but they've only been in her system for a short while and her body's still fighting. The nanites are designed for this exact thing. Then again . . . they *weren't* designed for humans."

"Edison is still out there. I think he's been communicating with . . ." I petered off, thinking of Jenner's delirious words. *Thinks he's talking to Earth.* "I have to stop whatever he has planned."

She didn't even blink. "Right. All the magnetic fields are still functioning and we didn't take out any of the tracks on the lower levels." Ada said. "Monitors show the magflys should be up and running down there."

She was flipping through schematics of the Dome and one caught my attention as it flashed across the screens.

"Wait. Show me that one again."

Ada flipped back, her voice hushed. "I've never seen this before. I wonder what else that LOTUS code gave us access to."

It was a map of Gabriel, recognizable and foreign at the same time. Familiar mountains ringed the valley. There were other landmarks too: Ad Astra Research Colony, with the curve of the Dome highlighted in blue. And nearby, a tiny semicircle of buildings—Pleiades

Hotel and Suites. And—where the open field of the Festival Grounds was—LOTUS Corporation Air Force Base.

Magfly lines crisscrossed the desert. But there were streets as well, lined with grids of rectangular buildings. There was a red circle encompassing most of the valley and at the bottom it read, **Emergency Protocol successful: 2084. 06. 20.**

The fist of God.

I pushed the thought out of my mind—concentrating on getting out to Tierra Muerta and stopping whatever Edison had planned next. "Okay, show me the map to the magflys again."

I jogged down several flights of stairs, ending at the double glass doors of a decontamination portal. This one was in disrepair—the sliding doors were opening and closing on their own. They were out of sync with each other, so I only caught little glimpses of the hallway on the other side. Damp cement floors. Dim lights. A sign above the doors read:

RESTRICTED ACCESS. LOTUS PERSONNEL ONLY. TRESPASSERS WILL BE PROSECUTED ON SIGHT.

I hurried down the hall, found the exit, and climbed on the magfly Ada had waiting for me. The doors slid shut behind me and it took off. All I could see was the black blur of the magfly tubes, but just as soon as we picked up speed, we were slowing down again.

Then I was gliding into a bright room—the magfly automatically slowing as it traveled through the usually busy Salvage Hall. There were bodies everywhere. Citizens strewn across the floor like scrap. My heart stopped as I spotted Sarika's face in the sea of corpses. Eyes open. A look of rapture on her face.

I tried to open the doors of the magfly. Prying at them, pounding on the button, but nothing happened. Then the magfly jerked into motion again. I was rushing down the tunnels and then out under the night sky.

The trip that would've taken days to walk took minutes. Ada had programmed the magfly to stop a mile or so away from the Indigno camp—we weren't taking any chances. And when the magfly finally slowed, I was grateful to climb out of the nightmare into the empty darkness of Tierra Muerta. I let it wash away what I'd seen.

As my boots sank into the sand, I turned instead to the stars. They were old friends and I clung to their constancy—as if I could walk the bright ribbon of light that unfurled across the sky. Tonight had already cost me so much and I didn't know what more was waiting for me at the Indigno camp, but at least the stars were still shining.

As I neared the clusters of boulders outside the camp, I thought I saw another shadow moving in the dark. I pulled my knife from my boot, but by then, the shadow was gone. I still hadn't seen any sign of Edison. Maybe I'd guessed wrong. Maybe he'd already been here and left? I gripped my knife tighter, almost hoping that was the case. Wishing I could be spared this confrontation.

I crept around the boulders, and remembering how the Indignos had posted guards up in the foothills, I glanced up. But the moon was bright and it threw a hundred more suspicious shadows across the landscape.

Then my foot caught on something and I went sprawling. I managed not to shout, biting my tongue in my effort to keep quiet. It was only scraped hands and bruises but I stayed down, feeling around for my knife. My hand hit soft fur instead.

"Please. No." I couldn't face losing another friend tonight.

I crawled over the wet sand. And there, lying in the grit, was Jaesun's dog. The pup's tongue lolling out. A gash across her belly.

CHAPTER 47

WHATEVER WAS LEFT of my heart hardened against Edison. I buried my hand in the pup's fur. "You didn't deserve this."

I was answered with a low whine. The dog managed to open her eyes, though I could only see the whites. "Oh, pup!"

She whimpered and gave another pitiful whine. It was a mournful, agonized cry and I raised my knife—steeling myself to end her suffering. But I didn't have it in me. Not after this night. Not after the terrible things I'd already seen and done.

Kneeling there, I let my head drop. Let myself grieve for just a moment. I was exhausted, my body ached, and my hands burned from my fall. I ran my fingers over my ripped palm. It was already starting to scab over a little, the nanites working fast. And I had an idea.

I winced as I sliced my palm with my knife. A dark red line welled up and I made a fist. Blood seeped between my clenched fingers—dripping down my hand—and I let it trickle into the dog's wounded underbelly.

She whimpered, straining to lift her head. I scratched her chin. "I know, pup . . . it hurts. I know."

Then she slumped back to the ground again. Eyes shut. Was it enough? Was it too late, like with Tasch? Or had the pup just passed out?

I pushed myself to my feet. I'd done all I could. Well, not everything—I added the pup to the list of things I would make Edison pay for.

As I came over the crest and descended into the small valley, the lights of the Indigno camp greeted me. I didn't see anyone moving around down there, but I could hear the hiss of the radio. And in the center of camp—where the bonfire had been—sat a smaller version of the shuttle we'd found in the sand dunes.

I stuck my knife back in my boot and pulled out my scope to get a better look. I recognized the aged metal. The markings on the door. This wasn't a *version* of the shuttle . . . it *was* the shuttle. Only it'd been taken apart and cobbled back together into a smaller machine.

Two wings jutted out on either side of a tiny cockpit. The engines that'd been close to the sides of the shuttle before had been reattached so they were sitting at the ends of the wings now, pointing down. Food replicators and stacks of storage drives were piled around an open door. I heard voices, and Edison came into view, wearing an isolation suit.

Then Nik, without one.

Dammit. Back in my bedroom, I'd *told* Nik where Edison was headed. Of course he came out here. I should've guessed. No matter what'd happened, Edison was still Nik's brother.

They were arguing as Edison loaded up the shuttle, but I couldn't hear what they were saying. Pulling off my boots and socks, I crept through the maze of tarp-covered ruins. Rocks dug into my soles, but my bare feet were silent and sure of the ground beneath them. Then I was only five or six meters away. I crouched behind a crumbling wall, assessing the situation.

The shuttle was sitting in the middle of the central clearing. In addition to the small cockpit, there was a second compartment where Edison was stowing supplies. You could access the compartment from either side of the shuttle and Edison had both doors open as he loaded up the ship.

". . . and I already said, *I'm leaving*." Edison carried a food synthesizer to the shuttle.

"But that's what I'm trying to tell you—you don't have to! The nanites can allow us to survive outside the Dome," Nik said.

They were completely absorbed in their debate and I realized this was a much better situation than I could've imagined. I ripped open my hem—pulling out the pouch of explosives. Nik was the perfect distraction. But I'd still have to sneak around to the other side so I wouldn't be seen.

"Don't you see?" Nik touched Edison's arm. "*This* is what we imagined all those years ago. We can start over! We can fix Gabriel!"

All the tents and buildings faced this central area and I retreated back into them—winding through the camp. Working my way around to the far side of the shuttle. I was terrified of making a noise, but I concentrated on the heft of the bomb in my hand. Letting it steady me.

"But this is bigger than we ever imagined." Edison's voice drifted through the Indigno camp. "You *have* to come with me! We owe it to ourselves to do this together."

I reached the other side, the rebuilt ship sitting between me and the brothers now—only a few meters away from the wall I was crouching behind. From this vantage point, I could see Edison on the far side, framed by the open doors of the compartment. And there was a look on his face as he loaded the final bits onto the shuttle—one I couldn't quite place. Doubt? Regret?

Then he plastered a wide smile on his face and he turned to Nik. As soon as Edison's back was to me, I scurried across the open ground to the shuttle—stashing the explosives behind a stack of drives. Pulling the detonator out of my pocket.

"These people are desperate for technology and those nanites of yours are exactly what they're looking for. I mean, look at what it's already done for you . . . I assume that's why you aren't wearing an isolation suit?" There was a false casualness to Edison's voice as he asked his last question.

And hearing it, I froze—half in, half out of the shuttle—danger prickling at my neck. If Nik had come straight out to Tierra Muerta, then he had no idea about Edison's Decontamination Protocol. He had no idea what his brother was capable of. But *I* did.

If Edison wanted Nik to come with him—wherever he was going—it could only be for one reason. The nanites inside Nik's veins.

Nik was going to get himself killed. He was going to get us both killed.

I pocketed the detonator and eased out of the shuttle. Edison's back was still to me, but he'd moved to his brother's side, so now I could see both of them through the doors. I tried to get Nik's attention.

"But our people need this technology too!" Nik gestured toward the shuttle and his eyes went wide when he saw me there. He recovered quickly and managed to keep talking. "Are you telling me that Earth is more deserving than them?"

Edison let out a bark of laughter—a dry, humorless thing. "That's the thing, Nikola . . . the joke's on us. We're already *on* Earth."

CHAPTER 48

"I KNOW IT'S IMPOSSIBLE to believe . . . it was for me at first too. But somewhere on the other side of those mountains"— Edison turned, pointing to the ridge behind me and I dove out of sight, hoping I was fast enough—"there are people."

Now I pressed my back flat against the wall of the shuttle—the cold creeping through my thin dress. *Earth?*

Edison was insane. He *must* be.

Then an image came into my mind—the bottle of wine Edison had shared with me that first night. The valley and vineyards of California.

That bottle had felt important. Familiar somehow. And now I understood why . . . I had *recognized* that ridge line. That picture on the bottle had been of *our mountains*. Our valley.

"*Think* about what you're saying." Nik's voice was strained— trying to understand what Edison was telling him. Trying to figure out what to do about me. "If there were other people on this planet, we would have seen them . . . seen *some sign* of them."

"Not if they'd abandoned us here. Not if we *wanted* them to forget. Remember . . . remember when we realized that Red Death was a hybrid . . . that someone had *made* it on purpose? Tell me you didn't guess at least a little of the truth that day. *We* made that virus. Well, not us, but the Dome's scientists, hundreds of years ago."

"That's what the underground laboratories were for . . . *that* was LOTUS." Nik was putting the pieces together—faster than I was.

Edison nodded, keeping his eyes on his brother as Nik paced a little to the left, effectively angling Edison away from me.

"You're looking at ground zero!" Edison gestured dramatically at the valley around him. "Ad Astra wasn't some utopian planetary colony. It was a prototype. Scientists living and working inside the sealed environment, studying food replication, terraforming, swarm robotics—but it was all just a front for the real work.

"Red Death was the crown jewel of the LOTUS Corporation's biological weapons division. The scientists couldn't wait to show off their creation to headquarters in Washington, DC. But they underestimated it." Edison flicked his head at the shuttle. "The crew was already infected by the time the plane even got off the ground."

And I remembered the broken orange cases Suji found inside the shuttle. No, not shuttle—I corrected myself—Edison said *plane*.

"And how did the LOTUS Corporation reward their loyal employees for creating such a stunning success?" Edison asked. "By bombing the hell out of this valley and hitting the Dome's self-destruct button."

I thought of the date of the first Decontamination Protocol. 2084. That's where Edison got the idea. From my hiding spot, I clutched the detonator hard—the prongs biting into my palm.

"But they survived," Nik said, the whole picture unfolding in his mind. "The scientists sealed in the isolation labs . . . the Citizens in the valley . . . they survived. No wonder we could never break into Ad Astra's computer system. They locked themselves out on purpose. The only way to keep the LOTUS Corporation from coming back and finishing the job was to stay invisible."

"What can I say? Life wants to live!" I could hear the glee in Edison's voice. "But when we discovered this plane, we rediscovered the access codes . . . though it took me a while to figure out how to use them. Turns out they're activated by proximity keys. Brilliant!"

And I thought of Lotus's necklace—unsealing the Lab, turning off the Decontamination Protocol.

"But once I finally got the codes working, the whole Dome simply laid itself bare. Nik, you should've seen it. Everything we've ever tried to change or fix or understand for the last fifteen years was there! Schematics, data files, maps. All right at my fingertips!

"But Ad Astra had kept its secrets well. According to the files, after LOTUS Corporation declared this whole area a dead zone and started shooting anyone who tried to get in or out, the survivors made a pact. They threw away the passcodes to the LOTUS computer system and radios—*anything* that would connect them to the outside world—and they made up a history that would keep them safe. This valley"—Edison spread his arms wide—"bombed and crushed and abandoned, became Gabriel. Anyone who protested—inside *or* outside the Dome—was deemed Corrupted and exiled to Tierra Muerta."

"And the next generation grew up safe, listening to stories about how their ancestors had journeyed across the stars to the planet

Gabriel. Brilliant." Nik echoed Edison's admiration. He sounded awestruck—caught up in the story Edison was weaving. "And Ad Astra Colony became a lone settlement on an infected planet. The perfect cage for people who had no choice but to stay trapped."

I could tell by Nik's tone that he'd forgotten where we were. What was happening here. But Edison hadn't—I was sure of that. He was doing everything in his power to pull Nik back into a time when it was the two of them against the world. Giving Nik the satisfaction of piecing together the mystery they'd been born to solve.

I'd have to think for both of us, then. I peeked out from my hiding spot next to the open door—checking if it was safe to make my move. The two of them were in profile now, and as I shifted, I discovered I could see their reflections in the window of one of the food synthesizers. Squatting next to the plane in safety, I watched, waiting for my moment.

"Only . . ." Confusion clouded Nik's face. "What makes you think they're going to welcome us back now?"

"Because they *need* us!" Edison's voice was suddenly infused with compassion and it was clear he was intent on drawing Nik into his scheme. "The dead zone did nothing to stop the spread of Red Death. Los Angeles was infected in a matter of hours. The west coast in a matter of days. They kept expanding the dead zone, but Red Death kept spreading. And with a ninety percent fatality rate, it only took a few months for the whole world to fall apart."

Nik played right into Edison's hand, his face filled with horrified fascination. "Even if there was still electricity, anything with a computer in it would've broken down in a matter of years or even months . . . and there would've been no one to fix it."

"And nothing to fix it with." Edison stepped toward Nik, reeling him in, and I tensed. *Turn toward Nik! Go on! Look away!*

"They would've been too busy just trying not to starve," Nik said.

"You see it now, don't you? We were *never* meant to save the Dome." Then Edison threw his arm around Nik. "We were meant to save the world!"

And I could see it too. Gabriel—our valley—had survived because the Dome's technology had remained intact. It'd kept us all alive. But the rest of the world wouldn't have had anything like the Dome to safeguard them. And now Edison was going to take our incredibly advanced tech back out into the world. He wouldn't just be a hero. He would be a God.

"Then Jenner was right . . . *this* is what we were made for." Nik was smiling, but his eyes flicked to me as he threw an arm around Edison. Pivoting his brother away from me and the plane.

I jumped up, scrambling into the compartment, and plunged the detonator into the bomb. I hit the timer—red numbers flashed three-zero-zero. Then they started counting down. Edison would not get the chance to destroy another world.

Through the doorway, I flashed three fingers at Nik and he nodded. We both knew that Edison would never let Nik share any of the power this new tech would bring. Edison liked to rule alone.

I backed out of the compartment and, keeping low, crept toward the nose of the plane. Trying to stay hidden. Trying to hurry. Trying to stay silent. Two minutes, forty seconds.

Nik kept talking, distracting Edison while I put distance between myself and the bomb. "If the whole world was infected, why keep the dead zone?"

"Same reason the Dome never let in the Citizens. The outside world never came up with a cure, but they weren't saturated in the contagion like we were. With strict quarantine procedures, they managed to eradicate the disease. They haven't had a case in—"

A squawk of feedback blasted through the plane's radio as I slipped past the cockpit. I leapt back, my skirt swishing around me, and the squealing stopped. My stomach dropped as I looked down at my dress and realized what I'd done. Grimm's feathers. I'd *decorated* myself with a whole array of shiny *antennas*.

I ran.

But Edison ran faster. He had me by my arm and was dragging me around the front of the plane before I'd made it three steps. "Why, Leica! How lovely of you to join us! I should've known a little bonfire wouldn't stop you. Though you put on quite a show for my Curadores."

Edison thought he'd won. But my mind was on the clock, running down the seconds. There couldn't be more than two minutes left. I'd rather not die, but I was willing to.

"I suppose Nik bestowed his little miracle upon you too."

I needed to keep him talking—distract him while the clock ran out. And I knew just the spot to hit. "Yeah . . . too bad for you that Nik turned out to be the smart brother."

Edison laughed, pulling me close so my face was pressed against the speakers of his suit—his words rumbling through me. "Intelligence isn't everything."

Nik was only a few feet away, but his voice was very soft when he said, "Let her go."

"Of course, brother . . . in a minute."

As Edison smiled at Nik, I pulled my dagger from my pocket,

wanting to cut the smug smile off Edison's face. But Edison seized my wrist and twisted hard, turning the knife on me.

There was a glint of silver as he forced me to slice my own arm and then his hand—tearing a gash through the white isolation suit and into his palm. Blood flowed down my arm, dripping on the sand. Staining my skin.

Nik was moving, but Edison had already clasped his injured hand around my bleeding arm. My mind went blank with the agony of it—the pain finally catching up with me. And by the time Nik had closed the distance between us, Edison had got what he wanted. The nanites.

He threw me at Nik, my limp body slamming into Nik's chest. My dagger flying. The two of us skidding into the sand.

"I guess I should thank you for sparing me the task of killing my own brother." Edison stripped off his isolation suit as we scrambled to our feet.

But I barely heard him over the refrain in my head. *One minute. One minute. One minute.*

Nik's hands curled into fists. But I grabbed his arm, stopping Nik from going after Edison. "Don't! Can't you see that he's won?"

But Edison's face changed as I pulled Nik away, seeing through my pleas of surrender. "I *told* you we were the same, Leica. And neither us would ever give up."

Edison seemed to think for a second, then climbed into the plane and rooted around. A moment later he said, "Ah, here it is." And came out holding the pouch of explosives.

"Thirteen seconds. You definitely don't disappoint." He pulled out the detonator and, almost amused, he tossed it on the ground. "I've asked you once before to come with me . . . here in this same place." Edison looked around the Indigno camp. "And now I'm asking you again. You know there's nothing . . . no one . . . left for you inside that Dome."

"They were your own people!" Rage shook my voice and I didn't try to control it. Let him think he'd succeeded with his Decontamination Protocol. Let him stay cocky.

Fear tinged Nik's words. "Edison, what did you do?"

In a cold voice Edison said, "I simply finished the job."

I didn't need a bomb or a self-destruct button. My second knife was already in my hand. My feet already moving.

I would've killed him. *We* would've. But Marisol suddenly burst into the clearing, flinging herself at Edison's feet. "Don't you dare leave me here!"

Her eyes were wild. Face caked with grit and tears. "They're dead. All of them." Her shredded dress dragged in the dirt as she clung to Edison's legs, begging him. "You can't just leave me here to die."

There was a madness in her, and even Edison took some kind of pity on her. Or maybe her prostrations made him feel more powerful. Either way, he helped her up, wiped off her face, and lied. "You know I'd never leave you."

I met Nik's eyes. If we wanted to stop Edison, we'd have to kill them both now—if Marisol had proven anything, it was that she was a fighter. And they'd be painful, violent deaths—fists and knives. But I was a fighter too.

I adjusted my grip on the knife, six fingers wrapping tight around the hilt. Then I heard the *shick-shick* and I saw Edison's gun pointed directly at my face. "Not tonight, sweet Leica. As much as I'd like one last dance, there's simply no time."

His gun was smaller than the Mother's, but I guessed just as deadly. And like that, it was over.

"Like I said, life wants to live." Edison shrugged, and gave us a smug grin as he helped Marisol onto the plane and slammed the doors. After all the planning, after all the fighting, there was nothing more to do. Numb with shock, Nik and I backed away as the engines roared into life. And through the shimmering waves of heat, I saw the pup running toward me. Tail wagging. Wonderfully alive.

Even as Edison and Marisol lifted off the ground—the wind of the engine scalding my face and throat—a tiny hope blossomed in my chest. With Edison gone, we could start over. The outside world would get what they wanted . . . and maybe we would too.

Edison had forgotten his own lesson—he'd underestimated us. If the pup had been saved, maybe Riya had been too. Maybe they all could be.

I crouched down, wrapping my arms around the pup as she barked madly at the rising plane. Then I saw it. Or rather, didn't see it. The explosives, the detonator, they were gone.

Marisol. She'd played the devoted Kisaeng so convincingly.

"Don't look!" I grabbed onto Nik and pulled him to the ground just as the sky exploded with a flash of white. The plane combusted in a great orange fireball. Raining debris and ash and death down on all of us.

CHAPTER 49

MY VOICE WAS HOARSE, but I raised it up anyway. The words rasping against my scorched throat. "May the fire cleanse you. May you take wing from the ashes and be remade. You are worthy."

A tear streaked down my cheek as I knelt in the grit. Mourning the girl I'd known. The ruthless, unflinching woman Marisol had become. And the courage she'd died with.

I wished this was not happening again. I wished this was not how our new world had to begin—built on the bones of the old. But maybe that's how worlds are made.

Nik and I clung to each other, there in the sand. Each lost in our own complicated grief. Until a cold, wet nose wedged itself between us. Nudging my arm up and out of the way. Insisting that she be included in the hug.

And when she couldn't stand it any longer, the pup bowled me over. Humid, stinky breath in my face. Cleaning off my tears with her sticky tongue.

"Okay. Okay!" I laughed, pushing her away. "Enough."

And it was.

• • •

Nik and I held hands as we climbed the steep hill out of the valley in silence. The pup led the way with a wagging tail. Impatient with our slowness, she ran ahead, then doubled back to check on us. Then ran ahead again.

"Do you think that's who I was talking to on the radio, then?" I asked, thinking out loud. I had so many questions, but this one had been with me since I first discovered the plane. "Do you think it was someone from the LOTUS Corporation, way on the other side of the mountains? Can they really not have known we were here . . . all this time?"

Nik was quiet for a moment. Then he said, "If you infected and then murdered millions of people, I doubt you'd go looking very closely at the end results. Especially if things generally appeared the way you expected them to. I think you'd just try to bury what happened and get on with the job of putting the world back together."

I nodded. "Do you think our people ever imagined we'd still be hiding here, believing our own lies five hundred years later? Do you think they'd even recognize who we've become?"

We crested the ridge, and we could see fragments of the burning plane strewn all across Tierra Muerta. Pillars of smoke staining the early dawn—black against the fading grey.

"I don't know," Nik said. "But we're alive, aren't we?"

"Well," I said, gazing up at the open sky, "we certainly are now."

We hiked out to the magfly I'd left behind. But when we reached it, I had to coax the pup aboard, holding her while Nik closed the door. She whined a little.

"I know." I buried my face in her soft fur. "But we're going home."

The sky turned pink and ash floated down across the valley like snow. Nik and I stood hand in hand watching the burning wasteland slide past. There were more fires on the Festival Grounds and fear clutched at my heart. What would be left of Pleiades? I hit the emergency brakes, the magfly dragging its rudders in the sand.

But when I got out, I was relieved to see they were simply bonfires, granting light and warmth to the crowded grounds. Behind the crackling flames, the nine buildings of Pleiades stood tall and untouched, shimmering in the rising sun. I had no prayers left in me—I had given Marisol my final one. So I simply let the words float up on the morning air.

"Thank you."

People were everywhere. Carrying bodies on cots and improvised stretchers. Corralling groups of children. Asking for news of loved ones. And Lotus stood in the middle of it all, her voice booming across the Festival Grounds.

"Conscious patients in the north corner! Unconscious in the east. Dead in west. And if you come across anyone you suspect might not have been dosed by the flys, take them to the south corner."

Alejo touched Lotus's arm gently and pointed to Nik and me, crossing the field. Her face lit up and her body, which had been bent with exhaustion, suddenly lifted and stretched taller. She made a tiny understated wave—a happy, sad, perfect gesture in the midst of all the turmoil.

As I returned the wave, I was surprised to realize that she no longer looked anything like Taschen had. Lotus only looked like herself now. And it made my heart hurt and glad at the same time.

But when we reached her, Lotus was all business. She looked at Nik first. "Ada's gonna be glad to see you. She's in the south corner dosing people with nanites and I know she could use your help."

"Of course." Nik squeezed my hand, already turning and jogging across the field.

"Alejo, can you take the pup down to the tunnels? If anyone can find Jaesun down there, it'll be her."

"Jaesun's missing?" My chest tightened. I had lost too many people over the course of the day.

"The whole tunnel collapsed while they were getting the last folks out," she said. "We've been digging for hours, but there's so much rubble, it's hard to know where to look."

Alejo and another Indigno had already jumped into action—finding a bit of jerky, enticing the pup out to the Reclamation Fields—and I noticed the way they looked at Lotus. With complete confidence. She'd become someone people were happy to follow. She'd become someone *I'd* be happy to follow. And I was glad to call her my sister.

But once we were alone, the face of the fearless leader dropped away and there was my little sister underneath. Her shoulders caved in and weariness crept to the surface.

I pulled her to me, smiling even in my own sadness. "You're alive!"

"Actually, I think *I'm* the one who's earned the right to be surprised." She hugged me tight. "You were already reported dead once tonight . . . and then, when I saw the explosion, I was sure."

"You know about Taschen?" My voice was soft.

Lotus nodded. "I was one of the first ones Nik treated, so once

I recovered, I was able to help other Indignos clear the labs. They found Tasch in that first hour too, but . . ." And she let herself cling to me for a second before pulling herself upright again. "We lost so many of them . . . probably lost a third of the wards."

A third. It was a sobering figure.

Inside the Dome, the story was the same. Thanks to the nanites, most people survived the Decontamination Protocol, but not all.

June met me at the door of the Genetics Lab, where an exhausted, but very much alive, Riya was hovering over a sleeping Oksun.

"Are they okay?"

"Yes," June said, with a tired smile. "Thanks to Ada's quick thinking, everyone who was in the streets was fine; the concentration of the toxin wasn't strong enough to kill them. But the gas was piped directly into the Salvage Hall . . ."

"Sarika and her followers." And I thought of the look of rapture on Sarika's unmoving face.

June nodded.

It hurt that my last real memory of Sarika was her abandoning me to a mob. Still. She'd been true to own her beliefs. She'd sacrificed herself for them.

"There must have been fifty Citizens down there," I said.

June took my hand. "I know."

There had been other tragedies too. Planck and one of the Ellas had died in the riots, along with a handful of other Curadores. And there was Jenner, of course.

But there was good news too. The pup found Jaesun and his group alive and unharmed, if a little hungry and thirsty. Olivia

SARA WILSON ETIENNE went to college in

Maine to become a marine biologist . . . but when her research transformed itself into a novel, she realized that she loved fantasy more than fact. So she gave in to it and wrote *Harbinger*. She now lives in Seattle, Washington, with her husband and two dogs. *Lotus and Thorn* is her second novel.

had been found and revived in Ward C. The Dome was trashed, but intact—along with the Meat Brewery, the water pumps, the generators, and the Salvage Hall. And all through the day, Nik's nanites continued to win the battle, healing the Citizens and inoculating the Curadores and Mothers.

I was also spared the task I'd been dreading since I'd stepped out onto the Festival Grounds—how to tell people about Earth. It turned out that while I'd been out in Tierra Muerta, Ada had been combing through the LOTUS files and learned all about it, the same way Edison had. News had spread through the Dome like flys and by dawn, everyone knew. All day, I overheard snatches of conversations—curious, disbelieving, angry, even a few people excited about the revelation. But in truth there was so much to do, no one had time to really absorb the idea. That would be for tomorrow. And the next day. And every day after that.

Today was for saying good-bye.

By the time the sun set, everyone was either strong enough to stand, or they were on the pyres.

Lotus and Alejo were at my side, and as torches were laid on the graves, Lotus took my hand. Tasch wasn't out there in the field, but we were both thinking of her. Mourning her for the second time. Nik took my other hand and leaned in to kiss my head. Nearby, the pup whined from where she sat on Jaesun's feet, making sure he wasn't going anywhere.

The Festival Grounds became a field of flames. Blocking out the stars. Even those who could barely walk were there to bear witness to what had happened.

Ada, June, Oksun, and Riya all watched together. Behind them, the ranks of Kisaengs and Mothers were shoulder to shoulder. My pain was reflected on each of their faces and somehow that made it more bearable. The weight of it shared among us all. And I saw it—strong and bright and real this time. What our new world would look like. Who would usher it in.

It would be built out of pain and love, and loss would be its foundation. A house of air and light.

Because that's how worlds are made.

We slept out there—Nik and me and the pup—huddled together for warmth. I'd wanted to stay with those we'd lost. To make sure that the fire freed them from this place that'd been their home and their cage.

A noise woke me just after dawn—a harsh beating of the air. My breath puffed out in the chill early morning.

Nik was awake now too. His hair wild. His sleep-fuzzed face searching for danger. "What's wrong?"

"I'm not sure. You hear that?" The noise was getting louder and I got to my feet, looking east, toward the crest of the mountains.

It was a low steady pulse now, throbbing through me. Shaking my bones.

Thooom-thooom-thooom-thooom.

And over the ridge—glowing orange in the new sun—rose three monstrous machines. Their propellers cutting against the air. Descending on the valley.

As they got closer, I could see they were ancient and dilapidated. The bodies had been patched and repatched, until they were nothing but an overlapping quilt of steel and rust. The only thing shiny on them were gun turrets bolted to the sides. I linked my hand with Nik's and tucked the LOTUS necklace back under my shirt—the cold metal burning like ice against my skin.

After five hundred years, Earth had remembered us.